A PECULIAR KIND OF LOVE

LISA WALKER MCCRAY

Printed in the United States of America

ISBN: 9798356487750

10 9 8 7 6 5 4 3 2 1

EMPIRE PUBLISHING
www.empirebookpublishing.com

Table of Contents

Have you ever wondered how Yah (GOD) hears everyone's prayers and requests at the same time? Well, like many of you so has Drewlynn McCain. Oh, I'm sorry that's who our story's about, and I'm her Guardian Angel, Abigail. I report to the Creator everything I see and hear; from prayers to complaints, laughter, and tears. You name it, I announce it when concerning Drewlynn McCain.

Everyone has a Guardian Angel or two, maybe even twenty, but I belong to Drewlynn McCain, and it's been fascinating being her Angel.

Drewlynn has always been an interesting person, with an interesting life. Nothing extraterrestrial or anything, but peculiar. Since birth I've been with Drewlynn, watching over her, protecting her, guiding her, and comforting her; if there's a Being that can tell you everything it is to know about Drewlynn it's me, but I can't do that all at once; it'll ruin you slowly falling in love with Drew, and I'll need you to slowly fall in love with Drewlynn L. McCain. I want her personality, character, and love to reach beyond the pages of this novel and conquer your heart, as you share in Drewlynn's laughter, tears, smiles, pain, and fears.

Drew's story starts off... Oh, forgive me, Drew is what I and those dear to Drewlynn call her for short. Anyway, I'm going to start Drew's story off when life started to wake up for her; it's a time when Drew had to face the realities of life. At a time when Drew's heart was put through the test of love, hate, excitement, adversity, grief, and happiness. Drew overcame things she didn't believe were possible.

At this time Drew's *definite maybes* were no longer considered maybes, but a *sure thing*. Drew's choices were no longer hers, but choices the Creator made for her long before she was born, and although Drew thought her choices were her own they weren't they were part of The Most High's plan for her life.

So, friends, if you've gotten this far you might as well stick with me and cuddle up to this novel; I Promise you won't be disappointed. You're going to laugh, cry and you may even get mad, but above all you'll be encouraged and enlightened, with a chance to fall in love with a new character.

CHAPTER 1
Ramen Noodles & Oreo

You could hear the music ringing through the college dorm from miles away, make-up scattered on sinks, clothes laid out on beds, attitudes because hair wouldn't cooperate, the exchange of clothes amongst friends, and the change of mind at the last minutes. It seems the entire Tubman Dorm was preparing for a night out except for Shantel Reid, Drewlynn McCain's college roommate of four years.

"Come on Shantel you have to go," Drew admired herself in the mirror trying to convince Shantel to attend their class of 2000 graduation party at Randy's: Drew's favorite bar and grill.

Drew left her image for a moment to give Shantel pouty lips, thinking it would change her mind if she saw how disappointed she was. "Please, Shantel, we have worked our asses off four years," Drew threw up four fingers. "And finally we have our bachelor's in Advertising. Why wouldn't you want to celebrate."

Shantel plopped down on the blue bean bag holding a bowl of Ramen Noodles and a package of Oreos, shaking her head. "Exactly Drew, worked our asses off; that's why I wanna spend these next few weeks straight chilling, not putting forth any effort for anything."

Shantel twirled some noodles around the fork and slurped them up. "Drew, the only thing I wanna do is enjoy my Ramen noodles & Oreos, listen to some jazz, relax, and finish this year out in solitude. You'll learn to appreciate moments of peace like this."

Drew looked back at Shantel with disgust. "That's the nastiest combination I've ever eaten. I had to be a fool to try that crap," Drew paused thinking back on the day Shantel tricked her into trying the disgusting snack. "You Owe Me," Drew yelped out in excitement.

Shantel was confused as to what Drew was talking about. "*Umm,* explain sis, how do I owe you?"

"Girl, don't act like you've forgotten; four years ago, when you tricked me into trying that nasty ass combination. You said if I tried it, then you would owe me."

Throwing an Oreo into her mouth Shantel wasn't surprised Drew would reach back four years to blackmail her. “Girl boo, that was four years ago, you should’ve cashed in on that when you had the chance."

"Well, you didn't put an expiration date on it," Drew did a victory dance with her image, while holding the qualifying outfit for the night. "Come on Shantel you owe me, besides, Jay's my best friend, and he's coming all the way from Texas to celebrate with us, so it's only fair he meets my Atlanta best friend."

"Some best friend, he hasn't been to see you once since you've been here; he didn't even make your graduation."

"That was out of his control. Jay wanted to be here, but his job needed him more. Besides, it's expensive to fly out here. Are we a little jealous," Drew grabbed an Oreo from Shantel's bag, and quickly kissed her cheek.

"No, I'm not, and Ewe,” Shantel wiped Drew's kiss away. "I just think he could've made more effort; it's been four years."

"Geesh Shantel, chill,” Drew ran to Jays' defense. "Does all that matter anyway; every time we needed something Jay always came through,"

Drew looked at Shantel, reminding her Jay's money also bought those Ores she’d just wolfed down.

Well, if that's not the ice burg that sunk the Titanic. Ok, I'm in, but don't you dare try and hook me up,” Shantel pointed her finger at Drew, ordering her to behave.

"Girl chill,” Drew nudged Shantel, walking past the bean bag sighing. "Ugh, I will not miss this small room." Drew hurried to escape the conversation because that's what she'd planned to do, hook her best friends up.

Shantel got up to search for something to wear.

"Oh no hunny." Drew observing Shantel rummaging through her closet. "You will not pull anything from that spinster's closet tonight." Drew grabs Shantel's shoulders and guides her over to her well-organized closet. "Pick something, I can't have you meeting my boy all jacked up."

Shantel looked at Drew sideways.

"Don't look at me like that hunny, you represent me tonight, so fix yo face." Drew chuckled.

Shantel paused, eyeing Drew. "So, all the other times who was I repping?"

Drew laughed hysterically. "I plead the fifth."

"Tell me more about Jay." Shantel was excited to meet Jay in a small way.

"You know almost everything it is to know about Jay; we first met at the age of eight, It was 1986, I was living with my foster parents, Curtis & Sheila James. Curtis's new position required him to relocate to Texas and run their home office, so we moved from Georgia to Texas, and I must say, meeting Jay was the best thing about our move."

Drew laughed, reliving her first memory of meeting Jay. "Meeting Jay for the first was funny. I was taking boxes to the storage shed behind our house when I heard the laughter of Jay and his older brother Shawn." Drew, now laughing hysterically, "Gurl, they were playing cops and robbers in their underwear." Drew laughed even more as the memory became clear. "I was watching through the space in the fence, I giggled; the sight of the two of them in their underwear was priceless and funny. Anyway, Shawn heard me on the other side and yelled out, '*Hey, Who's Over* There?' I didn't want to be humiliated, so I hid behind the shed, and stayed until they were back playing. It was embarrassing." Drew laughed at the foolishness.

"Well, early the next morning I got up to let the dog out, that's when I saw Jay standing on their front porch; knobby knees and ashy elbows." Drew laughed. "Jay's body looked so fragile, if the wind blew hard enough it would've carried him away, and to make matters worse his country ass yells out, *"I LIVE HERE, MY NAME IS JENUS TATE; I SAW YOU SPYING ON ME AND MY BROTHER SHAWN YESTERDAY."* I was trying to ignore him because of my embarrassment, and then he yells out, 'DO YOU HAVE A NAME!' Suddenly their front door flew open, Shawn walked out, and quietly yells. *"Shut Up Boy, Are You Trying to Wake Daddy?"* It was Love at first sight, and before I could catch myself I was screaming, *'DREW, DREWLYNN MCCAIN IS MY NAME.'* The next thing I see is Shawn shooting me the bird and calling me a spy. From that day on I was known as Harriet the Spy."

Shantel could see the memory tearing at Drew's heart because tears started to fall. "Drew, are you Ok?" Shantel was now puzzled by the tears.

Drew wiped the tears, trying to bring herself from memory. "I'm sorry Shantel, just the memory of Shawn standing there and knowing I'll never see him again just hit me. The first time I laid eyes on Shawn I loved him, although he didn't know it." Drew was lost in her memory once again.

"I'm sorry Drew, I didn't mean to bring back painful memories."

"It's ok Shantel, tears cleanse the soul, and Yah knows I need the cleaning." Drew held up two dresses for Shantel to choose from. "Which one?"

Shantel grabbed the black dress, checking her image in the mirror. "May I ask what happened to Shawn?"

Drew exhaled. "Car accident; Jay seems to think it was suicide."

"Oh my, why?" Shantel was even more intrigued by the story.

Drew explained to Shantel the night it happened. "Shawn called Jay upset the scout from Zion University (ZU) informed him that his application had been denied. Even Jay didn't understand why Shawn was denied; he was star quarterback, all-American player, and class president, so being denied acceptance to one of Texas best colleges broke Shawn's heart. Anyway, Shawn drank that night, drowning his sorrow, and crashed. Jay said Shawn called earlier that night and apologized for his failure, going on and on about how he would right his wrongs, and how sorry he was for letting everyone down. Scared out of his mind Jay tried to convince Shawn to come home, but it was too late. The following day the police informed the Tates that Shawn died in a head-on collision due to drinking.

Drew shook her head in disappointment. "I spent most of my life trying to tell Shawn how much I loved him, but he never paid any attention." Drew smiled. "Well, enough about that." Drew hurrying from the conversation. "We have to move quickly, Jay's meeting us there."

"Man, I can't believe you didn't tell Drew I was coming." Marcus looked out the hotel's window overlooking the city.

Jay laughed to himself, looking at his image in the mirror. "Hey man, you're not nervous are you?"

"Hell Naw, I'm good. I just haven't seen her in a while."

Jay emerged from the bathroom wearing the hotel's robe, shower cap, and slippers.

"You trying to get the whole experience, Huh?" Marcus laughed.

"HELL YEAH! We paid good money for the entire experience, so I'm getting my money's worth. I'm ordering room service later."

Marcus looked at Jay and laughed out.

"Hey Marcus, don't worry she's still the same."

"How do you know, you haven't seen her in almost four years?"

Jay pranced around the room pretending to be royalty. "I know because we write and call, we stay in touch."

Marcus pulled a suit from the closet. "Man, you can't tell how a person has or has not changed like that."

Jay eyed Marcus. "I know my friend, and she's still the same." Jay looked at Marcus suspiciously. "Why are you so concerned about Drew anyway?"

Marcus hesitated to answer. "Cause, it's Drew."

Marcus wanted to be honest and tell Jay he'd been secretly in love with Drew since they were kids, but he didn't know how Jay would feel about it, so Marcus hurried and jumped the subject.

"So, Drew got some fly homegirls?"

Jay shook his head. "Nah, she got a roommate that she claims to be her girl Bff." Jay said sarcastically.

Marcus picked up on the envious vibe. "Dang, you jealous or something?"

Jay looked Marcus up and down. "No, not at all. It's Drew's roommate, the girl has a smug attitude."

"So, you've talked to her?"

"Yeah, she's answered the phone a few times when I've called."

Marcus became interested. "So, have you ever seen said homegirl?"

Jay could see Marcus's interest was personal. "Man, hold up, I don't know her like that, nor do I care to. Besides, we are two little fish in a big ocean tonight. I have to keep my options open."

"Finally, you are thinking like a man." Marcus gave Jay some dab and sprayed himself repeatedly with cologne.

"Damn, Marcus." Jay starts coughing uncontrollably. "I think that's enough cologne man."

Marcus eyes Jay and sprays the cologne once more. "Hey, I have to smell good for the ladies; this stuff pulls them in."

Jay took the bottle and examined it. "Night Love, smells more like Nightmare."

"You crazy, this stuff brings the ladies in. You know, tickles their nose a little bit."

"Marcus, that's not a tickle, it's a punch."

CHAPTER 2

Change & Champagne

What beautiful ladies I see before me." Randy complimented Drew and Shantel, handing them drinks. The two women never had to order drinks at Randy's because he always knew what they were having, Twisted Nipple & Sex on The Beach, with a twist of lemon in both.

Drew and Shantel had been coming into the bar off their fake id's since they started college in Atlanta. Randy was aware, but it didn't matter he'd grown to love Drew and Shantel. Randy wasn't fortunate enough to have children of his own, so he took Drew and Shantel under his wing the moment he met them.

"Randy got it lit tonight," Drew screams out over the music.

Shantel hurried to agree. "Most definitely."

The women sipped their drinks while grooving to the music played by the DJ; it seemed the entire college campus was in the bar ready to relieve the stress of four years.

"Shantel, you're rocking that dress," Drew admired Shantel's chosen look for the night. The dark blue off-the-shoulder dress set Shantel on display, complementing her dark chocolate skin. Shantel's jet-black hair swayed her shoulders like satin curtains. The dark blue eyeshadow added mystery to her almond eyes, while the matte pink lipstick lay upon her luscious lips like snow on a mountain top. Shantel's necks and shoulders claimed ownership of the pearl neckless she wore.

"You're beautiful tonight Shantel." Drew eyed her with amazement.

"I know girl," Shantel stated jokingly, trying to take the attention off herself. "You're as beautiful as always Drew," Shantel returned the compliment. "No one in here can touch my girl," Shantel stated proudly.

Drew quickly jumped to her feet, holding her glass in the air, joining Shantel in the hype, showing off her *coke-bottle* shape. The leopard print romper Drew wore seduced her perfectly shaped body. Drew's blond hair flowed down her back, infused with the leopard print. Drew turned around displaying her perfectly sculpted body for the crowd. The light hit her caramel-colored skin, massaging her face with grace and serenity. "GIRL, You Better Say That." Drew jumped around to the music.

Shantel laughed at Drew's foolishness, while grooving to the music. Suddenly, Shantel's attention was seized by a bronzed man of color, he was the epiphany of gorgeous. His medium-built body was sculpted better than any Greek god; this man had Shantel's heart racing. The closer he got the faster her heartbeat. In the four years she'd been coming to Randy's, Shantel had never seen a man so perfectly created by God. As he approaches, the gentleman deeply examines Drew, and a smile comes across his face.

Shantel is captivated by the dimples that pierced his cheeks, they were like two sinkholes in the desert. Being kidnapped by his soft lips and bedroom eyes, Shantel battled to pull herself from his grasp; then it dawns on her this had to be Jay.

The gorgeous man walks up behind Drew and covers her eyes, whispering in her ear, "That ass thumping tonight."

Drew recognizing the voice, boiling with excitement, turns and jumps into the man's arms. "JAY, OMG! You're here."

Tears wet both their eyes; the pair stepped back to give each other a once over. Jay was stunned at how much Drew had changed, picking her up with another embrace.

"Four years, and you grow up on me," Jay couldn't keep his eyes off Drew.

Blushing from Jay's compliment Drew looks up and smiles. "Well, look at you, Mr. GQ, smooth. Damn, where's my fragile little friend?"

Staring at each other in amazement neither of them could believe the new people that stood before them.

Drew snapping from the astonishment remembers Shantel. "My bad, how rude of me. Jenius Tate, I would like to introduce a good friend of mine, Miss Shantel Reid."

Shantel was pleased with Drew's introduction, throwing her a smile. Jay immediately extends his hand; Shantel leers at Jay with her chestnut brown eyes and takes his hand. Jay raises Shantel's hand to his lips and blesses her with the sweetest kiss. Shantel never taking her eyes from his.

"Wow, Drew's description didn't come with enough detail. Shantel you're beautiful."

"Thank you, Jay," Shantel could feel an immediate connection. "You're not what I expected either," Shantel took her hand back, and wanted to leave it at the same time.

Interrupting their stare session Drew yelps out. "Now that we've all been properly introduced, *LET'S PARTY,"* Drew danced around Jay and Shantel; meanwhile the pair were searching each other's soul's, exchanging energies.

Walking to the dance floor Jay pulls Drew to the side and whispers, "I didn't come alone."

Drew looks at Jay confused. "Who's with you?"

Shantel listened as Jay tried to explain who the unmentioned guest was, that's when Shantel notices a dark-skinned, well-built man walking up behind Drew, taking the meaning of gorgeous to a whole new level. Shantel assumed this was the unmentioned guest, and if it was Drew should be delighted. Shantel sure was, as she looked upon the six feet and something well-groomed brother, bald by choice, and owning it.

"Hello, Drewlynn McCain," The deep captivating voice summoned Drew's attention.

"Marcus, Marcus Tidwell." Drew stood in disbelief. "What are you doing here?"

Marcus gave Drew the sweetest smile. "Well, Jay needed some company for the trip, so I volunteered."

Drew looked at them both, confused. "Wait, did I miss something; when did you two make amends," Drew Pointed at them both, trying to process how two best-known enemies stood before her being civil.

Jay knew the conversation Drew wanted to have but quickly stopped it. "Well, it's a long story, a story that can wait," Jay pulled Drew to the dance floor. "Come on bestie, let me see what you got."

After dancing to almost every song Drew yells over the music that she needs to sit, pulling Shantel from the dance floor.

Jay yells in disappointment. "What The Hell Drew." Jay was just beginning to fall into the groove with Shantel.

"Come on, just a minute or two, I need to sit." Drew scanned the bar for a table. "Let's hurry and find a table before their all gone," Drew hurried to a vacant table she spotted by the bar.

Obediently Jay and Marcus follow behind the two women.

Drew plops down and immediately starts to rub her hurting feet through the red thigh-high boots. "My feet are killing me."

Shantel agreed. "I'm going to need a soak and message after tonight."

Jay jumped at the opportunity, grabbed Shantel's feet and started rubbing them.

"Oh no, that's quite alright," Shantel took her feet back. "I have a massager back at the dorm." Shantel was impressed by Jay's gesture.

"You have a massager right here," Jay took Shantel's foot back and continued rubbing.

"That's what I'm talking about friend, show her the man ya daddy raised." Drew looked at Shantel and gave her a wink.

"So, how about some champagne, so we can toast to the graduates." Marcus offers.

"Sure, why not if you're buying." Drew accepted Marcus's offer, throwing him a wink.

"I'll buy anything you want Drewlynn McCain."

Drew eyed Marcus, she wanted to tell him to get outta there with that weak line, but she didn't wanna ruin the moment, so she sat on it. "I can be expensive."

Shantel pinched Drew's thigh under the table, Drew jumped from the sting, knowing that was Shante's way of saying be nice. Drew and Shantel had been on a few double dates, and this was Shantel's way of getting Drew's attention when she was being rude or judgmental.

"Anyways," Drew rolled her eyes at Shantel. "Sure, we'll have some champagne, this will give us time to gossip about you two." Drew teased the men.

"Make sure you add sugar to mine," Jay stood and tipped his invisible hat to the ladies.

"Move around crazy," Dew pushes Jay away from the table.

"Hey Shantel, let me tell you something funny Drew did in seventh grade."

Drew hurried to push Jay from the table, scared he'd reveal something that would embarrass her in front of Marcus and Shantel. "Go get the drink boy, ain't nobody trying to hear that."

Jay laughed hysterically, his dimples got deeper, pulling Shantel in like a hypnotic swirl.

"SHANTEL, SHANTEL," Drew was now yelling, snapping her fingers to gain Shantel's attention. "Dang girl, you're already married with a kid."

Honestly Drew loved the pair's energy, it saved her some time doing precisely what Shantel asked her not to do, try to hook them up.

Drew looked at Marcus and decided to do a little flirting of her own, grabbing his hand, gently stroking it. "Marcus, could you be a dear and bring back tall glasses?"

Marcus held Drew's gaze, returning the flirtatious vibe. "Anything you want, Miss McCain."

The men walked off on their mission to the bar leaving the women alone to gossip.

While waiting for their chance at the bar Marcus kept eyeing Jay and smiling. "What's up, why are you smiling all weird," Jay knew something stupid was about to come from Marcus's mouth.

"Why didn't you tell me Drew Barrymore is now Drew Sidora," Marcus was amused at the woman Drew had blossomed into.

"Man, come on," Jay shook his head. "You know I don't see Drew like that; she's like a sister to me."

"C'mon Jay, I know how you feel about Drew. I watch both of you growing up."

Jay became slightly offended by Marcus's statement. "Look man, it's never been anything but brotherly love for Drew; she's extra special to me, and the situation she grew up in wasn't always great, so I promised myself & Drew I would be her keeper, never letting anyone hurt her or disrespect her."

Marcus held his hands up as to block the hostility coming from Jay. "Respect man, calm down. I just had to make sure I wasn't stepping on any toes."

Jay eyed Marcus. "Stepping on toes, what are you saying?"

Marcus cleared his throat. "Look Jay, I've been in love with Drew since we were kids, and seeing her tonight brought back old feelings."

Jay gave Marcus a side-eye.

"Why did you think I jumped at the chance to come on this trip."

Jay's eyes were bucked, and his jaw on the floor.

"You act like I said something wrong."

"Nah, I just never knew you felt that way about Drew."

"Neither does she." Marcus ask the bartender for a bottle of Dom Perignon. "Drew was always so wrapped up in Shawn I figured I never had a chance."

Jay agreed, especially with the Shawn part; Jay was always Drew's ear when it came to Shawn. What he was doing, what he wasn't doing, who he was dating, and who he wasn't dating (Drew).

"Why haven't you told her?"

"Man, we're talking about Drew; her response to me admitting that would've been brutal. "I can hear her now; You stupid Marcus, get out of my face, you don't know what love is."

They both laughed.

"Besides, after Rebecca confronted Drew about the note, and Drew being so wrapped up in Shawn; it was hard to get her attention."

Jay laughed, "Yeah, we're going to talk about that note, and you're right about Shawn; a few times I thought Drew only hung out with me to get his attention." Jay chuckles. "But his death proved me wrong. Hey man, I can't tell you how to feel about Drew, but I can tell you not to hurt her, because you will answer to me."

Marcus could tell by the look on Jay's face he wasn't playing around with that statement.

Jay wondered about Drew's love for Shawn, and how she'd held herself back from getting to know any other guys besides Rodney Shed, and Jay believed he was just a cover-up so people would stop questioning Drew's sexuality.

"Sometimes I wonder if Shawn ever knew how much Drew loved him; I hated how he led her on." Jay shook his head in disappointment, thinking about how cruel Shawn was, and how much Drew loved him.

To lighten the conversation Marcus puts the spotlight on Jay's vibe with Shantel. "I see you feeling Shantel." Marcus reminding Jay of the connection he saw between them.

"Yeah, it's crazy, I've never connected with a woman this fast before," Jay smiled. "Shantel has something different about her."

"Well, are you going to get at her?"

"HAHAHA," Jay laughs loudly. "Wouldn't you like to know," Jay yells at the bartender for two bottles to avoid the question.

Shantel eyed Drew as she freshened up her make-up, she couldn't wait for the guys to leave so she could get the scoop on Jay. "Gurl, why wasn't I informed Jay was that fine, and good looking," Shantel stated with excitement. "And does he have a girl?"

"First of all, ewe, I look at Jay like a brother," Drew put the make-up compact back in her purse. "And second, if Jay had a girl he wouldn't be all over you."

Shantel blushed from Drew's statement, embarrassed the vibes she and Jay were giving off were noticeable. "Mumm, and loyal too," Shantel smiled.

Drew could see Shantel was intrigued by Jay. "You're digging my friend, aren't you?"

"Yeah, I don't know what it is, he's a different kind of man."

"He has to be if you're interested; girl, I've never seen your eyes light up like that, not even with Tracy."

"Hush," Shantel cringe., "I see you flirting with Marcus." Shantel made Drew's little secret public.

"Well, it's something to do," Drew eyed Shantel and smiled. "Though I must say he's not the Marcus I grew up with; he's still a little arrogant and wears too much cologne, but he's gotten fine girl."

And he'll buy you anything you want."

The women laughed.

"So, what's funny," Marcus threw his gorgeous smile at Drew.

"Ah, nothing, just a little girl talk," Drew gave Shantel a wink.

Jay popped the cork on the champagne, pouring everyone a glass, toasting to the lady's graduation and new success, without ever taking his eyes off Shantel.

Jay grooved to the music, *D'Angelo* was making a statement tonight. "Shantel, would you like to dance," Jay gave her a gentle smile.

Shantel didn't hesitate; just the invitation alone had her doing flips. Shantel Jumped to her feet; which no longer needed care, and followed Jay to the dance floor. Meanwhile, the two onlookers remained at the table reminiscing about old times.

Marcus eyed Drew; he still couldn't get over how much she'd changed, he was almost nervous being alone with her. "So, Drew, you remember when I put my Iguana in your locker?"

"YES, OMG!" Drew yelped out. "You had me running down the hall like a mad man. I knew for sure I was being attacked by an alligator. You were always so mean to me." Drew pinched Marcus's arm.

"Only because I liked you."

Drew gave Marcus a soft smile while trying not to blush. "So, Marcus, why the change of heart? Why does it seem like you and Jay have been friends forever?"

"Well, Drew." Marcus brushed lint from Drew's hair while taking in her beauty. "Our newfound friendship came about at a very awkward time."

Drew was about to bust, wanting to know every detail. "Share for goodness sakes, Marcus."

"Ok, keep your panties on; I see you're still nosey as hell."

Drew blew Marcus a kiss. "Come on, stop stalling and spill the tea."

Marcus was captivated by Drew's interest in the story. “One night I was out with friends; it had to be about a year after you left for college."

"Wow, you kept up with when I left for college?" Drew was shocked and impressed.

"Can I finish my story," Marcus chuckled. "Anyway, we were hanging out at Shades, and Jay comes in, already lit; the bartender must have sensed he’d already had too much because he wouldn’t serve him. Jay got upset and started to make a scene, so I go over and suggest he calm down, and take the bartenders advise; we might not have been the best of friends, but even I know when to intervene."

As Marcus carried out his story, Drew became captivated by his heroic acts. Pulling herself from the illusion of Marcus hanging from a rope in the jungle, Drew interrupts him briefly. "It was honorable for you to watch out for Jay; you're the sweetest.” Drew planted a soft kiss on Marcus' cheek.

Marcus, stuck in a moment of confinement from Drew's soft lips, took a deep breath and concluded his story, "Unaware it was the anniversary of his brother's passing; I suggested he cool out on the alcohol. When Jay looked at me, I could only see pain in his eyes, and after recognizing who I was, he took a swing at me, and the rest is history." Marcus laughed at how drunk Jay was trying to swing on him. "The best thing about that night was in the process of me taking Jay home; we hashed out a lot of our differences. We talked about his brother, Rebecca, his dad, and you."

Drew was even more interested in the story now that she’d heard her name. "What was the topic when it came to me?"

"Damn, interested a little,” Marcus stated sarcastically. "We talked about how much Jay missed you, and how scared he was that someone would take advantage of you. Jay didn't have anyone after you went away to college; it was like he lost you and Shawn at the same time. Y’all were the other half of him. After our conversation, I understood my dislike for Jay, and it wasn’t because of Rebecca, it was because of his relationship with you. He was to you everything I wanted to be."

Drew was speechless and taken by Marcus's confession. "Marcus, I didn't know you felt that way; I thought you were always in love with Rebecca."

"Rebecca, HA! Rebecca was only there because I couldn't have you. That's why she hated you so much, and she played Jay and me against each other. Rebecca was in love with me, and I was in love with you."

Drew held Marcus's stare. "*Wow,* I'm speechless."

"Drew, I've loved you since Mrs. Wilson's 8th-grade Theater Arts class, and I should've said something back then."

"HAPPY GRADUATION!" a small crowd began to shout, which started a wave throughout the bar of college students. Meanwhile, Drew and Marcus were locked into a world of their own. Marcus took Drew's hand and caressed her cheek guiding her lips to his, gently placing a kiss on her lips. Drew was charmed by Marcus's soft lips and firm grip that held her body close; she was like melting caramel in his arms.

"Wow," Jay and Shantel stated simultaneously after sharing a kiss.

"I'm sorry Shantel, no disrespect, but I've been wanting to do that all night."

"I'm not complaining; it was sweet. I've never been kissed like that before," Shantel blushed still trying to recover from the kiss.

"Shantel, do you have any plans for the rest of your life?"

Shantel laughed, "What do you mean, Jay?"

"Marry me?"

Shantel was honored, "Sure, I'll marry you." Shantel laughed uncontrollably, she knew Jay was just caught in the moment, but she played his game anyway.

Jay stared into Shantel's eyes and stated with confidence, "You will be my wife one day, I promise," Jay stated the words as to speak them to Shantel's soul.

CHAPTER 3

Grown People & No Chaperone

The way Drew pulled up to the five-star hotel for her ten-year high school reunion was priceless; you'd thought a celebrity had just pulled in. Everyone's attention was on the pearl white Mercedes Benz E-class that rang out the lyric from *Kelis's, Bossy*. The crowd waited with curiosity for the driver to exit, each one asking the same question, *"Dang, who doing it big like that?"*

After making the group of inquisitive onlookers wait a few minutes Drew emerged from the vessel giving the crowd an exit that would last them another ten years. Drew tossed back her jet-black hair, allowing the light to dance upon her soft golden skin like rays of sunshine; Drew wore an elegant off shoulder black evening gown that appeased her body, announcing every curve she introduced. The invisible split exposed her legs in a game of pick-a-boo. Each step Drew took in the black stilettos seemed to glide her to the attendant's podium.

"Good evening, Tevin." Drew observed the name on the young man's vest.

The young man stood motionless, in disbelief that a face could hold so much beauty. "Good evening, Miss." The words tumbling from his mouth.

"Darling, will you be my knight and shining armor tonight?" Drew gave the young man a wink.

"Yes, I'll be assisting you this evening. Are you here for the class of 96' Frederick Douglas high school reunion?"

"Yes I am." Drew dropped her keys in the young man's hand. "Take care of *Maggie*."

Drew sashayed off to the hotel's lobby leaving the young man baffled. Walking into the lobby Drew could see the observation was still on her as a couple of her classmates whispered amongst themselves *"Game on Haters,"* Drew whispered to herself while checking in.

Drew started to the ballroom when she felt her ankle bracelet twist; fearing it would break, she stops to adjust it. While checking the jewelry Drew felt the presence of someone standing over her; looking up Drew's eyes were fixed on a pair of black Stacy Adams that stood before her. Rising to explore the character that boldly stood in her midst, Drew became nervous. *"Marcus."* His name was escaping her lips before she could catch it.

"Well, Miss Drewlynn McCain." Marcus took Drew's hand, lifting it to his lips, gently kissing it.

"'Why are we so formal, Marcus?" Drew licked her lips; quickly gaining Marcus's attention. "Marcus, you know better than anyone, it's Drew."

"Yes indeed," Marcus replies with a playful grin.

Marcus leans in to kiss Drew's perfectly blushed cheek; she quickly pulls back and eyes him as the crowd of onlookers watches them like a hot romantic flick. "Come on now Mr. Tidwell, you wouldn't want to give these gossips anything to talk about, would you?"

The couple's eyes locked.

Marcus pulled Drew closer and blessed her with the sexiest kiss he could give her. "I could care less about what people have to say."

Drew was dazed for a moment; the kiss Marcus had planted on her caused confusion in her soul. Drew was caught in a whirlwind of thoughts, feelings, and hot flashes, until she heard a familiar voice.

"Hey, Party People, Jenius Tate in the building." Jay strutted through the lobby, loudly introducing himself.

Drew, overwhelmed with joy, quickly forgets her interaction with Marcus. "BASTIE," Drew yells, running into Jay's arms. "I missed you."

Jay stepped back to admire his friend. " I've missed you too Miss Drewlynn McCain. I see life's been a blessing to you." Jay spins Drew for a once-over.

Drew, trying not to blush, hurries to take the attention off her. "Friend, I see life's been good to you as well, and different." Drew observed Jay's new look. "I knew you were going into ranching, but Jenius, do you have to dress the part?"

"My man here trying to be on the next cover of Cowboys & Indians." Marcus was making his way into the conversation. "What's up Jay," Marcus extends his arms for an embrace.

Drew shook her head. "Well, I'm not sure what Cowboys & Indians is, but Jay is most definitely wearing the cowboy part, looking like he's about to ride out with Mario Van Pebbles and the rest of the posse." Drew and Marcus looked at each other and burst into laughter.

"Oh, so y'all got jokes," Jay gawked at the pair.

"Well, Well," A familiar voice sarcastically speaks from behind the trio. "I see a lot, but so little has changed since school."

The three of them were repulsed by the comment, and the annoying voice.

"Rebecca Sims, what a delight," Drew states while gritting her teeth.

"Drew, fix your face darling, you wouldn't want to add any more wrinkle lines, now would you," Rebecca rudely states, trying to get a reaction from Drew.

Drew tried to remain a lady, but the *Ghetto Queen* was screaming to get out. "Rebecca, how are you, aren't we lovely."

"Yes, I am, sorry I can't say the same for you; seeing that ten years has done a number on you."

Freely the thoughts danced around in Drew's head, *"I'm killing this trick, she's talking about wrinkles, trick looks like to me if you miss one session of Botox your face would fall like those breasts, without the push-up bra. TRICK I'M KILLING YOU."* The words were prying at Drew's mouth trying to escape.

Marcus noticed Drew struggling to remain a lady, so he cuffed her in the waist to calm her, which worked immediately; the soothing touch of Marcus's hand quickly sent chills through Drew's body humbling her.

"Marcus Tidwell & Jenius Tate, I fancy seeing you two acting civil. It's been a long time." Rebecca eyed them both.

Jay takes Rebecca's hand and gently kisses it. "I'm impressed; glad to see one of you has grown up."

Marcus steps to Rebecca, glares into her eyes, and whispers. "Fancy or shocking; being a grown man permits you to put childish things behind you, and I can see that you haven't learned that after ten years, Rebecca."

Rebecca's face was loaded with disgrace, thinking the two men would still be ready to challenge each other over her after all these years. Rebecca gave the trio a once-over and walked off with little hesitation.

"I'll see you in a bit, Rebecca," Marcus yells out.

"Good come back, Marcus." Drew slapped him a high five.

"Childish things?" And the both of you standing here giving each other high fives." Jay shook his head at the irony. *"Grown people and no chaperone."*

"*Wow*, fellas, I'm pleased to see you two are no longer letting TRICKS come between y'all," Drew states sarcastically.

"Be quiet Drew," both men suggested.

Jay looked over at Marcus, he didn't want to be rude, but he needed to speak with Drew privately. "Hey bro, let me holla a Drew for a moment."

"Sure thing, I'm about to find Rebecca and give her a little of the hell she gave us in school," Marcus leered at Drew. "Drewlynn McCain, we'll continue our conversation later." Marcus took Drew's hand and kissed it gently. "I'll be expecting a dance from you later as well."

Drew was taken in by Marcus's bedroom eyes. "I promise, Mr. Tidwell."

Marcus walked off in search of Rebecca.

"I don't know why you do him like that; you know he's still crazy in love with you."

"He's not, stop it." Drew denied the allegation. "Anyway, what's the deal, how have you been?" Drew waited with anticipation to hear what had been going on in Jay's life.

"I've been good Drew, a few changes here and there." Jay pulled at his bolo tie. "I bought a place out in Promise Texas, so I don't have to rent pastures anymore. I got a few heads of cattle, a couple of horses, and a John Deer tractor. I must say business has been good for us. We didn't expect too much with us just starting out, but we've stayed afloat for the last couple of years."

Drew questioned Jay, "What do you mean us and we?" Drew took Jay's cowboy hat and placed it on her head.

Jay hesitated. "Me and Marcus."

"Wow, you and Marcus are in business together, and you've moved to the big country of Promise Texas."

"Yeah, Promise was my best move, and Marcus has been a great investor; he really has a good head for business."

Drew could tell Jay was proud of his accomplishments. "I'm happy for you Jay, you're doing everything you said, and I'm thrilled you're doing it with Marcus."

"Thanks Drew, that means a lot." Jay hugged her.

Drew analyzed Jay for a moment, she could tell there was something he wasn't telling her.

"So, Drew, what's been going on with you?"

Drew was almost embarrassed to say, seeing that Jay and Marcus were living their dreams. "Other than trying to become a partner and working my ass off to live this lavish lifestyle, nothing. I work more than I play, I'm at the office more than home."

"Is that why you sent Marcus back to Texas heartbroken?"

Drew took a breath; she knew this question was coming. "*OMG* Jay, that happened almost five years ago. What Marcus and I had was sweet, and I didn't mean for things to end like that."

"I know Drew, but they did, and you left Marcus discombobulated."

"Jay, I never meant to hurt Marcus. Besides, he understood I wasn't ready for a relationship. Jay, I went to school for a career, and starting a relationship just didn't fit at the time. I'd just started my internship at Cambridge and needed to keep my head in the game."

Jay couldn't believe Drew's excuse. "Drew, it took a year to figure that out. Then, after you did, you just put Marcus on a plane back to Texas and wished him well."

Drew pulled Jay to a corner to have more privacy. "Ok, Jay, to be honest, I figured Marcus was getting tired of waiting on me."

Jay looked at Drew, puzzled. "What do you mean waiting on you?"

Drew hesitated, trying to find the right way to explain. "You know, to give him some."

Jay was speechless; he'd thought for sure Drew had done the nasty before. "Drew, you never did the do?" Jay covered his mouth in disbelief. "Drew, you're almost thirty."

"SHUT UP, JAY!" Drew hated she'd even said anything, she knew Jay would make a big deal of it.

"I can't believe you've never…

"Shut up, Jay. It's not a big deal." Drew's face now blushed with embarrassment.

"Drew, you have to tell him."

"Are you crazy, I can't tell him that. It's embarrassing." Drew covered her face in shame.

"What's embarrassing about it, there's women out here wishing they could get that part of them back, and Marcus, would find that more admirable than any woman that will just throw herself at him. Drew, you were with this man a year, don't you think he deserves an explanation?"

Jay could see Drew starting to feel uneasy, so he took her in his arm changing the subject. "You know I watched you pull in," Jay laughed. "And I must say, quit and entrance Drewlynn McCain; left that young man speechless."

"Well, Jay, you know me, I'm always looking to give these country-ass folks something to talk about."

"Watch it, I remember when you used to be one of these country folks Ma'am." Jay grabbed his hat from Drew's head and tapped the tip of her nose.

"Speaking of country, when did you become the spokesman for Stetson?"

Jay cracked up at Drew's comment. "Drew, you're still crazy."

"And that will never change." A soft and gentle voice coming from behind Drew warmed her heart. Overwhelmed with excitement, Drew turned around to make sure her ears were hearing correctly, and to her surprise, they were. "OMG, SHANTEL!"

The two ladies embrace each other, ecstatic and surprised, as the tears fall from their eyes.

"Shantel, what are you doing here, how long has it been?"

Before Shantel could answer one question, Drew asked another. "Wow, it's been almost a year how have you been? What are you doing here? Somebody, please tell me something." Drew was overjoyed with excitement.

"Can we find a table first," Jay suggested.

The trio couldn't sit down fast enough; Drew waited with anticipation for someone to explain. "Are y'all together?"

Shantel looked at Drew. "I love you Drew, you give me so much energy." Shantel prolonged the conversation to taunt Drew.

"Come on you guys, stop playing with me." Drew was about to launch like a rocket with excitement.

"Ok, I'm here because me and this fabulous man are in love, and we're getting married in two weeks. Would you be my maid of honor?"

Drew was stuck, speechless, and confused.

"Drew," Jay calls her name for the third time.

Drew tried to process the words that had just come from Shantel's mouth. "Stop lying." The excitement grew more intense for Drew.

"We're not lying," The couple said simultaneously.

Drew observed Jay and Shantel holding each other. "When did this happen?"

"Well, Drew," Jay took her hand. "Remember my trip to Atlanta for the Farmers Convention about a year back? Well, I ran into Shantel one night at the hotel's bar, we started to catch up, and one conversation led to another, and here we are."

Drew thought back to that week Jay was in Atlanta. "Hey, is that why you stood me up for dinner that one night?"

"You'd better think back, you stood me up, that's how I ended up at the hotels bar in the first place. You were so busy at work you didn't have time for ya boy."

Shantel chuckled. "I can witness to that; she's stood me up plenty times."

"Hey, it's not about me, it's about you two." Drew pointed at the couple. "What I wanna know is, how y'all manage to keep it secret from me this long?"

"Now, that was the hard part," Jay kissed Shantel. "You don't know how many times I wanted to pick up the phone and call you. It burned at my soul not being able to tell you, but we agreed not to tell anyone until we knew for sure."

Drew understood their reason, and it didn't matter long as they were happy. "I couldn't be any more content for the two best people in my life, congratulations." Drew stood to her feet with her glass in the air. "Now, it's a celebration we have a wedding to plan."

Marcus held Drew just right as they danced their promised dance. Drew looked around the room, it seemed all eyes were on them. Drew could see Rebecca amongst the crowd with a smug look on her face; Drew could tell this wasn't the outcome she'd expected. Rebecca probably imaged herself in Marcus's arm at the end of the night, but life has a strange way of doing its own thang.

"I missed you, Drew," Marcus whispered in her ear inhaling her sweet aroma.

"I missed you too, Marcus," Drew responded.

"What happened to us Drew, I thought we had something special."

Drew thought about taking Jay's advice and telling Marcus she was a virgin, but the fear of rejection pondered her heart. "Marcus, I thought we had an understanding; we both wanted to focus on our careers and starting a relationship would have compromised that."

"That was your understanding Drew, not mine."

Drew couldn't say a word because she never asked Marcus what he wanted.

Drew looked over the room, thinking of a way out of the conversation, only to spot Jay motioning her to tell Marcus her secret. Drew took a deep breath and exhaled. "Marcus, I'm a virgin."

CHAPTER 4

A Dime for What's on Your Mind

Shantel, what's wrong?" Drew hurried to wipe Shantel's face before she ruined her make-up. It had been two weeks, and finally, the day had arrived. Drew and Shantel had run themselves senseless, planning the perfect wedding in the little time they had.

"Drew, it's all moving so fast." Shantel started to take deep breaths on the brink of a panic attack. "What if Jay and I are rushing things? What if this isn't a part of Yah's plan? What if...

Drew stopped Shantel in mid-sentence. "What If Shantel? None of that matters you're just getting cold feet, and besides, it's too late for that, we're here at the day in the moment, and I'm killing this dress," Drew said, trying to cushion the moment with her comedy. "Shantel, you have nothing to be afraid of, Jay is in love with you. Every time he talks about you, Jay gets this smile that the worst news couldn't break. I remember the first night you guys met; I never said anything, but Jay promised me he would marry you one day."

Drew wiped Shantel's tears. "Now, here we are. You're about to become Mrs. Tate." Drew gave Shantel a comforting smile. "I know you're wondering if y'all are ready for this, and it's okay, but Jay loves you Shantel, and never questions that. Enjoy Yah's blessings and honor him. Put all your trust in Yah and know he'll make the both of you great. Nothing happens by chance; it's all designed by his plan."

Shantel was now able to regain stability after her breakdown. "Thanks Drew, you have always known the right words to say."

"Aw girl, you know me." Drew winks at Shantel while making sure her make-up is still intact.

"Hey ladies, can I interrupt?" A middle-aged woman peeks in the door.

"The ladies welcomed Jay's mother into the room.

Jay's mother was a beautiful person inside and out, a well-kept woman, a woman of dignity and sophistication. Mrs. Tate was a purpose-driven woman, but if needed she would pull out the hammer; raising two boys she had to be tuff at times. Mrs. Tate always told it like it was, she believed in the statement, *"Honesty is the best policy,"* and for Drew, Mrs. Tate was the most honest person she knew.

Mrs. Tate stops suddenly and glares at Shantel. "Oh my, what a beautiful sight you are, mesmerizing." Mrs. Tate salutes Shantel with a kiss on the forehead.

"Thanks Mrs. Tate." Shantel gave her a gentle smile.

"Now Shantel, if I've told you once, I've told you a hundred times, call me Momma."

Shantel corrects herself, "I'm sorry, Momma."

"Now that's more like it." Mrs. Tate turned to look at Drew. "Drewlynn darling, you're gorgeous as always, spin one time for me."

Mrs. Tate knew all it took was a little hype to get Drew to her feet, and just like clockwork, with no hesitation, Drew jumped to her feet and gave Mrs. Tate a spin.

Enjoying the moment, the three ladies share in their laughter.

Mrs. Tate looks at Shantel, "Now that's the kind of smile you're supposed to wear on your wedding day."

Knowing Mrs. Tate's reasons for the intervention, Drew gives her the biggest hug, whispering in her ear. "Thanks, Momma."

Mrs. Tate trying to hold back the tears looks at the two women. "I couldn't have asked Yah for two better women in my son's life." Mrs. Tate stroked Shantel's cheek, looking into her eyes. "And in you, he chose a wife, and my dear, that alone speaks volumes."

At that moment, looking into Mrs. Tate's eyes, Shantel's *"What If's"* never existed.

"I'll give you ladies a moment." But before Mrs. Tate exited, she looked back at Shantel and stated. "No backing out now, girl I look good in this dress."

Shantel points at Drew and laughs, "That's where you get that from." Both women laugh.

"Ok, before we go, I have something for you." Drew pulls a box from her things. "Shantel, you are one of the best people in my life, and I had this made for you."

Shantel was delighted and amazed at Drews's gift, a bouquet of teal green flowers with white baby booties embedded.

"Omg, Drew, this is the cutest thing ever, so thoughtful and unique." Shantel examined the bouquet. "It's so you." Shantel couldn't help but ask. "Are the booties to hurry us to have a baby?"

Drew laughed. "No, just my way in asking Yah to bless you guys when it comes to starting a family; just something special from me to you."

Shantel could hardly hold the tears back. "Drew, you have been more than a friend to me; you've been a sister. Losing my father and dealing with my mother's depression was hard; being an only child made it even harder. Not having anyone to talk to was the hardest, until Yah blessed me with a sister."

Drew fanned the tears back as they collected in the wells of her eyes.

Shantel continued. "Going to college was never my dream, it was my father's dream for me; if I could've just faded into the background of life, that would have been suitable enough for me. Had I not honored my father's dream for me, I would've never met you, therefore never meeting Jay. Drew, I want to thank you for all the years you've been here. Within those years, you've allowed Yah to use you in helping me, and I'm grateful. I've often asked myself, why Jay did choose me when he's had this perfect woman in his life almost his whole life, why me?"

Drew kissed Shantel's cheek. "Why not you?"

As the wedding ceremony ran its course, there wasn't a dry eye in sight.

Not only did the coral and teal green decor set the mood, but the love Jay and Shantel shared also filled the room with its essence, and Drew felt every bit of it. Although she sat three seats down from Marcus, Drew could somehow feel his energy. Drew had caught him staring at her a few times, and he seemed to catch her eye every time.

Ding, ding, the sound of the wine glass sang as Marcus stood to make his best man speech. "Excuse me, everyone." Marcus cleared his throat to gain the guest's attention.

At that moment, Drew notices a group of women whispering & admiring Marcus; she tried not to care, but her alter ego dared him to give notice.

"Good evening, everyone, I would like to make a toast to this beautiful couple."

Drew couldn't keep her eyes off Marcus. The more she fought against him, the more he drew her in.

"Most of you may know me and Jay haven't always been the best of friends." Marcus laughed, and so did the crowd. "Fortunately, we learned to put our differences behind us and be what we needed to be, Brothers. Big ups to Yah for allowing us to correct things, because without that opportunity I wouldn't have never known how good a person this man is. Jay, you've been more to me than I ever could imagine, and Shantel, you are the beat of this man's heart. You are a lovely, wise, intelligent woman, and Jay couldn't have made a better choice. I remember the night he met you, Jay promised to make you his wife, and today we celebrate because he made good on that promise. I wish both of you the best in life, much success, love, and prosperity. May those searching for love one day find it as you two have."

Marcus raises his glass while leering a Drew. "Here's to Mr. & Mrs. Tate."

While the spotlight was on Jay and Shantel as they shared in their union dance, Drew made a way to the open bar, seizing the opportunity to drown her thoughts in a twisted nipple.

"Bartender," Drew calls out, becking for his assistance.

The bartender hurried to Drew's call, eager to take her request. "Can I get you something beautiful." The bartender wasted no time trying to gain points with Drew.

"She'll have a twisted nipple." Marcus interceded on Drew's behalf.

Drew was impressed, eyeing Marcus as he took a seat beside her. "Wow, remembering drinks, are we?"

"I know what you like, Miss McCain." Marcus removes a hair from Drew's face, while visiting her soul through her eyes.

For a moment, Drew fell captive to his search. Noticing the abduction, she quickly looks away, downing the drink and asking for another.

"Why do you do that?" Marcus took hold of Drew's chin and guided her eyes back to his.

"Do what, Marcus?" Drew blushed trying not to lock eyes with Marcus.

"Fight me, like you're fighting me now, Drew."

"Marcus, I'm not fighting you. I'm simply resisting you."

"What do you mean by that?" Marcus was confused at Drew's comment.

"I mean, there's not a woman that can resist you, except me." Drew took a swig of her drink, making Marcus aware of the female fans he'd gained throughout the evening sitting at the end of the bar.

Marcus never looked in their direction, Drew was the only one he was interested in. "Drew just let it happen," Marcus pleaded, placing his hand on her thigh.

Drew swallowed the knot in her throat as chills ran from her toes to her head from Marcus's touch. "Let what happen, Marcus?" Drew pretended to be lost in the conversation.

"Us, Damn Drew, I've been trying to love you since we were kids. All I ever wanted was for you to feel the love I have for you. I moved 15 hours away for you Drew, putting everything on hold. Let me love you Drew, let me show you things you've never seen. Let me give you a love you never had."

"Marcus... Drew tries to speak.

"No Drew, I want you to hear me for once; let yourself go; allow me to love you."

Drew was feeling overwhelmed; she couldn't tell if it was the liquored down drink, the Freddie Jackson, or merely the heartfelt words coming from Marcus's mouth. Either one, Drew's heart was in maximum overload; she was feeling things she'd never felt before. Drew was trying to find the words to say, but with all her emotions requiring her attention at one time, she was befuddled. Drew leered into Marcus's eyes.

"Marcus." Drew, still trying to find the words, but couldn't, so she immediately jumped to her feet and walked off, leaving Marcus sitting there with his thoughts.

Drew observed a couple having a moonlit picnic on the lawn just below the overlook outside the wedding venue. This was the kind of love Drew's heart desired, and something told her Marcus was the one to give it. Although Drew was reluctant, recalling Marcus's confession had her wanting him more.

"Drewlynn, what are you doing out here; Please, Please! Don't Jump." Jay sat a couple of drinks down on the bistro table and grabbed Drew around the waist, pretending to save her from jumping.

"No jumping today, I wouldn't want to spoil their intimate moment." Drew points at the couple.

"Marcus told me you were out here." Jay handed Drew one of the drinks.

Drew sighs: Jay could tell something deep was on her mind. "What's wrong with my friend?"

"Just getting some air," Drew said, accompanied by another sigh.

"Ok, that's the second sigh, what's wrong?" Jay grabbed Drew's hands and started to dance. "Come on now, this isn't the Drew I know. The Drew I know would be on the dance floor showing off her moves."

Drew took a drink. "Jay, have you ever been so confused by life that you didn't know what direction it was taking you?"

"Yeah, but thank Yah, it led me here at this moment, marrying the love of my life."

"Yeah, well, we're not all that blessed."

Jay rumbled through his pockets, pulled out a dime, and handed it to Drew. *"A dime for what's on your mind."*

Drew gave Jay a gentle smile, "I can't believe we're still doing this."

As children, Jay & Drew would put dimes on their forehead, thus the coin would magically cause them to reveal their thoughts.

Drew takes the dime and places it on her forehead; her and Jay laughing at the foolishness of their youth, then Drew states in an unemotional voice. "Marcus wants to love me, he wants me to let myself go so he can show me things I've never seen and give me a love I've never had."

Jay couldn't believe Drew's nonchalant attitude towards Marcus's confession; he could clearly see it was time for a little tough love, after hearing the unregistered details about Drew and Marcus's conversation. Jay grabbed Drew's hand, rubbed it, patted it, then rubbed it again all while shaking his head.

"What!" Drew yelped out; she couldn't stand all the mystery.

"Drew, don't you think it's time you let someone love you?" Drew starts to defend herself, but Jay interrupts. "No, Drew, it's time, it's past time. Drew, you have passed on love your entire life because of fear. Now, you have this man wanting to show you there's nothing to be afraid of, and you stand here mocking him. Drew, Marcus might not be the perfect man, but he's a decent man, a man that's willing to love you with all your fears and flaw. Alright Drew, you gonna miss out on love."

Jay took the dime from Drew's forehead and replaced it with a kiss. "Marcus is a good man, and because of your parents, foster parents, and Shawn; you've put a limit on who you love and who loves you."

Drew fixed Jay's bouquet, explaining her reason. "Jay, love doesn't come as easy for me as it does you."

"It's because you won't let it, Drew." Jay crushed Drew's excuse.

"Jay, I have welcomed love my entire life. Don't you think if I had control over love, I'd have a happy marriage, kids, a dog, and a beautiful home."

Drew's reason had Jay speechless. He never knew Drew had those kinds of dreams; she'd always played it tough when it came to settling down and having a family life. All Drew ever talked about was having this bomb career and living her best life. For the first time, Jay could see Drew wanted more. He could finally see Drew, after so many years camouflaging her feelings. "I never knew you wanted those things, Drew."

"How could you, I never talked about it with you; I never talked about it with anyone. What does it look like for the girl with no family trying to have a family?"

"It would look normal to me."

Jay was hurt Drew felt this way; all the years they'd been friends, Jay never knew how damaged, and broken Drew was. "It would be you, defeating all odds Drew."

"Dang Jay, I don't even know how family works. The closest I've ever come to family was your family."

Drew reminded Jay that Shelia and Curtis weren't always the loving type. They constantly reminded her that she'd never be part of their family, nor would she ever have one of her own.

"Words can really do a number on a person." Drew shook her head. "Sometimes, I believed Shelia blamed me for not being able to have children. She would constantly remind me if she wasn't raising me, she could probably relax enough to get pregnant with a child of her own; not ever second-guessing if Curtis hadn't had those affairs, she might have gotten pregnant as well, but I guess it was just as easy to put the blame on me and cures me from ever having a family."

Drew wiped the tears from her eyes. "Now, I have this man that wants to love me, and I don't know how to love him back. "I'M A FREAKING VIRGIN JAY AND HE STILL WANTS ME!" Drew yelled out.

Marcus sat at the bar, sipping a drink, still in disbelief that Drew could just walk away from him after confessing his love. Everything in Marcus wanted to just get out of there, but for some reason he just sat there.

While gathering his thoughts, a sweet voice tickled Marcus's ear. "Your toast was so sweet." One of the ladies Drew pointed out from before sat beside him.

"Thank you." Marcus smiled.

"It's hard to tell you and Jay ever had any differences."

Marcus could tell she wasn't interested in talking about the toast, or he and Jay's story by the young lady's stare.

The young lady placed her hand on Marcus's knee, pretending she wanted to know more. Instantly, Shantel grabbed the young lady's hand, taking it from Marcus's knee. "Ski, excuse yourself." Shantel looked down at the young lady with a look of frustration; the young lady excused herself as to know that Shantel meant business.

"Marcus, I apologize." Shantel gave him the sweetest smile. "My cousin Ski is such a flirt, beware."

The pair laughed.

Marcus took Shantel's hand, "Well, I'm glad I have the enforcer here."

"You know I have to put the strong arm down sometimes." Shantel held up a fist in her laughter. "Why are you sitting her alone, I have the perfect friend who I think would enjoy your company."

Marcus gave Shantel a gentle smile. "If that friend is Princess Drew, you better rethink it."

Shantel examined Marcus more closely. "Oh my, do I detect trouble in the palace?"

Marcus hesitated, regretting he'd said anything; he'd never talked to anyone about Drew other than Jay. Besides this was Shantel's wedding day, and she shouldn't be worried about him and Drew's *situationship*.

"It's ok Marcus, I understand if you're not comfortable with talking to me."

Marcus couldn't take it anymore; he'd talked to Jay, but he really needed a woman's perspective. "You shouldn't be dealing with this on your wedding day."

"It's fine Marcus, we're family, and besides, I'm no stranger when it comes to you and Drew." Shantel chuckled.

Marcus rubbed his head. "Drew is driving me crazy. I don't know what she wants from me."

Shantel understood exactly where Marcus was coming from; she knew Drew could be complicated when it came to love, and even more complex about Marcus.

"Shantel, I've tried to love this woman, and she's shut me down every time. To be honest, Shantel, I'm about ready to let go. I feel like a sucka sometimes, but I love her so much."

Shantel could see Marcus was confused. "Sweetheart, I've been team Marcus for six years now, and I know Drew can be complex, but her heart is in the right place. We've had plenty of conversations over the years, and most of them were about you. Marcus, y'all have history, and sometimes having history makes the best love stories."

Shantel pleaded that Marcus didn't give up but to go harder. "Marcus, I know you might not think it's worth it, but in the end, it will be. Drew's a good woman, be patient with her. I'm looking forward to you making our Princess your Queen one day."

Shantel and Marcus joined Drew and Jay out on the over-look.

"Hey, you," Shantel danced, teasingly towards Jay, pulling him into her arms to share the dance.

Marcus stood back watching Drew observe the couple.

Drew watched the newly married couple express their passion for one another in dance. Shantel and Jay shared a beautiful love, and Drew was happy for them.

"It's beautiful, isn't it?" Drew's heart jumped, she didn't feel Marcus behind her.

"Yes, love is beautiful when you share it with the one Yah designed for you; I'm happy for them both."

Marcus took his hand and rubbed the small of Drew's back, she exhaled, laying back into Marcus's arms. " Let me show you love like that," Marcus whispered to Drew.

CHAPTER 5

A Perfect Love

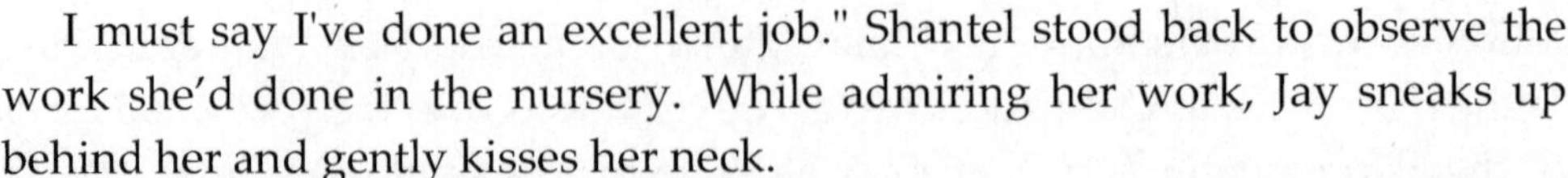

I must say I've done an excellent job." Shantel stood back to observe the work she'd done in the nursery. While admiring her work, Jay sneaks up behind her and gently kisses her neck.

"Wow, this safari theme looks like something out of a magazine. You've done an excellent job, and to think our baby boy will be here soon to enjoy it."

It delighted Shantel to hear the excitement in Jay's voice as she pulls him closer for a more intimate embrace.

"Ok, love bug, I ran you a bath, so wrap things up and come relax."

"Let me finish this, and I'll call it quits." Shantel took the paintbrush and stroked the tiger's tail.

Jay ignored Shantel's excuse; he grabbed the paint, put them on the Chester cabinet, turned off the light, and guided Shantel to their bedroom, where he undressed her.

Upon entering the bathroom, Shantel was amazed. Jay had a bath bubbles ran with rose peddles, vanilla scented candles lit the room, and smooth jazz set the mood.

"Jay, this is amazing, when did you do this." Shantel gives Jay a very seductive kiss.

Jay found himself blushing from the affection. "I know my wife, and things like this turns her on, and I need her turned on tonight."

Jay and Shantel share in another passionate kiss. Trying not to indulge, Jay pulls himself away. "Ok, get in the tub, Hott Sally."

Shantel laughs at Jay's comedic remark.

Before leaving Shantel to relax, Jay requests that she join him after her bath for a little TLC.

"Yes, my Mandingo warrior." Jay was intrigued by Shantel's reference.

After soaking and relaxing, Shantel finally decides to remove herself from the bath and join her husband. While making herself ready Shantel's mother crossed her mind. Shantel had tried on several occasions to contact her, but she never responded, so Shantel figures, why not give it another try?

Reaching for her phone, Shantel began to feel light-headed and dizzy; the spell came on so sudden, Shantel had to sit immediately before passing out.

"Ok, baby boy I know you feel cramped, but can you give mommy a break, we both have to share this body a bit longer." Shantel rubbed her belly to calm the baby growing inside, while dialing her mother's number. The phone rang a few times, but no answer. Shantel waited a moment, she didn't want to hang up prematurely. Shantel imagined her mother answering, and she announces the good news that she'd gotten married and expecting her first child.

The phone rang once more before it went to her mother's answering service. Shantel didn't understand why her mother wasn't picking up; she'd missed the wedding, now the birth of her first and only grandchild. Shantel started to become upset as tears streamed down her face.

Nearing the end of the hallway, Shantel could hear Jay singing along to Zapp and Rodgers. Shantel chuckled; she knew Jay couldn't hold a tune if you strapped it to his hand, but you couldn't tell him that. Jay thought he sound like Luther Vandross, and Shantel never said a word; she loved him singing to her while rubbing her to sleep.

Shantel gathered herself; she didn't want Jay to notice she'd been crying. "Baby, where are you," Shantel yells out.

"In the den, come join me." Jay said.

Shantel was surprised beyond words when she entered the room. Jay stood bare in his *birthday suit,* holding a tray with a bowl of Ramen Noodles and Oreos. Shantel couldn't have been more amazed at his effort to make her feel like a queen; Jay had done something special for her each month they'd been married, showering Shantel with a *perfect love.*

"Happy five months anniversary, come here and let me grant your every wish." Jay put the tray down and cuddled his wife.

Shantel loved Jay's romantic moods. "Jay, you're the best, happy anniversary." Shantel blesses Jay with a kiss.

"Shantel, I know we didn't get to honeymoon, and baby, I promise we will," Jay kissed Shantel. "But for now, welcome to Big Daddies house of wishes, your wish is my to do."

Shantel couldn't focus on anything but Jay's well-toned body that enticed her imagination; she could only think of one wish that would satisfy her right now. What a dangerous game Jay played with Shantel's hormones in a rage.

Shantel couldn't even be excited about her favorite snack, because her hormones wouldn't allow it. "Anything I want," Shantel asked with a seductive tone.

Jay, already knowing what Shantel wanted, took her hand and led her to a blow-up mattress covered with fur; candles lit the room, accompanied by streaming led lights, lining the ceiling. The wood-burning heater set the mood just right. Jay begins to kiss Shantel's body, starting with her belly and making his way to her thighs, kissing every inch of her.

Shantel's body was exhilarated by Jay's touch; her lips longed for his kiss as Jay tenderly placed his lips to hers. Shantel finding it hard to control herself wails with excitement. Jay was becoming more electrified by the passion flowing from Shantel. "Please make love to me." Shantel making that her only wish.

"Good morning," Shantel greets Jay with a kiss when he enters the kitchen for breakfast. Jay took Shantel in his arm, still aroused from the night before; he starts to grind on Shantel, kissing her neck and shoulders.

"Oh no Mr. Tate, we have a busy day, so we must make time for that later," Shantel said, prying herself from Jay's grasp.

"C'mon Mrs. Tate, you do this to me." Jay sat Shantel on his lap, still trying to persuade her to feed his craving.

"Raincheck, my love, we have a lot on schedule today." Shantel squirmed from her husband's grasp again, hurrying to retrieve plates from the cabinet, hoping the breakfast she prepared would satisfy Jay's appetite for now. When getting the plates Shantel felt the same dizzy spell come over her as it did the night before. "Whew, this little boy is doing a number on me this morning."

"You ok, bae?" Jay was now concerned about the complaint Shantel made.

"I'm fine, just the pregnancy bug. No worries."

"Shantel, if you're not feeling well, I think you should call Dr. Jones," Jay suggested.

"Jay, I'm fine, just pregnant, there's no reason for that." Shantel leans in to kiss Jay, assuring him she was okay. "After I speak with Drew and Momma Tate, I'll get some rest, I promise."

Jay sits Shantel on his lap rubbing her stomach. "I'm gonna need you to do that, seriously."

Jay noticed Shantel drift off for a moment, her face holding a look of concern. "Are you sure you're, ok?"

Shantel hesitated to respond; she didn't want to tell Jay she was worried about her mother. Shantel knew he would get upset with her for being anxious. "Jay, I tried to call momma again last night."

"Shantel," Jay stayed calm, not wanting to upset Shantel any more than she already was. "Did she answer?"

"No," Shantel responded with disappointment.

It hurt Jay to see his wife in so much pain; he'd tried everything to make her feel better about her mother, but nothing seemed to work. Jay's biggest fear was Shantel going into depression after their baby was born, just as her mother did when she was born, and after her father died. Jay read depression could be hereditary, and Shantel stood a risk, especially after the baby was born.

"Shantel, I know you want your mother to be a part of your life, but you can't make her, nor can you keep worrying yourself. I know it's easier said than done, but baby, I'm begging you, please don't let this stress you out," Jay shook his head. "This is why I told you to let it go, now you're upset."

Shantel could hear the concern and frustration in Jay's tone, and although she assured him she was ok, she could tell he was disappointed. Shantel placed a kiss on Jay's lips to humble his heart.

Drew grooved to the sounds of Luciano while applying an Aloe Vera facial treatment; she had taken the day off for self-care and taking full advantage. "Hey, can you answer that," Drew yelled from the bathroom; her phone was on its fourth ring and she was expecting a call from her bosses, congratulating her on becoming a partner. Drew hadn't officially been asked but she was optimistic about their decision between her and another prospective employee.

"Hello, you've reached Drewlynn McCain's phone," Marcus greeted.

A light giggle came from the receiver. "Marcus, is that you?" Shantel began to meddle. "So, we're playing secretary for Drew now?"

"Oh, we got comedy?" Marcus chuckled, catching Shantel's voice. "Drew's in the bathroom, is everything Ok, Shantel?" Marcus was concerned from the mid-day call.

"Things couldn't be better. So, how are you and Drew?"

"We're good Shantel, I can't complain. Drew's up for partner, and I have an Atlanta opening for a new barbershop in a few months. Things couldn't be better."

"Wow, you guys are really thriving, congratulations. How have things been with you and Drew; how's she treating you?" Shantel chuckled. "I know Drew can be challenging."

Marcus laughed. "Yeah, she can be at times, but I must say Drew's been great, and her letting me stay in the guest room until I get this shop underway has been a blessing."

Drew emerges from her bedroom. "Who's on the phone?"

Marcus faked a confused look on his face. "I don't know, a lady trying to sell timeshares in Florida."

Drew motioned for Marcus to hang up the phone, but instead, Marcus did the opposite and handed her the phone. Drew looked at Marcus side-eyed walking back to her bedroom; he knew she wouldn't be rude and hang up, but he also knew Drew didn't like talking to telemarketers, they always challenged her skills, being they were in the same line of work. "Hello, Drewlynn McCain speaking."

"Good afternoon, Miss McCain." Shantel went along with the prank. "How are you today, would you be interested in…

Suddenly Drew recognized Shantel's voice. "Good afternoon, Shantel, put me down for five." The women laughed. "Is everything ok," Drew inquired about the mid-day call as well.

"Everything is fine." Shantel is amused by the concern coming from both Drew and Marcus.

"Great, how's Jay and the baby?"

"They're lovely. We're just getting ready for this little boy's arrival. I finally finished the nursery."

"Oh, wow, I can't wait to see it; that's been your projects since before you were pregnant. I'm so excited." Drew began dancing around her bedroom with excitement.

"Gosh Girl, send some of that energy to Texas, because this little one consumes all I have."

Drew laughs. "I'll bring it when we come for the baby shower."

“Let me be the first to say, I love that it’s we now.” Shantel giggled. Anyway, I'm out picking up a few things and need your input. I was thinking about going with the Toy Story theme.”

"Ahem, I thought I was in charge of the baby shower?"

Shantel chuckles. "I just had an idea."

"Oh, you just had an idea, and it was Toy Story,” Drew inquired.

Shantel could hear the sarcasm in Drew's voice. “What, I love Toy Story.”

"Shantel, this is your first baby, and it should be an elegant shower.”

Shantel shook her head; she knew with Drew in charge she was powerless and would probably be in a *Tiffany Rose* maternity gown by the end of the nigh. “Fine, do you, just make sure I’m comfortable.” Shantel stated her request.

“I can do that,” Drew overheard the city in the background as she spoke with Shantel. "Why are you out, anyway, it’s in the 40’s there. You need to be resting."

"UGH,” Shantel growled; she was getting irritated at everyone telling her what to do. "You and Jay are on my nerves. I'm pregnant, not dead." Shantel spoke with frustration.

"Oh, sorry, is someone a little cranky?" Drew made Shantel aware of her rudeness.

"Sorry Drew, I’m just a little overwhelmed with everything."

"Exactly, overwhelmed, that's why I said let me handle the baby shower."

"It's not about the baby shower, Drew. I called my mom last night, and she still didn't pick up." Drew could hear the disappointment and worry in Shantel's voice. "With the holidays approaching, you’d think she'd answer, but still no answer—Drew, she's about to be a grandmother in a few months, and she doesn't care.” Shantel began to cry.

"Shantel, listen to me, I see where the frustration is coming from.” Drew putting two and two together. "I know how much you want your mother to be part of your world, and it's tearing you to pieces that she's not. Even more so because you're pregnant."

Drew could feel Shantel's sadness, and if she could jump through the phone and hold her, she would. "Shantel, please don't cry, I know the hurt you're feeling, but you must let it go. You have a whole life of your own. If your mother wants to be a part of that, she'll find her way to you. Until then, stop putting so much energy into her not being there. Besides, Jebba needs all your energy.

Shantel screamed with laughter as the people in the store observe her. "You will not call my baby JEBBA." Shantel is astonished by Drew's name.

"What's wrong with Jebba, That's my nickname for him; he needs a nickname."

"Ok, that's fine, but as long as it's not Jebba."

"You suck," Drew chuckled. "Anyway, while we're on the subject of names, have you guys thought of one."

"Nothing has been set in stone." Shantel browsed through the infant clothes at *Carter's*. "I wanted to name him for Shawn and my dad, but Jay's convinced he must have his own identity. Gabriel is one we've both agreed on, and we're considering Yaheim for his middle name."

Drew screamed and did another happy dance around the bedroom. Marcus chuckled; he didn't know what the excitement was about, but he knew if had to be big considering Drew's actions.

"Shantel, that's my name, what an honor you guys would give him the name Yaheim, one that I chose. You know that name means raised up in Hebrew."

"Wow, I didn't know that; may my son be raised up to follow the Highest Yah, and I thank his godmother for being a part of his naming."

Drew was so honored she could hardly say a word.

"Drew, are you ok?"

"Gabriel Yaheim Tate, my godson, I'm honored, Shantel."

"Well, it's not yours alone, you have to share it with Marcus."

Shantel removed the phone from her ear, another dizzy spell was coming on, but this time more intense, accompanied by a flood of hot flashes and sweats. Shantel could barely hold herself up, holding on to the clothing rack in the department store, trying not to fall. "Drew," Shantel called her name softly.

"Hello, Shantel, are you there, are you ok," Drew asked, now worried.

Shantel could hear Drew's concern, and with barely enough energy put the phone back to her ear, informing Drew that she didn't feel so well.

Drew's voice quivered with fear. "Shantel, sweetheart," are you Ok?"

"Call Jay," Shantel could barely get the words out. Suddenly, there was silence.

Drew stood in the middle of the room, screaming hysterically. "Shantel, say something, please."

Marcus ran to Drew's bedroom when hearing the terrifying scream.

"Baby, what's wrong, are you ok?"

"It's Shantel, she's not responding, she wasn't feeling well, she's not answering me back." Drew tried to explain but couldn't get the words straight.

Marcus took the phone from Drew, hoping to get a response from Shantel. "Shantel, are you ok?" Marcus repeated himself again when a bystander responded from Shantel's phone.

"Hello, I'm Misty, your friend has passed out. The manager called for medical assistance, and they're on the way."

After speaking with the woman, Marcus immediately called Jay.

Jay paced back and forth, waiting for news about Shantel and the baby; he was distraught, no one had come out to give him any updates in the last hour. Jay thought to himself, how could a hospital be so poorly staffed they couldn't send at least one person out to update him.

"OH MY GOD SHANTEL," Jay cried out. The images of their love was on repeat in his mind; that seemed to be the only way Jay could keep from flipping out. Jay thought back on the first time they met, to the first time she told him about the baby. Jay didn't know what to do; he was lost. Tears streamed from Jay's eyes, he could feel something wasn't right.

Mr. and Mrs. Tate ran through the double doors in search of Jay and Shantel when they spotted Jay at the end of the hallway. Mrs. Tate ran to comfort her son; she could see from a distance he was struggling.

"Jay, are you just fine, how's Shantel and the baby," Jay's mother inquired.

"I'm not sure, no one's come out to tell me anything." Jay was growing more impatient by the millisecond, and his mother could tell.

"Jay, calm down." His mother suggested.

Jay stepped away from his mother. "Momma, please no orders right now, just let me handle this."

Mrs. Tate understood how Jay felt, so she backed off and plowed into the arms of Mr. Tate, with her eyes full of tears.

"Come on Jay, your mothers just concerned." Jay's father motioned for him to calm down.

Jay looked at his parents and could see they were just as afraid, he apologized for his frustration, pulling them into his arms for an embrace.

Jay tried to pray but couldn't get the words together. The memories of his and Shantel's love replayed one after another. Jay couldn't believe what was happening, he held his parents trying to stay strong for them and himself, but the task was becoming harder and harder.

The double doors swung open and emerging from them was a nurse; Jay left his parents comforting each other hoping he could get information. Walking toward the nurse, Jay wanted answers about his wife and child, and would no longer remain calm. Either the nurse would give him answers, or he would go through the double doors and get them for himself.

"Excuse me, nurse, can you give me information about my wife, Shantel Tate."

"Mr. Tate," The woman scrambled for words. "Mr. Tate, the only information I have is that your wife's in surgery. They're trying to do all they can for your wife and child."

"What do you mean she's in surgery, and they're doing all they can. What's going on with my wife and child?" Jay was having a hard time processing the data.

The nurse couldn't give him any more information, so she informed Jay that he'd have to wait for the doctor with any more updates. The nurse took her place behind the nurse's station, where she proceeded to answer the busy phone line.

Jay stood in the middle of the waiting area shaken; his confusion, fear, and regret formed a fist and punched him in the stomach, knocking the wind out of him. Jay fell to the floor, gasping for air; he couldn't stop the uncontrolled tears that fell from his eyes. Jay's parents ran to comfort him. The nurse offered to get a doctor, but Jay's parents refused. They knew what he needed, and it wasn't a doctor. Jay's parents cradled him as he cried and began to pray.

Jay and his parents waited in worry for an update on Shantel; it had been almost three hours, and they still hadn't heard any more than what the nurse told them. The hours of waiting felt like years.

Jay was about to start another round of pacing when the double doors opened. Jay could tell by the look on Dr. Jones's face the news wasn't good. Jay couldn't move from the spot he held; his parents stood with him to receive the information.

Jay's heart stopped; he tried to shake himself out of the nightmare he was experiencing, but he couldn't. Jay's whole body shook, what he feared most had come to haunt him. Jay nor his parents could believe the news they'd just received.

CHAPTER 6

Stand By You

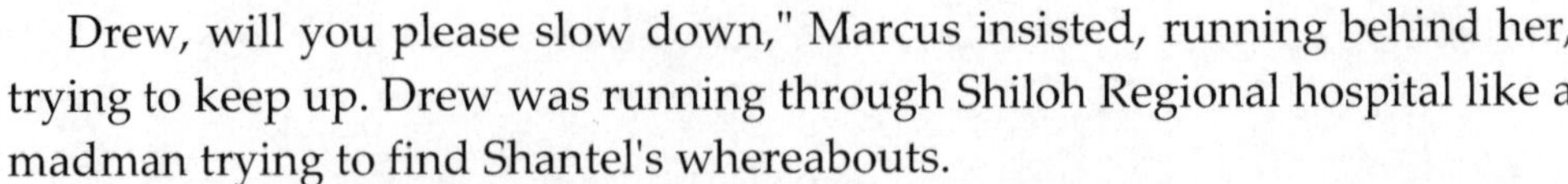

Drew, will you please slow down," Marcus insisted, running behind her, trying to keep up. Drew was running through Shiloh Regional hospital like a madman trying to find Shantel's whereabouts.

Drew ran even faster when recognizing the Tate's standing at the end of the hallway; she could see their faces soaked with tears as she approached. "Ma Tate." Drew hurried in for an embrace of comfort.

The way Mrs. Tate held Drew, she could tell something was off. "Ma Tate, how's Shantel, is the baby ok, where is Jay?" Drew asked question after question.

Mrs. Tate couldn't answer any of them. Every time she tried to speak, crying was all she could do.

Mr. Tate took hold of Mrs. Tate and cradled her in his arm. Drew knew something wasn't right; the last time she'd saw them like this, they had received the news Shawn passed.

So many questions ran through Drew's head, and no one there to answer them; there were no doctors or nurses in sight. "Where's the freaking staff," Drew yelled out.

Marcus gripped Drew's shoulders, trying to calm her. "Drew, baby, you have to calm down."

Drew appreciated Marcus for trying to be there, but calm wasn't something she couldn't be right now. Drew began to become perplexed when finally, she noticed a doctor. Drew quickly walked towards the doctor, confused and not knowing what question to ask first.

"Excuse me, Doctor, can you give me any information on Shantel Reid, I'm sorry Tate, it's Tate." Tears began to fall from Drew's eyes. Marcus held Drew, worried about the news she was about to receive.

"Are you related to the patient?"

"Yes, she's my sister," Drew stated with no hesitation.

While explaining, you could hear the hurt in the doctor's voice. Drew was paralyzed, the only words stuck in her head were, *sorry for your loss,* everything else was muttered.

Drew and Marcus stood there in utter disbelief. Drew tried to process the news but couldn't. Marcus was even more distraught.

Drew could feel herself getting light-headed and her legs becoming rubber; she began to fall. Marcus swiftly turns to catch Drew before she falls.

The doctor assisted Marcus in getting Drew to a chair. "Let me check her vitals." The doctor took her stethoscope and got Drew's vitals.

The Tates were even more distraught watching Drew go through her episode.

"Her vitals are fine; the shock from the news was too much for her to handle. Give her a few minutes, and she'll be fine. If not, have someone page me. I'm Dr. Jones."

Marcus was unsure about letting the doctor leave. "Are you sure you can't stick around, she's never done this before."

The doctor assured Marcus Drew would be fine, and he should relax for her sake.

Marcus held Drew tight; he'd been so busy staying vital for her Marcus didn't realize how hurt he was until he felt tears hit his hand. Marcus's thoughts couldn't be gathered; he asked himself a million questions and prayed a million and one.

After a short while, Drew slowly regained consciousness, examining everyone around her.

"Drew, are you ok?" Marcus was thankful she was back from her episode.

"I'm fine Marcus." Drew stood to her feet quickly.

"Drew, take it easy, you just...

Drew blew Marcus off, her only concern was Jay. "Ma Tate, Pop Tate, where's Jay?"

Mrs. Tate was finally able to communicate with Drew. "He's with Shantel."

The agony in Ma Tate's voice crushed Drew's soul. "What happened?" Drew really didn't want the Tate's to relive the trauma, but she needed to know what happen; the explanation from the doctor had literally gone in one ear and out the other.

Mr. Tate explained that Shantel's blood pressure was extremely high, and she developed a preeclampsia condition, making it hard for the doctors to control her blood pressure, resulting in an emergency C-section.

Mrs. Tate started crying. Drew rubbed her back to comfort her while Mr. Tate continued explaining the tragic events.

After listening to the story and looking at the hurt and exhaustion in the Tate's face, Drew suggested he and Ma Tate get some coffee and fresh air.

Mr. Tate agreed; in the thirty years he and Brenda had been married, he'd never seen her like this. Shawn's Death didn't affect her as this had. "Brenda, let's get some coffee."

Brenda pulled her face from Mr. Tate's chest where it had been buried all day; Brenda could barely stand. Mr. Tate had to practically carry her down the hall.

Drew stood in place for a moment, trying to muster enough courage to face Jay. Drew knew she would have to be strong for them both.

Marcus held Drew's hand as they walked down the hallway. Drew paused.

"Are you ok, you don't have to do this right now." Marcus suggested.

Drew stares into Marcus' eyes. "I need to do this alone."

Marcus tried to contest Drew's decision, wanting to be there for them both as well.

"No, Marcus, I need to do this on my own; please understand."

Marcus stood down and allowed Drew to go alone.

"Thank you." Drew kissed Marcus and walked down the hall to Shantel's room.

Jay didn't hear Drew enter the room, so she stood back to assemble more strength. Drew observed Jay with Shantel, pain was all she could feel. Drew was numb to everything else.

Jay sat there holding Shantel's hand, sobbing a silent cry that made Drew helpless. Drew prayed to herself. "Please Yah, I need you now." Taking a deep breath, Drew walks over to comfort Jay. Drew held Jay in her arms with no sound; they cried together silently, and Drew wouldn't let Jay go until he was ready.

After a while, Drew finally suggested they get some air, but Jay wouldn't leave Shantel's side; he began to cry out. “Shantel, Shantel. Please Baby, Wake Up." Jay laid across Shantel, sobbing.

Drew tried to pull Jay away, but didn't have enough strength. Drew was defeated, so she ran from the room in search of help. "Can someone please come and take him, he's not letting her go." Drew was bewildered about what to do; she just knew it was time for Jay to leave Shantel's side.

Marcus and Mr. Tate tried to help Jay to his feet, but he couldn't stand. Drew had never seen him so weak.

“No daddy, I can’t leave her like this, it’s not right." Jay pleaded for his dad to let him stay, as he tried to get free from their grasp, so he could hold his wife. “Wake up Shantel, baby please,” Jay screamed out.

Drew could see it taking everything in Mr. Tate to remain strong.

Finally, after a few minutes of struggling, the two men were able to walk Jay outside the room. Drew went back in to say her goodbyes.

Looking down at Shantel, Drew had never seen a glow so beautiful and perfect. Drew shook her head, not wanting to accept her friend was gone. Drew allowed the tears to flow freely taking a deep breath and exhaling. "Somebody pinch me, this can't be real.” Drew cried out. "Shantel, you were one in a million; you hurt us with this one girl. What are we supposed to do without you.” Drew stood over Shantel shaking her head, the hurt had settled in the pit of her stomach and wouldn’t move. “I promise to protect that little boy with all my heart and soul. I dedicate myself to him; I make you this vow, my friend." Drew cried more with each word. "You’re my best friend Shantel."

The more Drew searched for words, the more she cried; Drew knew she had to leave Shantel's side, but there was so much she wanted to say.

Drew was startled after Marcus touched her shoulder. "I'm sorry Drew, I didn't mean to scare you." Drew grabbed Marcus's hand and held it tight. "Come on, baby, time to let her go."

Drew could understand Jay's feelings at this point, because she didn't want to leave any more than he did. Drew buried her face in Marcus's chest and cried out. “OH MY GOD, Marcus, this is not right."

Drew watched Jay as he stared out the window. The tears were falling from his face unrestrained; all she wanted to do was help him, be there for him, but Jay wasn't responding to anyone, not even his parents. Jay was broken and didn’t know how to put himself back together.

Brenda walked over to Jay trying to comfort him once again. "Jay, let's get some air, maybe go check on the baby."

Jay didn't move or respond; he just stood there like a statue.

"Why don't Marcus and I take Jay home for a while; maybe get him a shower and change of clothes."

With no hesitation, the Tate's agreed; the only obstacle was getting Jay to agree. Ma Tate stroked Drew's face. "Thanks sweetheart, this will give me and Joe time to see the baby."

Jay's parents embraced him, but he gave no response to their comfort. Drew could see the worry in their eyes; she assures them he would be ok once he took a shower.

Mr. & Mrs. Tate sat in the waiting room, awaiting permission to see their grandson. The pair sat in silence, still in disbelief that Shantel was gone.

Brenda took Joe's hand, "Joe, tell me it's going to be Ok."

Brenda was seeking comfort from her husband's encouraging words.

"Brenda, I promise you everything is going to be just fine; we've seen worse days." Joe pulls Brenda closer to give her physical comfort as well.

The door to the waiting room sprung open; a middle-aged female Doctor stepped into the room. "Hello, Mr. & Mrs. Tate." The doctor extended her hand to them both. "I'm Dr. Russell, your grandson's Doctor. I'm sorry for your loss; Dr. Jones informed me about the mother."

"Thank you, Dr. Russell, how's the baby?" Both Mr. & Mrs. Tate inquired.

Dr. Russell updated Joe and Brenda on their grandson and the risk of having a premature baby. "I'm going to be honest, with him being 24 weeks and only weighing a 1pound and 10oz, it going to be touch and go for a while, but on a positive note." Dr. Russell gave the Tate's an assuring smile. 'He's a strong baby, and he's in the best care. There will be some bumps on the way, so get yourself ready for a very emotional journey."

Dr. Russell escorted the Tate's to a wash area outside the nursery. "This is where you'll wash up before each visit entering the NICU. You have to do it each time; it keeps germs and infections out." Dr. Russell also gave the Tate's masks, hospital wear, and extra hand sanitizer for additional protection. The Tate's followed Dr. Russell's every instruction.

Dr. Russell walked the Tate's over to their grandson. "So, will the father be joining us."

After sitting in Jay's driveway for over an hour, Drew suggested Jay go in and get cleaned up for the fifth time, but Jay wouldn't get out of the car. Drew didn't want to push him to go inside, but they were making no progress. "Jay, sweetheart," Drew spoke in the softest voice she could. "Would you like to go in for a change of clothes and shower?"

Jay muttered, "I can't go in there."

Marcus could see how hard this was for Jay, so he intervened. "Hey man, give me the key, I'll go in for you. Is there something special you need." Marcus took the keys from Jay's jacket pocket.

"Please, take me to my parent's house. I can't go in there," Jay states once more as tears stream down his face.

Marcus had never seen Jay this broken, not even when Shawn died. "Ok bro, I got you; I'm going to run in real fast, get you some clothes, and then we going to your parent's crib." Marcus eyed Drew before exiting, hoping she could handle things while he was gone.

Drew looked back at Jay, all she could see was the eight-year-old boy she'd met ten years ago, so fragile and timid. "Jay," Drew called his name, but Jay didn't look up. Drew reached back and clutched Jay's chin so she could see his eyes. "I want you to listen to me; you will get through this."

Jay pulled away from Drew. "No Drew, not this time. Not without Shantel."

"Jay, you have a son; you have to find the strength."

"Not without Shantel," Jay repeated the words over and over, growing more frustrated because he couldn't hold his wife. "I want Shantel. Drew she can make it better." Jay cried out. "PLEASE DREW, I Need My Wife." Jay began to pull at the door, not aware Drew had put the child lock on. "OPEN THE *DAMN* DOOR, DREW!" Jay screamed out. "I NEED MY WIFE!"

Jay continued to pull and tug at the door trying to get free, so he could find Shantel. Drew jumped in the back seat to comfort Jay. Drew could see he was about to lose it, so she took Jay into her arms and started a rocking motion trying to calm him, but nothing worked. Jay had the entire car rocking trying to escape.

The trio finally pulled up to Jay's parent's house; after the struggle Drew had just endured, she was exhausted, and ready to lay down. "I'm going to stay with Jay until his parents get here." Drew informed Marcus.

Marcus was troubled by Drew's proposal, he had waited all day for a chance to comfort her, but instead, she would rather console Jay. "Drew, I figured we'd go to my place and get some rest as well."

"Marcus, there's no way I'm leaving Jay like this." Drew started to gather her things.

"I understand your reason Drew, but we flew from Atlanta."

Drew began to get frustrated with Marcus's selfness. "Marcus, if you're tired, then go."

The words stung Marcus like a yellow jacket coming from Drew's mouth.

"Drew, Marcus is right, you need to get some rest; you guys can stay at my house."

"No Jay, that's out of the question, there's no way I'm leaving you." Drew argued.

Jay could see Drew was becoming upset. "Drew, I'm fine." Jay handed his house key back to Marcus. "Look bro, you don't have to drive back to Shiloh; just stay at the ranch." Jay eyed Drew. "You need to go with Marcus and get some rest."

"I'm fine, why can't y'all see that. Jay, you need me here with you, please don't push me away. I can't be alone tonight; I need to be with you." Drew pleaded.

There was silence amongst the three. Marcus felt worthless; Drew had made him feel less of a man. Marcus was crushed; he didn't care if Drew went with him or not. Better yet, he would rather she stay after the statement she'd just made.

"Drew, it's fine stay with Jay, I understand." Marcus wanted to express how worthless Drew made him feel, but this wasn't the time or place.

Drew sat in the Tate's living room, trying to fathom how her friend was gone. They were both just on the phone a few hours ago planning a baby shower, now she was lying dead in a morgue by herself. Sitting there, Drew could hear Jay wailing from the bathroom. Drew felt powerless; there was nothing she could say or do to comfort Jay.

After showering, Jay came and sat next to Drew on the sofa. Drew made small talk to fill the void of silence. "Sitting here brings back memories." Drew looks at Jay and smiles. "I remember all the trouble we got into around here. We drove *The Parents* crazy with all our shenanigans."

Jay never said a word; he just sat there looking into space while tears flowed from his eyes like an open faucet. Drew didn't know anything else to do but hold her friend and let him mourn his wife's death.

Joe and Brenda had been sitting beside the incubator for over an hour. They were astonished at the tiny life fighting before them; the baby was so small you could literally hold him in the palm of your hand.

"Oh Joe, he looks just like Shantel, and he's so tiny." Brenda was pressed against the glass bed; if she could've gotten in with the sweet angel, she would have.

Dr. Russell explained to the Tate's all the different machines, monitors, and tubes. Dr. Russell then opened the incubator's door. "You can touch him if you want." Dr. Russell strongly suggested they do so; she informed them from just their touch alone would give him a greater chance of survival.

Dr. Russell could see the Tates were slightly concerned, so she gently caressed the baby's arm. "See, it's okay, you won't hurt him."

"Oh my, he's so tiny, Joe." Brenda was trying to get up enough nerve to touch him. Gabriel Yaheim Tate," Brenda whispered to the tiny baby while rubbing his little leg. "This will be your name; the name your mother wanted for you."

Brenda looked up at Joe watching the tears fall from his eyes; she hadn't seen him in this much pain since he buried their son eleven years ago. "Go ahead, touch him Joe." Brenda encouraged her husband hoping the touch alone would calm his aching heart.

Joe was hesitant about touching the tiny baby, but he had to feel that he was real. The moment Joe touched him, his heart filled with joy. Yah had taken one son and given him another. Joe played with the baby's tiny hand; his entire hand fit around Joe's index finger. Joe was amazed at the grip the baby had on his finger; he could tell Gabriel was a fighter.

For the first time all day, Joe & Brenda smiled. They put the hurt aside and enjoyed the life Shantel left behind.

&

Drew could feel her phone's vibrations from the nightstand; she hurried to grab it before another round of pulses went off. It was the fourth text from Marcus that night. Drew dimed the light on her phone to review the messages. Drew didn't want the light to wake Jay; he'd finally drifted into sleep mode, and she didn't want to ruin it.

Drew scanned her messages.

#1 *"Where are U? I thought U were going to call."*

#2 *"No response? WOW, Drew."*

#3 *"Drew, I know you're hurting right now. I'm just trying to stand by U"*

#4 *"Drew, please call me when U get this message; baby, where are U."*

Drew looked at the phone shaking her head; she had no desire to speak with Marcus. He was becoming annoying. Drew couldn't understand why Marcus didn't realize Jay needed her right now. Drew turned to look at Jay, and although he was sleeping, Drew could still see the grief on his face.

Drew thought back to the last time she was in Jay's bed. It was the night before she left for college. She and Jay had stayed up all night talking about their childhood and their future. That was a special night for Drew, it was the first time she'd ever been kissed. Drew smiled at the memory, remembering she was nervous about college and never being kissed, so Jay made it his business to make sure his best friend didn't go off to college and had never been kissed. Jay made the kiss as special as he could. Jay got some of his mother's scented candles, which he later got chewed out about, popped in his 112 cd, took Drew by the hand and led her in a dance to his favorite song, *"Cupid."* The pair danced almost the entire piece, but just before the song ended, Jay softly placed his lips to Drew's. The kiss was over, and Drew's eyes were still closed; she'd never experienced anything like it before.

CHAPTER 7

Strengths & Weakness

Brenda stood at the door greeting friends and family as they filled Jay's house for the repass. The hardest part was over, now it was time for healing, which Brenda knew would be a hard task as she looked out at Jay still standing at Shantel's grave, weeping. Brenda felt powerless, all she wanted to do was hold her son and take away the pain. Sadly, Jay had barely spoken a word to anyone besides Drew; she was the only one fortunate enough to get any interaction from him.

Brenda was so focused on Jay she didn't hear Miss Sue talking to her.

Miss Suzanne Cummings was a long-time, nosey, outspoken family friend, who often said a little too much but meant well. "Brenda, what a lovely service." Miss Sue grabbed Brenda's hand, snapping her from the trance.

"I'm sorry Miss Sue, you were saying." Brenda, unaware of the words that came from Miss Sue's mouth.

Miss Sue carried on and on about the service and eulogy. "Brenda, it's such an honor, Jay burying Shantel out here on their ranch, choosing the perfect place under that beautiful Oaktree."

"Thank You, Miss Sue; that tree was the first thing Shantel noticed when they decided to build here." Tears began to fall when Brenda informed Miss Sue that she and Shantel planned to plant flowers around the oak in the summer.

"It's ok, Brenda, you go ahead and plant those flowers; it'll bring peace to the soul." Miss Sue patted Brenda on the shoulder. "Now don't you worry, God has a way of turning everything around; you keep praying and plant those flowers anyhow."

"Thank you, Miss Sue." Brenda helped Miss Sue across the door's threshold, allowing the other guest to enter.

Drew sat in the rocker imagining Shantel decorating the nursery; she'd bragged countless times to Drew about bringing the jungle indoors. Drew smiled examining Shantel's work; Shantel didn't over-exaggerate, Shantel had brought the wilderness indoors. Shantel didn't leave anything to the imagination; she had lions, tigers, giraffes, elephants, trees, waterfalls, tropical birds, and flowers. Anything you could name to make her jungle theme come to life; Shantel had put it and herself in the room. Drew smiled, Shantel had every right to boast.

Drew took a baby book from the table beside the rocker; she was in tears looking at the photos of Shantel, Jay, and sonograms of the baby. Drew took a pen and began to fill out the pages. Gabriel Yaheim Tate was the first thing Drew wrote down then the name of his parents. Drew was to make sure the baby knew everything it was to know about his mother.

Drew was so involved in the book she didn't notice Marcus standing at the door.

"Knock, Knock," Marcus stated while tapping on the wall to gain Drew's attention.

Drew looks up with tears in her eyes.

"Aww baby, come here." Marcus walked over to Drew, pulling her from the rocker with an embrace. "Hey, baby, how are you?" Marcus removes the tears from Drew's face, gently kissing her where they had fallen.

Drew pulled away from Marcus, rejecting his affection. "Will you look at the job she did in this room, Isn't it amazing?"

Marcus looked the room over; it amazed him the detail Shantel had put into the room. "This room is excellent," Marcus replies. "She would have been excited to see Gabriel lying there."

Marcus pulled Drew close; looking into her eyes he could see she was mentally drained. Marcus kissed Drew passionately, wishing he could take away her pain with one kiss. Drew pulled away once again. Marcus didn't understand why she kept rejecting him. "Drew, I feel disconnected, I feel like you've been avoiding me. You haven't answered any of my calls, and now you're rejecting me." Marcus gazed into Drew's eyes. "Can't you see I'm trying to be here for you?"

Drew didn't interrupt, allowing Marcus to state his case.

"I know you're trying to be here for Jay, you're loyal that way." Marcus removed his cowboy hat. "Drew, I'm hurting as well. You have made me feel worthless since we arrived. Drew, I'm trying to be here for you, and you keep rejecting me, why?"

"Marcus, Jay needs me right now."

"Drew, I Need You Right Now!" Marcus was vexed; how could he express himself like this, and she still didn't understand his pain.

"Marcus, can we talk about this later?" Drew exits the room leaving Marcus standing there.

Drew walked through the kitchen on a mission to the back door; she was trying to get away from Marcus and his needs as quickly as she could. Drew was almost home free when she was stopped by Ma Tate, asking her to take Jay the plate of food she held in her hand.

"Sure Ma Tate." Drew took the plate.

"Please, make sure he eats."

Drew looked back to make sure Marcus wasn't on her tail.

"Is everything ok hunny?" Ma Tate could see the strain on Drew's face

"Yes ma'am, everything is fine; I'll make sure he eats." Drew gave Ma Tate a half smile.

Ma Tate looked back and noticed Marcus standing in the hallway glaring at Drew. "Are you sure everything's okay?" Brenda eyed Drew.

Drew could feel Brenda trying to read her, so she quickly set out on her mission to find Jay.

Drew walked out to Shantel's grave in search of Jay, she was sure he was still standing there, but Jay was gone. Drew looked around amongst the few guests standing outside, but she didn't see Jay anywhere. Digging for her phone to call Jay, Drew heard banging coming from the barn.

"Jay, you out there," Drew calls out, making her way into the barn where she found Jay hammering away on a metal sculpture.

"JAY!" Drew hollered out for the hundredth time. Jay couldn't hear from all the banging, so Drew walked over and took the hammer from his hand. "Ma Tate wants you to eat something."

Jay glanced at the plate. "Thanks, but I'm not hungry." Jay took the hammer back and continued to beat on the sculpture.

" Jay, you have to keep your strength up." Drew insisted he ate something as well.

"I'M Not Hungry!" Jay hit the sculpture once more.

"Jay, I'm not leaving here until you eat something." Drew stood unmoved with the plate in hand.

"FINE!" Jay dropped the hammer. "You want me to eat?"

Jay snatched the plate from Drew's hand and began stuffing his face using only his hands. Drew was paralyzed; she couldn't believe Jay's actions, there he stood with meatloaf, mash potatoes, greens, cornbread, and corn on his face.

"There, you happy, now you can tell everyone I ate."

Drew could feel the blood boiling inside—first, her encounter with Marcus, and now dealing with this foolishness coming from Jay. "Look, *Dammit!* If you don't want to eat okay, if you're going to keep crying fine, if you're going to bang the hell outta stuff, cool, but you will not patronize me."

Drew took the plate from Jay's hands. "Jay, we've all tried to be here for you. We've all tried to comfort you in some way, and you've made it your business to reject us all. Well, I'm sick of it, buddy. You're not the only one hurting. Shantel's death also troubles us, and I'm not about to stand around and let you abuse me or our friendship. You have a baby fighting to live, and all you want to do is die. If Shantel could see you now, she'd be so disappointed."

Drew stepped closer to Jay, taking the plate of food and smashing it in his face. "Now, I'll tell everyone you ate." Drew flung the dish to the ground and began to walk away.

"Drew," Jay called out. "I'm sorry, please don't go."

Drew stopped to hear Jay out; although he'd hurt her, Drew knew he was hurting just as bad.

Jay exhaled. "Drew, this is a hurt I never felt before; even when Shawn died, the pain wasn't this bad. It's like pressure on my chest. I can't breathe. Every muscle in my body is knotted up; I smell her, I taste her. I can hear her calling my name."

Drew takes a rag from Jay's workbench and gently wipes the food from his face. "Jay, no one expects the pain to stop immediately, but you have to allow the healing to begin."

"Drew, it's only been a week. I'm a lifetime away from being healed." Jay eyed Drew weirdly.

"Jay, the healing starts when you let go."

Jay laughs uncontrollably. "Are you serious, Drew, do you hear what you're telling me. You want me to let go?" Jay eyed Drew. "I just latched on."

Jay couldn't see the reason for the conversation if Drew wanted him to let Shantel go. Jay thought: how could Drew tell him to let Shantel go, and what good would come of it, but more grief.

"Jay, listen to me, you never have to forget about Shantel; how could you with Gabriel here to remind you every day." Drew eyed Jay, summoning his attention, hoping he'd understand her reason. "Jay, there will come a day when you'll have to let Shantel go in order to move on, so focus on the angel Yah left in your life, because he could've taken them both, and left you with only memories; look at Gabriel as your walking memory of Shantel."

Jay started to feel regret when Drew talked about his son.

"Jay, this will be hard for us all, but I promise you we'll get through it."

"You know she liked this ugly thing." Jay swiftly changes the conversation, putting focus on the sculpture.

Drew admired the sculpture; it looked familiar to her, and it was defiantly something Shantel would find interest in.

"Shantel said it reminded her of the artwork outside Randy's."

Drew smiled, remembering Shantel always adored the piece of art outside Randy's. Shantel would rub the sculpture every time they went into the bar; believing if she did, she wouldn't get wasted.

Jay rubbed the sculpture. "Shantel always said I was in the wrong business; she believed I could sell my sculptures."

"Well, Shantel was right; you could sell this as art, it's incredible." Drew rubbed a smooth spot that had been sanded.

"Drew, this hurts so bad. I think about what we would've been, what we should've been. I think about us raising the baby together. Making bottles, changing diapers, feedings, pre-school, first lost tooth; how can I do that without her? How can I make all her dreams come true?"

Drew didn't know any other way to be with Jay than direct. "Jay, there is nothing you can do for Shantel but be the best father you can, and how you do that is by letting Yah and your family be there for you." Drew takes the hammer from Jay's hand. "Understand, best friend, I got your back even if I have to come back to Texas. Jay, before I said goodbye to Shantel, I vowed to love and protect Gabriel with all my might." Drew embraced Jay. "You have always taken care of me; now it's time for me to take care of you."

Finally, the last of the guest were gone, leaving Drew and Ma Tate with a messy house to clean, so Drew geared up for the task at hand. Drew also hoped this would stall the conversation between her and Marcus. Drew saw him walked through a few times when she was catering to the guest, probably hoping to catch her empty handed to finish their conversation, but Drew made sure to keep her hands full. Drew shook her head; she never could understand how people could be so careless with their trash.

While cleaning the den Drew heard a rumble in the kitchen, so she hurried to check the matter, worried Ma Tate had fallen. Upon entry Drew saw Ma Tate hunched over cleaning up a casserole that had fallen from the counter. "Ma Tate, I got this, go sit down and rest." Drew could see the exhaustion in Ma Tate's face.

"Drew, if I sit still, I'm going to think, and if I think, I'm going to cry." Ma Tate continued to clean the mess.

"I understand entirely, so let's do this together," Drew stated.

Both women shared a laugh.

Drew and Ma. Tate spent the rest of the night cleaning and reliving memories of Shantel; they laughed a while and they cried. Both women could appreciate the mental and emotional therapy they received from one another; it was helping them more than they could imagine.

"Thanks for your help Drew, I appreciate all that you do."

"No problem, Ma Tate it's been my honor."

Ma Tate glanced at Drew as she swept the floor; she figured it was good a time as any to address Drew about her actions with Marcus she'd witnessed earlier. "Drew, sit down, let me talk with you for a moment."

Drew took a seat on one of the island chairs, so Ma Tate got right to the point.

"Drew, earlier, when I asked you to take Jay his plate, Marcus came through the kitchen behind you, and honey, I couldn't help but notice he looked devastated. Now Drew, you know I've always tried to stay in my lane when it came to you guys love lives, but you also know when I feel like intercession is needed, I will change lanes. Drew, you have unquestionable loyalty for Jay, but darling Marcus is also a part of your life. Honestly, he's the more significant part of your life. Now, Drew, I know everything you had to endure growing up, it wasn't always sunshine and roses; you've faced many obstacles, and conquered most of them. I guess what I'm trying to say is, I've always looked at you as my own daughter and would never tell you anything wrong. I only want the best for you."

Drew felt honored that Ma Tate saw her that way.

"Drew, let Marcus love you, I see him, I know the love he has for you, and he wants all of you like any man would. Drew, a man doesn't like to share his woman with anyone, and you're making this man share you with Jay. Marcus is a good man Drew, and you're entitled to have a good man." Ma Tate took Drew's hand. "I know you're worried about Jay, and it's ok, but you need to focus on your own life."

Drew sat quietly and took every piece of advice Ma Tate had to offer.

Marcus and Jay sat on the dock enjoying their solitude. Jay noticed the stars shined brighter than he'd ever seen them before. Jay thought back to the first time he and Shantel walked the land. Shantel looked out over the small lake, and she knew it was the perfect spot for their home.

Jay glanced over at Marcus; he could see Marcus had a lot on his mind as well. "What's good, you alright over there?"

Marcus was so deep in thought he didn't hear Jay reaching out, so Jay backhanded Marcus's arm to gain his attention. Jay chuckled when seeing the look on Marcus's face.

Marcus cringed from the sting of Jay's slap. "Damn Man, What's Wrong with You!"

Jay laughed out, Marcus still had that same look of surprise on his face. "Why are you looking more depressed than me?"

Marcus tried to analyze what was going on at that moment; Jay had barely spoken a word in the past week, and now he was concerned about him. Marcus rubbed the sting from his arm. "Nothing Man," Marcus shook his head in disgrace.

"C'mon, do I have to give you a dime." Jay rattled his pockets.

Marcus laughed at the idea. "Yeah, it's one of those Drew things."

Both men laughed.

Marcus took a deep breath and exhaled. "Jay, I don't want to burden you with my problems. You have enough going on with Shantel and the baby."

Jay gestured for Marcus to stop." Hey man, it will be my pleasure to deal with someone else's life besides mine."

Marcus agreed, but still doubtful about pouring his and Drew's problems on Jay. "As I stated before, it's one of those Drew things."

Jay looked towards the heavens. "Oh lord, here we go."

Marcus eyed Jay. "Yeah, one of those."

Jay nodded his head in agreement.

"Jay, I understand Drew has this specific commitment to you, but bro, she has completely blown me off since we got here. I've tried to be here for her, and she's rejected me on every turn. I understand the love you two have for each other, but damn. I'm trying to get in where I fit in, and it seems to be nowhere when it comes to Drew."

Jay thought back to the night they were in his parent's driveway, and the statement Drew made would've had him in his feelings too.

"Back up," Jay responded.

Marcus's addled brain appears to be playing tricks on him, because he couldn't grasp what Jay was implying. "I don't follow."

Jay turned to face Marcus to understand his concept of Drew. "Look, you got to back up. Drew's not the one to receives comfort, she's the one that gives it. It's one of her strengths and weaknesses." Jay continued to explain. "Drew didn't get a lot of that nurturing mother's love as a kid, so basically, she tries to give it to everyone she feels needs it, even if they don't. Understand, Drew's wall is well guarded, with only one entrance. You can't knock it down, go under it, climb it, or go around it. There's only one entry, a small wicket gate that only she controls, and the only people permitted in that small door come few and far between."

Hearing Jay's explanation, Marcus was at crossroads. He knew he love Drew but was it worth all this. Shantel said it was, but Marcus couldn't see the point.

Jay could see Marcus was still torn about what to do. "Look bro, take your time and think about it, but don't analyze it for being more than what it is." Jay got up to leave Marcus alone with his thoughts. "Hey, at least you got someone here to fight with."

CHAPTER 8

Yah It's Me

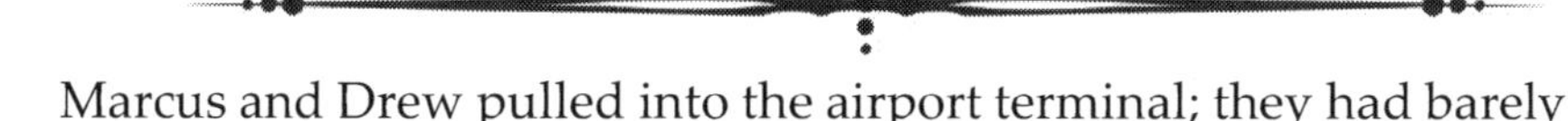

Marcus and Drew pulled into the airport terminal; they had barely spoken a word to each other all night or that morning. The tension between the two was terrible. Marcus got out of the car to retrieve the luggage from the trunk. Drew sat in the passenger seat, heartbroken she had to leave Jay, but she considered Ma. Tate's advice and set out to go back to Atlanta and patch things up with Marcus.

Marcus stood outside the car with the bags, waiting for Drew to exit. Drew glared out at him; she could tell by his actions that Marcus still had a chip on his shoulder, and she wasn't in the mood to deal with it; she was already leaving her best friend hurting what more could he want.

Drew exited the car. "I'm going to check our fight while you return the rental." Drew suggested, trying to escape Texas before changing her mind.

Marcus kissed Drew softly on the cheek, handed her a key, and proceeded back to the car. Drew looked at the gold key lying in her hand trying to process what was taking place.

"Why are you giving me this?"

"Drew, I'm not going back with you."

Drew was astonished at Marcus's statement. "What do you mean you're not going with me?"

"I'm not going," Marcus repeated himself. "Drew, you need to get your priorities straight, I love you, but I refuse to be your second pick. I endured this as a kid, but I'll be dammed if I go through a repeat as an adult."

A single tear fell from Drew's eye as the words Marcus spewed out cut her deep.

"I'm aware of your loyalty to Jay, and I will always respect that, but I will not come second to anyone, not even Jay."

Drew had a blank look on her face, trying to understand the events taking place.

"I'll be back in Atlanta for the grand opening of my shop, and I'll come by then to get my things."

Drew didn't utter a word; she grabbed her luggage, glared at Marcus, and walked off.

Marcus called her name numerous times, but Drew didn't respond; she just kept walking. Marcus snatched the cowboy hat from his head and threw it to the ground. "DAMN!" He yelled.

ൟ

Drew spent the entire flight processing everything happening in her life, from Shantel's death to Marcus ending things. The more she pondered on all that happened, the sicker she became. A small part of Drew just wished the plane would take a nosedive and kill them all, but who was she to kill the other 332 passengers.

Drew went through the photos on her phone, dating all the way back to the sixth of June, her high school reunion. Looking at the pictures, Drew logged every memory into her heart as tears flowed from Drew's eyes without permission, each one hitting the screen of her phone.

Drew was stuck on a photo of her and Marcus when a handkerchief covered her cellphone. When looking up to see who held the hanky, Drew was greeted by a warm smile.

"It's not my business as to why you're crying, but that's an expensive phone, and those Beautiful tears will ruin it."

Drew glanced at the neatly stylish, well-groomed man. "Thank you," Drew responded while using the hanky to wipe her tears.

The guy extended his hand. "I'm Zae Kingston."

Drew returned the introduction excepting Zae's greeting. "Drewlynn McCain."

"You know, I didn't think someone could actually cry tears of beauty."

Drew didn't know how to feel about Zae's statement, so she gave him a soft smile; she wasn't open to conversation.

"I see you're in advertising," the guy notices the *Cambridge Advertising* logo on Drew's laptop.

Drew shook her head in agreement.

"Your agency handles a lot of my dad's business; he's C.E.O. of Stylish Country Living Magazine. I know you're probably thinking how someone from the city writes about country life, well my dad is originally from a small town in Texas. My dad always felt like city folks didn't know what they were missing, so he started a magazine that would give city folks a taste and glimpse of country life."

Drew took a deep breath and exhaled, thinking to herself. *'I didn't ask, and I wasn't wondering, and I don't want to hear anymore stories about your dad or his magazine.'* Drew gave Zae a soft smile, hoping he'd take the hint, and just *shut the hell up.*

"Excuse me, could I get either of you anything?" The flight attendant was right on time, Drew was glad she'd interrupted the autobiography of *"My Dad."*

Zae glared at Drew; he could see she was hurt by something or someone, and much as he wanted to say something to make her feel better, the cold shoulder Drew had given him made Zae stay in his lane the rest of the flight.

Marcus walked into the studio apartment connected to his parent's garage. Marcus couldn't believe he'd broken things off with Drew. Dropping his bags on the floor, Marcus walked over to the French doors and pulled the curtains back; the sun rising in the east revealed the small dusty apartment. Marcus examined the small space shaking his head in disgrace. "What was I thinking," Marcus yelped out, then taking a deep breath to calm himself.

Marcus thought back on the few months he'd been in Atlanta with Drew and began to lecture himself. *"Fool, you love that girl, how could you let her go like that. Especially at this time, she just lost her best friend. Why man, you already know how she feels about Jay. If you just had been patient with her and taken your time, you could have made her love you the same way, if not more, but nah, you had to go mess it up. DAMN, Marcus, How Could You Be So Stupid and Selfish?"*

Marcus looked out over the balcony at his parent's house, he could see the glow from his mother's reading lamp. Marcus laughed to himself, thinking it had to be a good book or his father's snoring had gotten the better of her, because it was early for reading. Then Marcus notices the withering Ivy on his nightstand, and his question was answered, *it had to be a good book.* Marcus grabbed a water bottle from the fridge and gulped it down, only saving enough to share with the dried-out Ivy.

Grabbing his bags from the floor throwing them on the bed Marcus thought to himself, *'Might as well get comfortable.'* Marcus knew once he'd breaken things off with Drew, there was no turning back. Considering it was Drew, and she really had to love a place to visit it twice, Marcus didn't think Drew had that much love for him that she would ever revisit their relationship. So, when deciding to let Drew go, Marcus knew he wouldn't ever stand another chance. Especially the way it went down.

While unpacking his things, Marcus thought back to when Shantel pleaded for him to go harder and fight for Drew. Tears fell from Marcus's eyes, thinking back on their conversation. In a way, Marcus felt like he'd let Shantel down, and that was added grief. Scanning the apartment Marcus decided to direct his restless energy into cleaning it up; grabbing a V8 from the fridge, Marcus set out on his mission to restore the semi-abandoned apartment.

Drew walked into her condo and collapsed; she just wanted to lay there and forget about everything, but she couldn't; Shantel, Jay, Marcus, and the baby were in power, and they were not giving up the throne. Drew couldn't believe Shantel was dead, she could believe Jay was a single grieving father, and she couldn't believe Marcus had broken things off with her. Drew screamed a silent scream; the hurt was in the pit of her stomach, and it couldn't be birthed.

Drew finally got enough strength to drag herself to a shower, where she spent almost an hour crying and sobbing over her pain.

Staring at her image in the mirror Drew wondered how she would bounce back from the hurt that bound her. Tears began to flow from Drew's eyes as she watched them go down a dark drain to nowhere, and that's defiantly how she felt about the last few months invested in Marcus; they went nowhere. Reflecting on the time wasted Drew's hurt turned to anger and her heart crossed over to the cold side. Drew began stating these words, *'I will not let this hurt succeed,'* and she stated them repeatedly until the words stuck in her head.

Drew walked into the guest bedroom; she could still smell Marcus's sent in the air. Drew had only been in the room a few times since Marcus had been there, and somehow, he'd left his mark. Drew looked at the unmade bed, the hand weights in the corner, a pair of joggers, and his flip-flops that lay in the middle of the floor. "Leaving me with this mess," Drew stated while walking into the bathroom.

Scowling down at Marcus's things occupying the sink, rage grew in Drew; she ran from the bathroom to the storage closet on the balcony. Drew rambled through the closet moving things around and pouring stuff out before pulling out an empty box. “Get your stuff and go back to Texas,” Drew yelped out, running back to the bedroom gathering Marcus's things and throwing them in the empty box.

While making a sweep of Marcus’s things, Drew could only think about the months he’d been there, and she got even more upset; speaking to Marcus's things as if they were him. “How could you come into my life only to leave me like this? How could you tell me you love me and then leave?” Drew grabbed everything from Marcus's business suits to the toenail clippers, while on a continuous vent. "I can't believe you Marcus, you said you would never hurt me. You said you would never make me cry. You said you would always be here for me. Broken promises, broken promises Marcus, that's all they were."

For the first time in years, Drew felt alone; she had gotten so comfortable with Marcus being there she’d forgotten how it felt to be alone. Drew paused in her tracks looking down at the overflowing box, the anger turned back to hurt. Drew withered like a flower, wedging herself between the toilet and sink. The sobbing was uncontrolled so as the tears; Drew had never felt hurt like this before. The pain of not knowing her parents didn't hurt this bad, then it dawned on her that Jay had to be feeling just as bad.

Managing to pull herself from the floor, Drew grabbed a towel from the rack and whipped her face. Looking at her image in the mirror Drew wore the pain she endured on her face and posture. Quickly grabbing solidity and strength, Drew held a firm position. "CHIN UP,” Drew stated, raising her chin only to meet determined eyes. “CHEST OUT,” Drew voiced, taking a firm stance and pushing her chest out as far as she could get it. *“NOW STEP,”* Drew stepped away from the mirror, took a deep breath, and proceeded to gather Marcus’s things.

After collecting Marcus’s belongings, Drew put them in a pile and proceeded to the kitchen, where she grabbed a bottle of wine. " It's five o'clock somewhere," Drew said to herself while popping the cork.

&

After Marcus finished cleaning, he decided to go ahead and let his parents know he was back in the apartment. Marcus gave the apartment a once over before walking out the door. Shaking his head Marcus still couldn't believe he was back to being a Batchelor.

Marcus's mother was so involved in her book that she didn't hear him come in. "It must be a good book." Marcus stated.

Marcus's mother was shocked to see him. "Baby, what are you doing here? I thought you and Drew were heading back to Atlanta this morning?"

Marcus embraced his mother.

"When are you going to let us meet Drew? You've been with her long enough. I can't stand this oath you made."

Marcus thought about the oath he'd made years ago when he almost married *The Past;* a woman Marcus almost married out of high school. The pair attended the same barber college, and while in attendance, he and *The Past* sparked up a flame, and called it love, which led to Marcus's proposal and *The Past* turning it down. After that, Marcus swore he'd never bring a woman home to his parents again, unless he knew for sure she'd be his wife. So, Marcus was glad his parents never formally met Drew; he'd spent countless hours telling them about her, but never introduced her.

"How's Jay, I was hurt to hear about his wife. I sent flowers to Brenda. It's been so long since me and your father have seen her and Joe."

Marcus's mother kept talking, never taking her eyes from the book. Marcus never understood how his mother could be in a full-blown conversation with someone and still read a book. Marcus tried to get a word in, but she had already said five by the time he said two.

"Is daddy here?"

"Aww, baby, you just missed him, he and your brother just went to the shop. Speaking of the shop, I thought you were opening a Kingz Cutz in Atlanta?"

Marcus didn't want to relieve the last week, so he spared little detail. "I'll be going back in a few weeks." Marcus informed his mother hoping it would feed her need for answers. Marcus wanted to talk to his mom about everything, including Drew, but he needed his father. Marcus loved his mother's advice, but she could be slightly biased when it came to her boys, and right now, Marcus needs someone to be honest with him, even if it hurt.

☙

Rise & Shine,' the animated voice yelled from Drew's phone. Drew fought with the covers to release her so she could stop the annoying voice. "I have to get a new ringtone." Drew muttered, sitting up in the bed, trying to recall how she'd got there. The last thing she remembers was taking a bottle of wine from the fridge, sitting in the middle of the floor crying, popping popcorn, and crying some more.

Drew sat for a moment before making her way to the bathroom; it felt like someone had her head in a bench vice. Drew started to the bathroom, when she seen the empty wine bottle and a trail of popcorn from the bedroom to the hallway that told the story of why her head hurt, and how she'd got to bed.

Emerging from the bathroom, Drew grabbed a water bottle from the fridge, retrieved her mail from the floor, and plopped down on the sofa to examine it. While going through her mail, Drew came across a letter addressed to Drewlynn Rivers but without a stamp. Drew became puzzled at the letter and why it stated Rivers instead of McCain; she gave the letter a once over before opening it. Drew didn't know what to expect and feared anything else happening.

Drewlynn, I hope this letter finds you in the best of health. I was hesitant about reaching out; I didn't know how you would process it. Drewlynn, it has taken years for me to muster enough courage to contact you. I'm rambling; I tend to do that when I'm nervous about something. Drewlynn, my name is Carl McCain. and am your father. I know you don't understand, and I don't expect you to. Drewlynn, I met Joy at a very awkward time in my life. I was going through many things. I and Joy, your mother, hadn't been dating long before she disappeared. I didn't know she was pregnant at the time. Drewlynn, I have been afraid of contacting you. Afraid of the questions you might have, and I didn't have the answers. This is something I've been afraid to face for a while, but here I am facing it. Drewlynn, I will understand if you don't respond; I can't do anything but respect you for that. Drewlynn, I can't find all the words to say, but I felt they would come to me if I could reach out first. I'm not searching for a relationship, but I did feel it vital for you to know who I was. I will respect your feelings and will not contact you anymore until you're ready

Sincerely yours,

Carl S. McCain.

Drew peered at the letter, the words and letters jumped around the paper in chaos and so did Drew's emotions; she didn't know how to feel. This had been a day she'd waited on her entire life, but now Drew's feelings were awkward. Drew didn't know if she was excited, scared, angry, or she just didn't care anymore, but the letter was thin ice, and Drew had just fallen through. Before Drew knew it, she was pacing back and forth, hollering out her chant. "I WILL NOT LET THIS HURT SUCCED," Drew kept this up until she was out of breath.

Suddenly, Drew's doorbell rang, bringing her back to reality. Drew pulled herself together enough to answer the door. Looking through the peephole, Drew could see her noisy neighbor waiting to continue her investigation. Drew loved there were only two condos per floor, but sometimes wished her neighbor wasn't a sixty-something old lady, with nothing better to do but watch Family Feud and her apartment all day. Drew's first thought was to let her stand there, but her heart wouldn't allow her to be so cruel. As Drew opened the door, she muttered to herself, "thin ass walls."

"Mrs. Evens, how are you this morning," Drew greeted with a pleasant smile, pulling her robe together to keep from exposing the silk nighty she wore underneath.

"Good morning Drewlynn, I heard some hollering coming from your apartment, so I figured I would check it out. Are you ok, sweetie, I thought you were coming back next week?"

Mrs. Evens looked over both Drew's shoulders, trying to find something out of place.

"Well, I was Mrs. Evens, but I needed to take care of some things."

"I'm glad to see you're back, how's that guy of yours?" Mrs. Evens took another glance over Drew's shoulder.

Drew was getting bothered with Mrs. Evans's investigation, but she was pleased the nosey little lady was concerned. "He's fine, Mrs. Evens," Drew answered fast as she could, "if you don't mind, Mrs. Evens, I'm swamped. Thank you for your concern, all is well."

Mrs. Evens continued to look over Drew's shoulders. "OK, if you need me, I'm right across the hall."

"Yes Ma'am, Mrs. Evens, I'll keep that in mind."

Mrs. Evens started back to her apartment when she paused her tracks. "Oh, Drewlynn, I almost forgot." Mrs. Evens turned around to face Drew. "There was a man here looking for you, a nice-looking man. I told him you were out of state, and he should come back.

Drew couldn't help but think it must have been Carl. "Thanks, Mrs. Evens. I appreciate you watching things for me."

"No problem, Drewlynn." Mrs. Evens disappeared inside the dark apartment.

Drew closed her door; she didn't know which situation to handle first, so she did the only thing she knew to do; Drew faced the east and fell to her knees.

"Yah it's me, Drew. First, I wanna ask for forgiveness, I don't feel worthy of this opportunity to bow before you. Yah, I need you to remember Solomon's prayer when he asked that any Israelite facing your temple crying out be heard. I'm here Yah trying to get an understanding. Ma Tate told me years ago if I put my trust in you; you would always keep me. Yah, I haven't been feeling kept lately with all the pain I've had to endure these last few days; I don't feel you care for me as you did. Yah, my best friend is gone, Marcus left, and now my father is adding to the confusion and pain. Why are you being so cruel? I've always tried to do the right thing. I don't do too much wrong. Yah I'm trying to figure it out. What am I doing wrong? Yah, I need you to please lift this burden of hurt. Please. Help Me Yah, I Need You." Drew cried out.

Getting up from her knees, Drew's face was stained with tears; she knew Yah heard her prayer, but in Drew's mind she thought of ways she could assist him. This was one of Drew's bad qualities; she would go to Yah for assistance but didn't trust him enough to give it completely over to him.

Drew picked the letter up and examined it when noticing the letterhead read *'Unlimited Resource Solutions,'* a staffing company out of Texas. Drew was surprised to know it was from Texas; she wondered had her father been in Texas this whole time. So many thoughts and questions ran through Drew's head, once again making her overwhelmed with life and the fire that tried her like gold. There was only one other thing Drew knew to do; she loaded up on snacks, got back in her bed, put on old reruns of *A Different World*, and binged watched. Drew knew if nothing could take her mind off things the old retro show could.

THIS HAPPENED NEXT....

Drew laughed uncontrolled at Dewayne throwing Whitely over his shoulder attempting to save her from a burning *Heights Hall;* Drew had seen this episode a hundred times but still it humored her how Whitely worried about the materialistic things, like the Denzel Washington's photo that hung on her wall, and all Dewayne worried about was her well-being. *"Let that man be yo hero gurl, maybe I should've let Marcus be mine,"* Drew yelled at the tv. Two weeks had gone by and she'd made *A Different World, Drew's; World;* placing herself in every episode. *Drew's World* seemed easier to control; she already knew the problem and solution, but only if it were that easy in real life.

Drew went to retrieve a cheese puff from the bag and shook hands with air; looking in the bag hoping to have at least one left, Drew's feelings were hurt when there was none.

Drew thought about making a trip to the kitchen for more snacks, but she'd made an agreement with herself that after two more episodes she'd get up and clean the condo. Drew had candy wrappers, cookie packages, ice cream containers, empty fast-food bags, etc. trailing from the kitchen to the bedroom. The condo was in much need of a make-over.

After finishing her last two episodes Drew kept her vow and suited up to clean the untended apartment. Readying herself for the mission, Drew threw on an old, oversized college t-shirt, a pair of sweats, and a bandana. Drew then walked into the living room and put on some old-school music. The music flowed through the surround sound pumping enough motivation and energy into Drew she could've cleaned her place and another.

Drew plopped down on the barstool and inspected her work; she'd done so much cleaning the apartment was almost as clean as when she first moved in, and now it was time for a makeover on herself, after smelling the stench of onions coming from her armpits. "Oh, girl, you got to do better," Drew said to self, grabbing a bottled water from the fridge, heading to the bathroom.

Before Drew started self-care she called Jay; she'd tried calling him a few times before but didn't get a response or call back. Drew ended the call and redialed the number; she was puzzled at the message she received, thinking it may be a mistake, but received the same recording. Jay's phone had been disconnected, now she was concerned. Drew quickly called Ma Tate for information.

"Hello, Brenda Tate speaking."

Ma. Tate's voice sounded so comforting to Drew.

"Hello, Ma Tate, how are you?"

"Drew, is that you." Ma Tate was just as excited to hear Drew's voice. "I've been meaning to call you. Are you just fine?"

“I’m good Ma Tate, just got done cleaning,” Drew started running her a bath.

Ma Tate knew Drew wasn’t fine by the tone in her voice, but she wouldn’t make it a thing just yet.

“I’m calling because the recording tells me Jay’s phone is off.” Drew grabbed some milk bath and added it to her bath.

"Oh, sweetheart, that’s why I meant to call you; Jay has cut himself off from everyone, including me and Joe."

Hearing the sorrow in Ma Tate’s voice had Drew speechless.

"Drew, Jay *is* not ok; he hasn't been to see Gabe once, and he's almost a month old."

Drew smiled at the nickname Ma Tate gave the baby.

"Jay's letting the ranch go to *hell.* He hasn't taken a step into their home since Shantel passed. He’s out all night drinking,” Ma Tate let out a sigh. “His father tried talking to him; even Marcus has tried, but he refuses to hear anyone's advice."

Drew was upset that Jay was taking his parents through so much and even more upset that he’d turned his back on the only piece of Shantel he has left, Gabe.

"Is there something I can do?” Drew suggested she take a few more weeks from work and fly back to Texas.

"Drew, I couldn’t ask you to do that. Joe and I are handling things just fine. The only thing I need from you is prayer.”

There was a moment of silence between the two. Drew could tell Ma Tate wanted to say something, anytime she started humming during conversation she wanted to say or ask something. “What is it Ma Tate, is there something you need to say?”

“Sweetheart, Marcus told me about the break y’all are taking.” Ma Tate tried to be as discreet as she could not wanting to push Drew’s buttons.

"I see Marcus has given his version already." Drew tested the water for her bath.

Ma Tate chuckled, "I'm tired of you two."

Drew began to defend herself. "Ma Tate, I know you think it’s me, but I assure you it wasn't. Marcus sprung this, break, on me last minute."

"What do you mean, last-minute, and spung it on you?"

Drew didn't wanna relive the whole airport scene knowing it would make her cry, but this was Ma Tate, and she had to spill the tea. "When we got to the airport, Marcus informed me that he wasn't coming back with me," Drew exhaled, fighting back the tears.

"Oh, Drew, I'm sorry baby." Ma Tate hated they were going through this. "Well, maybe this break, is a good thing." Ma Tate tried to make better of the situation.

Drew wiped the tears that had escaped her eyes. "It's not a break, it's a break-up. Marcus. left me at the airport alone, do you think I would take a break from behavior like that? Marcus can call it a break if he wants, but far as I'm concerned, we're no longer in a relationship, and I understand that to be a break-up."

Ma Tate didn't interrupt, she knew Drew needed to vent; she'd always told her, it was better to vomit it out, than to let it sit on your stomach.

"Drew, I know you're hurting right now, and it seems life is stuck on rewind, but I promise you it's going forward. You just can't tell right now, but if you just hold on, you'll see life slowly taking you along and bringing you to a place of purpose."

Drew chuckled. "Seem like my only purpose is befalling heartache and pain. I'm finding it harder and harder to put my trust in a God that takes us through so many trials. I don't understand why Yah takes us through so much so we'll trust him. Don't get me wrong, I love Yah with all my heart, and I've always felt his presence in my life. I guess what I'm trying to say is, me and Yah have always had a peculiar kind of love; one minute we're good, and the next we're not. To me Yah has a strange and uncanny way of showing his love for me."

Ma Tate hated hearing Drew talk like that; she knew for sure with all the teachings and prayers she'd installed in her, Drew's attuited towards Yah should be more exhilarating.

"Drew, Yah takes us through trials and tribulations for us to trust him. Yah wants to know during those times we'll put our complete trust in him and allow him to guide us. Now, for as your love for Yah and his love for you; there are no two people that will explain identical love stories concerning Yah. Everyone's relationship and story when it comes to Yah is different and special in its own way. What you must do is make sure you're spending enough time with Yah for that love to grow into something beautiful, then that peculiar love will start to make since."

Drew stored the words of wisdom in her heart and took self-accountability; knowing she hadn't given Yah all the attention or time he deserved, and somehow needed to get better with their courtship.

"Thanks Ma Tate, you've opened my eyes to a lot of things, and I must say I have to do better about my time and efforts when it comes to Yah, but the Marcus thing is out of my control." Drew ran more hot water in her now cool bath.

"Drew, love comes when you least expect it, and when you allow it. While you were here, I watched you the entire time, and every time Marcus got close, you pushed him away. Drew This man makes it easy for you to love him, and you make it so hard; if you get out of your own way, you might have a successful relationship with someone other than Jay."

The words Ma Tate spoke were harsh, but Drew needed to hear them.

"Now, I'm not saying you have to take Marcus back; maybe you two need a break, before damaging your friendship. Take this time and renew your bond with Yah, it offers more benefits."

Marcus spun the barber chair around and permitted the music to guide his hands while cutting his client's hair. *Tyress* always seems to get him in the mood to cut hair, and right now, Marcus needs all the help he could get.

"Damn, bro, she got you feeling like that," Marcus's brother stated jokingly.

Marcus could hear a few of his regulars joining in the comedy, but he continued to perfect the fade he was working on, ignoring his brother's comment. Marcus's client looked at his image in the mirror and couldn't help noticing Marcus wasn't his usual self.

"What's up, Young Buck, you good?" The middle-aged man looked back at Marcus, waiting on a response.

"Yeah Sarge, I'm good." Marcus never takes his eyes off the man's head. Sarge could see Marcus was avoiding eye contact.

"That didn't sound convincing, how long have I been coming in here?"

Sarge was one of Marcus's father's former clients, and when his dad retired and gave him the shop, Sarge let Marcus continue cutting his hair, seeing that Marcus' dad passed the skill down to him.

"I've been coming in here 25 years, so I can tell when you got something on ya chest."

Marcus shook his head; he didn't know where to begin. "My girl and I are on a break, I mean, I'm pretty sure now it's a break-up."

Marcus shook his head again getting closer to Sarge, so the conversation would be between them. Marcus loved his barbershop family, but he kept some things private, his money and his relationship. "Sarge, I have done some stupid stuff, but nothing this stupid."

Sarge could see Marcus was sorry for whatever decision he'd made. "Aye, Young Buck, we all do, say, or make the wrong decision at least once in life; don't be so hard on yourself."

"I'm trying not to, but a woman like her only comes once in a lifetime."

Sarge looked in the mirror, examining the fresh new cut. "To be honest with you, my one-in-a-lifetime came and left almost thirty years ago. I guess what I'm saying is, if you can do something about it, then do, but if you can't, don't waste time and energy on it. Move on in search of new opportunity."

Sarge's advice was solid. Marcus knew he loved Drew and wanted to be in her life, but if she wasn't willing to forgive him, he would have to take the *L* and move on. Admitting those words dropped a weight in Marcus's stomach.

"Listen, Marcus, if you want that women go get her. You see it in the movies all the time."

Both men shared in a laugh.

After Ma Tate was finished lecturing Drew, she gave her an update on the baby. Ma Tate informed Drew that Gabe was eating more, weighing 2lbs and 10 ounces, and moving faster than most babies born at 25 weeks; Ma Tate praised Yah when she told Drew Gabe opened his eyes and cried out for the first time.

Drew laughed with joy, looking at the pictures Ma Tate sent to her phone. "Wow, look at him; he's grown so much since the last pictures, it's hard to believe it's been almost a month."

Drew went on and on about how much the baby looked like Shantel but held his father's dimples. Drew couldn't fantom Jay not going to see Gabe. "Ma Tate, I'm sorry Jay's not getting more involved. I wish I was there to help."

"Drew, as crazy as it sounds, I believe in some way Jay blames Gabe for Shantel's passing."

The revelation wasn't shocking to Drew; she could tell by Jay's actions and some previous comments he blamed Gabe, and Drew was glad his parents saw it as well. "He'll come around Ma Tate."

"I know he will, Yah's dealing with him. Well Joe and I were praying Gabe home by January," Ma Tate hurried to change the subject. "But Dr. Russell told us it wouldn't be until after."

Drew listened to Ma Tate go on and on about Jay and the baby. All the details started to sadden her; Drew knew if Shantel was here, none of this would be happening. The more Drew thought about it, the more upset she became. Drew hurried to end the call using her bath as an excuse.

CHAPTER 9

New Doors

Drew had been back at Cambridge for a week, and she still hadn't got her mojo back. Maybe if she'd stopped going through her photos, she could concentrate long enough to get something done, so Drew placed her cell phone on the Paris mouse pad and went back to work. Drew worked all of two minutes before the letter from her dad called for her attention. Glancing down at the letter Drew wondered, why now, and why drop a note; we're living in the days of cellular phones and computers, he could've just as easily sent a text or email. Drew thought about flying back to Texas and confronting him, but she didn't have the time nor energy.

Drew mentally left her office for a moment, traveling to a place where she stood face to face with her father, asking him the questions she'd written down in her journal through the years. The first question that came to mind was, '*why they didn't want her*.' For years Drew wondered why her parents walked out on her, and today she would find out.

Drew searched the letterhead on google, hoping to find answers, but couldn't find anything on Carl or his company. "Maybe he doesn't do social media," Drew said, glancing down at the letter. "He did send a letter," Drew chuckled.

Suddenly there was a knock at the office door, startling Drew bringing her back to the office. Drew gave permission for entry, sliding the letter under her keyboard.

"Good morning, good morning." a very chipper woman walked through the door.

Rachel Jones was her name, and she was one of Drew's bosses. Rachel was a happy free-spirited kind of woman; she knew what she wanted in life and wouldn't give up until she had it. Rachel, Shantel, and Drew had interned at Cambridge during their last year in college, but somehow Rachel became partners after two years. Some say she slept her way to the top, but Drew didn't care to bother herself with rumors. Drew knew Rachel knew her stuff, and whether she slept her way to the top or got there by her own ethical qualities, she was Drew's boss, and she respected that.

"Good morning Rachel, how are you?" Drew gave her a welcoming smile.

"I should be asking you that; glad to see you made it back." Rachel stood before Drew with two cups of expresso. "How was your trip?"

Drew thought to herself, *'I went to bury my best friend, how do you think it went.'* But instead, Drew smiled, accepting the expresso from her boss.

"We started to get a little worried about you; we thought you were trying to step out on us," Rachel stated with concern.

"Rachel, I would never do that, I just had a hard time coping with my friend's death. Dying is one thing but leaving a precious baby behind is something different."

Rachel looked at Drew with sympathy. "No need to explain, Drew. When my mom died last year, it took me almost three months to come back in."

Drew wished she had that much time, then she could help Ma Tate out for sure.

Rachel took a seat in one of Drew's chairs. "Drew, with you being gone these past few weeks, Isaac and I have noticed how much of an asset you are to Cambridge, so we were wondering if you'd like to be a partner."

"Wow, yes, I would be honored." Drew held a look of surprise. I knew you guys were considering, but this is surprising. I thought Carla had a better chance for sure."

Rachel glanced at Drew and chuckled. "Have more confidence in yourself, Drew. Isaac and I agreed it was time for you to come on board with us. You brought in the most numbers and clients this quarter and last." Rachel gave Drew silent applause.

Drew thought to herself, 'Todah Yah, it's about time they recognized her skills and hard work.'

"Drew, you have shown loyalty and a fantastic response; it will be our honor to welcome you."

Drew was boiling over with excitement; what she'd worked so hard for was finally hers. "Rachel, I'm so grateful. Thank you so much."

"Don't thank me, it was your hard work and loyalty. Give Isaac and me a few weeks to sort out the paperwork, and you'll be on your way."

Rachel stood up to exit, extending her hand to Drew. "Congratulations, Partner, I know we made the right decision." Rachel gave Drew a thumbs up as she walked out the door.

Drew pulled the letter from under the keyboard and stated, "I guess Texas will have to wait."

Drew was excited about Issacs and Rachel's decision to make her partner but couldn't enjoy the moment. Sighing, Drew thought to herself, '*Marcus was an ass, Jay was MIA, and Shantel was dead.'* Drew had no one to tell or celebrate her promotion with.

Drew looked out over the city from her office window; downtown was extra busy this time of year, everyone scrambled trying to get ready for *Xmas*. Drew looked down at the people and wonder if anyone else's life was as messed up as hers. Drew's heart skipped a beat when noticing the *Kingz Cutz* sign going up on the corner storefront. "Wow, Marcus did it," As disappointed as Drew was with Marcus, she couldn't help but be happy for him. Marcus had been working in the barbershop for months, and now his hard work was paying off. Drew noticed a few onlookers admired the new attraction, so she picked up her phone and attempted to call Marcus with congratulations, but her stubbornness got in the way. As much as Drew wanted to celebrate hers and his new levels in life, she decided it would be less humiliating to swing this one by herself.

Marcus looked out over the city from his hotel room imagining what Drew was up to, and if she'd consider having a conversation with him. The last time Marcus seen or talked to Drew was the morning he'd left her at the airport. Marcus mumbled, "Shh, I better call first." Marcus turned to retrieve his phone from the nightstand when noticing Michael standing behind him shaking his head in disappointment.

"Look bro, forget about that girl and come out with the crew." Michael danced in the mirror. "I know it's going to be some fine ladies out in Atlanta tonight."

Marcus shook his head. "Is that all you think about?"

Michael looked at Jay with a smirk. *"YEP!"*

"Nah, I'm straight, y'all take this one." Marcus laid back on the bed.

Michael looked over at Marcus. "Bro, I hate to see you down like this, you should be the happiest man on earth right now. You're opening a new shop, buying a house, and you're single."

Marcus looked at Michael with disappointment. "Yeah, success with no one to share it with."

"Look Marc, remember when you said you'll never let a woman bring you down again like *'The Past.* You back in that spot bro." Michael eyed Jay.

Michael spent the next few minutes trying to persuade Marcus to cheer up and come out with him and the guys, but Marcus declined, so Michael took the hint leaving Marcus alone to sort out his thoughts.

Marcus looked at his phone, debating if he should reach out to Drew or just let the entire situation play itself out. Marcus was really feeling the absence of Jay at this point, he really missed and needed his friendship and advice. Marcus thought about what his brother said and jumped to his feet. "Michael is right, I can't let this bring me down." Marcus looked in the mirror, dusted himself off, and walked out the door.

Drew stood in front of Randy's deciding whether to go in or not; she hadn't been in the bar or seen Randy in almost four months, and she knew he would have all kinds of questions about Shantel. Drew wanted to see Randy and tell him everything, but not tonight. Tonight, Drew wanted to celebrate her partnership, not sit around reliving memories of Shantel, leaving her heart broken, drinking tears with every shot.

Drew glanced across the street at the red and black Eclipse sign; she'd heard some of the ladies talk about the bar at work but had never gone. Drew was only loyal to Randy, but tonight looking at the Eclipse sign she thought. 'Why not try something new, celebrating with a new crowd might be just what I need.' Drew walked over to the bar.

Walking into the bar Drew was amazed, not only was the logo red & black, but the interior was as well. Drew was thrilled with the energy the decorator put in the bar; it had a soft, comfortable feel. Everything in the bar was red with a lining of black, from the lounge tub chairs, to the bar itself. The bar's lighting was also red. Drew was a long way from *Kansas,* this was a different crowd, a dignified bunch. Everyone was sitting, drinking, enjoying conversation; not jumping around, wasting drinks, and yelling across the bar, like at Randy's.

Drew noticed a sign saying seat yourself, so she looked for the most secluded spot she could find. Drew scanned the bar when she spotted a small private booth, small enough for her one-man celebration. Drew set out on a mission to claim the table when noting some interns from Cambridge. Avoiding an invite Drew kept her head down trying not to make eye contact.

Drew was just about to claim the table when a lively, smooth, well-dressed man took claim to the same table. "Excuse me, sir, but if you don't mind, I would really like this booth." Drew looked into the man's eyes.

“Beautiful Tears,” the gentleman stated.

Drew was confused by the guy's response. *‘Ok, let me just walk away,’* Drew said to self.

Drew started to walk away when the guy stated the words again.

“Beautiful Tears. You don't remember me?" The guy gave Drew a gentle smile.

Drew shook her head trying to get an idea of who this man was. "No, I don't."

"Damn, Miss McCain, I see you're still resistant."

Drew side-eyed the guy; she didn't have time for the game he played, and how did he know her name? "Look, guy, I'm sorry I don't remember you, so excuse me, I would like to...

Before Drew could finish her statement, the guy had his hand extended, reintroducing himself. "Zae Kingston, flight 333 to Atlanta."

Drew shook the guy’s hand, but still couldn't recall who he was.

"Oh wow, you really don't remember me." Zae took a napkin from the table and waved it. "Mr. Handkerchief Guy."

Then it finally dawned on Drew who the guy was. "Oh wow, I'm sorry it's been a hard month."

The pair exchanged looks.

"So, what are we going to do about this booth Miss McCain?" Zae gave Drew a flirtatious smile. "We could share it; it was designed for two people."

Drew eyed the handsome young man, thinking to herself, *‘what harm could it do,’* so she took a seat.

Zae was not only impressed by Drew's beauty, but now she’d captivated him with her free spirit.

Zae beckoned for the waitress. Drew removed her coat, making herself comfortable. Zae's words were stolen when looking at the gem that sat before him. Zae took mental photos of Drew, captivating her Asian eyes, full lips, perfect body, and her glowing skin. Zae was so involved with Drew that he overlooked the waitress standing before him.

"Excuse me, Sir, are you ready to order?" The waitress asked.

Drew waved her hand at Zae to break his trance.

"I'm sorry you were saying."

Drew chuckled. "I wasn't saying anything, the waitress was."

Zae hurried to turn his attention to the waitress. "I'm sorry, I got a little distracted."

After placing their order, Drew and Zae sit in silence for a moment, neither knowing what to say. This wasn't the way Drew planned to celebrate her promotion. *'What harm could it do,'* Drew mocked herself silently, while trying to feel out the stranger that sat beside her.

"I'm I that boring?" Zae finally broke the awkward silence.

"No, you're not," Drew smiled, "I'm just trying to get a feel of your spirit."

"Wow, so what does my spirit feel like." Zae eyed Drew, amazed at her aura.

Drew looked into Zae's eyes, searching his soul for the truth. While holding Zae's stare, Drew had taken something from him; he could say it was a small piece of his heart, but Zae didn't want to be labeled as crazy. Zae felt compelled by Drew's stare to open the doors of his heart, giving her every piece of him he'd never given anyone. Zae couldn't bring himself to look away. Drew had him hypnotized.

"Your spirit is warm with natural comfort," Drew looked deeper into Zae's eyes. Sometimes your spirit is misunderstood," Drew gave Zae a gentle smile. "You have an unconditional love for people that sometimes get you hurt. Sometimes you're hesitant, but when time and opportunity present themselves, you jump right in."

Zae was stunned, how could someone he's known less than 20 minutes know those things and be correct. "Wow, Beautiful Tears, that was amazing."

The waitress returned, eyeing Zae as she sat their drinks down. Drew could see he was a lady's man but tried to keep it on the low. Drew chuckled as the waitress walked off.

"What's funny, Beautiful Tears," Zae inquired.

Drew eyed Zae: the name he called her was really starting to bother her. "Can you please stop calling me that?" Drew took a sip of her drink.

"Why? Don't you like my name?"

Drew stared at Zae, debating if she wanted to share the story behind the tears. "If you knew the story behind those tears, you wouldn't call them 'beautiful tears."

Zae took Drew's hand. "I'm always ready for a good story."

Looking into Zae's eyes, Drew felt compiled; he had a familiar comfort that reminded her of Jay.

Marcus listened to the elevator music thinking back on a moment of passion he and Drew shared in the condo elevators. Marcus imagined Drew's touch, smile, kiss, and sweet smell; he was so deep in thought Marcus didn't hear the elevator stop.

"Marcus Tidwell, is that you?" The familiar voice summonsed Marcus back to reality.

"Rebecca Sims." The sight of Rebecca surprised Marcus. "What are you doing here in Atlanta?"

"I'm here on business, and you, Mr. Tidwell." Rebecca embraced him.

"Business as well Marcus stated. "I'm about to open a new barbershop downtown."

Rebecca was impressed. "Wow, how convenient; you can go from work to the barbershop, straight to happy hour."

Marcus shook his head in agreement. "Yep, in and out, in under an hour."

Rebecca eyed Marcus: she was truly impressed with the man he had become. Marcus wasn't that immature adolescent from high school; he was a grown man now, a grown man about his business.

"So, Marcus, are we putting down roots here, or just expanding?" Rebecca was anxious to know the deal with Marcus and his reason for an Atlanta shop.

"What's the deal Rebecca," Marcus asked, eyeing her suspiciously. "I know you, and there's an agenda behind your question." Marcus took a step back.

Rebecca eyed Marcus curiously. "I know Drew's here in Atlanta. Would that be your reason?"

Marcus could see Rebecca trying to pry. "My reason for what, Rebecca. Please don't tell me you're still hung up on the Drew thing?"

Rebecca took a step towards Marcus, pinning him against the wall of the elevator. "No, Marcus, I should be asking you that question." Rebecca stroked Marcus's chest, giving him no room to avoid the erotic behavior.

Marcus was relieved the elevator doors opened; he hurried to exit, but that didn't seem to bother Rebecca because her hand was still pressed against his chest.

"So, what's your reason, it's because Drew's here, right?" Rebecca waited for a response.

Marcus didn't want to give Rebecca any reason to gloat, so he didn't disclose any information about Drew or their relationship status. "I'm here on business, Rebecca."

Rebecca was pleased with the open-door Marcus left her. "Would you like to have a drink with me, Mr. Tidwell?"

Zae's eyes held Drew's gaze as she sang along to *Mary J's Sweet Thang;* he'd never seen karaoke like this before. Drew had the entire bar at attention as she rocked back and forth on the make-shift stage, as the crowd cheered her on.

Zae was mesmerized at Drew's unconstrained performance as she tossed her hair, rubbed her thighs, and licked her lip, all while seducing him with her eyes. Zae was so involved with Drew's seduction he didn't hear the applauding crowd until a group of men shouting encore summonsed his attention. Zae knew Drew wasn't his, but a small part of him felt threatened by the young men roars.

Zae hurried to Drew as she walked back to the table, hoping his actions would give the rowdy group a hint. "Wow, Drew, you were great." Zae assisted Drew as she took her seat.

Drew smiled bashfully. "I've always wanted to do that." Drew had an adrenaline rush; the crowd had her feeling like *Mary J* for real.

Drew took a sip of her drink while still humming the song. Zae could see the twisted nipple had a lot to do with the seductive performance. "You good Drew?" Zae eyed Drew concerned she might have had enough booze for the night.

"I'm fine," Drew chuckled turning her attention to a couple on the stage singing *Fire & Desire.*

As Drew sang along with the pair, Zae couldn't take his eyes off her; she was beautiful, intelligent, witty, and spontaneous. After hearing the story behind the *beautiful tears,* Zae couldn't understand how someone could be so foolish and let this *queen* go. Zae was like a fish caught in a net.

Drew was about to take another drink when she met Zae's leering eyes, and before she knew it, Drew was locked in an embrace that sent her soul into orbit. The kiss Zae blessed her with had control of Drew's body, paralyzing her in the embrace. After being released from the passionate kiss Drew was dazed and confused, thoughts spiraling, and words muted. Finally, after a few seconds of processing Drew could function, that's when she noticed all eyes were on them. Drew quickly grabbed her things, and ran for the door, on a mission to get away from this man who tried to open *new doors.*

Marcus and Rebecca sit at the hotel's bar, it wasn't the night he expected, but he was having a good time with Rebecca. Marcus saw a side of her he'd never known. Rebecca wasn't this vindictive, manipulative girl he dated in high school; actually, she was pretty cool.

Marcus laughed uncontrollably at the story Rebecca told. "Wow Rebecca, I never took you for the shy type," was Marcus's response after Rebecca admitted how she clammed up when meeting Drake for the first time.

"I know right, you'd think after interviewing hundreds of celebrities, I'd be calm and collective, but I'm telling you, Marcus, I was shaking like a wet chihuahua."

The pair laughed at the statement.

Rebecca clutched Marcus's hand. "I'm glad I ran into you Marcus. Tonight, I was going to celebrate alone. Remember the business I mentioned earlier? Well, it was an interview for editor-in-chief at one of Atlanta's bestselling magazines."

Marcus gave Rebecca soft applause. "So, did you get it?"

"We're celebrating aren't we," Rebecca laughed out.

"Oh, *is* that what we're doing?" Marcus looked around faking a confused look.

"Yeah, that's what we're doing. I just...

Marcus caressed Rebecca's arm. Nah, I'm just kidding, congratulations Tink, you deserve it."

"Wow, I haven't heard that name since we were kids." Rebecca eyed Marcus. I loved me some Tinkerbell."

"Yeah, you had a million of them." Marcus sipped his drink.

Rebecca moved her chair closer to Marcus. "You remember the first Tinkerbell you gave me."

"The stuffed one with the gold dress," The pair stated simultaneously.

Marcus tried not to get caught in Rebecca's web. "You know I still haven't forgotten what you did to me."

Rebecca settled her hand upon her chest. "Why, what do you mean, Marcus Tidwell."

"Rebecca, did you have to let everyone hear that recording? I admit I wasn't the best boyfriend, but you didn't have to disgrace me like that."

Marcus shook his head, still embarrassed about the humiliating recording of him begging Rebecca to take him back after breaking off their two-year relationship for Drew, who had no interest in him at all.

Rebecca chuckled. "You have to admit, it was funny, Marcus. But I do apologize, and in my defense, I was hurt. It's not easy finding out your boyfriend was head over heels for someone else. How did you get those letters mixed up anyway?"

The pair laughed as they continued their trip down memory lane.

Drew fondled her keys, trying to unlock the door, the five twisted nipples she'd consumed had her seeing twisted doorknobs. "I shouldn't have had that last drink, my goodness." Drew tried to stick her key in the knob and kept missing.

"I agree." Marcus grabbed Drew's keys to assist her in opening the door.

Drew turned and tried to focus her eyes; for a moment all she could see was a white ball bouncing up and down, back and forth. Once Drew's head stop moving, she could see the ball in focus, which was really Marcus's cowboy hat.

"What are you doing here? I thought we were taking a break," Drew laughed out. "Employees take breaks."

Marcus put his hand over Drew's mouth to quieten her. "Shh, you're going to wake the whole building."

Drew scrambled to remove Marcus's hand from her mouth. "Don't shush me, Marcus."

Marcus pleaded for Drew to quieten down but wasn't being too successful. Drew was on a rant about him being there. Marcus hurried to open the door; he didn't want Mrs. Evens to come snooping.

Drew staggered into the apartment after Marcus finally got the door opened, neither of them was aware Mrs. Evens had been watching them through her peephole.

Drew dropped her purse, then took off her shoes and coat leaving them in the middle of the floor. Marcus followed behind her picking the items up; he knew how Drew was about putting things away.

"You're Not Supposed to Be Here," Drew began to laugh, poking Marcus in the chest and taunting him about breaking up with her and leaving her at the airport. "Marcus, you had a diamond, and you let it go." Drew shook her head in disgrace while continuing to drive at his chest, repeating the word diamond.

Marcus was calling on patients now, Drew was really starting to bother him; he could take the venting, but the poking had to stop. Marcus had never seen Drew like this before, and he never wanted too again. Marcus couldn't help but take some of the blame. Besides, he did leave her at the airport after her best friend had just passed.

"Drew, sit down, you're drunk."

Drew screamed out. "DON'T YOU TELL ME TO SIT, I'LL SIT WHEN I'M READY!"

Marcus took a deep breath. Drew was really starting to push his buttons with the screaming and poking. "Drew, I know you're upset and mildly drunk, but the screaming and poking isn't necessary. Can you calm down, please?"

Drew searched the room for Marcus's things; she just about had enough of him. Drew picked up Marcus's items, shoving the box in his chest. Drew looked at him with tears in her eyes. "I'm not upset or drunk, I'm hurt."

"I'm sorry Drew, what else can I say?"

"Nothing, there's nothing to say." Drew eyed Marcus. "You know I made partner, and tonight I celebrated with a stranger, and do you know why I celebrated with a stranger, Marcus?" Tears streamed from Drew's eyes. "Because my boyfriend broke my heart, one best friend is dead, and the other is MIA. Have you seen Jay, Marcus?"

Drew became light-headed from her rant, so she sat down on the sofa. Marcus kneeled in front of her and Drew chuckled. "What are you doing, proposing. Wait, we're on a break."

Marcus could see the disappointment in Drew's eyes masked by the alcohol. "Drew, I didn't mean to hurt you."

"But you did," Drew quickly responded.

Marcus took Drew's hand and asked her forgiveness, but Drew remained silent; as much as she wanted to forgive Marcus and just lay in his arms, she held her chin up and stuck her chest out, thinking back on the day she was wedged between the sink and toilet. After the hurt Marcus caused, there was no way she'd turn and fold.

"My dad dropped me a letter." Drew shook her head in disappointment. He didn't call or email, he sent a freaking letter. After twenty-eight years, he sent a damn letter. I have spent my entire life wondering who my parents were, and if they were still alive."

Marcus could see Drew was overwhelmed with everything going on in her life, and now her father added to the pain. Marcus tried to comfort Drew, but she rejected it. Drew jumped up from the sofa, running to her bedroom, only to come back holding a green journal. Drew flipped through the pages on a rant about all the questions she had for her dad.

Drew paused remembering this wasn't Marcus's concern. "Can you take your things and leave?"

Marcus contested. "Drew, I don't feel comfortable leaving you like this."

"Marcus, you left me at the airport."

"Not drunk." Marcus was embarrassed by his actions being thrown in his face.

"Drewlynn, I'm sorry, what more can I say?"

"Good-Bye." Drew stood and slowly walked to her bedroom.

Drew could hear her alarm going off, but she couldn't move; she lay there looking at the ceiling suffering from the worst hangover ever. *"I'll never drink again,"* Drew said to self, trying to find her phone. Drew couldn't believe the event of last night as she thought back on her performance and the kiss Zae had planted on her.

Drew sat on the bed holding her head trying to stop the room from spinning but had no luck; it felt like Drew was on a rollercoaster ride after having nachos. Drew had to take this morning slow, because one wrong move and she'd be calling *Earl*. Drew slowly dragged herself to the shower hoping it would rejuvenate her.

After a long hot shower, Drew retrieved a water bottle from the fridge that's when she noticed Marcus asleep on her sofa. Drew was confused, she knew for sure he'd left last night after she'd put him out.

Drew walked over to wake Marcus; she began to think how noble it was for him to stay, then Drew kicked the sofa. "Marcus, get up," Drew demanded, nudging the sofa with her knee.

"Ok, I'm up, dang baby, I'm up."

Drew couldn't believe Marcus referred to her as *baby*. "I'm not your baby," Drew said sarcastically, still upset with Marcus.

Drew stood before Marcus still half hungover and mad, but it didn't stop her from noticing Marcus's well-cut body, and how bad she wanted to lay on his chest.

Marcus sat up to gain more consciousness, grabbing his shirt to cover his body. "Drew, can we please talk?"

"Marcus, you have been gone for weeks, there's nothing to say. Can you please get your things and leave?" Drew grabbed Marcus's things and sat them on the coffee table. "You know Marcus, I've always promised myself I'd never let a man mistreat me the way Curtis mistreated Sheila, and as much as I lo… Drew paused. "I'm not going to start now."

"Drew, please." Marcus grabbed her and held tight. "I was foolish and jealous. I didn't handle the situation well, and I'm sorry."

Drew was like melting ice in Marcus's arms. Searching Marcus's soul through his eyes, Drew could see the remorse, but the fact remained he hurt her.

Drew removed Marcus's arms and stood back. "The hardest part has already been tackled." Drew placed a soft kiss on Marcus's lips. "Marcus, I can't do this with you. Drew grabbed the box and handed it to Marcus.

Marcus was hurt, how could Drew be so cold, but what could he do, but take his things and leave. Marcus eyed Drew; she could see the hurt in his eyes but let him walk out the door anyway. Although everything in Drew was screaming come back.

Drew stood in the middle of the living room, silently throwing a screaming fit; she ran to the door on a mission to take back every word she'd said, but as her hand went to open the door, she locked it instead.

Marcus stood outside Drew's door trying to process what happened; had he really lost the love of his life, was it really over? The click of the lock confirmed it, Drew was really gone. Marcus banged the back of his head on the wall, "How can I be so stupid," Marcus asked himself.

Marcus stood banging his head a few more minutes when Mrs. Evens intervened. "Baby, that's not going to help anything; standing there banging your head against the wall is only going to give you a headache." Mrs. Evens chuckled.

Marcus was startled, for he didn't see her standing there.

"I'm sorry, Mrs. Evens." Marcus hurried to wipe his eyes.

"Here sweetheart, uses this." Mrs. Evens handed Marcus a silk hanky. "The hurt only lasts for a little while, and then it's gone, but it always leaves a scar to remind you."

Marcus looked at Mrs. Evens; no explanation was needed for her statement, he understood wholeheartedly where she was coming from.

Mrs. Evens gave Marcus a sweet smile. "You keep that hankey baby, she told Marcus, disappearing into her apartment.

Marcus's understood these were the consequence of his actions, and he would have to make this right; he would have to get Drew back somehow.

CHAPTER 10

Beautiful Rose

Marcus was shocked at the turnout for *Kingz Cutz* opening; the people were pouring in from everywhere. Marcus greeted each guest personally while trying to keep his head in the game, but the image of Drew kept haunting his thoughts. Although it had been 2months since their last encounter, the hurt on Drew's face was still fresh on his mind. Marcus didn't know what was going through his head, thinking Drew would accept his apology, and they would continue their mission of falling in love; he had to be out of his mind. The words of Mrs. Evens played in his mind as well; the scar still hadn't healed.

"Now see, if you would've just gone out with us, instead of groveling over her, you'd be enjoying the fruits of your labor, not standing over here feeling sorry for yourself." Michael whispered in Marcus's ear teasingly.

Marcus smiled. As much as he hated to admit it, Michael was right, he was feeling sorry for himself. Marcus couldn't understand how Drew could disregard his plea for mercy after throwing himself on the mercy of her court. "You right bro, I should've just stayed in the room like I said; not only did I go to Drew's and get rejected, but I also ended up spending the evening with Rebecca Sims."

"WHAT!" Are You Serious," Michael yelped out.

"Shh," Marcus motioned for Michael to calm down. "Nah, man, it wasn't like that, we had a few drinks and talked about old times. The night was going great until she kissed me."

Michael scratched his head. "She Kissed You, Bro!" Michael stated excitedly. "And you didn't tap that; she wanted it."

Marcus looked at Michael sideways. "Bro, I'm not over Drew; are you serious?"

Michael returned the sideways glare. "As a heart attack. You should've come out with us that night; you'd already be over this Drew chick. And do you wanna know why?" Michael put his arm around Marcus's shoulder. "Because you would've gotten to see what a real woman looks like. There was a Sista in the club doing a Mary J impression that would've taken your mind off Drew, Rebecca too."

Marcus could tell by the excitement in Michael's voice the entertainment was hot, and Marcus was glad he'd missed it. The only eyes Marcus had were for Drew and he didn't need his brother or some nightclub karaoke star changing that. Marcus shook his head; besides what did Michael know, he was a twenty-four-year-old *'Kidult'* without a care in the world. His advice for getting over someone was getting under someone else, and although they were raised to respect women, but somewhere along the way Michael lost his.

Michael was still talking about some chick in the club making Mary J look like a has-been when Marcus noticed Drew walking amongst the busy crowd; he wanted to run and take her in his arms, but his pride held back the action.

"You good bro," Michael broke Marcus's daze. "Get your head in the game; we got some hair to cut."

Marcus threw on some music, and readied his station for the inquisitive crowd, pulling out a satin purple barber's cape, a purple and gold carrying case that held his customized purple and gold marble clippers, scissors, comb and brushes. Drew gifted Marcus the customized set for his opening, so what better way to honor her by showing off his skills in styles. Marcus glided the clippers across the client's head smoothly, as the crowd cheered him on. Marcus demonstrated how he could perfect a cut in under 15 minutes.

I love you too Ma Tate, send my love to Pop Tate." Drew dropped the phone in her purse; after spending almost her entire lunch talking with Ma Tate, Drew felt eighty percent better. The other twenty percent was still being used by *Mother Nature.*

Drew neared her building when she heard a couple of her employees bragging about the new barbershop down the street and the fly barber that owned it. Drew had forgotten about Marcus's grand opening. Looking up at Marcus's work Drew was impressed, not only did he do an outstanding job, but he'd gotten these guys in and out before their lunch was over. *'He said in and out,'* Drew said to self, looking down the street at the line of people waiting to be amazed. As much as Drew wanted to go and congratulate him, the hurt wouldn't allow it. Drew wished him well in spirit and walked into the building.

"How was your lunch, Ms. McCain," The receptionist greeted Drew as she walked into the lobby.

"Too quick if you ask me Clarence," Drew laughed, exchanging pleasantries with the middle-aged gentleman.

Drew boarded the elevator, joining two of her interns. The two women laughed amongst themselves while viewing a new website known as *Facebook*. Drew chuckled to herself, the pair reminded her of she and Shantel, and Drew was feeling her absence right about now. Drew thought back to when she and Shantel were on the same elevator laughing at the stupidity on their *My Space* page.

When the trio exited the elevator, Drew noticed their flowers and mumbled to herself, *"It must feel good getting flowers on a Wednesday."*

Walking through the cubicle area of the office, Drew started to notice more flowers, teddy bears, boxes of candy, and greetings cards. Then it dawned on her, "Wow, I forgot it's stupid Valentine's Day." Drew was letting her bitterness get the best of her.

Drew sat in her office looking out at the employee's exchange laughs and giggles about the valentines they'd received. Drew had never been the one to allow a pagan holiday to control her mood, but for the first time, she felt the pain of the lonely spinster. Drew dreaded going home to an empty apartment; she'd become used to Marcus being there, and celebrating or not, it would feel good to go home and climb into his arms and watch a good movie.

Drew finally brought her head up from the computer, she'd been on a hundred for the last few hours. Drew looked out at the cubicle area and noticed it was empty; she was confused until she looked at the clock, and it read 7:18 pm. Drew saw all the valentine sticky notes stuck to her window and smiled. At this point she was grateful someone was thinking of her. Drew started getting her things together when Rachel poked her head in the door.

"Hey love, I thought I heard someone in here." Rachel looked at her watch. "What are you still doing here, don't you have a gorgeous man to run home to? It's valentine's day honey, work can wait." Rachel looked at Drew and politely smiled.

Drew removed the picture of Marcus from her desk and placed it in the drawer. "Marcus and I broke up."

Rachel glared at Drew with regret. "I'm sorry to hear that; you guys were so cute together."

Rachel held her chin up and stuck her chest out, holding up a fist pretending to protest. "Who says Valentine has to be about couples; hell, I'm dating myself, and I will not let a man validate who I am, or will I let him determine my happiness."

The two women shared a laugh, and although Drew laughed at the fake protest, it made a lot of sense to her, thinking about the words Rachel had just spewed out.

"Drew, I know you're not into the whole holiday thing, but a few of us singles were going for drinks tonight at Eclipse. Would you like to join our caravan, and get a new head on your pillow?" Rachel gave Drew a devious smile.

Drew thought: her pillows were just fine with her head, and then she thought back to her night with Zae and quivered. Drew wanted to decline in fear of seeing Zae, but she accepted Rachel's invite. Besides, a couple of months had passed, and it was better than going home to an empty apartment and stuffing her face with ice cream.

Drew stood in front of Eclipse glaring in the window, watching Rachel and a few more coworkers having the time of their lives, and much as Drew wanted to be a part of the fun, she couldn't bring herself to go in. The thought of her running out on Zae like a hooker runs from her pimp haunted Drew.

After pondering a few more minutes, Drew finally deciding to skip the invite and do her own thing. Glancing across the street at Randy's, Drew thought, *'what better way to spend the evening,'* so she shifted her loyalty back to Randy and walked across the street.

Drew stood at the entrance rubbing the sculpture Shantel always loved; she would stroke the piece of art every time they came into the bar. Shantel said it gave her good luck and kept her from getting too drunk. Drew laughed at the foolishness, seeing that it didn't take much for Shantel to get drunk; usually after one drink she was already buzzed.

Walking into the bar, Drew noticed all the couples and felt like a third wheel to everyone. *'I should've just stayed at home,'* Drew said to self, while looking for a break in the crowed so he could get out of there.

"Drew Boo, is that you," A voice rang out.

'Dang,' Drew said to self after being caught. "Hey Randy, how's your night going?" Drew turned to make her way to the bar.

"It's going great, now that I can look upon that beautiful face." Randy gave Drew the biggest smile reviling his shiny gold teeth.

Drew smiled bashfully. "Thanks Randy, you always know how to make me smile."

"That means I'm doing my job." Randy handed Drew a Twisted nipple. "Sorry I didn't make Shantel's funeral. The bar can't tend itself."

Drew accepted the false reason, knowing Randy had a couple of people to mind the bar. This was just Randy's way of saying *'I wasn't strong enough to face that kind of pain,* and Drew understood, not make it a thing.

"It's ok Randy, I know your heart was there." Drew gave Randy an assuring smile.

"If it's anything that baby needs, you let me know, you hear me." Randy started to get teary-eyed.

"I will, Randy." Drew cuffed his hand giving him a wink.

Randy studied Drew a moment. "Are you ok," he asked.

Drew looked at Randy and smiled; it amazed her how he could always feel when something wasn't right with her. "I'm ok Randy." Drew took her hand and lifted her chin. "Now go take care of your customers."

"And that's where it better stay." Randy kissed Drew on the forehead before walking off to tend to his customers.

Drew peacefully sipped her beverage while listening to the slow jams the DJ played for the lovers in the crowd. Drew thought about Marcus and wondered how his grand opening went. Then she thought about the last time she and Shantel were in Randy's together; it was about three years ago, and they were celebrating their full-time positions at *Cambridge.* Drew shook her head; it was also the first time she'd met *The Mistake.*

The *Mistake* was a true-to-the-earth narcissist in his fourth year of law school at *Crowdy University,* and dating him was the biggest mistake Drew ever made; not only did he almost influence Drew to quit her job, but he almost broke her and Shantel's friendship.

After Drew's reminiscing session, she began to feel the effects of the twisted nipple; her mind, body, and soul were relaxed entirely as she grooved to the smooth sounds.

"A beautiful rose, for a beautiful lady." Drew was interrupted by a deep, gentle, male's voice that hugged her heart. Drew spun around only to meet eyes with Jay. Drew was astounded; after months Jay stood before her.

"Damn, do I get a hug?" Jay stood with his arms stretched.

Drew glared into Jay's eyes, and a single tear strolled down her face; she was still in shock. Drew didn't know to be mad or relieved; she wanted to be angry at Jay for every reason, but she couldn't. Drew jumped around Jay's neck and wouldn't let go. The warmth from Drew's hug made Jay hold on to her as well.

"Jay, how are you here?"

"Well, I boarded a plane and rented a car."

Drew hit Jay playfully. "You know what I mean."

Jay laughed; it felt good to be in Drew's presence. "I've missed you so much, Drew."

"It's been months, Jay." Drew hugged Jay again and didn't let go.

Jay explained to Drew the only way he could deal with Shantel's death was to completely isolate himself from everything and everybody, so he kept his promise to Shantel and went on their honeymoon to Jamaica.

Drew shook her head as tears flowed from her eyes.

"I'm sorry Drew, I was so wrapped up in my own pain, feeling sorry for myself, blaming Yah, and didn't once think about those suffering with me."

Drew stroked Jay's face. "I'm glad you're ok, that's all that matters."

Jay pulled Drew's chin up. "I ran into Marcus, and he told me you were in a dark place."

"UGH, Marcus is overexaggerating," Drew replied in an annoyed tone.

"Calm down," Jay grabbed Drew's hand. "I was at his grand opening, and he mentioned to me that you had some things going on; he cares about you Drew."

"Jay, why go all the way to Jamaica, I needed you." Drew hurrying to change the conversation.

"Drew, I had to, the pressure from everything and everybody was consuming me."

"Even me, Jay?"

Jay laughed. "Especially you." Drew was confused by Jay's statement. "I could see that I was hurting you, and I couldn't take losing you too. So, I went MIA for a while to clear my head and allow Yah to direct me."

Drew punched Jay in the arm. "I needed you, Jay."

Jay could see Marcus wasn't lying about Drew being in a dark place. "Come on, let me get you home." Jay went to pay for Drew's tab, but Randy refused.

Can You Get That," Drew yelled from her bedroom as she changed into something more comfortable. Drew still couldn't believe Jay was there in her condo, alive and well; she couldn't wait to get caught up on things.

"I have an XL hand-tossed pizza for Drew."

"That's us." Jay pulled out his wallet to pay the young lady.

While making the transaction, Jay noticed the young woman checking him out; he was used to it, but it always made him feel uncomfortable. Jay couldn't understand why women seemed to always be the pursuer instead of letting a man be a gentleman and come at her, but it didn't matter Jay wasn't interested anyway.

"You have the sexiest dimples, has anybody ever told you that?" The young lady leaned against the doorframe sucking her teeth.

"Yeah, a few," Jay smiled avoiding eye contact. "All I have is a fifty, you can keep the change."

The young lady looked at the money and then at Jay. "Impressive, there's nothing like a big tipper, thanks dimples." The young lady poked one of Jays dimples with her index finger.

Jay closed the door in a hurry, finding Drew standing behind him laughing uncontrollability; she knew how Jay was when it came to women throwing themselves at him.

"Oh, has anyone ever told you your dimples are sexy." Drew teased Jay.

"Geesh, she was coming on strong," Jay chuckled. "Man, these females are crazy."

"It brings peace to my soul seeing you smile." Drew threw Jay a wink.

"It feels good to smile for a change," Jay admitted.

Drew ran to the kitchen to retrieve plates and wine, ordering Jay to find a good movie.

"What kind of movie?"

'Action,' they both said in unison.

"Why does it always have to be action." Jay flipped through the channels. "You need a little romance in your life, maybe look at the Notebook or something."

"Hell No, I Keeps It Gangster Baby!" Drew yelled from the kitchen.

Jay laughed, "That's the problem."

"What's the problem, Jay?" Drew stood before him, tapping her feet holding the wine and plates.

"It would help if you got a little romance in you; that's all I'm saying." Jay chuckled. "Drew, it's a shame you don't have a romantic bone in your body."

"I resent that; I can be romantic."

"Yeah, right." Jay took a bite of his pizza. "Marcus told me you made partner."

Drew shook her head. "I see he's not only your partner, but he's also the messenger." Drew poured a glass of wine. "And why was he the first person you seen?"

Jay blew Drew's question off by raising a glass in the air, toasting to Drew's new position.

Drew accepted his toast. "Yeah, ya girl finally got her forty acres and a mule."

Drew sipped her wine, wondering if Marcus told Jay about her dad reaching out as well.

"So, why did you reach out to Marcus, before me?" Drew asked not letting Jay escape the answer this time.

Jay could see Drew was feeling *some type of way,* so he explained. "Drew, Marcus and I are business partners, we have to talk. Besides, he was taking care of things."

Drew gave Jay pouty lips pretending to be upset that she wasn't first on the list. "Since Mr. Tidwell is so good at delivering messages, did he tell you about my dad?" Drew threw the question out there thinking Jay already knew, but she could tell by the look of surprise Marcus had left that part out. Either way, Jay was looking at Drew like she'd won the lottery, but that was not at all how she felt.

"No, are you serious!" Jay yelped, with excitement. "How do you feel about it?"

Drew took a sip of wine. "At first, it was confusing, and then I became curious; there's little to know about my parents, Curtis and Shelia only knew what the agency told them. I remember bits and pieces about my mom, but not her face."

Jay became even more anxious to find out who this mysterious parent was; he could remember he and Drew going on imaginary quests searching for her parents when they were kids; a voyage that never went beyond Miss Tess's candy house at the end of the block. Jay and Drew did this for years until one day Drew stopped. Jay never got an understanding of why Drew stopped; she came to him one day with all their notes, clues, and comparisons, handed them over to him, and said she was quiet.

"I tried searching for him, but nothing came up." Drew said with disappointment before running off to retrieve the letter.

Jay took a sip of wine; he couldn't believe Drew was going to find out after all these years who her father was. Drew had spent countless days and nights crying and worrying, wanting to know this information.

Drew handed Jay the letter so he could observe it closer. Jay was surprised to see the letterhead was from a staffing agency out of Texas, "Wow, he's been in the same state as you for all these years; no worries, when you ready we're going on another quest, but this time for real."

The pair laughed.

Jay and Drew sat for hours catching up and reminiscing about life; it was just the therapy they both needed. They laughed, Drew cried, they laughed some more, and Drew cried some more. Drew didn't want to ruin their good time, but she felt it time for her to intervene on Gabe and the Tate's behalf.

"Jay, can I show you something?" Drew took her phone from the couch table and found a picture of Gabe.

Jay refused to look at the picture.

"Jay, I need you to look at this picture." Drew pushed the phone in Jay's face, thinking he would fall in love if he just took one look.

"Drew, I can't, it hurts too bad." Jay pushed the phone away.

Drew kneeled in front of Jay so she could look at his face. "I don't understand Jay, Gabe is your son; he's part of you, and Shantel."

Jay became bothered as tears fell from his eyes. "If it wasn't for that baby, I would have my wife, here, with me."

Jay gulped down his wine and poured another glass. Drew's heart was in her stomach; she knew Jay blamed Gabe, but the anger he had behind it was heartbreaking.

"Jay, to love Gabe is to love Shantel, as if she were still here."

Drew placed her hand on Jay's chest to calm his spirit; she could see he was still working through the pain.

"Jay, you were the only person Shantel had in her life that made sense. You and Gabe meant the world to her, and I know all this has been overwhelming and tuff, but Yah didn't bring you through all this to leave you alone. Yah has tested all our faith with Shantel's death. Shantel came in our lives for a moment loving us unconditionally; she's the only person I know that could love like that, not even my own parents could do that. Jay, I know how it feels to grow up without my birth parents, and I don't want Gabe to ever experience that hurt."

The words Drew spoke massaged Jay's heart.

"Jay, this is not Gabe's fault, it was Yah's decision, and I know you can love Gabe with everything in you; you're just not allowing yourself because you're afraid. I know you Jay, and this rejection for your son is fear. You're terrified if you put that much love into Gabe as you did Shantel and Yah took him, you wouldn't survive."

Jay was amazed how Drew knew him so well; every moment he'd spent with her was worth it. Jay took Drew's phone and looked at the photo of the tiny baby; the tears fell uncontrollably this was the first time Jay had ever seen his son. Drew held Jay while he sobbed; not only was Jay hurt, but he was also ashamed of turning his back on Gabe.

"Drew, how could I be so selfish," Jay cried even harder.

Drew stroked Jay's face to wipe the tears. "Jay, you were sad and lost; no one can ever judge your reason."

Drew looked into Jay's tear-stained eyes; both began to feel forbidden feelings, so they hurried to pull away from the stare, resisting their emotions. Confused Drew jumped up to fetch the Kleenex from the kitchen counter, and puzzled Jay, sit in silence, thinking. It had only been three months since Shantel's passing; how could he be having these feelings for Drew? The pair wiped their tears and tried to pull themselves together.

"Thanks Drew, I couldn't be more grateful." Jay took another look at Gabe's photo.

"Yah has a way of working everything out, but you must first put your trust in him." Drew gave Jay a gentle smile.

"Drew, your trust in Yah has always been your strength. Against all odds, you always put your trust in him."

"Thanks Jay, but I can do better by trusting him more, so when I speak to you, I speak to myself. I remember the first time Ma Tate told me about Yah," A big smile came across Drew's face. "I'd broken Shelia's crystal serving bowel, and she made me kneel on the broom for almost an hour."

Drew shook her head, thinking back on that day, and how disgusting Shelia could be at times. "Anyway, afterwards I came looking for you; Ma Tate could see I had been crying, so she told me a story about when she was young and how Yah took care of her, and he would do the same for me. From that day forward I put my trust in Yah, besides he's all I had."

"I hate they did that to you, Drew." Jay shook his head.

"It just made me stronger." Drew held up a fist. So, let us talk about this handsome boy you got here."

Jay looked at Gabe's photo. "I have a lot of catching up to do.

"He's a fighter," Drew stated.

Jay continued to look at Gabe's picture, thinking to himself Gabe was the part of Shantel that was no longer here, and he would go through hell to make sure he was protected.

"Thanks Drew." Jay kissed her cheek.

Drew stood up and extended her hand. "Now, let's go look at A Different World."

CHAPTER 11

Acceptance is Healing

After a few days with Drew, Jay stood in front of Gabe's incubator, speechless; he couldn't believe how much of Shantel was in the baby; Gabe looked just like his mother. Jay couldn't fathom how someone so small could survive without their mother. Jay cried a silent cry.

"Hello, Mr. Tate, I'm Gabriel's nurse, Ami. The young lady extended her hand. "You have a fighter right there; he's one of our most vigorous babies, showing improvement daily. Every obstacle faced, Gabe conquers it."

Jay hurried to wipe the escaped tears before Ami noticed. "Thanks Ami, his mother was a fighter; she spent her last hours fighting for him." Jay smiled. "Fighting to make sure he had a chance at life."

"That explains a lot." Ami gave Jay a blushing smile.

Jay watched Gabe fight the white cloth covering his eyes and grew concerned. "What are the patches for?"

"Those are Argyle, baby shades," Ami explained. "They protect his eyes from the Bili lights.

"What's the Bili lights for?"

Ami explained the light was for jaundice, a condition particularly in babies born before 38 weeks, and he had nothing to worry about.

"Would you like to hold him?"

"Wow, that's possible; he's so tiny?"

"Well, he's 37 weeks now, so we encourage the parents to try skin-on-skin therapy; a lot of our parents aren't always comfortable with this at first." Ami continued to explain. "But it does wonders for babies' growth and development.

Jay agreed to the therapy; although he was nervous and reluctant, he would do whatever it took for Gabe to grow. Jay monitored the nurses taking the cords and tubes from one side of the glass bed to the other; monitors beeped, lights flashed, oxygen machines pumped, and nurses scrambled. Jay was in tears, he couldn't stand to watch the tiny baby go through so much.

Ami could see the fright and frustration on Jay's face, so she gave him a comforting smile, assuring him everything was just fine. Jay wanted to stop the nurses, but he knew Gabe needed the treatment much more than his fear needed calming, so he endured.

Going through all the changes was worth it when Jay looked down at Gabe resting on his chest. Jay took his index finger and caressed the baby's tiny arm; Jay was amazed that his finger was longer than the baby's whole arm. A smile came across Jay's face when Gabe gripped his finger, the strength Gabe had in his tiny hand gave Jay ultimate courage, and he didn't fear the road ahead. Jay laid his head back on the rocker and calmed himself, assuring Gabe he was safe. The thump of Gabe's tiny heart played a melody only a father could hear.

Jay held Gabe close, apologizing for blaming him for Shantel's death. "I promise I'll never leave you again," Jay whispered in the baby's ear.

Mr. Tate," Ami nudged Jay to wake him. "I'm sorry, we're about to change shifts, and I need to prep Gabe for the next nurse."

Jay didn't want to put Gabe down, but he complied. Once again, Jay watched closely as the nurses moved the tubes and cords around. It pained Jay to watch Gabe go through so much, but he stayed positive for the day Gabe would be free from the torture.

"You can wait in the family room until we're finished." Jay gave Ami a soft smile. "I see where he gets those adorable dimples." Ami returned the smile.

Jay sat in the waiting room amazed that so many families were going through the agony of having a premature baby; he watched all the different families, some with tears and some with smiles. Jay imagined everything that could go wrong but didn't allow the fear to control his thoughts, or emotions.

Joe and Brenda walked into the waiting room, scanning for a seat when they noticed Jay with his feet up in a corner, watching tv. Jay's parents were overjoyed to see him; Ma Tate crept up and rubbed his shoulder, interrupting his viewing pleasures of *Sponge Bob Square Pants.*

"Hey, baby, how are you?" Ma Tate gave Jay a sweet smile along with open arms, and with no hesitation, Jay stood up to embrace his parents.

Ma Tate stood back to examine her son. "Are you just fine?"

Jay stroked his mother's back, trying to explain his absence, but his mother shushed him, assuring him there was no need to explain.

"Have you seen the baby yet," Brenda asked.

"Yes, momma and he's awesome; I got to hold him, feed him, even change his diaper," Jay said with excitement.

"Wow, that's wonderful, Jay." Ma Tate was thrilled that Jay was so excited about his time spent with Gabe.

Jay rubbed his neck, trying to smooth out the soreness from the nap he took earlier. Joe could see his son hadn't had much rest, so he suggested they get coffee.

"I would, Pops, but I need to get back in there."

Brenda rubbed Jay's back. "Go get coffee with your dad."

"But Momma." Jay tried to decline his mother's orders.

"Jay, listen to me; your father and I have been doing this a few months, and the way you're going, you'll wear yourself out. Now go get coffee with your father." Ma Tate demanded.

Jay wouldn't dare argue with his mother. "I guess we're getting coffee." Jay eyed his father.

Jay and his father enjoyed their hot coffee from the *Java Café* located inside the hospital's cafeteria; it was just the eye-opener Jay needed. The two men sit in silence, Jay half-sleep and Pops trying to find words to say. Joe knew this was the moment he'd asked Yah for, and now it was time to speak his heart.

Joe cleared his throat, gaining Jay's attention. "Jay, can I tell you some good stuff?"

"Sure dad, you know you can." Jay observed his dad steadying himself.

"Jay, I've always looked at you and Shawn as my greatest accomplishment in life, and when Shawn died, it scared the hell out of me. I never thought I would bury one of my children; no parent does. Shawn's death weakened me, but it strengthened you. There was never any doubt in my mind that you wouldn't survive this."

Jay's father took a sip of his coffee, praying that Jay would understand his heart. "Jay, I'm sorry I didn't handle Shawn's death well."

"Dad, you've apologized for that." Jay wanted to spare his father's heart, knowing this was a part of his dad's life he wasn't proud of.

"No, Jay, let me say this." Jay's father refused the intervention. "My selfishness left you and your mother depending on one another. I was supposed to be the man that held his family together; instead, I almost tore it apart. I understand why you had to leave, and others may question your reason, but don't you pay it no mind; you did what was best for you and Gabe. The only thing that matters is you're here now, and son, I want you to know I have your back."

Jay looked at his father with nothing but respect; he knew it took a lot for his dad to say those words, considering he was a man of little words.

"Yah, I come to you asking for forgiveness, strength, and knowledge to be the best father I can be. Thank you for allowing my parents to be here in my absence. I ask for obedience in order to follow your guidance. Yah, this has been a tough road, but I thank you for making my heart content for what you have allowed. I pray for continued strength for what's to come. Thank you for the hospital staff and their efforts to care for my son. Yah, I pray you give Gabe the strength to fight. Todah *Yah."*

"That was beautiful." Ami complemented Jay on the heartfelt prayer.

"Thank you Ami, not only for compliment, but for also taking care of my boy."

"You're welcome, Mr. Tate." Ami gave Jay a big smile. "I have some good news before I leave, Gabe is two steps from release," Ami said with excitement. "We're looking at three to four more weeks if everything goes as planned, and he keep progressing."

Jay and his parents were excited about the news, giving Ami a warm smiles.

YOU' LL LOVE WHAT HAPPENS NEXT....

Jay spent the next few weeks at Gabe's bedside, making sure he was ready for the task of being a father, learning all that he could before Gabe was released.

Jay was finishing up skin-on-skin therapy when his phone chimed; it was the third alert and Jay was curious about who it was. Jay put the tubes and wires back in place; the process was much easier now, and Jay could do it himself, being that Gabe no longer needed all the machines. Jay's phone chimed again, he kissed Gabe's feet and lowered the top of the incubator. Removing the phone from its holster, it was Jay's mother informing him there was a problem at the ranch. Jay said a prayer over Gabe, thanked Ami, and headed for his house.

While in route Jay tried calling his mother for more insight about the issue but couldn't get her on the phone. Jay could only pray everything was ok.

After an hour-long drive of panic and worry Jay pulled up to his house; he explored the place but couldn't find anything unusual, so he exited the car to further investigate. Jay looked all over, and nothing was out of place. Jay stood in front of his house reliving the day he'd carried Shantel over the threshold; they'd been married three months living with his parents, so they were both relieved to finally have their own spot. Some days, it still seemed unreal to Jay that Shantel was gone.

Jay heard sounds coming from the barn, so he furthered his inspection. Jay walked up to the sliding barn doors and listened, slowly he slid the door back not knowing what to expect on the other side. *"SURPRISE!"* A small group of Jay's family and friends yelled. Jay was startled by the outburst, and surprised it was a baby shower.

Jay's mother embraced him. "Sorry, I lied baby, but I knew you wouldn't leave Gabe's side."

Jay looked around at all the familiar faces; his heart was filled with gratitude. It seemed the entire community of Promise had come out to celebrate. "Wow, thanks everyone, this is definitely a surprise."

While Jay addressed the guest, Drew walked through the crowd, revealing herself, giving Jay a sweet smile. Jay paused in speech, quickly taking Drew off her feet; the guest's hearts were touched by the reunion as they started a wave of Ooh's & Aah's.

"What's up girl, how are you here?"

"Well, I caught a plane, then I rented a car," Drew said jokingly.

"Oh, I see we got comedy." Jay embraced her once more, both shared in the humor.

"I know you had a part in this." Jay examined the decorated barn brought to life with a *Toy Story* theme.

Drew smiled bashfully. "Well, of course, you know we had to do something; we've been planning this for weeks. It was supposed to be something small, but you know how word gets around in Promise."

Drew took Jay to a gift table where gifts were piled on top of gifts, some were even falling on the floor. "Look at this, you have nothing to worry about, and check this out." Drew pointed at a young girl by the refreshment table. "That's Rainn Jacobs, she said anytime you need a sitter, she got you."

The young lady waved at Drew and smiled.

"I got your back Jay."

Jay pulled Drew into his arms and whispered, "And I have yours, best friend."

Drew and Jay headed over the refreshment table when they were stopped by Miss Sue.

"Drew, you and Brenda outdid yourselves with this one, you ladies make a great team. This party looks like something out of the movies."

Drew eyed Jay, both knew getting caught up in a conversation with Miss Sue meant they would need patience.

"Jay, I want you to know I'm proud of you, against all odds you made it; now you be a good father like your father was, and you'll do just fine."

Jay gave Miss Sue a gentle smile. "Yes Ma'am, thank you Miss Sue."

"I know this has been hard on you, and getting away was fine, but baby, don't do that again. That baby needs you, and you need him."

Jay looked at Drew and smiled, nodding his head in agreement. "Yes Ma'am, Miss Sue, I won't ever do that again."

Miss Sue patted Jay on his arm and made her way to the refreshments. Jay and Drew eyed each other. "Gotta love her," both said simultaneously.

The guest enjoyed themselves throughout the evening, eating, playing games, listening to music, and dancing. Drew and Mr. Tate were cutting up on the dance floor, they had the crowd jumping. Drew and Mr. Tate had three things in common: their love for Jay, a good stake, and the Gap Band. The crowd wanted more, but Drew couldn't deliver; she'd danced so much her sweat was sweating. Drew promised the crowed more later, but right now she needed air.

Drew stepped outside so the March winds could cool her; that's when she noticed Jay standing at Shantel's grave, so she stood back a moment to observe.

Jay looked down at Shantel's grave and straighten the freshly cut Dandelions; Jay made sure to put fresh flowers on Shantel's grave once a week. "Our little boy is perfect Shantel, he's us in one package. I know you would be crazy about him; off course, he has my good looks," Jay chuckled. "But, he has your witty sense of humor. He's so small Shantel, but I can already see what kind of kid he'll be. Yah has really been with us through this Shantel; I pray your soul is safe in his arms.

Drew rubbed Jay's shoulder. "Are you just fine?"

Jay looked at Drew and smiled. "You know Shantel put everything she had into that little boy."

Looking at Jay, Drew saw the same light in his eyes the night he met Shantel.

"When I look at that little boy, I didn't know I could love a person so much. The love I have for Gabe goes beyond natural. Shantel's served her purpose, Drew. I understand she was put here to bring Gabe." Jay went on to explain. "Think about the purpose Sampson served; Yah allowed him to marry Delilah so he could punish the Philistines. In that same way, he used Shantel to bring me, Gabe."

Drew was impressed at how Jay had new light about Shantel's passing.

"Shantel served her purpose, now it's time for Gabe and me to serve ours. Acceptance and healing Drew." Jay smiled. "You know, I never thought I'd find someone like Shantel. I always knew I wanted a woman like her, but never really trusted that I would find one; I knew from the moment I met her she would be mine. I asked Yah for her, now I have to give her back."

Drew noticed Jay hadn't dropped one tear, that's when she knew it was the right moment. Drew grabbed Jay's hand and struck out in a slow jog, pulling Jay behind her. "Come with me," she demanded.

Jay laughed out at Drew to slow down, he could tell she had gotten into something by her excitement.

Drew led Jay to the front door of his house, gazing up at Jay she could still see the light in his eyes, so she knew it was the perfect moment. "It's time Jay." Drew handed Jay his house key.

Jay looked down at the house key and laughed out. Drew had gotten the key costume made for his favorite team, *The New Orleans Saints.*

"Wow, this is so you." Drew gave Jay a wink; he took a deep breath and exhaled.

Walking in the place was quite an experience; Jay didn't recognize his own home. Shantel's decor was modern farm, now it looked like *the Ponderosa, bachelor's edition*. Drew had cowhide, bear rugs, stars, and leather furniture that told the home's story.

Jay observed all the pictures of Gabe's growth that hung in the living room and lining the hallway. The kitchen was different; Jay loved the black and gold decor. Jay's and Shantel's bedroom was totally different; just about everything had been changed.

"Do you like it?" Drew was nervous that Jay would freak out over the changes, as she nervously explained her reason for the intrusion. "I just thought you and Gabe needed something different; a place to call home, Jay."

Jay walked into the nursery to find it just how Shantel left it. Jay then looked at Drew, standing nervously in the hallway, awaiting his approval. Jay could only take Drew in his arms and hold her; he had no words. Drew was grateful that he was embracing her and not choking her.

Jay laid back in his new recliner; it felt strange for him to be back in his home without Shantel, but it definitely felt good, thanks to Drew. Jay thought about all that he had been through, yet he was grateful for it all. Beginning an inner praise, Jay was interrupted by a knock at the door; he tried to make out the face but couldn't see through the screen. Nearing the door, Jay could see Marcus holding a six-pack of beer.

"What's up Jay, you got a minute, your parents told me you were here." Marcus held up the six-pack and gave Jay a sad smile.

Marcus and Jay sat on the porch, drinking beers and talking about old times. Jay could see Marcus was in better spirit, which made him feel better; he hated seeing Marcus that way, Drew was really doing a number on him.

"Thanks Jay," Marcus shook his head in shame. "I messed up bad bro, I let jealously get the best of me; now Drew hates me."

Jay nudged Marcus. "Drew doesn't hate you, she's just being Drew."

"I don't know, it's been almost five months and she still hasn't come around. Damn Jay, I messed up." Marcus downed his beer.

"Look Marcus, I know Drew, and she's just being stubborn, so give her all the space she needs right now." Jay eyed Marcus. "But, when opportunity presents itself, act on it; act fast bro."

The men continued their conversation when they noticed a car pulling in. "Are you expecting company," Marcus asked, not knowing if Jay had put himself back on the market.

"Nah, that's just Drew," Jay eyed Marcus and smiled.

Marcus hurried to straighten himself. "Why didn't you tell me Drew was here?"

"Because you didn't ask." Jay laughed, watching Marcus nervously dust himself off. "Dang, you need bail money?"

"Bail money for what?" Marcus started gartering the empty bottles, putting them back in the container.

"Relax man, you act like you're going before a judge." Jay chuckled.

"Oh, you got comedy," Marcus replied, still dusting himself off.

Drew's heart skipped a beat when she notices it was Marcus sitting on the porch with Jay. Drew hadn't seen him in months and didn't want to see him now. Not because she had ill feelings towards Marcus or anything, but because Drew looked a mess; she'd been hosting a baby shower, dancing, and playing taxi driver for Miss Sue. If there were a bad time, this was it. "Dang Jay, a heads up would've been nice," Drew stated, while secretly looking at her compact, making sure her appearance wasn't a total loss.

While checking her status a reflection of light caught Drew's eye, she noticed a black Yukon parked beside her. "Ok, I see ya, Mr. Tidwell." Drew was glad he'd finally replaced his dad's old pickup truck with something more modern.

Marcus grew anxious with every second. "Why is she just sitting there?"

"I don't know maybe she's trying to figure out who's driving the Yukon," Jay shook his Jay head, in a way he wished Drew would just take Marcus out of his misery and marry him, but Jay wasn't sure either of them was ready for that.

Drew eyed the pair, she could imagine what their conversation had been. Drew gathered her things telling herself to be polite and kind. Drew exited the car, telling herself not to show to many teeth. Drew walked to the porch, telling herself you got this girl it's just Marcus, calm down. Drew got to the door and looked over at the men. "Good evening, gentlemen, nice car Marcus," Drew gave the men a wink and walked into the house.

Jay and Marcus eyed each other puzzled. "Well, at least she recognized you were here," Jay laughed, tapping the top of Marcus's beer.

CHAPTER 12

Anything For My Boys

Drew danced around Jay's living room to the old-school music; she'd been cleaning for hours, trying to make sure the house was in tip-top shape because today Gabe would be home, Drew had given herself entirely over to the task; fortunately, it gave her less time to think about Marcus. Drew knew the minute she saw him, all her feelings would come rushing back.

Drew wiped the surface of the marble counter repeatedly, unaware that *Earth* and *Wind* had started a *fire* inside that couldn't be tamed. Drew flipped through the images of Marcus the other night, sitting there in his cowboy hat, muscle shirt, bulletproof starched down jeans, accompanied by his gorgeous smile. Drew's body chilled. "No, No, No," Drew said, clearing Marcus's image from her mind.

Drew got back on task, walking down the hall to Jay's bedroom. Observing the room, Drew loved there was always little to do in there. Drew pulled the covers back on Jay's bed, it irked her nerves that Jay always left his bed unmade. Although he kept a neat place, Jay had a problem with making the bed. While fluffing the pillows, Drew's hand hit something. "Wow," Drew said, amazed at a photo of Jay and Shantel on their wedding day. Drew gazed at the picture, thinking back on that day. It was the most beautiful union she'd ever witnessed.

After hearing a car door close, Drew quickly stuffed the picture beneath the pillows and hurried to see who it was. Drew jumped up and down clapping her hands, she was excited to see Jay and the baby. Drew grabbed the cleaning things and put them away, then she ran to the guest bathroom to freshen up.

Drew opened the door just in time for Jay to walk through; she was more excited for Gabe's homecoming than he was. Drew had only seen Gabe in pictures, refusing to see him hooked up to all the machines, her heart couldn't take it.

Drew watched closely as Jay removed Gabe from the car seat. "Be careful not to pinch him."

Jay's heart warmed, he could see Drew's maternal instinct kicking in.

"Wow, you're good with him." Drew rubbed Gabe's leg.

Jay cradled Gabe in his arms, Drew could tell there was nothing Jay wouldn't do for Gabe. "You ready?"

Drew eyed Jay. "Ready for what?"

"Ready to get your feel of Auntie hood." Jay placed Gabe in the bassinet and showed Drew how to wash up when handling him. Jay also showed Drew how to make Gabe bottles, wash his bottles, change his diaper, and the place on Gabe's thigh he liked to be rubbed.

After the quick lesson, Jay picked Gabe up from the bassinet and attempted to put him in Drew's arms but Drew hesitated to take the baby.

"I'm not sure Jay, he's so tiny, and I don't want to crush him."

Jay laughed. "You're not going to crush him." Jay told Drew to hold out her arms, then placed the baby in her arms.

"Ok," Drew nervously accepted Gabe into her arms.

"Relax, he can feel your tension." Jay positioned Drew's arms in a cradle position and relaxed her back in the recliner.

Gazing down at Gabe, Drew was in love. "Omg, I see more of Shantel than anything, but he has your dimples," Drew rubbed the baby's cheek.

Gabe started to become agitated. "Oh, yeah, he doesn't like that either." Jay referred to Drew caressing Gabe's dimples.

"Like father, like son," Drew smiled.

Watching Drew with his son made Jay feel some type of way; it was those same feelings Jay had in Atlanta. Jay eyed Drew, he didn't want these feelings, he rejected these feelings.

"Jay," Drew called his name for the third time. "Where you at?"

Jay hurried to make something up, embarrassed by his feelings. "Just seeing how much motherhood fits you."

Drew laughed. "Are you crazy, I can barely take care of myself; we're not gonna add kids just yet." Drew tried to imagine herself with kids, but she couldn't fathom the idea. "I'll just spoil this one right now."

After putting Gabe down Drew joined Jay on the front porch. Gabe had only been home a few hours and Drew was exhausted; she'd changed a hundred diapers and made a thousand and one bottles. Drew was amazed at how much time and energy it took to take care of a newborn. "Whew, babies are a lot of work." Drew took a seat beside Jay and welcomed the March winds to gently massage her face.

"Yeah, I might have to get a nanny," Jay observed the baby monitor.

"Is he ok?" Drew leaned over to look at the sleeping baby.

"Look at you, all motherly and stuff." Jay teased Drew.

"I absolutely love taking care of Gabe, he's the perfect angel. If I had a choice I'd move back to Texas and take care of him myself; there wouldn't be a need for a nanny."

"Thanks Drew, you've done more than enough, so don't go quitting your job."

"I'll do anything for my boys." Drew eyed Jay for a moment before the chirp from his phone interrupted their stare.

"Hello, how are you," Jay greeted the caller. Drew could hear a female's voice coming from the phone. Trying not to eavesdrop, Drew grabbed the monitor and looked in on Gabe.

After a brief conversation Jay ended his call, and Drew couldn't help but investigate. "So, who was that?"

"Dang you nosey, all in my business," Jay stated sarcastically, looking at Drew wired.

"I'm not noisy, I'm just concerned about my friend," Drew chuckled.

Jay explains to Drew the caller was Gabe's nurse, and she was just making sure they got settled in ok, but Drew wasn't buying it.

"Oh, Ami makes house calls?" Drew probed Jay for more information.

"She's Gabe's nurse, that's all Drew."

Drew could see Jay didn't want to disclose any information, so she would leave it alone, for now.

Drew got up the following morning to find Jay in the nursery fast asleep with Gabe cradled in his arms, *cooing at the angles.* Drew carefully took Gabe from Jay's arms, startling him. Jay jumped up, thinking he'd dropped the baby.

"I got him." Drew hurried to calm Jay. "He's fine, go get some sleep."

After sleeping for hours, Jay walked into the living room fully energized; he noticed Gabe fast asleep in his bassinet and Drew in the kitchen on the phone. Jay admired the smile on Drew's face, only to wonder what she was involved in. Honestly, Jay hoped it was Marcus, maybe with him back in the picture he'd stop getting those forbidden feelings for Drew.

Ending her phone call, Drew began to dance around the kitchen. Jay sat down on the barstool laughing at her, still trying to awake from his sleep.

"Guess What," Drew said with excitement, dancing even more.

Jay threw a chip in his mouth and responded. "You and Marcus will stop this foolishness, get married, have some kids, and live happily ever after."

Drew paused, eyeing Jay. "Umm, no. Anyway, my partner Rachel just asked me if I was interested in taking my partnership to another level." Drew danced some more. "And wait on it."

Drew danced some more, making Jay anxious and impatient. "Will you stop and tell me, dang you play too much."

"Who's nosey now," Drew chuckled. "Ok, Rachel and Isaac want me to head their Texas division, *WOOP, WOOP!"* Drew announced excitedly, dancing a jig. Gabe began to cry, Drew immediately silenced her celebration, dashing to the living room to comfort him.

Jay couldn't have been happier; Drew had been there a few weeks on vacation, and Jay had gotten used to her, so the news was even more remarkable for him. Jay needed her more than she knew.

Jay jumped to his feet, now fully awake and did a silent happy dance. Drew danced along with him, the pair was grateful for the news.

Later that day Jay and his father were working out by the corral tagging calves when noticing a yellow sports car racing up the drive. Jay and his father eyed each other then looked back at the rushing car trying to make out the driver.

"You know who that is son?" Pop Tate held the fussy calf firmly.

Jay looked suspiciously at the car but couldn't recall anyone he knew with a car like that. Jay took his gloves off, leaving his dad to greet his unannounced guest. As Jay got closer to the vehicle, he noticed it was Aim. Jay thought to himself, how did she know his whereabouts.

"Ami, what are you doing here," Jay asked, walking over to her car.

"Well, I was on my way back to Shiloh City and thought I'd stop by and check on Gabe."

Jay looked at the front door hoping Drew didn't come outside. "How did you know where I lived?"

Jay eyed Ami suspiciously, and then checked to see if Drew had come out. By the time Jay turned his attention back to Ami, she'd cuddled up to him, holding a weird smile.

"I have my ways," Ami poked Jay's dimple.

Jay was uncomfortable with Ami's response, and her actions. Jay wanted to end their conversation but feared Ami would make a scene and Drew would come out with a bad understanding, so Jay stayed humble and patient.

"How's Gabe, I really miss you guys being in the NICU every day."

"Ami, your thoughts are sweet, but I have a lot of work to do." Jay tried his best not to hurt her feelings, but this unscheduled visit puzzled him.

"I understand." Ami opened her car door, so she could quickly escape her embracement.

Jay could tell Ami's feelings were hurt, but what could he do, he was caught off guard by the surprise visit, and she was partially throwing herself at him. Jay wanted to excuse Ami's behavior, considering she was younger in age, but found it hard to do.

"Maybe I'll call you later." Jay suggested, trying to smooth things over with her as she drove off.

Ami gave him a thumbs up and a disgraceful smile. Jay looked back at the front door, still hoping Drew hadn't come out; he was relieved to see she hadn't.

Pop Tate eyed Jay suspiciously as he walked back to the corral. Jay could feel his father's stare burning a hole in his face. Jay already knew the question his father would ask. *'Jay, you back on the saddle boy?'* Followed with a chuckle.

Pop Tate's face held a half grin. "You back on the saddle boy." Pop Tate chuckled.

Jay laughed at his dad's question. "Nah Pops, I guess she got a lil crush or something."

Joe eyed Jay once again, holding a bigger grin this time.

"What Pop's, for real, I made it perfectly clear I wasn't ready for all that yet."

"Let me ask you something, son." Jay's father looked him over with a playful look of suspension. "Have you slept with her?"

Jay laughed out, Pop Tate laughed along with him, but he was serious about his question.

Jay blushed. "Nah Pop's, I'm serious, it's not like that. The only parts of my body that have ever touched hers were my lips to her hand. I'm no fool."

Jay's father looked at him and smiled. "I didn't raise one either. Be careful where you park your car son, we represent a higher power and have an example to set, never take a woman unless you ready to be a husband to her. Remember the teachings of your father, son."

"Yes Sir." Jay heard his father's teachings, but it still bothered him that Ami just popped up like she did.

CHAPTER 13

Answered Prayers

Drew walked out the thirty-story building and lifted her face to the sun, it felt good to be out of that stuffy office with those whining, privileged, complaining *kidults.* Drew had been running the Texas office a month, doing more of the work than the interns. Drew couldn't understand how the branch held on for 16 years. Files were out of place, accounts had been mishandled, there were to many people on payroll, and Drew had to fix it all. Once again, she was over worked and under paid, but Drew didn't complain it was all worth it, being able to have a part in raising Gabe.

Drew searched downtown for a place to have lunch when she noticed condos were being leased. Drew thought about getting her own place, but Jay had gotten used to her being there, and it would also mean double rent. Drew still had her spot in Atlanta, she hadn't given it up yet, seeing she was still traveling to the home office once a month. Besides, she couldn't leave Gabe, so leasing was entirely out of the question.

Drew was still unsure about where to have lunch, so she settled for her usual spot, *Tammy's* a lovely sub cafe in walking distance of the office. Drew didn't feel like exploring downtown for other options, so Tammy's would be it.

"Hey Drew," a young lady greeted her as soon as she walked in.

"Hey, Becks, how are you?"

"Awesome!" The high-spirited woman replied.

"Wow, it looks like a pinata exploded in here." Drew side-eyed the sloppy, over-dressed job done on the decorations.

"Yeah, I kinda got a little carried away for Cinco De Mayo." Becks laughed.

"You Think." Drew made another observation.

"What can I get you today Drew." Becks told Drew the days specials that included a fiesta blast, a made up version of a *Mexican Torta,* Becks had put her spin on.

"As interesting as that sounds, I'm just going to get my usual sandwich." Drew gave Becks a soft smile, rummaging through her purse looking for her wallet. *"Dang, I took my wallet out at the office, trying to buy those freaking candy bars. Knowing I didn't need them."* Drew spoke with herself while searching her purse for loose bills and change. "Hey, Becks, I left my wallet at the office, can you credit me, I promise to bring it back."

Becks wasted no time voiding the order. "You're okay, I know you're good for it."

"I'll take care of it." A Tall, well-groomed, middle-aged man stood behind Drew.

"That's ok sir." Drew declined the gentleman's offer. Drew was thankful for his politeness, but wasn't the type to take hand-outs.

"It would be my pleasure as your father to buy my daughter lunch, Miss Drewlynn McCain."

Drew was appalled. Who was this man? Father? How did he know her name? Father? Had he been following her? Father? Father seems to be the only word Drew could and couldn't process.

"Father, excuse me." Drew addressed the man that stood before her, claiming to be her father.

The gentleman's heart was beating outside his chest. "I'm Carl McCain, your father." The man extended his hand as if Drew would willingly take it.

Drew was stone, the father she'd always wanted stood before her in the flesh. The father that only lived in her immigration stood before her. The father she wanted to pick her up when she fell stood before her. The father she wanted to attend the *father daughter* dances stood before her. The father she wanted to walk her down the aisle stood before her. The father that left her and forgot about her stood before her. Drew was stone.

"I know you have questions, and I will answer every one of them if you allow me the chance. I have...

Drew threw her hand up to stop the trembling man's explanation, then walked out of the cafe.

"Drew, you forgot your sandwich," Becks yelled out, unaware of the situation. Drew kept walking, disregarding Beck's call.

Carl grabbed the sandwich after paying and ran after Drew.

“Drew,” Carl pleaded. "Hear me out,” Carl yelled out, while trying to keep up with Drew through the moving crowd. "Drew, will you please stop and let me explain."

Drew stopped in her tracks, giving Carl her full attention, thinking. *'How could he possibly explain being an absent father for twenty-eight years,'*

Drew and Carl were at a standstill while the city continued functioning around them; not wanting to miss a word of her father's lame excuse, Drew tuned everything and everybody out.

"Drew, I'm sorry I never came for you, by the time I knew you existed you were already with a family that loved you more than I could. When I received the news that I could be your father, it frightened me. I wasn't ready nor responsible enough to take care of you, so I just left you alone." The out of breath man tried to explain best he could.

Drew was cut by every word coming from Carl’s mouth. Any explanation he could give would never be good enough for Drew, especially if it wasn't the truth. Drew applauded Carl on a well-rehearsed plea; clapping her hands gaining the crowds attention "Are you finished?"

Carl didn't push his case anymore, he could see Drew was not interested.

Drew looked at Carl with tears in her eyes, told him thank you, then turned and walked away, leaving Carl in the middle of the lunch rush.

Drew tried working through the hours but couldn't focus, every five minutes she found herself looking out over the city, trying to process everything Carl explained. The more Drew thought about it, the more upset she became. “Why couldn’t he just leave it alone, I did,” Drew said to the downtown crowd.

“Ms. McCain, there is a problem with the Connor Account!” A very energetic young man ran into Drew’s office in a panic, startling her.

“I have to get out of here." Drew gathered the files from her desk, assured the young man she would take care of the problem, grabbed her purse and laptop, gently pushed the young man out the door, turned off the light, closed the door and locked it, gave the young man orders not to call her, and called it a day. The young man stood in front of Drew’s office confused at what had just happen.

As Drew neared the exit of the building, the receptionist informed her that a gentleman came by and left his contact information. Drew knew it had to be Carl, so she took the information and threw it in her purse.

Drew was almost to the door when the receptionist remembered one more thing. "Oh yeah, he said make sure you eat." The woman held up the sandwich from *Tammy's*.

"You can have it," Drew gave the woman a wink, and proceeded to the door, leaving the middle-aged woman grateful.

A smile came across the woman's face as she eyed the sandwich. "I'm about to be all in yo business," The women spoke to the sandwich as if it could hear her.

Drew used the extra time to do a little shopping therapy, hoping it would calm her before picking up Gabe. Drew walked downtown window shopping until a cute little boutique caught her eye. *"Saddle Girls, hmm looks interesting,"* Drew said to self, never noticing the shop before.

Drew stood in front of the boutique admiring the visual merchandising used with the mannequins, they were on point from head to toe. Drew loved the unique rays of color the retailer used as an eye-catching gimmick. Drew wasn't into western wear, but this was a different style of western, it was more modern western with a mix of urban. Drew chuckled after visualizing the look on Jay's face if she walked in dressed like a cowgirl.

The bell above the door announced Drew's presence. *"Wow, this is nice,"* Drew said to self, checking out the classy shop. Drew was impressed with the different styles of clothing. Not only did the boutique carry western wear, but they also had causal, formal, street styles, some miscellaneous items, and shoes galore.

"Hello, how are you." A dashing young woman emerged from the back, extending her hand with a pleasant smile. "I'm Dina Cole, but you can call me Den, welcome to my boutique. If I don't have it, I can get it."

Drew was impressed with the young woman's introduction, and success. It wasn't many black business downtowns, so this was impressive; it also watered Drew's seed to one day be a business owner herself.

Drew eyed Den, she loved her lively spirit and unique personality. "Nice to meet you. I'm Drew, you have a nice place here," Drew returned the pleasant smile. "But I don't recall seeing it before now."

"Probably because I've only been open three weeks." Den chuckled.

That made since to Drew, she'd only been back in Texas a month and really hadn't gotten a chance to explore. Yeah, she was from Texas, but so much had changed.

Drew gave the young lady a smile and continued her boutique exploration. Den followed, giving Drew the layout of the little shop. It wasn't Macy's, but Den had lots of lovely things.

Den searched through a rack of assorted green shirts. What did you have in mind, maybe I can put an outfit together for you. Purple seems to be your soul's color."

Drew eyed Den. "What's a soul color?"

"It's a color close to your heart. Have you ever had a color that you were drawn to." Den took a purple scarf and wrapped it around Drew's neck.

"Yeah, purple, how did you know that?" Drew smiled while rubbing the silk scarf on her cheeks. For Drew, Den was very peculiar person.

"Purple is a color of extreme spirituality, wisdom, deep understanding, and psychic energies. I felt your energy when approaching you. You're aware of your surroundings and a very knowledgeable person."

Drew eyed Den. "Again, I ask, how did you know that?" Drew took the scarf off and gave it back to Den. "That's right on point, I couldn't have explained me any better."

Den observed Drew from head-to-toe, kind of making her feel uncomfortable. "I'm sorry for the close observation, but you have some sexy hips."

Drew looked at Den sideways. "Excuse me."

Den grabbed a violet blouse, a pair of jeans with lavender rhinestones, and a purple scarf. "I just helped you."

Drew was puzzled at the young lady's actions and statement. "How?"

"Say your boyfriend throws a last-minute date night on you, and you need something new. Well, you can call me or drop by, I'll put you an outfit together in 20 minutes flat, no hassle, no wait. Only if I have customers before you, but usually my clients call ahead." Den gave Drew a smile.

Drew looked unconvinced, but it didn't bother Den, she was familiar with looks like that, especially from those with their own fashion sense, and Drew looked the part.

"Seriously Drew, I can help you. I used to be a fashion consultant before starting my own business."

Drew was impressed at the young lady's accomplishments. "Wow, you're quite an entrepreneur, congratulations on your new business, but to be honest, I'm not that big on having someone dress me."

Den took the clothing from Drew's hands, wrapped the scarf around Drew's neck, then stood behind Drew with the blouse and jeans pressed against her body. "So, you're telling me this outfit isn't perfect for you."

Drew observed herself in the full-body mirror. The outfit was perfect, it made Drew look more like a woman and less like a college student. "Ok, make me hire you with the second outfit."

Den went right to work, pulling garments from almost every rack. Drew was mesmerized at how Den put the clothing together, it seemed every outfit was on point and matched Drew's personality.

"Gurl, you have a gift." Drew looked back at the mirror, pleased with Den's classy sense of fashion. "I may have found my own personal fashion consultant; you're hired."

"Yay." Den gave Drew and herself applause.

After hours of shopping therapy and conversation with Den, Drew headed to the Tate's so she could pick up Gabe. While in route Drew noticed someone starting renovations on the Cooper house, she'd always loved the *Victorian Home*. It needed a little work done, but Drew could tell it was a good investment.

Drew drove past the house slowly, trying to get a glimpse of the inside. Fortunately for Drew the door had been left open, now she could finally look into the home's soul. Drew's eyes lit up when she got a glimpse of the old staircase, it was a piece of art in Drew's eyes; the original wood and layout are what kept the heart beating in the house. Drew imagined herself gliding down the coffin corner stairs into Marcus's arms. *'Beep, Beep,'* the sound of the horn snapped Drew back to reality.

Drew entered The Tate's home finding Pop Tate on the floor playing with Gabe and Ma Tate in the kitchen, preparing dinner. "Hey, did you guys notice someone doing renovations on the Cooper place?" Drew joined Pop Tate on the floor stealing kisses from Gabe.

"Yeah, I noticed those fellas out there about three weeks ago." Pop Tate confirmed.

Pop Tate and Drew talked a little bit more about the home, Gabe, and her settling in at the office before she dashed off to the kitchen.

Drew plopped down on the vintage counter-high chair/step stool. Ma Tate could tell something wasn't right with her by the way she plopped down on the chair. Drew sighed, all the shopping in the world couldn't hide Drew's pain. Especially from Ma Tate.

"Talk to me Drew, what's wrong?"

Drew grabbed one of the carrots from Ma Tate's cutting board, she'd held on long as she could before releasing the hurt, fears, tears, and anger she had built up inside from Carl's visit. Drew looked at Ma Tate with tears in her eyes. "Ma Tate, how do you think Yah hears everyone's prayers at the same time."

Ma Tate paused from cooking. "That's a good question and to be honest I can't say. Maybe the angles he has watching over us tells him."

The women laughed

"But I know he hears them." Ma Tate assured Drew, handing her another carrot. "It hurts me to see you like this Drew, what's wrong.

"My dad showed up today."

"What, oh baby how do you feel?" Ma Tate paused her cutting.

"Angry, confused, and drained." A single tear fell from Drew's eye.

"Drew, time heals all wounds, so give it some time. There's nothing written that says you have to rush into forgiving or having a relationship with this man." Ma Tate gazed into Drew's eyes. "I know this is something you've been waiting on, and I'll stand with you no matter what you decide, just don't rush it."

Drew gave Ma Tate a soft smile, Ma Tate stroked Drew's face. "From the day I saw you moving in next door, I knew Yah had sent you to me."

Drew was honored to be the daughter the Tates never had but knowing her real father would bring closure.

After a brief counseling session, Drew started to gather Gabe's things when Jay walked through the door. "What are you doing here, I thought it was my day," Jay asked Drew.

Drew eyed Jay for a moment, trying to remember whose pick-up day it was. "What's today?"

Jay side-eyed Drew, shaking his head. "It's Wednesday."

Drew laughed out when remembering it wasn't her day for pick-up.

The Parents shook their heads.

Jay began to rant about everything that went wrong at the ranch, Drew struggled with Gabe and the car seat, Gabe cried because he didn't want to be in the car seat, Drew tried to calm Gabe, and Jay was asking his parents if they was paying attention.

The Parents could see both were overwhelmed with jobs, relationships, parenthood, and life's curve balls. "Y'all need a break," They said simultaneously.

"You two need a night out." Ma Tate helped Drew with the car seat. "Now call Rainn and set something up."

Jay and Drew both rejected the suggestion, neither wanted to leave Gabe, but after a few minutes of persuasion from *The Parents* the idea didn't sound too bad. Jay and Drew had practically given up their personal lives since Gabe had come home.

Drew and Jay sat on the front porch gazing at the stars in silence, while calculating the day's events; neither had the energy to tell the other about the shenanigans that altered their day. The silence seemed to tell it all.

Jay was about to break the silence when his phone rang. Jay seen that it was Aim and wasn't sure if he wanted to answer. The stunt Ami pulled had Jay rethinking a simple friendship with her.

Drew could see Jay's hesitation, thinking he might want some privacy she excused herself. Drew could tell by the frequent calls Ami was fishing for more than just information about Gabe. Drew pulled her exhausted body inside the house, at this point all she wanted was to soak in a warm bath.

Drew couldn't wait for her mini- spa session, she had her waterproof tub massaging spa on full blast, aromatherapy candles lit the room, the water temperature just right, and the soft sound of jazz set the mood, all that was missing was a glass of wine. Drew threw on her robe and dashed to the kitchen on a mission to conquer her last task.

While pouring up a glass of wine, Jay came in with the biggest smile on his face, he smiled so big his dimples had dimples, and as much as Drew wanted to pry, she left him with his fantasy.

Drew prayed and soaked a while before removing herself from the relaxing bath, it was just what she needed to end her day. As Drew readied herself for bed she thought about her father and their brief conversation. Then she thought about Den and their conversation, and although she'd only known Den a few hours, Drew felt comfortable talking to her. Not only did Den give Drew good fashion advice, but she also gave her some sound advice about Carl. Den thought it would be good for Drew to have a sit-down with her father and ask for the truth and nothing but the truth, but Drew was still undecided about the matter.

Before retiring for the night, Drew looked in on Gabe, she knew for sure he'd kicked his covers off. After tucking Gabe in, Drew reached for the monitor and noticed it was gone. Drew was puzzled, she thought it was her night with Gabe or did she have it mixed up like the pickup.

Drew knocked at Jay's door waiting for clearance, she could see Jay doing his nightly exercises through the crack in the door. Drew watched Jay admiring his physique, she'd never seen him like this; Jay might have been her best friend, but Drew wasn't blind to the fact her fragile little friend was now a *strong manly man.*

"Come in," Jay responding to Drew's knock. "What's up Drew, you good?"

Drew almost forgot why she was there, intrigued by Jay's perfectly cut body. Drew snapped from her illusion, eliminating the forbidden thoughts that danced in her head. "Did you take the monitor from Gabe's room?"

"Yeah," Jay replied, out of breath from his sit-ups. "I thought I'd take tonight, seeing how your day was a bit rough."

"Thanks, Jay." Drew was relieved for the break.

"Drew, you do know if all this becomes overwhelming for you, you're not obligated to either of us."

"ARE YOU CRAZY!" Drew yelped out. "I love that little boy, I couldn't go a day without him. I'll always be obligated no matter what."

"Drew, I've been thinking about what *The Parents* suggested, and they're right, we need a night out."

Drew eyed Jay suspiciously, she knew exactly what Jay was hinting at. "Ok, so where are you taking her?"

Jay looked at Drew and chuckled. "Taking who, where?"

"Where are you taking Ami," Drew asked again.

Jay started to blush. "Shades, I thought a night out at Shades would do us well, like Ma said."

Drew looked at Jay smug. "First of all, I'm not going to Shades." Drew went on about how the bar was too rachet for her, and only thugs hung out there. "And second, be honest, you're using me for an opportunity to take Ami out?"

Jay jumped up and crept over to Drew, handing her a charming smile. "Yeah, kind of."

"What do you mean kind of," Drew ask, detecting a motive in play.

Jay tiptoed around his answer because he knew Drew wouldn't go for the next part.

"Say it Jay." Drew grew impatient with him beating around the bush.

"So, Ami has this cousin…

"Nope, not going to happen Jay." Drew already knew what Jay was about to ask with the whole cousin deal, and she wasn't having it. Nope, not happening." Drew shook her head.

"Wait Drew, hear me out," Jay whispered, trying not to wake Gabe. "Ami speaks highly of him, he seems to be a pretty decent man."

Drew looked at Jay under-eyed. "Have you met him?"

Jay stumbled over his words, "Not in person."

"Nope, you know how I feel about hookups."

"I know, and it's not a hookup, It's just four adults hanging out." Jay tried to sugar it up.

"Is that what you call it?" Drew turned to leave Jay's room, only for him to follow her, begging that she go. Drew wanted to say no, everything in her was saying, *'Say No,'* but Drew could also see how much Jay wanted it, and who was she to deny him a night out. Jay had been through hell and back, he was an outstanding father, and he seem to really like Ami.

"Fine, Jay, I'll go, but this is not a freaking date." Drew closed her door in Jay's face, leaving him enjoying a solo victory dance in the hall.

CHAPTER 14

Relaxing & Reconnecting

Rainn watched Drew and Jay run around the house gathering everything she needed to sit with Gabe. Rainn shook her head, she'd heard of first baby syndrome, but this was ridiculousness. Jay and Drew were running around like disturbed ants; continuously reminding Rainn that Gabe was a preemie and needed to be watched closely. Rainn looked at Gabe, to her he looked nothing like a preemie; yeah, he was kind of small for six months, but not small enough for anyone to ever believe he'd weighed only a pound when he was born.

"Remember Rainn, Gabe is not like most baby's, he's a preemie." Drew reminded her for the hundredth time, while organizing Gabe's essentials for the night.

Rainn shook her head when looking down at the baby in her arms, Gabe was just as confused watching the panicked pair as she was, but also found it humorous; laughing as he watched his father and Drew run back and forth like two madmen.

Drew paused her mission for a moment, handing Rainn a piece of paper. "Rainn, here's our numbers, Ma Tate's number, and the number to the spot. Now if…

Rainn stopped Drew in midsentence. "You do know I have a cell phone, right?"

Drew stood there with a blank look. "Yeah, I know, but what if the power goes out?"

Rainn could clearly see Drew fished around for that answer, and if Jay didn't add to the confusion by taking Gabe from her arms, giving him endless kisses and hugs as if he would never see him again. Gabe laughed even more at the foolishness while Rainn grew sick of it, so she took Gabe in one arm and pushed the overbearing parents out with the other. "You guys have a good night." Rainn helped Gabe wave goodbye. Drew was still yelling out orders when Rainn closed the door.

Jay and Drew pulled into Brooklyn's, a friendly little jazz club in Shiloh City. Drew heard some of her employees talking about the place and wanted to check it out but could never find the time.

Drew looked at the line and knew it was a jumping spot; she could also tell by the distinguished men and women in line, the place was also elegant and sophisticated.

Drew pulled the sun visor down to freshen her make-up when she began to rant about how it was too soon for Gabe to be with a sitter. Jay chuckled, he could see Drew was just as opposed to the idea as he was.

Jay watched Drew, he hadn't noticed how much she'd grown until that moment. "Your beautiful Drew, inside and out."

Drew gave Jay a blushing smile. "Thanks, Jay."

"I mean it, Drew, you are a lovely lady with a beautiful soul; you've been my backbone through all this, and the way you care for Gabe is priceless. I'm grateful Yah put you in my life."

Drew finished touching up her makeup. "Aww, Jay, you're the sweetest, I couldn't let you to do this alone. Now, can we go in before I change my mind." Drew hurried to end their heart-to-heart before ruining her refreshed makeup.

As the pair approached the bar, Drew was impressed, Ami wasn't just your average nurse, she was gorgeous. Jay was also stunned by her beauty; he'd only seen Ami in scrubs with her hair pulled back, but the dress she wore tonight told a story the scrubs didn't. Ami's soft face gave off a glow that couldn't be deemed by any woman in the room.

"Wow, *Jay*, she's stunning, not at all what I expected." Drew began to feel a little territorial; she knew Shantel was gone, but an unquestionable loyalty was still there.

Ami was excited to see Jay, embracing him on arrival; her smile could launch a thousand rockets. "Jay, I'm glad you made it."

"Ami, I would like you to meet my best friend, Drew."

The ladies embraced one another, complementing one another on their beauty and clothing.

Jay looked around and began to wonder about Ami's cousin, and his whereabouts. Jay didn't want Drew to feel like a third wheel. "Where's your cousin," Jay asked.

Ami was so taken by Jay she hadn't explained her cousin's absence. "I'm sorry, how rude of me." Ami explained that her cousin had a problem at one of his shops and would be running late.

By Ami's explanation, Jay could tell she didn't know exactly what was going on, so he suggested they find a table so the ladies could be comfortable in their wait.

Drew eyed Ami, noticing how fascinated she was with Jay; she hadn't taken her eyes off him since they'd got there. Drew chuckled, it always amazed her how women threw themselves at Jay, and how he always blew them off.

The trio enjoyed the music while the band played. Drew started to feel like an extra as Jay and Ami veered off into a world of their own; they'd been sitting there almost 30 minutes, and her cousin still hadn't shown up.

Drew explored the cute little jazz club, it was her type of spot. Brooklyn's had a wonderful atmosphere, good music, a friendly crowd, and the food looked amazing. While looking the club over Drew noticed a rather charming guy checking her out from across the room. Drew tried not to make eye contact, but found it complicated with his ceaseless flirting; besides, it gave her something to do in the meantime.

About ten minutes into Drew's across the room *eyes and smiles conversation,* Ami and Jay emerged from their world long enough for Ami to notice her cousin at the entrance, searching the room for her whereabouts.

Ami stood and motioned for him to join them, so Drew hurried to end her ten-minute romance with the charming guy, not wanting to be rude.

Jay and Drew eyed each other, both were shocked to see the cousin was Marcus. "You got to be kidding me, did you plan this," Drew whispered to Jay, while kicking him under the table.

"No, I didn't, and Ouch." Jay rubbed his leg.

Drew eyed Jay she knew he had something to do with this reconnection set-up, and he would pay.

Approaching the table Marcus was just as surprised to see Drew and Jay. "Damn, what's up bro?" Marcus hurried to greet Jay, he was happier than a kid in a candy store.

“What’s up bro, you good.” Jay returned the love, embracing Marcus followed by some dap.

The men took a minute and laughed at the coincidence, but Drew didn’t find it humorous; she couldn't help but conclude this was a setup, and the culprits were Jay and Ami.

"What’s up cousin," Marcus embraced Ami.

Marcus eyed Drew, his insides jumped with excitement. "Good evening, Miss McCain." Marcus took Drew's hand and placed the sweetest kiss he could birth from his lips upon it.

"Surprising to seeing you here, Mr. Tidwell." Drew gave him a half-grin, taking back her hand. Jay kicked Drew under the table, she knew that was code for be kind.

The foursome sat in silence, listening to the live band; the tensions between Drew and Marcus was so thick you couldn’t cut it with a chainsaw. Drew hadn’t really talked to Jay about Marcus, and Marcus hadn’t said anything to Jay about Drew, so he didn’t know where they stood with one another.

"So, how do you all know each other?" Finally, Ami spoke. Drew was relieved because she still didn't have much to say, especially when it came to Marcus.

Marcus enlightened Ami on their connection, and she was too thrilled they’d all grown up together. Ami asked question after question; Drew started to feel like she was being interviewed and needed Ami to chill.

Jay must have sensed Drew getting tired of the questions, so he gave her an out by suggesting they all hit the dance floor. Jay assured Ami they would get caught up later, but now was the time for them to enjoy themselves and all Brooklyn had to offer.

Ami was game to Jay's idea, she stood up, took a drink, and pulled Jay to the dance floor; while Drew and Marcus declined.

Drew and Marcus watched the band in silence, neither had much to say. Drew began to feel awkward, she and Marcus had always found something to talk about, even if it was a disagreement. Suddenly, a thought went through Drew's mind that frightened her.

"So, you're starting to date again," Drew inquired.

Marcus didn't know what to say, he just knew he had to handle Drew delicately and answer the question correctly. "Nah, my cousin needed a favor.”

Drew was relieved at Marcus's answer.

"So, are you dating again?" Marcus couldn't restrain himself from the question, noticing the eye conversation Drew held with the guy across the room.

"No, just here supporting Jay."

Both couldn't have been happier, knowing neither of them were considering moving on.

"How have you been, Drew?" Marcus tried to make small talk, avoiding going back into silence.

"I've been good, Marcus, and you," Drew gave Marcus a pleasant smile.

Marcus's heart beat a hundred beats a second; the advice everyone he sought comfort in flooded his thoughts. Marcus kept in mind all the steps it would take in winning Drew back, and the first was open conversation. Marcus left the floor open for whatever Drew wanted to discuss, hoping she'd tell him how she felt, and how he could fix it.

Marcus motioned for the waitress. "Congratulations on your move back to Texas, welcome home."

"Yeah, one of the perks of becoming partner. Congratulations on your new truck, and the new shop."

Marcus smiled: he was glad Drew noticed. "Thanks, I had to get something so I could keep up with Jay, in the fields.

Drew smiled and nodded.

"Jay tells me you're doing a great job with Gabe." Marcus asked the waitress for a twisted nipple and a beer.

A smile came across Drew's face, just the mention of the baby's name melted her heart; at the same time Drew became a little worried, remembering he was alone with Rainn.

"Excuse me, Marcus." Drew hurried to call Rainn, spending ten minutes on the phone going over everything she'd already told her. Rainn's only response was, *'Un Huh and ok.'* Drew could tell by the young lady's tone she was over her and just wanted to do her job, so she said her goodbyes.

"Everything ok," Marcus inquired; Drew seemed to be a little worried.

"It's our first time leaving him alone with a sitter, so it's kind of challenging." Drew looked at her phone as if she was waiting for something to go wrong.

"Relax, I'm pretty sure the sitter will take good care of him; besides, you wouldn't have left him if she wasn't responsible."

Drew allowed Marcus's advice to lay upon her heart. "You're right, Rainn's a responsible young lady for 16, but, she's also a teenager." Drew gave Marcus a welcoming smile.

Marcus was fascinated with the motherly instinct Drew had obtained, he'd never seen her this humble and patient. Suddenly Marcus started to see Drew in a different sight; Drew didn't look like the girl he'd left at the airport. This Drew had matured from the hurt he and life had inflicted on her. This Drew was more beautiful than he'd ever seen, and he needed to know this Drew.

As the night went on, the group spent most of their time reminiscing about old times; Ami was smitten at all the stories she heard. Ami was also amazed at the idea of Drew and Marcus; she'd always heard about Drew, but never got the chance to meet her.

"So, what happen to you guys, why the split?" Ami threw the question on the table with no disregard, leaving Drew and Marcus speechless.

Jay eyed the pair, he knew how sensitive the subject was, so before emotions got high, he hurried to intervene. "Can we go for another round," Jay yelped out.

"It's ok bro," Marcus noticing Jay's intercession. "I need to say something." Marcus took Drew's hand, holding her stare. "Drew, I'm sorry, the way I left you at the airport was wrong. Your friend had just died, and I was so busy in my own feelings I neglected yours. I understand why you reacted the way you did, and I'm sorry."

Ami was in tears from the apology, waiting for Drew's response.

Drew looked around the table, her pride tried to overpower Marcus's sincere apology, but she conquered it, and accepted. This wasn't the beginning of a new friendship, but more of a casual situation, realizing she'd have to see Marcus at the ranch from time to time.

The clique stood in the parking lot readying themselves to part ways, when Marcus extended his hand, offering to escort Drew to the car. "Are you going to let my hand fall off?"

Drew smiled bashfully at the *Billy Dee Williams* line, handing Marcus her hand. "Thank you, Mr. Tidwell."

Marcus opened the car door. "Good night, Miss McCain." Marcus gently kissed Drew's cheek, helping her into the vehicle; he wanted to ask her for a nightcap but resisted. Marcus didn't wanna move too quickly. Besides, he knew Drew wanted to get back to Gabe.

"Good night, Mr. Tidwell." Drew gave Marcus a soft smile; she wanted to extend an invitation for him to join her back at the ranch, but she didn't wanna seem thirsty. Besides, it was her night with Gabe.

Drew waited patiently for Jay and Ami to say their goodnights, but she could smell the rain coming and wanted to make it home before it started. Thunderstorms in Promise could sometimes be savage, and Drew wanted to be home out the way before it started.

Drew continued her observation of Jay and Ami cuddle up at her car. Drew laughed, wondering if Jay would steal a kiss before letting her go. Then Drew thought about her own sweet kiss given by Marcus and she got chills.

Drew lay on the floor listening and watching the rain hit the sky window, the night-out was just what she needed. Drew closed her eyes and let the sounds of the rain take her to a place of peace. Finding herself basking in the goodness of Yah, a twister of blessings flooded Drew's thoughts; each one slowly revealed themselves, carrying a tear that cleansed her soul. Drew's heart welcomed Yah in, allowing his love and kindness to rest upon her heart, as it cried out in praise. Yah's mercy and grace became reality to Drew, thinking back on the months he'd carried her and held her close.

Drew was interrupted by a light knock. Leaving her world of peace, Drew gave permission for entrance, wiping the tears from her eyes.

Jay walked in and stood over Drew looking up at the sky window. "Wow, Shantel used to do the same thing in her here."

Drew rubbed her face after a drop of cold substance hit her nose. "Ewe, what's that?" Drew hurried to sit up, thinking the roof had a leak, but to her surprise the leak was Gabe, cradled in his father's arm, laughing at her. Drew was shocked but delighted to see Gabe up so late.

"Hey, my baby." Drew took Gabe and started their baby talk conversation.

"So, what do you think of Ami?" Jay threw the question out there, catching Drew off guard.

"She's ok, I guess," Drew stated, with little enthusiasm.

"That was dry." Jay was anticipating more feedback from Drew.

"I'm sorry, what do you want me to say, how do you want me to feel." Drew sat on the chaise lounge, jumping Gabe on her lap. "Anyone that can make you smile like Ami had you smiling tonight is alright with me."

"Come on, Drew, tell me the real." Jay began to get anxious.

"Jay, what do you want me to say." Drew quickly analyzed Jay. "You want me to give you a reason." Drew knew all Jay needed was a good reason not to pursue a relationship with Ami.

"I need you to tell me the truth."

"My truth is this, she's a lovely young lady with a good head on her shoulder, she has a career, she has morals, and she knows what she wants in life. Bonus, she's good with kids. In my opinion, she's a good fit, if that's what you're looking for."

"Ok, I get it." Jay could see Drew wouldn't give him an out.

"Look Jay, if you're not ready for all that, it's fine. Take your time and explore; Yah has the perfect woman for you, so don't rush it."

Drew eyed Jay: she could see he was still unsure about the whole situationship, so she comforted him, encouraging him to follow his heart.

Drew's phone chimed, singing along with the birds chirping outside her window. The cool morning breeze gracefully climbed through the window, placing sweet kisses on Drew's body as she basked in the ambiance of Yah's glory. Drew sat up, remembering the chime was a reminder for *Sunday Fun Day,* and as much as she wanted to lay there, Drew knew she had to ready herself for the day out at the pier.

Drew grabbed her phone to clear the alert when she noticed Marcus had sent her a good morning text. Drew started to blush as she returned the text. Drew sat there for a moment, thinking about the kiss he'd given her a couple weeks ago when she was interrupted by Jay yelling.

"Get up Drew, we got to get an early start; I heard your alarm go off."

Drew jumped to her feet, there was a thousand things she had to do, starting with Gabe, which she knew would be a task. Gabe was just like his mother and wanted nothing to do with sunrises or birds singing, noon was the start of their day and nothing earlier.

Jay and Drew were loading the SUV when he noticed Ami driving up. Jay was puzzled he couldn't remember inviting her on their outing.

"Well, I see you made your decision," Drew said jokingly.

Jay assured Drew he hadn't decided or did he invite Ami.

Ami jumped out the car excited. "Hey handsome," Ami pierced Jay's dimple, kissing him on the lips.

"What are you doing here, Ami?"

Ami Looked at Jay with high spirits. "You mentioned the pier today, so I thought why not tag along."

Drew and Jay looked at each other in disbelief; if neither one of them had a reason for Jay not to pursue a relationship with Ami they did now.

"Ami, it's a private day for just me and my family."

"Aww, I'm sorry Jay, I just thought since you mentioned it... Ami fondled her words and her keys.

Jay eyed Ami: he could see she was embarrassed, so he went against his better judgment and invited her anyway.

CHAPTER 15

Ferris Wheels & Pinwheels

Drew listened to Ami exchange baby talks with Gabe in the back seat, she couldn't fathom how Ami had intruded in on their family outing. Drew shook her head, Ami seemed to be pushing her way into Jay's life and Drew didn't like it. Drew felt it to be a little stalkerish, and she questioned Ami's actions. Drew thought about Jay and held her tongue knowing how he felt about discretion.

The trio pulled into the parking lot of *Mystic Pier, The Parents* awaited their arrival. Drew hurried to exit the car, knowing Ma Tate would have plenty of questions and all the answers.

Jay hurried to unload the vehicle, wanting to get the day over quickly as he could. Looking over at his father Jay knew he had questions.

"Nurse Ami, is that you?" Brenda embraced the young lady, shocked to see her there. Drew could see the look of confusion on Ma Tates face as she eyed her to explain.

Drew shrugged her shoulders to communicate that she was just as confused.

"Hello, Mr. & Mrs. Tate," Ami smiled with excitement. "It's good to see you all again."

Mr. Tate greeted Ami and walked off, he wanted no part in the interrogation his wife was about to commit to.

"Hey, where's my big boy," Ma Tate turned her attention to Gabe, trying to occupy her mind with something other than the situation at hand.

The group set out to enjoy their day at the pier, it was something they'd done every Sunday for years, and now that Gabe was here, it was time for the family to restart the tradition. Drew was extra excited for Gabe to experience the pier, because right along with Jay and Shawn, it had become her tradition with the Tates as well.

The group searched the pier trying to decide what to do first, when they noticed the Mr. Early puppet show: the show tended to always keep babies entertained, so that's what they enjoyed first; while Jay and his father set out on a mission to find turkey legs.

Jay and his dad enjoyed their turkey leg while exploring the pier, both relieved to get away from the strange looks being tossed around by Ma Tate and Drew.

"Thanks Pop, for getting me outta there." Jay gave his dad some dap. "She did it again Pops."

Jay's father looked at him sideways, chuckling. "She did what again son."

"Ami, she just popped up again." Jay shook his head.

"Son, looks like you got a stalker on your hand," Jay's father laughed out.

Jay eyed his dad. "Stop playing man, I'm serious."

Pop Tate could see this Ami situation had his son bothered, so he suppressed his laughter. "Alright son, talk to me."

Jay explained to his father despite Ami popping up out of nowhere, he still went out with her, giving benefit over the doubt, and then she turns around and does the same thing again.

Pop Tate tried his best not to laugh, but he couldn't hold back; Jay's little fatal attraction had him entertained. Jay couldn't understand why his situation was so funny to his father, and as much as Jay wanted to be upset with his father for not taking him seriously, he couldn't. Pop Tate was laughing so hard Jay couldn't help but join in.

Pop Tate finally calmed down enough to respond to Jay's complaint. "Let her down easy son. Ami is the type of girl that reads into things a lot deeper than you do; she's looking for it to be something more, and clearly you're not ready for that." Pop Tate chuckled. "Before it ends ugly, allows it to finish fast."

After the puppet show the women headed to the Ferris Wheel. Ma Tate grew anxious and could no longer resist; she was curious to know the business between Ami and Jay and what was really going on. Ma Tate didn't like to bother in Jay's situationship, but by the looks on his and Drew's face when they drove up, she needed to do a little snooping.

"Ami, it's nice to see you again. I see you and Jay have gotten closer."

Ami bashfully smiled at Ma Tate. "Yeah, all the time he spent with this little fella right here allowed it."

Drew played with Gabe while also eavesdropping, she'd get answers one way or another; even if it meant listening to Ma Tate's interrogation.

"Jay didn't tell us you were coming along." Ma Tate felt her way around the conversation, trying not to come off rude.

"Yeah, I kinda surprised him," Ami looked at Drew and smiled.

'You think,' Drew thought to self, returning the smile.

Ami explained to Ma Tate how she popped up on him and Drew while loading the car.

"I didn't know you and Jay were dating." Ma Tate waited anxiously for Ami's response, so did Drew.

"Oh no, Mrs. Tate, we're not dating," Ami made clear.

Ma. Tate was even more confused. "Well, sweetheart, if you're not dating...

Drew stopped Ma Tate in mid-sentence, she knew what came next. Ma Tate always told it like it was, and Drew didn't think Ami could handle it.

"Ma Tate, would you like some popcorn?" Drew threw the question out there while the vendor was in sight.

"Sure Drew," Ma Tate eyed Drew. "Ami, would you like some popcorn?"

"Sure, I would love some."

Ma. Tate glared at Drew once more, disappointed she didn't give her enough time for interrogation.

Jay and his dad joined the women at the Ferris Wheel, and while waiting to board the ride Drew noticed Gabe had made friends with a lady in line. The two of them exchanged baby talk; it was adorable to Drew how Gabe had begun seeing other people and interacting with them.

The middle-aged woman held up a pinwheel holding Gabe's attention long enough to get a smile. "Is it ok for him to have this," The lady asked.

Drew didn't wanna seem rude, so she accepted the gift. Gabe and the lady played back and forth until Drew and Ami boarded the ride. Drew insisted Ami board with her, this would give her time to talk with Ami.

Drew tried to keep her conversation short in fear of saying something to hurt Ami's feelings, but the questions pulled at Drew and wouldn't let go.

"Ami, I have to ask you something."

"Sure, ask me anything."

"What are you doing here?"

Ami looked puzzled at the inquiry, while struggling to justify her reason. "Well, Jay mentioned going to the pier last night while in conversation, so I thought I would Join."

"Ami, I think you should've run it by Jay first?"

"I didn't think it would be a problem."

Ami had a blank look on her face. Drew could tell it was taking her a moment to process what she'd just said.

"Ami, can I give you a little advice?"

"Yeah Drew." Ami feared what Drew was about to say.

"Jay is a very private person that takes things slowly, and with you just popping up on him today may have been overdoing it. Jay isn't a big man on words, and he will always consider your feelings first, but Ami, pushing yourself on him like this will quickly lose his interest. Ami, I know you like Jay, and I know the two of you have spent a lot of time together, but sweetheart, if Jay hasn't made a verbal agreement with you about a relationship, you need to pull back."

Ami felt a warmth come over her, she wanted to cry at this point; she'd done it again, pushed herself on yet another man. "I'm sorry Drew, I didn't mean to make Jay feel pressured; I guess I've jumped the gun a little."

Drew started to feel bad when seeing the embarrassment on Ami's face. "It's ok Ami, I feel like you and Jay need to talk."

Ami agreed she would speak with Jay while continuing to apologize.

Exiting the ride, Drew noticed Gabe had found the lovely lady that gave him the pinwheel. Drew was amazed at how fascinated Gabe was by the lady. Drew took Gabe's hand and helped him wave bye to the lady as they went their separate ways.

Ma Tate quickly jumped in Gabe's view. "No baby, we don't play with strangers."

Drew notices Ma Tate eyeing the lady. "Ma Tate, you just fine," Drew asked with concern.

"I'm fine, Drew, just being cautious."

Ma Tate had a pained look on her face; Drew had never seen that expression before, and it worried her. Drew's thoughts got hungry, why did this woman have Ma Tate acting so suspicious, why did she look so ruffled.

Drew didn't know, but hopefully Jay got a good look at the lady so she could ask him later.

Drew gazed up at the sky through the moon roof, the ride home was much more pleasant than she thought it would be. From what Drew saw and heard, Jay and Ami seem to be hitting it off just fine; maybe they could have a thing for each other Drew thought, or perhaps Jay was just softening up the blow for when he told Ami to hit the dusty trail.

Pulling up to the house, all Drew could think about was a nice long soak in a hot bubble bath, and with the Tates taking Gabe for the night, it was about to go down. Drew hurried from the car leaving Jay and Ami to sort out their issue; the bubble bath was calling her name, and she was answering.

Drew didn't realize how long she'd been soaking until she heard Jay knocking at her bedroom door.

"Are you ok in there," Jay yelled out, not sure if Drew was decent.

"I'm okay, Jay," Drew yelled back from the bathroom.

Jay entered the room and sat on the teal-green chaise lounge. Jay examined Drew's room; he hardly ever came in there, and he was blown away by Drew's taste. The teal green blended well with the blush pink, and the outline of black exposed Drew's dark side. Jay growled at the pink-dyed polar bear rug that lay in the middle of the floor; Jay couldn't understand Drew's taste in décor.

Jay got up and walked over to Drew's dresser, he was stunned to see so many bottles of perfume. *'You can only wear one,'* Jay said to self, while shaking his head at Drew's ludicrous behavior concerning the perfume; he'd only smelled one fragrance on Shantel, and he hadn't smelled it since she died.

Drew emerged from the bathroom to find Jay on her dresser. "Excuse me, can you be helped, why are you in my business?"

Jay turned and looked at Drew, holding an astound face. Drew was confused about Jay's expression.

"What's wrong with you, crazy?"

Jay held up a teal blue and yellow checkered handkerchief. "You kept this?"

"Of course," Drew grabbed the hanky and put it back in the wooden box. "It has sentimental value."

"Wow, I can't believe you kept that, I remember when I gave it to you," Jay thew out a flakey laugh. "Eight-grade prom, Shawn hurt you bad that night when he took Samantha Blake. And then, to add injury to insult, you walked in on them kissing. What were you doing in the gym?"

Drew punched Jay in the arm. "Shut up, I was hurt that night, so I went in there to cry."

"Yeah, you messed up my million-dollar suite."

Drew laughed out. "That Morris Day suite."

Jay smiled. "Oh, you got comedy."

"Jay, you know that suit was horrible, and Ma Tate should be ashamed for letting you out the house in it."

"Well, Staci thought it was fly."

"First of all, we don't use fly anymore, and second, Staci doesn't count." Drew grabbed some lotion from the dresser and took a seat on the chaise lounge.

Jay was still in debate over Drew's comment. "Stacie was fine."

"Staci had big cha-cha's, that's the only thing she had going for her. "Drew laughed.

Jay stood at the mirror picking at his face." She was cute too."

"No, she wasn't, and get off my dresser," Drew ordered Jay.

"Get off my dresser," Jay mimicked Drew's words in a whining voice, joining her on the chaise.

"What's the deal with Ami?" Drew held the question long enough.

Jay rubbed his face with both hands, letting out a sigh.

"Was it that bad," Drew asked with concern.

"It wasn't terrible, just stressful; trying to let someone down easy is very hard." Jay nodded his head agreeing with himself. "I told Ami showing up like she did was out of line, and it was making me rethink my decision about starting a relationship, amongst other things."

Jay still hadn't told Drew about Ami popping up weeks before.

"Well put, Mr. Tate." Drew clapped her hands silently.

Jay looked at Drew with his lips turned up.

"Wow, I just clapped for you."

"Yeah, but we both know you were about to be derisive."

"Jay, you handled Ami well." Drew took some lotion and began to rub her legs.

Jay could help but follow Drew's hands as they gently massaged the lotion over her legs. The fragrance tugged at Jay's nose, snapping him from his daze. "Damn that smell like Shantel," Jay whispered to himself.

"Jay," Drew called his name for the second time. "You good, what you say?"

"Man, that smells just like Shantel."

"Yeah, it was her favorite, One Wish." Drew applied more cream.

Jay asks Drew why she kept the handkerchief; Drew was puzzled, and wasn't ready for a question like that, but she could only be honest with Jay.

"You took care of me that night, you saw how upset I was, and you never judged me. You knew Shawn didn't see me like that, hell I knew Shawn didn't see me like that. Everyone laughed at me that night, but you never left my side. I remember you taking the hanky out and wiping my tears. No one before then till now has ever wiped my tears but you, Jay."

Jay found himself caught in Drew's stare; trying to contain himself became an obstacle; before Jay knew it he'd taken Drew in his arms and kissed her.

Drew sit on the deck sipping a glass of wine, watching the sunset over the lake; she couldn't command the kiss Jay planted on her two nights ago to leave her thoughts. Drew didn't know how to feel about the kiss; it was nothing like the kiss they shared before she went off to college, and as much as Drew didn't want it to happen, a small part of her welcomed it.

Drew looked at the sunset admiring the pink clouds that sheltered around it. The calm evening wind directed the wind chimes to play a soft melody that had Drew utterly relaxed. Drew's thoughts brought back the kiss, she shook her head rejecting any lustful feelings. Drew knew it was better for the kiss to happen now, and nothing happen, rather than later, and it ruined she and Jay's friendship.

Drew was in deep thought when Jay's touch startled her. "Geesh, Jay, you scared the crap outta me."

"I'm sorry, I didn't mean to scare you." Jay sat in the vacant Adirondack chair next to Drew. Jay glanced at her a few times before speaking, trying to find the proper explanation for his actions was impossible.

Jay took a deep breath and exhaled; Drew chuckled, she could see Jay was struggling, about to make a big deal out of nothing.

"Let's get right to it, Drew, I don't know why I kissed you. I guess seeing how much that hankey meant to you, smelling that lotion, and you always being there been having me in my feelings lately."

Drew didn't speak a word, she loved the torment Jay was putting himself through.

Jay looked at Drew, waiting on a response.

"Was the kiss pleasant," Drew asked; she was cracking up on the inside, trying not to show any emotions.

Jay was befuddled at the question, hesitating to answer. "It was ok, I guess."

"I dare you rank my kiss as just ok." Drew began to laugh at Jay, the look on his face was priceless.

Jay laughed along with Drew, relieved she was taking the matter well and didn't have any ill feelings.

"Jay, it's okay, I know how you are." Drew teased Jay by sticking her index finger in his dimple, "And there's no reason to be awkward with each other."

"Whew," Jay exhaled. "I was just worried about our friendship."

"That's been a long time coming." Drew threw Jay a wink.

Drew looked out over the water, Jay could see much more than a kiss was on Drew's mind.

"If it's not the kiss, then what is it?"

"I'm going to reach out to Carl," Drew stated apathetically, while gazing at the sun's reflection on the water as it went down.

"Are you sure about that, you don't seem to be very excited."

"I don't know how to feel, but I have questions and I want answers."

CHAPTER 16

Moonlight & Sunrises

Marcus eyed Sarge through the mirror as he put the finishing touches on his haircut. Marcus could tell by the awkward silence Sarge had a lot on his mind. Usually, Sarge was the life of the barbershop, cracking jokes, imitating people or just clowning around, but today he'd been strangely quiet.

After watching Sarge swipe the unlock button on his phone for the fiftieth time Marcus finally intervened. "It's June 15th, 5:25pm."

"Huh,' Sarge responded, confused as to why Marcus was giving him the date and time.

"I thought maybe you needed to know, seeing how you've swiped your phone over fifty times only looking at the date and time." Marcus chuckled.

Sarge let out a sigh. "Young Buck, have you ever been so afraid to face someone that it had your stomach in knots."

Marcus laughed out loud. "Sarge, I had to face my girl with that same fear. It wasn't easy either, made me have to use the bathroom."

Everybody in the shop laughed out, even Sarge laughed along with the crowd.

"Yeah, something like that," Sarge responded.

Michael paused from cutting his client's hair to share his story, informing the shop of a time he'd felt the same way after breaking his mother's crystal vase. After Michael's share it was open floor in the shop, everyone had a story to tell.

Marcus and Sarge left the open conversation and talked amongst themselves. That's when Sarge informed Marcus about the meeting with a young lady from his past, and it had him a little disconcerted and concerned about the questions she'd ask. Offering his advice, Marcus told Sarge to be honest and speak from his heart, he also advised Sarge that he should probably pray before going, because dealing with *matters of the heart* could be tricky. Sarge could appreciate Marcus's advice because *honesty* was all he had, and praying was something he didn't do often. Sarge wasn't entirely on board with Marcus's beliefs about *Israelite culture* and the *Torah*, but he believed in a higher power, and knew good sound advice when he heard it.

Drew waited with anticipation for Carl, it had been a few weeks and she'd finally decided to have a sit-down & explain with him. Drew tried thinking of all the questions she wanted to ask her father, but for some reason couldn't think of any. Drew rummaged through her purse and pulled out the journal which held all her questions; flipping through the pages Drew tried to store as many questions as she could, categorizing them from most important to least important.

Carl sat in his car staring at the entrance to Brooklyn's, everything in him wanted to get out of there and just go home, but he couldn't bring himself to do it. Carl thought about Drew and how she would react to being stood up, so he shook off fear and armored himself with courage. Carl knew there was no other way to deal with his past but to face it head on or risk his relationship with Drew altogether. Carl banished the thought from his head, turned the car off, let the sun visor down, checked his image in the mirror, took a deep breath, and stated, "This is not a mountain, it's only a hill."

After the brief consoling session, Carl grabbed a black gift box from the dashboard; he'd thought about giving it to Drew as a peace offering, but figured it may be intimidating, so he took the gift and placed it in the glove box. “This is only a hill,” Carl stated as he exited the car.

Drew watched the hostess station for her father; she'd gone over most of the questions in her journal and now needed a drink to relax, so she scanned the room looking for a waiter. Drew was amazed to see the weekly functions of the casual jazz club, it was nothing like the weekend operations. The place seemed to be structured and organized, more like a cozy restaurant and less like a club.

Drew noticed a waiter coming her way so she hurried to stop him.

"Good evening Ma'am, may I help you?" The young man gave Drew a sweet smile.

"Yes, you can Tevin." Drew noticing the young man's name tag, eyeing him suspiciously. "Have I seen you somewhere before." Drew inquired, also noticing the young man had a familiar face.

"I'm not sure," Tevin eyed Drew, amazed at her beauty. "Fredrick Douglas, Class of 1996." Tevin stated, instantly remembering Drew, and the way she'd stole his heart that night. "Yeah, your class reunion at the Sheraton Suite." Tevin had held the warmth of Drew's beauty since that night, and was delighted to be in her presence again.

"Wow Tevin, good to see you again." Drew was amazed the young man remembered her.

"So, what can I get you, Miss McCain?"

"Wow, you even remembered my name." Drew was even more impressed. "You can bring me a Merlot Wine, tall glass please." Drew gave the eager young man a wink.

"My pleasure, Miss McCain." Tevin gave Drew a soft smile.

"Please, call me Drew, it feels like I know you well enough now."

They both shared in a laugh. Tevin dashed off to fetch Drew's request.

Drew glanced at the door and noticed Carl talking with the host; seeing how intrigued the waitress was with Carl, Drew could tell he was a real lady's man. Drew observed Carl from head to toe, standing there in his midnight blue Kenneth Cole suite, Italian dress shoes, and your essential jewelry to liven his image. Drew was amazed at how well-preserved Carl was for an older man; he even wore a small diamond earring that held his youth. Carl stood at about 6'3 and was very handsome. Drew could see where most of her features came from, holding the same eyes, nose, and complexion as Carl.

"Here's your Merlot Miss... Tevin caught himself. "I mean Drew."

"Thank you, Tevin." Drew chuckled noticing his correction.

Walking over to Drew, Carl felt the sweat creeping down his face and his stomach making waves; the feeling Carl had made him wanna run past Drew straight to the bathroom, but what kind of impression would that make. In Drew's eyes Carl was already a horrible person, he didn't wanna add embarrassment.

"Good evening, Drew." Carl sat across the table from Drew, making sure he could see her eyes.

"It's Drewlynn, thank you."

"Good evening, Drewlynn." Carl corrected his mistake; he could feel the tension in the air and his stomach getting tighter.

Drew took a drink of wine, ready for the shenanigans to begin. Drew had no intentions on making this meeting pleasant; if she could've made Carl feel the 28 years of pain she'd endured, that would've been the icing on her cake, making this reunion sweet.

Carl started the meeting with an apology; he apologized for not reaching out sooner knowing Drew existed and could've been his since the age of four. Carl also apologized for not stepping up taking full responsibility for her. Carl told Drew about his and Joy's brief love affair, informing Drew him and her mother hadn't been dating long before she disappeared without a trace.

Carl stunned Drew with the next piece of information; she felt like a member of the Gap Band, and a bomb had just been dropped on her. Not only were Shelia and Curtis her foster parents, but they were also her real aunt & uncle. Shelia was Carl's sister, and her involvement came when Child Protective Service called her, informing her that a child had been left at Mystic Pier carrying a purse containing her name and number, along with a picture of some woman.

Drew was smitten, remembering a time going through Shelia's things trying to find information about her parents, and coming across this picture of a lady in bell-bottoms and a haler top. When Shelia walked in and saw Drew holding the picture she scolded her, ordering her to never touch her things again. Drew had often gone against her wishes in a continuous search for her parents, but she never saw the picture again. Drew could barely remember what the lady looked like, but now that Carl confirmed there was a picture, Drew couldn't help but believe it was her mother.

Carl explained to Drew that Shelia felt it was best to raise her as a foster child; making it easy to give her back if she didn't want her anymore. That confession pierced Drew's heart. *'How could someone be so heartless,'* Drew asked herself, taking a drink, noticing nothing wet her lips. Drew looked at the glass and chuckled, she'd drunk the whole glass, unaware. Drew becked for Tevin to attend.

"Yes Drew, are you ready to order?"

Drew informed Tevin that she wouldn't be eating right away and asked if he could bring the whole bottle of Merlot. Drew really wanted to walk out, not knowing how much more she could take, but decided to endure, hoping the wine would shield her from the blows of reality.

Carl perceived Drew was upset, and he didn't blame her. Carl hated he'd waited so long to reach out; to see Drew breaking before him hurt more than her not saying anything at all.

Drew was relieved that Tevin wasted no time bringing the wine, she hurried to gulp down another glass.

"Excuse me sir, would you like anything." Tevin awaited an answer from Carl.

"No, I'll have some of hers." Carl moved the bottle of Merlot to his side of the table.

Tevin looked at Drew as she raised her glass and toasted a great night. Tevin could see Drew's spirit had been broken as he walked off.

"Why didn't you take me?" Drew threw the question at Carl like a curveball.

Carl adjusted his tie and cleared his throat; it appeared he had been waiting on this question the whole night, and now it was time for the answer. *'Honesty'* rang in Carl's ear, and that's what he would be, honest.

"I'm going to be straight with you, Drewlynn. I wasn't ready to be a dad." Carl wiped the sweat from his face. "I 'd just completed four years in the army and needed to start my career; there was no way I could've done that with a child."

A tear fell from Drew's eyes and sweat poured from Carl's face; the question they'd both been waiting on had been asked and answered.

Drew sat in silence processing and saving, taking a sip of wine with each pill she had to swallow.

"Where am I from, Carl," Drew asked, with an angry tone.

Carl cleared his throat once again. "Originally, you come from Texas." Drew became even more confused. "Let me explain, Shelia and Curtis where living in Atlanta when they received the call from CPS, so they traveled here to get you. It wasn't until later Curtis's job relocated him to Texas.

Drew took another drink of wine. "What's my mother's full name?"

"Joy Rivers," Carl confirmed with a slight grin.

Drew eyed Carl: he looked as though he might still have a thing for Joy, which confused her.

"We were in our sophomore year of college when I met your mother. Your grandparents were very strict on Joy, all she ever talked about was getting away from them.

Drew thought to herself, *'grandparents, wow, I'm out here feeling alone, and I belonged to everybody.'* Drew shook her head in disgrace. "Where are my grandparents now.

Carl informed Drew last he heard her grandparents lived in Texas, and their names were Joab and Ruth Rivers. Drew always wondered about her grandparents and if they ever knew she existed.

Carl eyed Drew: the hurt she held in her eyes made his heart drop.

"What about the Rivers," Drew asked. "Are they aware I even exist?"

Carl hesitated to answer, he knew the answer would crush Drew even more.

"Well," Drew awaited his response.

Carl cleared his throat once again. "When you were about ten Shelia reached out to your grandparents, but they never responded back."

Drew thought back to when she was ten, that's when Shelia found out Curtis had an affair and fathered his mistress child; Drew was convinced Shelia was going to give her up, and that's why she'd reached out to the Rivers.

The more Carl told Drew, the more heartbroken she became, putting the missing pieces together. Drew poured herself another glass of Merlot.

Carl became concerned at how much wine she was drinking. "Drewlynn, I think you should slow down on the wine; that stuff can take you fast."

Drew sat the bottle down, stared at Carl for a moment, raised her glass, and knocked back the entire beverage. Carl was not surprised at Drew's behavior and wanted to console her, but he knew she would reject anything coming from him at this point.

"Drewlynn, I know you're upset...

"UPSET!" Drew yelped out, stopping Carl in Mid-sentence. "I'm furious; you, Shelia, Curtis, and my mother took my whole life and made it about yall. All these years, you knew I existed, and you did nothing. And Aunt Shelia," Drew chuckled. "She knew my mother and father were alive this whole time and never had the common decency to tell me anything. And my grandparents," Drew shook her head repeatedly. "Treated me like yesterday's news. And you say upset, no Carl, I'm beyond upset."

Carl had no defense because Drew was absolutely correct and had every right to feel the way she did.

Drew explained to Carl how hurt and angry she was as tears streamed down her face. Tevin noticed Drew's tears, so he made his way over to make sure she was ok. Noticing a few onlookers, Tevin stood in front of Drew to shield her, pulling out a napkin so she could wipe her tears.

After Drew finished wiping her tears, she set her emotions on calm. "Carl, I appreciate all the information you've given me tonight, it was very beneficial." Drew stood up from the table. "You have been a great help, thank you for your time, but I've heard enough."

Drew pulled the journal from her purse, handed it to Carl, and proceeded to the door.

Tevin approached Drew. "Would you like to settle your bill?"

Drew looked at Carl. "My father will be glad to take care of it." Drew threw Tevin a wink and walked out the door.

Drew strolled downtown trying to make sense of all the things her father told her, but the more she thought about them the more Drew's soul hurt. At this point all Drew wanted was to feel numb, so she walked into *Moonlights*, the closest bar she could find.

Soon as Drew sat down at the bar she yelled for the bartender to make her a Twisted Nipple, gaining the attention of the entire bar.

The bartender hurried to wait on Drew, trying to make a conversation happen. "Someone having a rough night?"

Drew blew him off, taking the drink and downing it. "Can I get another one?"

"Sure, Ma'am." The bartender was pleased to be serving Drew, dashing off to make her another.

"Drew looked around the bar trying to find her peace, but it wasn't there; Randy was in Atlanta, and she was in Texas. Drew sobbed on the inside, she really needed Randy right now.

"Here ya go ma'am, another twisted nipple for the beautiful lady."

Drew eyed the determined bartender, he wasn't Randy, but he would have to do. "You know Mike." Drew giving the guy a name that he didn't own. "Mike, you know I've lived life for everyone else." Drew began to vent. "For real, Mike, I've lived life with so much baggage, now it's time for me to unload this luggage."

Drew downed her drink and slammed the glass on the bar, protesting that from now on she would live her life baggage-free.

The bartender handed Drew another drink he'd stored under the bar. "Looks like you can use another one."

Drew looked at the guy and smiled. "You don't even have a clue." Drew threw the guy a wink. "You know what Mike, My Parents SUCK!"

"That's enough, you can close out her tab." A male's voice came from behind Drew.

"I Beg Your Pardon!" Drew turned and looked into the eyes of the last person she thought she'd see.

"MARCUS!" Drew yelled out, gaining the bar's attention again.

Marcus slid two fingers over Drew's lips, shaking his head with disgrace, wondering what had her in this state.

"Look, Marcus, I'm not for your crap tonight, I got a lot of things going on, and I just wanna deal with them my own way."

Marcus removed the hair from Drew's face. "No judgment."

Drew took a drink, holding Marcus's stare. The tears that flowed from Drew's eyes confirmed this was a moment sent by Yah, and Marcus would have to handle it delicately.

Marcus was speechless after Drew told him everything Carl had revealed to her, he could feel Drew's pain, and all he wanted to do was take it away. Marcus spent the next half hour listening to Drew, allowing her time to vent and sober up in the process.

"Drew, let me take you home," Marcus suggested.

Drew looked at Marcus with tear-stained eyes. "I don't wanna go home."

Marcus was confused as to where Drew wanted to go if not home. "Where you wanna go, because I'm not letting you leave here by yourself." Marcus eyed the bartender.

Marcus loaded Drew into his car, put her seat back, clicked her seatbelt, cracked her window, put on his Musiq Soulchild cd, and set out on a journey to bring Drew serenity and peace.

While making blocks Marcus pulled up to an old brick building on the city's south side.

Drew woke from her ten-minute nap. "Where are we?" Drew investigated her surroundings.

"It's my pop's place, well used to be before he gave it to me." Marcus got out the car and went to the passenger side, opening Drew's door.

Drew looked around, she hadn't been to the south side since before leaving for college, and from what she'd heard, it was nothing like their old neighborhood.

"Are we ok over here?"

"Anytime you're with me, you're ok." Marcus took Drew by the hand and escorted her inside the antique building.

Marcus hurried to turn on the lights so he could disarm the alarm system.

Drew couldn't believe her eyes, she'd never been inside a barbershop. Drew looked around in amazement at the different workstations, everyone holding a piece of the barber that owned it.

"So, this is where the magic happens for you guys?"

"And women," Marcus corrected Drew. "Yeah, we service females like yourselves."

Drew was embarrassed that she'd never supported Marcus's business.

"And I must say we do a damn good job too," Marcus gloated.

"Respect." Drew admitted Marcus had his stuff together.

Drew sat in one of the barber chairs and took a spin; she stopped the chair immediately, spinning on liquor didn't mix. Drew began to get sick. "Ugh, I shouldn't have done that."

"You ok, I have a Ginger Ale in the back?"

Drew looked at Marcus, a single tear traveled down her face. "Carl and Joy are the worst parents ever." Drew started to vent all over again.

Marcus walked over to Drew, took her head in his hands, and massaged her temple.

"Drew, I know you're hurting right now, but you have to deal with the pain better than drowning it in alcohol. I know it doesn't sound heartfelt, but I'm coming with good intentions." Marcus looked down at Drew. "I've seen you like this twice, and I'm sorry, but not sorry; Drew it's not ladylike." Marcus hated to be harsh, but Drew needed to hear it. "Drew, hurt comes and goes, so know that it's coming, and don't be surprised when it gets there. You gotta know who's in control.

Drew rested her head on the chair; she'd heard everything Marcus said, but right now all she wanted to do was relax her mind. Marcus continued to massage Drew's head, he could tell it was precisely what Drew needed from the way she moaned.

"Marcus, all I ever wanted in this life was to know my parents, find love, get married, have a few kids, and start a cute little B&B, is that so much to ask?"

Marcus wanted to tell Drew he could give her all that and more but held back; Marcus felt it wasn't the right time to try and ease back into Drew's life. Although it was tempting, still Marcus wanted their reconnection to be pure.

Looking down at Drew, the beauty she held inside and out was the reason he loved her so much. "Drew," Marcus whispered. The relaxing massage had calmed Drew down, almost putting her to sleep. Marcus gently took Drew in his arms and headed to the door, he could clearly see it was time for her to call it a night.

"Marcus, can we just stay here a bit longer," Drew asked.

Marcus hesitated but gave in to her plea. "Sure, Drew, I have a quiet spot set up in the back, you can rest there."

Marcus carried Drew to his hideaway in the back of the antique barbershop.

"Wow, this I nice." Drew approved of the ducked-out area; it was small and cozy.

"Yeah, this is where I come to relax between clients."

Marcus sat Drew on the red futon while retrieving a towel from under the sink that occupied the small space as well.

Marcus ran some cold water on the cloth. "Here, put this on your forehead."

Drew thanked Marcus for taking care of her. Marcus was embarrassed to admit it, but it had been his pleasure, so he just nodded his head.

Drew rushed in and kissed Marcus in a fiery passion. Marcus and Drew had never shared a kiss so intense before, and as much as Marcus was enjoying the moment, he pulled away.

"No, Drew, this is not the way to feed your pain."

Ignoring what Marcus said Drew tore at his clothes, trying to gain access to his perfectly chiseled body, begging Marcus to make love to her."

Marcus couldn't contain himself from the passion Drew threw at him, and for a moment he gave in, but quickly caught himself. Marcus had never been with Drew and didn't want it to be like this. Marcus ordered Drew to stop.

"Look Drew, as much as you want to feel something other than pain right now, I can't do this with you." Marcus sat back on the futon, took Drew in his arms, and held her until sunrise.

Good morning, beautiful." Marcus bent down and kissed Drew's forehead.

Drew struggled to bring herself from the night's sleep. "Aw, my head hurts so bad." Instantly, Drew's memory replayed the night before. "Marcus, I'm sorry and embarrassed. I can't believe I acted so undignified. I should go."

Drew searched for her shoes and realized they weren't there.

"Um, did I come here with shoes?" Drew tried to gather her thoughts of the night before.

"Here, drink this." Marcus handed Drew a glass of Ginger Ale.

"No, I can't drink that, I already feel sick." Drew shook her head, rejecting the drink.

Marcus handed Drew the drink once more and insisted that she drink.

"UGH, I'm going to vomit," Drew complained. "Marcus, I want to thank you for last night. I was a mess, and I handled the situation recklessly and immature. You have every right to judge me."

"Judge you," Marcus stroked Drew's face. "You were hurt, so I'll give you a pass this time."

Drew laughed.

"Drew, I know forgiveness is hard, believe me I can contest. I'm still trying to forgive the man that shot my parents."

Drew was saddened by Marcus's revelation. "Marcus, I'm sorry I didn't know."

"Well, it's not something I go around broadcasting." Marcus laughed to fill the void; thinking back on that night still controlled his fears.

"Marcus, are you ok?" Drew became concerned about his absence.

"Yeah, Drew, I'm fine just thinking back on that night." Marcus swallowed his tears.

Drew gazed into Marcus's eyes, speaking to him with her heart. "I'm here for you Marcus, here like I've never been before." Drew softly kissed Marcus's lips.

CHAPTER 17

Time & Place

Drew and Ma Tate finally finished planting the last of the flowers around the oak tree, standing back observing their work; both women were glad the task had been completed. Planting the flowers gave Ma Tate a sense of peace, knowing she and Shantel had made plans to do this before her untimely death.

"I think we did a pretty good job." Ma Tate admired their work. "What do you think, Gabe?"

The women looked down at Gabe and noticed he'd crawled from his blanket to Shantel's grave. The two women were amazed at how Gabe sat there so calm at his mother's headstone playing with his toys.

Drew smiled at life, because at that moment her soul set well with it; being in the sun, breathing fresh air, consuming nature, and listening to words of wisdom from Ma Tate helped Drew understand many things. Most of their conversation had been about Carl, but why wouldn't it be, he was the only thorn in Drew's side at the moment. Drew dealt with her father the best way she knew how, and that was prayer.

Life was great for Drew, the office was running smoothly, she and Marcus were back seeing each other on standard terms, but more involved. It was crazy for Drew, Marcus had seen her broken, and for whatever reason it made him love her more. The last month with Marcus had been the most peaceful for Drew since she'd been back in Texas.

Drew watched Gabe, it amazed her when he laid upon Shantel's grave, seemingly getting comfort from the soft St Augustine grass that lay over it. Drew watched Gabe even closer when she noticed a tear fall from his eye. Drew didn't know if it was from the wind and dust or if Gabe felt some sort of connection laying there; either way, Drew hurried to provide him comfort.

Ma Tate notices Drew's swift movement. "Is everything ok?"

"Yeah, he's fine, I think dust flew in his eyes." Drew checked Gabe eyes.

Ma Tate walked over to examine Gabe; she suggested taking him in to wash out the dirt, hoping it would calm the fussy baby. Drew kissed Gabe's eyes before handing him over to Ma Tate, where he continued to make a fuss over the dust in his eyes. Ma Tate returned the baby talk while trying to console him.

Drew started gathering the tools she and Ma Tate used to beautify the oak tree when she heard Jay's truck pull in; the rattling cattle trailer always announced his arrival. Drew got excited, leaving the tools where they lay. Jay and Marcus had been on a four-day trip to South Carolina to retrieve cattle Jay purchased at an online auction, and that was long enough for Drew; she couldn't take not seeing Marcus one more day.

As Drew got closer to the Chevy double cab pick-up truck, she could see both men look disturbed. Drew walked to the passenger side where Marcus had ejected, greeting him with a hug. Drew wondered why the men looked so down.

"How was yalls trip?" Drew eyed Marcus, with a need to know the reason for the long faces.

"It was good, not much to tell, got the cattle, came back," Marcus responded.

Drew eyed both men suspiciously, Marcus didn't say a lot, but she could tell something had happened. "So, is anyone going to say anything?" Drew grew frustrated with the men.

Marcus grabbed Drew and embraced her once more. "I'm sorry baby, the trip was great. Jay got some pretty healthy cattle out there." Marcus tried to make small talk, but Drew could clearly see him holding back information.

Marcus started taking his things from Jay's truck and putting them in his car when noticing the confused look on Drew's face, so he pulled her close, placing a kisses on her cheeks, one after another.

Drew laughed at his affection. "Someone missed me." Drew blushed, accepting the kisses.

"And that someone is me." Marcus gazed into Drew's eyes. "How about I take you out tonight?"

Drew gave Marcus a pleasing smile. "Of course, you can take me out, I would be honored."

Marcus got in his car to leave, but before driving off, he gently placed a kiss on Drew's cheek, whispering in her ear that she needed to talk with Jay.

Drew ambled to the back of the truck where Jay was disconnecting the stock trailer. "Hey, a dime for what's on your mind." Drew pulled a dime from her pocket and handed it to Jay.

Jay looked at Drew and knitted his eyebrows, then sucked his teeth. Drew had been Jay's best friend for almost twenty-two years, and for him to blow her off like that, standing there with a freaking *dime* in hand, had rubbed her the wrong way. Drew didn't like Jay's attitude but would be patient and let him throw his fit. For all Drew knew Jay had overpaid for the stock of cattle he'd traveled days to get and was now upset with his decision. Drew left Jay alone with his thoughts returning to her task.

Drew gathered the last of the tools when Jay walked up with his hand out. "I'll take my dime now," Jay peacefully stated.

Drew didn't deny him; she quickly took the dime from her pocket in exchange for Jay's thoughts.

Jay took the dime and placed it on his forehead. "First off, I'm sorry." Jay took his cowboy hat off, covering his heart. "Drew, I spent my entire life putting others before myself, making sure I gave everyone a fair chance, but at this moment, right now, can I cash all that in and be selfish."

Drew didn't understand why Jay was expressing himself this way, but she listened and let him vent. After about five minutes of Jay trying to justify how it wouldn't be wrong for him to be a complete *ass,* Drew finally interrupted and asked.

"Jay, where is all the hostility was coming from?"

"Drew, I received a call today from the Infamous Miss Madam Loraine, The Houdini of Mothers, The Queen of MIA."

Drew was in the dark about who Jay was talking about, but she kept listening.

"How does a person feel they can pick up where they never started. Drew, I'm about this close to flipping." Jay threw up his thumb and index fingers to measure the depth.

Drew still didn't say a word, watching Jay pace back and forth, muttering under his breath. Ma Tate must have heard Jay venting because she emerged from the back patio doors demanding to know who'd pissed him off.

"Jay, I can hear you in the house," Ma Tate called out. "What's the matter, sweetheart?"

Jay continued to vent, ignoring his mothers concern.

Ma Tate started to bring about a fuss. "Jay, if going away dose this to you, why don't you consider staying home next time, and let Marcus go."

Jay really didn't want to hear his mother fussing, but he dared not say a word.

Ma Tate asked Jay to come up and grab a seat on the wooden deck, Drew followed behind him, saying the name Loraine repeatedly in her head. Drew wondered why the name sounded so familiar, but Jay hadn't given her enough clues to figure it out; he was too busy on his rant.

Jay scowled his face in a way Drew had only seen once since she'd known him, and that's when he'd caught Curtis trying to grope her in the backyard one day; it took Shawn, Mitch, and Marcus to calm him that day.

"Ok, Jay, what's wrong?" Ma Tate asked with patients.

Ma Tate knew it would take a little understanding once Jay got to this point, for Jay hardly ever stepped out of charter like this.

"I got a call from Shantel's mother today."

Drew and Ma Tate looked at each other stupefied, then both women eyed Jay; both taking a deep breath, neither knowing what to say. Ma Tate suggested Jay be reasonable and keep understanding, reminding him Gabe was a part of this woman. Drew agreed with Ma Tate, but she could also understand Jay's feelings as well.

"WHY, MOMMA!" Jay stood and began to vent for a second time.

Ma Tate kindly interrupted. "Look at your friend." Ma Tate caressed Drew's face. "Drew is a prime example of why you should keep understanding. Look at how her parent's decisions almost destroyed her."

Jay was speechless, everything his mom said made sense.

Ma Tate pulled Jay in for an embrace. "Sit down son, let's reason together."

Jay told Ma Tate and Drew every word spoken in his and Loraine's conversation. After hearing all the details, Ma Tate couldn't be biased.

"Well, Jay, sounds like she's remorseful for not being there for Shantel and wants to be here for Gabe."

Drew agreed with Ma Tate, but still a small part of her sided with Jay. Looking at Jay with empathy, Drew could see this situation had him torn up inside.

Drew cleared her throat to speak. "I understand why you're upset, hell, I'm upset, but we have to consider Gabe in the situation."

Jay stared at the sun's reflection on the water as it went down, contemplating the words his mother and Drew dropped in his ear.

Ma Tate rose from her chair and rubbed Jay's back; she could tell he didn't want to discuss it anymore. "I'm going to check on Gabe." Ma Tate walked off, leaving Jay and Drew on the deck.

"It's going to be ok friend, pray about it." Drew took the dime from Jay's forehead and lifted his chin. "It's ok for you to feel the way you do, just don't let it stick around long enough to become unpleasing to Yah. Seek His guidance Jay, you know he got your back."

Drew allowed the wind to kiss her face and the music soothe her soul, as she and Marcus set out to enjoy date night. Drew loved when Marcus planned nights out, he always made them fun and mysterious. Drew figured they'd end up at an escape room or casual restaurant, but it didn't matter long as she was with him.

Drew adored the sundress and matching shoes Den hooked her up with, shed really gotten her right with an all-purpose dress. Den had been a life saver for Drew; not only did she keep Drew in the hottest trends, but she'd also become a good friend and listener. Drew couldn't count the times she'd went to the shop on a therapy run, but instead end up venting to Den. Drew could appreciate Den and all the advice and time she'd given.

"You good over there," Marcus asked, noticing Drew had slipped into a world of her own.

"I'm awesome," Drew leered at Marcus, caressing his cheek.

"Good, the night is only going to get better." Marcus took Drew's hand and kissed it.

Drew had her eyes closed, head tilted back, arms in motion, and voice chiming, as she song along with Kisha Cole. Marcus shook his head; Drew was so involved with Kisha Cole she didn't notice the car stopped. Marcus didn't interrupt, he allowed Drew to finish her performance while he enjoyed the entertainment.

The song ended, so Drew thanked her audience of one, blowing Marcus kisses and bowing like she'd been preforming for a crowd.

Drew finally noticed the car had stopped, so she looked around to see what her night had in store. Drew's mouth dropped when noticing they were at the old Cooper home. Drew noticed renovations on the Victorian Home months ago, but why was she and Marcus here.

"Why are we here?" Drew gazed at the home; she'd always pictured herself in a house of this sophistication. The design and details of the house were immaculate. The antique white paint glowed in the moonlight, while the wrap-around porch held the place in comfort like the arms of a mother sheltering her child. Solar lights lit the driveway and sidewalk leading to the French doors that held the old home's soul.

Marcus eyed Drew, the excitement on her face made his heart warm; he'd been planning this night for a long time, and now that he and Drew were on the same page, it was time for him to bring it to light.

Marcus escorted Drew up the sidewalk lined with a garden of assorted flowers and hedges. "Wow, this is beautiful." Drew picked one of the roses.

Inside the home was like something out of *Southern Living Magazine.* Drew could've fainted taking in the beauty of the traditional staircase; she'd gotten a glimpse of them before, but it was nothing like seeing them up close. The home was breathtaking, Drew fell in love with the home's modern upgrades which complimented the original essence of the house.

Marcus only gave Drew a moment to indulge in the beauty of the home before leading her across the original hardwood floors to more French doors leading to the backyard.

Drew's eyes lit up like the stars when Marcus opened the doors. The backyard stored a secret garden designed for a queen's palace. "Wow, Marcus, this is beautiful." Drew noticed the changing lights in the pool and ran with excitement to enjoy the show.

Marcus stood back watching in silence as Drew ran her hands across the waters in the pool; the smile on Drew's face had him floating, and nothing could bring him down.

Drew noticed a picnic set up on the pool house lawn; she'd never had an outside picnic before, especially one entertained by the moonlight. Drew was amazed at all the thought Marcus put into this beautiful night.

"Marcus, this is awesome, you did all this? Whose home is this, Marcus?" Drew asked.

"Calm down, Drewlynn McCain." Marcus rubbed the small of her back to relax her. Drew loved when he touched her there, it sent chills to parts of her body that had never been explored.

Marcus walked Drew over to the blanket where he had all kinds of treats. Drew could hear The *Isley Brothers* coming from the trees; this amazed Drew, she'd never heard of anyone putting speakers in the trees. It felt like they were at an outdoor concert.

The night was perfect in Drew's eyes, she and Marcus enjoying each other's company. Drew thought of Jay and how he must be feeling throughout the night, but she couldn't allow her thoughts to intrude on the intimacy she and Marcus shared.

Marcus held Drew as they watched the fourth of July entertainment hosted in the night skies, listening to the music being pushed out through the trees. "I love you, Drewlynn McCain," Marcus whispered in her ear; he'd told Drew this a times million but Drew never said it back. Obviously, she loved Marcus, but Drew was never the one to be careless with those word. Marcus was aware Drew still held part of herself from him, but didn't make a deal of it; he knew there was a time and place for everything.

The sounds of the O'Jays pulled Drew from the blanket where she proceeded to have a solo dance with herself. Marcus admired how Drew allowed the music to take her away to a place that had no limit. Drew snapped her fingers and grooved as if she had someone enjoying the moment with her, yelling out, 'THAT'S MY SONG.' The melody from the song had Drew feeling some type of way.

After watching for a moment Marcus got up from the blanket and joined in, cuffing Drew in his arms, kissing her gently. The pair allowed the music to narrate their endless romance. Marcus could live in the moment forever; his love for Drew burned deep within his soul.

Marcus spun Drew around, the magic in her smile boosted his energy levels to the unknown. Marcus could spin Drew all night just to indulging in her smile.

Drew looked into Marcus's eyes, searching his soul, pulling out all his hidden affection. The moment of passion they shared was stored in their hearts' memories that would last forever.

"So, you gonna tell me whose house this is." Drew was having the time of her life but still questioned who house this was.

"It's yours." Marcus took Drew's hand and slid a ring on her finger. "Drewlynn McCain, I've loved you for a long time, and I want to keep loving you for the rest of my life.

Drew was psyched; she couldn't believe what was taking place. "Marcus," she whispered softly.

Marcus continued with his speech. "Drew, I'm in love with you, and I want you to be my wife, share my life, have my babies, go on vacation, make decisions, have arguments, make up." Marcus cuffed Drew, holding her stare.

Drew was overjoyed and hesitant. "Marcus I....

"Drew, I asked you a question." Marcus waited for her answer.

Drew looked at Marcus, how could she say no, he'd displayed his love for her in ways no man had ever done. "YES," Drew replied. "Marcus, I'll marry you."

Marcus was pleased with her answer, before Drew could exhale Marcus had her in the air spinning her around. "I love you Drewlynn McCain."

Drew leered into Marcus's eyes. "I Love You too, Marcus Tidwell."

CHAPTER 18

Older & Wiser

It had been a couple of months since Marcus's proposal, and Drew was still on cloud nine; things between her and Marcus were better than they'd ever been, and she was enjoying every bit of it.

"UGH!" Drew grumbled from the dressing room, she had an all-out war going on behind the royal blue curtains. Drew had grown frustrated; this was her fifth outfit and she was convinced she'd put on twenty pounds. "Why did I let them talk me into this," Drew mumbled.

Drew was having a whole conversation with herself behind the curtains, and Den was on the other side cracking up. Den crept over to the dressing room and asked Drew if she was ok; she grew concerned when noticing the curtains fighting each other. Den shook her head, this was always the case when Drew came in indecisive.

"No, I'm not ok," Drew yelped out, emerging from the dressing room wearing an off-the-shoulder white western dress, held in place by a tan belt.

Looking at her image in the mirror Drew let out a sigh. Den noticed Drew's frustration and hurried to assist her.

"Gurl, what's up with you, is everything ok?"

"No, Den, everything is not ok, look at this gut and butt." Drew grabbed the body parts and shook them. "This is the price you pay for having an intermate relationship with snickers ice cream bars." Drew stuck her lip out. " I know I've put on at least twenty pounds."

Den chuckled, adjusting the dress around Drew's waist. "Drew, stop it, this dress looks good on you." Den wasn't surprised at how Drew's body complemented the clothing; she'd been shopping there for a while now, and Den knew Drew's body and what it liked.

Drew tugged and pulled at the dress. "Will, you stop," Den ordered. "You'll never see the fit if you keep pulling at it like that."

"Den, you don't understand, this Sunday is my 29th birthday, and I must be flawless." Drew grew more frustrated. "I went to sleep a size eight and woke up a size ten."

"Wow, happy birthday Drew, you don't look older than 25."

Drew pulled Den in for an embrace. "Oh, my love, you're sent from heaven."

Den shook her head; she could always count on Drew to bring her a smile.

"So, does this look like a rodeo-style dress?" Drew began to explain to Den that Jay and Marcus were throwing her a rodeo-themed birthday party, and she needed the perfect outfit for the occasion.

Drew gave the dress another once-over. "I still can't believe I let them talk me into this. I guess it's their way of saying it's time to convert from stilettoes to boots."

Both women laughed.

"Wow, that's going to be lit." Den was excited for Drew.

"Why don't you come, it's going to be mostly family & close friends."

"Sure, I would love to."

"Awesome, I'll text you the info."

Drew looked at her image in the mirror, disappointed about the weight she'd gained. "UGH, this is horrible, I'm rethinking this dress; Mother Nature and *PMS* will not let me be great."

"To be honest I can see you in something totally different, especially for a rodeo theme." Den dashed to the store's front to retrieve the perfect outfit for Drew's birthday bash.

Drew looked in the mirror and gave herself another look; she confirmed the dress wasn't the best outfit. Drew looked around for other options while waiting on Den to return when she noticed a middle-aged woman walk in. Drew noticed the women, and Den began to have a conversation that was none of her business, so she explored closer to the back of the store.

Den yelled to Drew that she would be right back before disappearing into her office, leaving her and the middle-aged woman to browse.

Drew watched the classy lady from the back of the shop, she couldn't help but notice the woman had a very familiar face. Drew browsed the racks, reframing from making eye contact; she didn't wanna seem weird or anything, but there was something about the lady that desired her attention.

&

"Shh, y'all chill." Marcus motioned everyone in the shop to calm down. "Y'all gonna get me kick out of here." The shop had another one of their heated debates going, and everyone was trying to get their point across. The shop quieted down for a moment, and they were right back to it, tossing their options around like balls.

Marcus brushed the hair off Jay's shoulder, admitting if he knew discussing the Torah would bring this much confusion, he'd saved the conversation for his southside shop; the people from their old neighborhood seem to be more open to the Israelite way of life than the people from his uptown shop.

Jay shook his head in disappointment. "Look man, you can lay the material before the builder, but it's up to him to build the house."

Marcus agreed, but it didn't stop him from educating his people on who they were and where they came from. Marcus himself thought the Torah was the most essential part of the bible (the first five books written by Moses) it held Israel's ancient history, the agreement between Abraham, Isaac, and Jacob, the Exodus, Ten Commandments, and the Laws of Leviticus that governed the Israelites as a nation. So, Marcus stood firm on educating as many of his people as he could about their heritage and history.

Jay examined his trim, admiring Marcus's technic on the beard, it was just how he liked it. Marcus always made sure his cuts stayed within the Law of Leviticus, and he made them look good. Most of Marcus's clients didn't care for a taper fade or bald fade; the way Marcus cut their hair made those cuts look like a thing of the past. Marcus's cuts were unique in their own way, and his clients were satisfied.

"Yeah, ya boy coming along." Jay stretched a four-inch dread, admiring its growth. "You see that hang time, as Drew would say."

Marcus laughed at Jay's impression of Drew, because that's precisely what she'd say.

"Hey Gabe, you see your old man's hang time," Jay looked over at Gabe playing in the portable playpen. "Get ready son, when you get old enough Uncle Marcus gonna hook you up too."

Gabe laughed at his father, babbling the words *Dada* like he understood the words coming from his mouth.

"Speaking of Drew, have you talked to her?"

Marcus paused from cleaning his tools, recollecting if he'd spoken to her or not.

"Dang bro, you don't know if you've talk to ya girl."

Marcus laughed at the expression on Jay's face. "Nah, I've been so busy with this party I forgot when I talked to her last. Someone was supposed to help me." Marcus threw out a hint.

Jay chuckled, noticing the emphasis Marcus put on *someone.* "Respect Marcus, my bad, since my parents have been out of the country I haven't had time to commit to anything else. Gabe keeps me busy.

Marcus knew Jay's parents played a significant part in his support team, so he didn't make a big deal of it. "It's cool, overstood bro." Marcus was now sweeping the floor. "So, are your parents going to be back from Tanzania for Drew's party?"

Jay checked his phone for their arrival date; *The parents* had been in Tanzania for almost two months on mission work. The Tate's were founders of a small organization called *H.U.G.* (HELPING US GROW). The organization reaches out to families in crisis; whether it be financial, emotional, spiritual, or mental. The Tate's made sure the needs of those seeking help from the organization were met, with an added bonus of Torah teaching.

Jay's parents started the organization in their old neighborhood when they lived in Shiloh City; after a few years the program became so successful the Tate's began traveling worldwide, helping struggling families all over the world. *H.U.G.* had attracted the attention of so many people, even a few celebrities contributed to the cause. Jay's parents established the organization over 20 years ago, and it was a success from day one. The Promise community was also a great support, everyone was always committed to giving for one reason or another.

Jay informed Marcus that his parents were due back on the 26th, giving them three days until Drew's party.

"Perfect, just enough time for momma to get back and help you." Jay took Gabe from the playpen looking at Marcus out the corner of his eye.

Marcus looked at Jay sideways as he backed crabbed to the door. "You're full of it, how you gonna throw your duties off on moms like that?"

Jay took Gabe's hand and threw it up at Marcus. "Say bye to Uncle Marcus, Gabriel."

Marcus shook his head, he knew not to expect anything more from Jay other than the cake he was told to buy.

While continuing to back out of the shop and his duties, Jay backed right into Sarge. "What's up Sarge," Jay greeted him with a salute.

Sarge returned the salute. "At Ease Soldier, and who's this handsome young man." Sarge played with Gabe's dimples.

"This my boy, Gabriel Tate," Jay said with proudness.

"And a fine boy he is, a boy with strength and dignity." Sarge held a fist in the air. "But only if you instill it in him, keep that in mind Young Buck."

Jay chuckled, he always expected two things from Sarge, advice and to be called a *young buck*. "I got you Sarge." Jay gave Sarge another salute as he exited.

Drew was still waiting for Den, she'd gone in her office almost twenty minutes ago and Drew hadn't seen her since. Drew didn't want to seem impatient or demanding, but it was starting to aggravate her in a small way. Drew thought about other things she could've been doing. *"Come on Den,"* Drew hummed to herself while pretending to look through the racks.

Drew jumped when the dressing room curtain flew back and the middle-aged women from before came out. Drew had forgotten the women was still there. The lady glanced at Drew and complimented her dress. Drew thanked the lady for her compliment and pretended to still be shopping.

'UGH, Den where are you,' Drew questioned in her head.

Drew watched the lady as she admired herself in the mirror, checking out the denim Maxi dress she'd tried on. "That's a beautiful dress. I see you have an eye for fashion."

The lady looked at Drew and threw her a wink. "Thanks sweetness."

Drew checked the lady out from head to toe, she was classy and sassy. Drew couldn't waver the fact that she'd seen the woman before but couldn't put it together.

Drew hesitated to ask, but before she could stop the words had already escaped her mouth. "Do I know you from somewhere?"

The woman looked at Drew with a smile. "I don't think so."

At that moment Den stormed up with an outfit she'd put together for Drew. Den apologized for her unprofessionalism, explaining to Drew she had to fill some orders and go through some things in the back to complete the outfit.

Drew accepted Den's apology, but her interest was in the mysterious women. Drew looked back to continue their conversation, but the women had already disappeared into the dressing room. Drew couldn't shake the feeling that she knew the woman from somewhere.

After getting her attire together Drew decided to drop by *Kingz Cutz* for a little interaction with Marcus. It was just up the street from *Saddle Girls,* so she decided to walk; the autumn breeze was just what Drew needed after being cooped up in Den's shop for over an hour.

Drew was grateful for Marcus's downtown shop, it was only a block from Cambridge which gave her free access to Marcus whenever she wanted. Marcus spent a lot of time at his downtown shop, it had more sentimental value; it was the first shop he'd opened on his own. Of course, his dad's shop was unique and where he learned his technique, but this was his shop.

Drew struck out on her mission to the barbershop where she used to be a stranger; now it had become her own personal adventure. Drew loved going into the shops, staring up the barbers and beauticians with some crazy conspiracy theory she'd throw at them. It always amazed her how they'd latched on to a subject, boosting and debating all their different opinion they had stored up, waiting to present them to anyone that would listen. Although Drew liked the people and atmosphere at the downtown shop, she loved the southside shop even more; the crowd seemed to be more open to gaining knowledge about their history and heritage. Versus the downtown crowd who basically wanted everything sugar-coated and unaware of the reality around them.

The topics of conversation were always better at the southside shops as well. Drew never had to throw out an issue, there was usually one up for debate whenever she came into the shop.

"Hey, Drew." Everyone greeted her as she walked through the door. Drew always felt like she was on an episode of *Cheers* when they did that. Drew returned the greeting hurrying to kiss her man.

Marcus was always happy to see Drew walk in, it gave him reason to smile. "Hey baby, how's your day?" Marcus kissed Drew's neck.

"Don't do that." Drew always became coy when Marcus showed affection in front of the crew; their Ooh's & Aah's always made her blush. "My day was interesting, I guess you can say." Marcus had a client in his chair, so Drew didn't detail her day, especially the part about her gaining twenty pounds, so she just told Marcus the basics of her day while watching him cut the client's hair.

Drew was always amazed at how Marcus owned the clippers; he was so good and professional with them he could make a blind man see his work. Marcus looked at Drew and smiled, she was so focused on his work she didn't notice him staring at her.

"So, are you ready for your rodeo?" Marcus pretended to ride a horse.

Drew shook her head; she still couldn't believe she'd let Jay and Marcus talk her into these ridiculous rodeo shenanigans.

"I rented a mechanical bull and everything."

Drew shook her head. "I know you don't expect me to get on a mechanical bull?" Drew eyed Marcus.

Marcus looked at Drew and licked his lips seductively, whispering in her ear. "I expect you to get on that bull and ride it."

Drew's cheeks grew warm, and it wasn't long before Michael yelled out the first *'Oohs.'* Drew smiled at Michael with embarrassment, considering the words only she heard. Drew eyed Michael putting one finger to her lips, silently telling him to be quiet. Michael blew Drew a kiss and cut his client's hair. Michael and Drew weren't particularly favorable of one another but tolerated each other for Marcus's sake. Michael held a resistance towards Drew after remembering her being the *Mary J* impersonator that night at Eclipse. Michael never told Marcus about the performance or the kiss, considering his feelings. But he'd made sure Drew was aware he knew her little secret. Drew had only met two of Marcus's family members, and both were questionable; she only hoped the introduction to his parents would have a more positive outcome.

Drew turned her attention back to Marcus. "I'm not getting on that bull sweetheart, not Drewlynn McCain."

"Well, how about Drewlynn Tidwell." Marcus stole a kiss.

Drew hurried to cover Marcus's mouth. “Shh, before someone hears you.” Drew whispered.

Marcus removed Drew's hand and kissed it. "Drew, I don't know why you're keeping it quiet. Don't you want to share the good news?"

"Yes Marcus,” Drew pouted, "But I want to tell everyone together."

Marcus respected Drew's request, so he would keep quiet for now.

Marcus spun his chair to finish his client's hair when Drew noticed Carl sitting in the seat. Drew and Carl's eyes met, both in shock that either of them was there, together, in the barbershop.

Drew continued to glare at Carl until Marcus finally interrupted their stare by asking if she was ok. Everyone's attention was on Drew, the humiliation was too much for her. Drew glanced at Marcus then at Carl before she ran off to the ducked-off spot in the back. Marcus didn’t know why Drew ran off and didn't hesitate to run after her, leaving Carl bewildered.

Opening the door to the secluded room Marcus could see Drew was in some form of distress. "Baby, what's wrong?” Marcus grabbed Drew's arms and began to cress them, trying to calm her shaken spirit.

"Why is he here?" Drew pointed to the door.

Marcus looked back at the door. “Who’s, he?" Marcus had no idea who Drew was referring to.

"Carl, the man sitting in your chair." Drew eyed Marcus waiting on a response.

"What are you talking about Drew, that's Sarge."

"No, Marcus, that's Carl, my father."

Marcus was shocked, how could this be Drew’s father; he’d been cutting this man's hair for years and never imagined him to be Drew's father, or his name to be Carl.

"Sarge is your father?"

"No, Marcus, Carl is." Drew folded her arms, eyeing Marcus becoming annoyed.

Marcus walked over to the door and peeked out at the confused man trying to compare, that’s when he noticed Sarge walking towards the room. Marcus closed the door just as fast as he opened it.

"Well, he's coming this way."

Drew paced back and forth, biting her nails. "I don't wanna talk to the dude."

Marcus could understand Drew's frustration, but for him she was acting like a child and needed to face her pain. Marcus decided to put his foot down, it was time for Drew to release this hurt, and he wasn't letting her out until she did.

Carl knocked at the door, he was finally over Drew not being reasonable with him. Carl had finally made up his mind that Drew would either accept him or not. Being the older wiser one Carl felt it his reasonability to nip this whole situation in the bud, and now that he had Drew in a corner this was his chance.

Drew begged for Marcus not to answer the door, but Marcus went against her wishes and opened the door anyway. Marcus apologized to Sarge for his unprofessionalism, explaining that he had to make sure his fiancé was ok. Carl was very understanding of the matter and disregarded Marcus's actions

Carl asks Marcus for a moment alone with Drew but he refused. Marcus wasn't going anywhere until Drew finally released the hurt she carried from this man, so Marcus allowed Carl into the room and closed the door. The trio spent seem like hours in the ducked-away room trying to resolve their issues; by the time the three of them emerged from the room Michael was sweeping up, and everyone else had gone home for the night.

Michael didn't know what was going on, but he could see lots of tears had been freed; even Marcus looked as if he'd been crying. Michael and Drew's relationship wasn't the best, but even Michael hated to see her upset like that.

"You good Drew." Marcus gave Drew a gentle smile.

"I'm good, thanks Mike." Drew gave him a gentle smile.

Michael nodded his head and continued the cleanup.

Marcus cradled Drew in his arms as Carl said his goodbyes; he knew she was good, but it didn't stop him from securing her.

Carl gazed at Drew before leaving, admitting that Marcus was a good man and she'd made a wise choice to marry him.

Drew gave Carl a pleasant smile, looking up at Marcus. "I know."

Not everything had been worked out between Drew and Carl, but they understood each other better and agreed to work past their differences.

CHAPTER 19

It's my party, I'll dance if I Want To

Marcus escorted Drew inside the event center where everyone awaited her arrival. Marcus couldn't take his eyes off Drew, she was beautiful, more stunning than he'd ever seen. Drew was also pleased, Den really came through with her wardrobe.

Drew wore a white off- the-shoulders ruffled blouse, some denim jeans with turquoise stones on each pocket, turquoise rose in plated cowgirl boots with a belt and cowgirl hat that matched, and to bring the entire outfit together Drew wore turquoise stone jewelry which complemented the glow of her skin.

Marcus stopped and embraced Drew before meeting the crowd.

"What was that for?" Drew was puzzled by Marcus's actions.

"I'm just grateful to have you by my side. Happy birthday Drew."

Drew started to tear up; her birthday never really meant much to her, but here stood Marcus, making her feel like September the 30th was the day a queen had been born. "Stop, Marcus, you're going to ruin my makeup." Drew fanned her eyes to dry the tears before they fell.

Drew was amazed at Marcus and Jay's energy put into the rodeo theme. Observing the room, Drew saw hay bales, gun powder barrels, salon doors, and stuffed cattle in various places. Drew also noticed Marcus wasn't playing about the mechanical bull; the guest was already giving it a try. Drew was pleased to see everyone dressed in their western attire which really brought out the theme all together. Drew was greeted by her guest with the loveliest birthday wishes. Everyone was there, even old high school friends. Drew had never felt so loved in her life.

After Drew greeted most of her guests Marcus then escorted her to meet his parents. Drew was so nervous her stomach was in knots; the closer they got to the table the tighter Drew's grip got around Marcus's biceps. Marcus leaned in and kissed Drew's ear, and with a whisper he assured her there was nothing to be nervous about; his parents were good people.

Marcus and Drew stood behind his parents awaiting their attention. Marcus's father entertained the entire table with his impression of Jamie Foxx and Jim Curry. Marcus cleared his throat to gain his parent's attention, which acquired the entire table's attention. Drew tightened up on Marcus's biceps once more. Marcus assured Drew it was fine by rubbing the small of her back.

"Good evening, everyone." Marcus greeted the table, kissed his parents, and introduced Drew. "Mr. and Mrs. Tidwell, I would like for you to meet my gift from Yah, the love of my life, the apple of my eye, the sun to my shine, the beating in my heart, the beautiful Miss Drewlynn McCain."

The table applauded Marcus's introduction. Drew also felt compelled to join Marcus in his comedy by presenting his parents with a *Royal Curtsy* and a head bow fit for a king and his queen.

"Please to meet you, I'm sure." Drew greeted them with an English accent. Marcus's parents applauded Drew; they were impressed by her witty personality, and by the way Marcus gazed at Drew he was too.

Marcus's mother jumped to her feet with no hesitation, taking Drew in her arms blessing her with the most tender embrace. "Aww, how precious are you, happy birthday Drew; it's finally good to meet you." Marcus's father was just as elated, throwing compliment after compliment at Drew.

Drew was amazed, she thought with Marcus's parents being shot and his father paralyzed due to a violent robbery they wouldn't be very sociable, but Drew was wrong, these two people had more life in them that had been taken away.

After finally meeting Marcus's parents the pressure was off, and Drew was ready to let her hair down and enjoy her party. But, before Drew was to do that Marcus had a surprise for her.

Marcus took Drew by the hand and guided her to the bar, asking the bartender to give Drew a twisted nipple. Drew looked out at the crowd having a good time, dancing to the music and enjoying themselves. Drew smiled, she'd never had a party before, so this was exciting and new.

"Twisted Nipple for the lady." The bartender handed Drew her drink. Drew turned to retrieve her drank when she noticed it was Randy. Drew was flabbergasted, she couldn't believe Randy was there to join in the celebration.

"Randy, I can't believe you're here." Drew wasted no time wrapping her arms around Randy's neck. Randy was in tears, blessed to see Drew so happy; recalling the last time he saw her Jay had to practically carry her out of the bar.

Randy looked at Drew, admiring the smile on her face. "Well, Drew Boo, I couldn't miss my most important girl's birthday."

Drew looked at Marcus, presenting him with a gentle kiss on his cheek. "I know you did this."

Drew took a sip of her drink and indulged in its goodness. "Randy, no one can make a Twisted Nipple like you."

"Always my pleasure, Drew Boo." Randy kissed Drew's cheek.

Drew watched Jay dance his way through the crowd, making way to the bar where she and Marcus sat enjoying the festivities. Drew was glad to see Jay enjoying himself, he'd come a long way from tears to smiles.

"What's up birthday girl, are you enjoying yourself?" Jay gave Drew a kiss.

Drew shimmed her shoulders. "I'm enjoying myself. I can't believe you and Marcus pulled this off."

Jay gave Marcus some dap. "Well, you know how we're coming behind you." Both men kiss Drew's cheeks.

The trio were engaged in conversation when Jay noticed a *blue rose* walking through the crowd headed their way. Jay had never seen a face so unique and beautiful. Jay examined this rose from head to toe. Who was this woman? Where had she come from; she walked with grace and sophistication. Jay could see confidence in every step she took. The natural essence of her beauty captivated Jay, from the natural way she wore her hair to the natural way she wore her make-up. This woman sparked a flame in Jay he didn't want to put out. Jay was a sucker for a natural woman. Jay became disabled when catching a glimpse of her smile; this gorgeous woman offered a smile that could change your whole mood from sad to happy in seconds.

"Wow, how well do you look in that outfit. My goodness, where did you get it?"

"Um, this cute little boutique called Saddle Girls, I know the owner, she's really sweet and knows her stuff."

Both women laughed at the inside joke.

"Happy birthday Drew," Den kissed Drew's cheek. "I see the rodeo theme came together perfectly." Den admiring the decorations.

Den and Drew held their own conversation while Jay and Marcus talked amongst themselves. Drew could clearly see Jay inquiring with Marcus about Den, so she fed his craving of need to know.

"Forgive me Den for my rudeness." Drew intruded in on the fella's conversation pulling Marcus to her side. "Let me introduce Marcus Tidwell, my ever-so-loving boyfriend, and Jay, my handsome yet single best friend. Fellas, this is Dina, my stylist slash life savior."

Jay and Marcus laughed at the lively introduction. Marcus greeted Den in return while Jay stood in a daze, trying to get his line together. *'Was this a match,'* Drew thought to herself, and if so they would have to do it themselves, because tonight it was about her.

Drew's attention was taken off Jay and Den by Mr. & Mrs. Tate ripping up the dance floor. The crowd cheered as they danced to *R Kelly's Step In The Name Of Love.* The Tates didn't miss a beat. Drew could see the crowd was entertained because everyone started to join in, even Marcus's parents were on the dance floor.

Marcus grabbed Drew by the hand and pulled her to the dance floor. "Come on girl, it's your party and you can dance if you want to."

Drew looked around at her family and friends, her heart was filled with joy; Drew gave Yah inner praise at that moment, grateful that he'd put people like the Tates, Miss Sue, Jay, Den, Randy, and now Marcus's parents in her life. Drew realized in that moment she might have been abandon as a child, but Yah had given her so much more in return. Yah had given her people that loved her unconditionally.

Drew and Marcus spent almost half an hour on the dance floor enjoying the music, and now it was time to rest. On their way back to the bar Drew noticed Jay and Den enjoying each other on the dance floor; it looked like a match in Drew's eyes. Drew refreshed herself with a ginger Ale Randy had waiting on her when she got back to the bar; it was just what she needed to cool down.

Ma Tate grabbed the mic and called for everyone's attention. Drew didn't know what was going on and grew anxious with every second. Marcus took Drew's hand and led her to the middle of the floor. Drew looked around at all the guests waiting with anticipation along with her. What had Marcus done now?

Ma Tate handed Marcus the microphone then gave Drew a gentle kiss. Drew could tell whatever Marcus was about to present, Ma Tate had a hand in it. Marcus also placed a soft kiss upon Drew's cheek, starting echoing 'Ooh's & Aah's through the crowd.

Marcus twirled his hand in a rolling motion at Jay when an 85-inch projector screen fell from the ceiling. The suspense was killing Drew; what had Marcus and Ma Tate done so great that it needed an 85-inch screen.

"Our Love," Marcus announced to the guest and a video began to play.

Drew was amazed, the video started with pictures of her and Marcus from kids to adults. It also included video clips and pictures of Drew and Marcus's seven-year courtship. Drew was stunned when she saw the night Marcus proposed being replayed before her eyes; Marcus had recorded their entire night. The guest viewed the movie, and not a dry eye was in the hall. The love Drew and Marcus shared was now on the big screen.

Drew watched as the proposal scene played out; she was still moved by Marcus's actions that night as tears began to flow from her eyes. At this point Drew didn't care about ruining her makeup, Marcus had just made her the happiest woman in the world. The applause had Drew blushing as the video came to an end; the guest was honored to share the couples love.

Marcus took Drew's hand leading her in a heart-touching whirl when the DJ played *Let get married by Jagged Edge*. This was the moment Drew had always dreamed about; being loved by a man with no limits, and Marcus had proven he would do that.

Marcus and Drew got lost in the moment, holding each other exposing their love to the guest. As the song ended, the guest applauded, then everyone rushed in to give their congratulations to the couple.

Meanwhile, Carl sat in his car debating about going in or just going home; he knew Drew was still unsure about furthering their relationship which made him hesitant, but it would be now or never for him. Carl opened the glove box and retrieved the gift from months before. Twirling the box in his hand Carl smiled, this would be the first gift he'd ever given Drew, and he hoped it was something she'd cherish.

Carl sat a few moments more watching the people go in and out of the building; he could tell by the smiles and laughter everyone was having a good time, so who was he to interrupt. Carl pulled the sun visor down. "You've climbed the mountain, tackled the hill, now it's time to glide the speed bump." Motivation was what Carl needed to hear, whether it came from someone else or himself.

After all the fuss was over Drew escaped to the lit deck connected to the hall. Drew was pleased with the evening, looking over the county side basking in the love everyone had shown. The night had been perfect; there was nothing that could ruin it for Drew.

Carl stood behind Drew holding the gift in hand. "What a beautiful young lady you are."

Drew turned to identify the unfamiliar voice; she was shocked to see Carl standing there. "Carl, what are you doing here?"

Carl explained that Marcus thought it would be a good idea to come out. Drew couldn't bring herself to be upset with Marcus because she always knew his heart was in the right place. Besides, Drew felt it time for her to build a relationship with Carl.

Drew walked over and embraced Carl; he was unsure how to handle Drew's affection. Carl swallowed his fear and doubt, wrapped his arm around Drew, and indulged in her warmth, almost consuming her. The fearless lion had turned into a tiny cub. Drew's embrace touched places in Carl's heart only a daughter could.

Carl thought to himself, after twenty-nine years he finally held his daughter for the first time. Carl pulled Drew closer and held her tighter; if he could bottle this moment he would.

Carl detached himself from the hug and cleared his throat before the tears fell. "Drew, I got you something."

"Wow, Carl, you shouldn't have." Drew opened the box reveling a platinum neckless with a *center of me* diamond pendent attached. "Oh, Carl you shouldn't have."

"It's the least I could do." Carl congratulated Drew on a beautiful proposal and expressed how happy he was for her and Marcus. The father and daughter were having a conversation; it was quite an experience for them both.

Jay waked through the hall searching for Drew and she was nowhere to be found. Jay had searched the kitchen, bathroom, office, and the dressing rooms, but Drew was nowhere to be found. Jay noticed a couple come in from the deck when it dawned on him Drew had to be getting some air. Jay walked out on the desk when he noticed Drew talking with an older gentleman; he didn't want to be rude, but Marcus's needed her inside. Jay waved his hands in the air trying to gain Drew's attention when just about the fourth wave he was cold busted; both Drew and the unknown gentleman had caught him in the act.

"Jay, what are you doing?" Drew and Carl both laughed at his foolishness.

Jay situated himself from the humiliation, cleared his throat and spoke. "Drew, you're needed in the hall."

Drew wasted no time introducing Jay to her father; Jay was shocked to see the man Drew introduced was Sarge.

"What's up Sarge." Was all Jay could say, he had more questions, but they would have to wait.

Sarge embraced Jay with excitement; he was just as shocked to see Jay. "What's up Young Buck."

Drew had a look of curiosity on her face. "Wow, you two know each other?" The men updated Drew on their connection while making sure she returned to the party.

Drew could see Marcus standing in the middle of the floor; all she could think was how Yah had favored her, and she was grateful, but if he was trying to get her on that bull he could forget it.

Drew was in the kitchen preparing lunch; she blushed when reliving the night of her party, still on cloud nine. Although it had been weeks ago Drew still got chills.

Drew glanced over at Gabe when she noticed him walking to the end table; it was ironic because the table held a photo of Shantel. Before Drew knew it, she was screaming for Jay to come see.

Jay emerged from his bedroom startled by Drew's scream, hurrying to see the matter.

"He's walking, Jay." Drew was excited, encouraging Gabe to keep going.

Jay was just as excited. "Come on Gabe, walk to daddy."

Gabe took three steps towards his father and fell into his arms. The trio danced around with excitement. Drew ran to the nursery and retrieved the baby book, there wasn't one milestone she hadn't written down.

After half an hour working with Gabe, he became fussy; Drew could see he was tired and ready for a nap, and if she didn't hurry to rescue him, Jay would kept pushing him to walk. Drew took Gabe from Jay's arms, mimicking Gabe's baby talk. "Come on baby boy, cause daddy doesn't know when to stop."

After putting Gabe down for his nap, Drew hurried back to finish lunch but found Jay already completing the task. "Thanks, you're my hero," Drew was delighted that Jay had taken over.

"I've missed you, Drew." Jay poked at the hamburger helper cooing in the pan.

Drew was puzzled at Jay's statement and hesitated to comment. "What do you mean, you miss me, I'm right here, every day." Drew thumbed the back of Jay's head, taking the fork from his hand.

Jay took a seat at the counter. "I don't know Drew, it seems like you're not around as much." Jay explains to Drew that she didn't have much time for him and Gabe anymore since the engagement, and Gabe had spent more time with Rainn than with her.

Drew could understand why Jay felt that way.

CHAPTER 20

Past & Present

Hurry up, Jay, you're going to make us late," Drew yelled out at Jay while wrestling with Gabe on the sofa; he and Drew had quite a match going, Gabe wanted to play, and Drew insisted he put the jacket on. "Come on Gabriel don't be difficult today of all days," Drew pleated with the determined baby.

"I'M COMING!" Jay yelled from his bedroom. Jay took a deep breath, kneeled, and bowed his head, searching for the words to say, but nothing came to him, so he relaxed and let Yah speak for him. Clearing his mind and opening his heart, Jay surrendered.

Yah, I come to you right now first to say thank you. This has been a long, challenging, emotional journey, but you kept me, and I thank you. You gave me the perfect woman, and then you took her; not giving us enough time to fully love each other, and I will not question your decision, but give you all the glory. Yah, I thank you for the opportunity to be Gabe's father and for him to be my son. I ask that you continue to build our relationship, and you give me the teachings to provide him with a good life. Yah, today is a tough day, and I need you to give me the strength to stand firm before my family and friends in the remembrance of my wife, Shantel. I thank you, and I trust you, Amen, Todah Yah."

Drew looked around the room; she was overjoyed by the turnout for Shantel's memorial service. So many people came to show their respects, even people Drew had never seen before. Drew glanced at the Tates; she could see the tears about to fall as Ma Tate looked at Shantel's picture on the easel. Drew handed Ma Tate a Kleenex to catch the tears before they fell.

Trying not to drop tears herself, Drew focused her attention on Gabe. She pointed at Shantel's picture softly, whispering, "Wave at mommy," Gabe smiled at the photo muttering the words *momma* as if Shantel was waving back. Drew looked up at Jay standing behind the podium coaching himself to stay strong and allow Yah to guide him. Drew was so very proud of her friend, he'd been broken in a million pieces, and to witness Yah put him back together before her eyes was amazing.

Jay cleared his throat, summoning the crowd's attention. "Shalom, family and friends, I'm glad to see everyone made it here safe." Jay wiped the nervous sweat from his forehead. "I would like to thank each of you for coming out joining us in this blessed event."

Jay talked a while about Shantel and the love they shared; he spoke about Gabe and their new journey without Shantel and how hard it was, then he topped it off with praise to Yah for being with him and Gabe, surrounding them with a great support system.

Drew was amazed at how strong Jay was; she could clearly see he had healed from Shantel's death.

Jay completed his presentation then opened the floor for anyone else that wanted to share words. Drew hesitated knowing she would probably cry more than talk, and the butterflies were also making kung fu moves in her belly, but Drew didn't let that stop her. Soon as Drew started to address the crowd the waterworks began. Drew cried her entire speech which created a chain reaction in the crowd; she tried her best to continue, but Drew couldn't. Marcus could see it was becoming more difficult for Drew to speak, so he went and guided her back to her seat.

After a few remarks from the guest Jay retook the podium, informing the guest that he had a special guest he wanted to introduce. Looking amongst the crowd Jay motioned for a woman sitting in the back to come up. As the woman approached the podium many guests began to talk amongst themselves. Drew thought to herself the middle-aged woman looked so familiar, but she couldn't process it. Drew wondered who the woman was and what she had to say.

As the woman reached the podium, Jay introduced her to the crowd. "I would like for you all to meet Loraine Reed, Shantel's mother." Drew was overtaken by shock, and so were a few guests.

"Good afternoon, everyone." Shantel's mother greeted the people.

Drew could tell she was nervous and wanted to run out, but held firm and continued.

"I would like to thank the Most High for being in front of you all to celebrate the memory of my daughter Shantel." Loraine searched for the right words to say, and the only words she could find were her truths. "As many of you may know Shantel and I lost my husband, her father when Shantel was very young; shortly after that I went into Bi-polar Depression and detached myself from the world and my daughter."

Loraine didn't feel obligated to explain, but felt it would be fair to Gabe, Jay, and Shantel that she explained her absence.

Drew was in full-blown tears hearing that Loraine's sister moved in with her to care for Shantel until she went off to college; shortly after passing from a stroke. Hearing this brought back the memory of Drew holding Shantel all night while she cried over the death of her Aunt Sharron.

Loraine wiped the tears. "I had a choice to live or die." Loraine admitted to the group her suicide attempt and how Shantel was the one that found her. "I was too broken to live and too selfish to die."

Drew knew how Loraine felt, she'd experienced the same feelings a few times herself. Drew remembering a time she stood in the Tates bathroom holding a bottle of Shelia's anti-depressants, hoping she could get enough strength to take them after Curtis tried forcing himself on her again. The only reason she didn't go through with the attempt was because Pop Tate knocked on the door demanding she open it; it was like he knew something wasn't right. After Drew opened the door Pop Tate took her in his arms assuring her she would never have to worry about Curtis again. Drew didn't know what happen, but later that week Curtis came home with a busted lip and three broken ribs. After that, Drew never had to worry about Curtis again.

Drew never understood how Pop Tate knew what happen between her and Curtis, but she was grateful for his protection.

Drew snapped back to the present looking over at Pop Tate thankful that Yah had put him in her life. Focusing her attention back to Loraine, Drew could tell the words coming from her mouth were sincere; she could tell by the pain in her voice Loraine was remorseful for not being there as she should've for Shantel.

Loraine looked over at the Tates and thanked them for stepping in taking care of Gabe and Shantel; reassuring them she wasn't there to take over, but simply right her wrongs. Drew could tell by the smile and tears on the Tates faces they were forgiving.

Then Loraine fixed her eyes on Drew; no one had to tell her who Drew was, by the kind words and letters Shantel sent home she knew precisely who she was.

Loraine raised her hand to the rose gold cowgirl hat she wore. "I tip my hat to you Drewlynn McCain; you have been more than a friend to my daughter. You stepped in and took care of her son with no questions to be asked. You've proven that you and Shantel were more than just friends. You guys were sisters, and I tip my hat to you Drewlynn McCain."

Drew gave Loraine a gentle smile, blowing her kisses, mouthing the words thank you; she was grateful for the respect shown from Loraine.

Before Loraine ended her speech she motioned for Jay to come up. Loraine took Jay's hand and began to express how blessed she was that he didn't turn her away but instead welcomed her in and didn't judge her reason. Loraine presented Jay with a photo album/ scrapbook she'd custom made. The book held pictures of Shantel from the day she was born until she left home for college. The book also had a cd with old home movies of Shantel, old drawings, report cards, plane tickets and much more.

"Jay, please take this part of Shantel and share it with Gabe; my daughter might not be here in the present, but her past memories live on through you and me." Loraine handed Jay the album with tears rolling down her face.

Drew clutched Marcus's hand trying to hold back the little tears she had left, but it was pointless they flowed uncontrollably like her tear ducks had been refilled.

Ma Tate walked Gabe over to Loraine so she could meet her grandson. Upon first look Loraine could see Shantel had put every bit of herself into the child. Sorrow came over Loraine; this child had been in this world a year, and this was the first time she'd ever laid eyes on him. Gabe and Loraine gazed at each other getting an immediate connection. "I'm so sorry Gabriel, I should have been here."

Gabe began to cry for Loraine, Drew thought maybe it was the rhinestones in her hat, but once Loraine took him, Gabe simply laid his head upon her bosom. Drew wasn't surprised at Gabe's actions, he'd always had the ability to connect with people.

"Oh, my, how sweet is he?" Loraine kissed Gabe's forehead, and in that moment her sorrow had turned to joy.

After the memorial service the entire family agreed on Mystic Pier for Gabe's birthday celebration. It was a perfect November day, the sun shined bright, and the breeze was crisp and clear. Shantel's memorial brought many tears, but now it was time for laughter. Drew honored Jay for being thoughtful enough to invite Loraine on their outing; she could tell by the smile on

Loraine's face that it was a perfect day for her as well. Drew knew it took a lot for Loraine to be there, so she'd make sure Loraine had the best day ever.

Loraine struggled to lock Gabe down in his stroller; he was giving her the fight of her life as he struggled and pulled to get free. Drew noticed the tussle and ran to help; she didn't want Loraine to become overwhelmed.

"Are you just fine Loraine," Drew asked.

"I'm okay, I remember Shantel not wanting to ever be strapped in either."

Gabe was really giving the ladies a hard time; Drew knew Gabe didn't like the stroller, but this was unusual behavior.

Jay looked over at Gabe giving the women a run for their money, so he left his parents unloading the car to assist them.

Loraine looked at Jay with embarrassment that she didn't know Gabe well enough to calm him. "Jay, I'm sorry, I don't know what to do." Loraine tried to explain.

"There's no need to apologize." Jay retrieved Gabe from the stroller and handed him to Loraine. "He wants what he wants."

Loraine was pleased that all the fuss was about her; soon as she took Gabe in her arms he calmed down. At once Loraine's embarrassment turned to honor.

The group looked for an open spot in the picnic area of the pier but wasn't having much luck. It seemed everyone was taking advantage of the beautiful fall weather.

Drew called to the small group. "Here's a spot, you guys." It was a bit secluded but perfect for their private celebration.

The ladies put down some blankets to set up their picnic area; Drew notices Den walking towards them, she was shocked to see her there. Drew shook her head, was this another Ami episode?

Drew walked over to embraced Den. "Hey girl, what are you doing here?"

Den eyed Jay and smiled. "I was invited."

Drew couldn't help but question the blush on Den's face. "Ok, well join us."

Drew gawked at Jay; how could he ask Den here today of all days. Drew looked at Jay and secretly motioned for him to walk off.

"Are you crazy inviting her here?" Drew's tone held frustration.

"No, what's the problem." Jay eyed Drew.

"What's the problem? Are you serious Jay, Loraine is here?" Drew was concerned that Loraine would have a problem with it.

"Will you calm down; Den is the reason Loraine's here."

"How did Den have anything to do with this?" Drew was confused.

Jay assured Drew he would explain later, but until then they should just enjoy themselves. Drew eyed Jay: she would let it go for now, but Jay knew he had some explaining to do.

After the group had eaten lunch, enjoyed birthday cake, shared stories about Shantel, and opened gifts, the ladies agreed it was time to leave the men and explore the pier.

Drew kissed Marcus goodbye, thinking this would be the perfect time for a little snooping, so she allowed Ma Tate and Loraine to walk ahead with Gabe so she could do just that.

"Den, I didn't know you and Jay had gotten so close." Drew beat around the bush a little before diving in with questions.

"Yeah, ever since your party we've seen each other none stop." Den answered with optimism and a smile.

"Wow, he didn't say a word to me." Drew thought how could Jay keep something this important from her; he'd moved on, him and Den where in a whole relationship. Drew didn't wanna make it a thing so she held back her true feelings, not wanting to make Den uneasy.

Den threw light on the relationship seeing how Drew was questioning things in her head. "So, for the last couple of months me and Jay have been seeing each, dating, getting to know one another." Den volunteered the information.

Drew could tell by the excitement in Den's voice she held some feelings for Jay already.

"I can't remember how it happen; we were at your party on minute and the next having coffee, talking about Gabe's grandmother." Den explained to Drew how Jay was at a crossroad whether to let Loraine into Gabe's life.

Now Drew understood, Den had been the one to convince Jay that it was ok to let Loraine in. Although Drew felt some way about Jay not telling her about Den, she could fully understand. All Drew wanted was for Jay to be happy, and by the look of it he was, so there was no reason to question that.

Drew joined Jay on the front porch after putting Gabe down; both gazed up at the sky; it seem to hold a unique beauty that night. The clouds were illuminated with an unusual back light making the sky look navy blue and purple. The stars peeped out from behind the clouds in a game of pick-a-boo. Drew and Jay sit in silence while speaking to each other's hearts. Drew had questions for Jay, and Jay wanting to answer each one.

Jay spoke. "Drew, I know you're disappointed that I didn't tell you about Den." Drew sat in still silence, allowing Jay to express himself. "I didn't tell you about us because I needed to be sure it was right, before bringing her to the family."

While Jay explain a single tear rolled down Drew's face.

"Say something, Drew."

"Jay, there's nothing to say you're happy, and that's all that matters to me. Yeah, I admit I was a little salty at first, but when I saw you two together and the smile on your face, nothing else mattered. Anything understood doesn't have to be explained."

The pair eyed each other, and for the first time, in a long time, they were both happy.

After a beautiful day at the pier Den walked into her office at the boutique. Plopping down in her chair Den was still excited about her day out with Jay, but even more excited about her time with Drew.

Den pulled a picture from her purse she, Jay, and Drew had taken in the photo booth at the pier and smiled. Den had grown close to them both over the past few months and hoped it was the beginning of a lifelong friendship.

"What are you doing, who's that in the picture?" A man's voice came from the dark shadow in Den's office, startling her.

Den exhaled. "Why are you in the dark?" Den quickly put the photo back in her purse.

"I was just sitting here thinking." The voice said calmy.

"What are you thinking about." Den asked nervously.

"Thinking if you're going to be honest and tell me who's in the picture."

Den eyed the young man.

CHAPTER 21

Questions & Answers

Carl looked at his watch again, he'd been waiting on Drew over twenty minutes for lunch.

"Mr. McCain, would you like to go ahead and order; if I know Drew she's caught up at work." Becks stood before Carl with her notepad awaiting his order.

Carl looked at his watch once more. "Sure Becks, that'll be fine my girls cutting it close today."

Just as Carl was about to order Drew walked in, rushing. The six months she'd gotten to know her father Drew knew he was a very punctual man; Carl had addressed her a few times on tardiness.

"Sorry I'm late Carl," Drew began to explain the obstacles that held her up. "I have an advertising ad due yesterday for the 2008 Obama Campaign, and it's taking so much of my time."

Becks stood patiently as Drew explained; she didn't wanna leave knowing Carl was ready to order. Becks already knew what Drew was having, it hadn't changed in almost a year.

Drew finally settled down long enough to notice Becks standing there. "Hey Becks, how are you, sorry I didn't see you standing there. This job got me crazy girl."

"It's ok, I know where you're coming from." Becks looked over at a timid young man about to drop a bucket of ice.

"Have you ordered Carl?" Drew looked at the menu as if she was going to change her regular order.

"I was just about to when you rushed in."

Drew smiled at Becks with a wink. "You know what I'm having."

"Of course, the same as every day; a smoked turkey sub with the works, on toasted rye bread, and a water." Becks took Carl's request then hurried off to produce the order.

While the pair waited on their order Drew went on and on about the wedding and her job; venting to her father that she didn't have enough time in a day for all she had to do. Drew complained about the wedding being only four months away and having so much more to do, then she complained about her career not allowing her the freedom she needed for her wedding.

Carl suggested Drew start her own business if she would be working her butt off like that. Carl always encouraged Drew in the matter of owning her own business; he'd ran his own staffing company for over 20 years, and nothing felt better than answering to himself.

Becks returned with their order, but before walking off she asked Drew about the wedding. Drew buried her head in her purse and began to whimper.

Becks looked at Carl. "Did I say something wrong?"

Carl smiled at Becks. "No, not a thing, I just think our little bride is overwhelmed right now."

Drew looked up from her purse with a snicker wrapper holding on to her eyelash.

Becks laughed uncontrollably, pulling the wrapper from Drew's eye. "If she keeps eating these snickers there's gonna be more to worry about than just flowers." Becks slapped her hips and walked off laughing.

Drew's father took her hand and kissed it. Drew loved when he did that; it made her feel like a princess.

"Drew, you have to stop overworking yourself, and make your employees work for you. Be kind, but firm."

Carl gazed at Drew; now she hated when he did that. It made her feel like she was under a microscope. Drew bashfully looked down at her phone to pass the moment.

"I know it makes you feel uneasy when I stare and believe me I try not to, but when a man has a daughter as beautiful and intelligent as you he can't help but be proud. Your mother was beautiful as well."

Drew looked up from her phone. The words *your mother* had summoned her attention. Carl never talked about her mother, so this came as a shock to Drew.

Responding with a smile and nod, not wanting to say a word to interrupt any knowledge and truths she could obtain about her mother, Drew didn't say a word.

"You even have smile." Carl took Drew's hand, he felt it was time for her to know the truth about his and Joy's relationship.

"Drew, I must be honest with you, at our first conversation there were a few things left out. I only answered the question you asked. Drew, I told you me and your mother were never an item, but we were. I must admit Joy held a part of me that no one could release; that's partly why I went to the military after she ran off. It was the only way to escape the hurt of her leaving me."

Drew looked at Carl growing more involved as he began to tell her the backstories of his and Joy's relationship. Drew could see for the first time in her father's eyes that Joy's disappearance hurt him.

Carl pulled his chair closer so he could look into Drew's eyes; they made him think of her mother, because they were the same eyes he'd stared into for months. The same eyes he'd fell in love with.

"Drew, you're as beautiful as your mother; I can remember the first time I saw her. I'd been at Zion University 'ZU' for almost two years, and I'd never seen your mother until the evening of January 2, 1977. Everyone gathered in the rec hall on campus to watch the premiere of Roots." Carl started to laugh. "You would've thought someone famous was coming the room so packed. Anyway, everyone was mingling until the show started. I noticed Joy as soon as I entered the room; she and another young lady were joking around on the piano, but honestly Joy sounded unbelievable. Drew, your mother had the voice of an angel, and the way she commanded the keys on that piano to sing in harmony with her was pure talent."

Drew listened to her father's story growing more excited with every word. Drew also notices Carl becoming just as excited telling her.

Carl continued. "After the movie a few of us students went to an off-campus party." Carl told Drew he didn't wanna go but a few of his buddies insisted, so he gave in to peer pressure. "After seeing Joy." Carl smiled. "I was glad I went. I had never been this infatuated with a female before until Joy." Carl looked up at the lights as though he could see her face. "Basically, I was still a virgin."

Drew was amazed that Carl saved himself for so long, now she didn't feel so weird about her virginity. Seeing that her and Marcus still hadn't done the due; they'd came close, but always stopped before any damage was done.

Drew turned her attention back to Carl. "The night had passed, and while everyone was enjoying themselves, I had spent the night in a corner, fighting the boy in me that wasn't man enough to even say hello to your mother." Carl shook his head. "Joy was so beautiful, I thought she'd laugh at me for sure."

Drew yearned for more; she'd finally got an image of her mother, a real one, not one created by her imagination.

"After the party I got in my car to leave when I noticed Joy standing at the bus stop smoking a cigarette. The way she glowed under the moonlight you would've thought she had a special light that only shined for her. Joy looked like she'd just stepped off a runway, her jet-black hair flowed down her back like dark waters, her skin was smooth as sweet honey, her eyes spoke to you without saying a word, her smile sweet and soothing, her spirit humble and meek."

By the way Carl's eyes lit up when he described Joy, one would've thought he was still secretly in love with her.

"So, I pulled over to ask if she needed a ride back to campus. Believe me, being a black woman back then you didn't wanna get caught alone at a bus stop. Joy hesitated at first, but I guess she must've thought about it, so she got in." Drew's father chuckled. "She didn't waste any time and came right out with her question.

'Why did you stare at me the whole night and never ask me to dance'

"I was speechless; did I make it that obvious? I didn't know how to answer, so I just laughed. Joy insisted on an explanation, but I didn't have one; at least one that didn't make me seem like a scared little boy. So, I was honest and told Joy that I thought she was too beautiful to be interested in someone like me. Joy laughed so hard it made me feel even dumber. Are you kidding me was your mother's reply. Joy assured me if I was beneath her she wouldn't have wasted time being left at the bus stop purposely, just to see if I would be the gentleman she thought I was."

Drew interrupted. "She gets left purposely?"

Carl answered with excitement. "Yeah! She was spontaneous like that. After that night we were inseparable. Your mother was a driven woman." Carl looked deep into Drew's eyes. "You are your mother's daughter."

Drew didn't know how to feel about Carl's statement.

Carl went on to tell Drew how her mother wanted to dance, but the River's (Joy's parents) were strictly against it. "Your mother often talked about just packing up and leaving, but I never took her seriously. Besides, we'd been together a little over a year, and she hadn't gone anywhere, so I blew it off as venting. The last day I saw your mother she was upset, almost disturbed. I tried to comfort her, but she rejected me. I thought she may have had another falling out with her parents, so I gave her time to cool down."

Carl informed Drew how Joy acted out every time she and her parents disagreed.

"Drew, if I had known Joy was pregnant, I would've never left that night. I loved your mother, but I figured she needed time to cool down. I checked on Joy the following day and her roommate informed me she'd packed up that night and left. I went looking for her, but the doors were slammed in my face. Your grandparents treated me like crap when Joy and I were together; they would always try to convince Joy I wasn't good enough for her. So, after that I went to the army; four years later I get a call from Shelia that you had been abandoned at a pier in Texas."

Drew began to feel uneasy. It was the way her mother just dropped her off, not knowing if she was safe or not. Drew couldn't understand how Joy could take care of her for four years and abandon her like that.

"How did Shelia know you were my father?"

"I had taken your mother over to Shelia's a couple of times. I guess from the picture she left in the purse Shelia put two and two together."

Drew was grateful to her father for sharing his story, but now she despised her mother even more. Drew knew she had to let go of the hurt and hate in her heart in order to move on, but she just couldn't understand Joy's actions enough to do so.

After a stressful day at work and the confession lunch with her father Drew needed a small shopping spree, so she dropped in on Den.

Den was checking out a customer so Drew shopped around to give her time to finish up.

"Thank you so much Mrs. Fancy, come again." Den gave the customer a smile. "Hey lady, how are you?" Den quickly embraced Drew.

Drew replied with a gloomily fine.

Den grew concerned; this wasn't the lively soul she usually encountered. "A dime for what's on your mind." Den took a dime from a pink bowl that sat by the register and handed it to Drew.

Drew was shocked at Den's actions. Had Jay let Den in on their secret. As much as Drew wanted to know she put it to the back of her mind. Drew really needed a female's perspective on her and Carl's conversation, which was way more important than *ten cents*.

Drew took the dime and placed it on her forehead; both women laughed at the silliness.

Den flipped the open sign to closed and took Drew to the lounge area. Den designed this area for stressed-out husbands, although very few men ever came in the boutique with their wives.

Den held Drew's hand allowing her to gather her thoughts. After a few minutes Drew finally spoke, telling Den every detail about her life, not leaving out one piece of information. Drew literally summed up twenty-nine years in less than twenty minutes.

Den welcomed the ventilation; she was honored to be there for Drew. This was the first time she'd actually opened up to her.

"Den, I've forgiven Carl for what he did, and now that Carl has told me more I blame Joy even more. How could she be so cruel and selfish not to even let Carl know she was pregnant."

Den eyed Drew; the woman that sat before her was everything she wanted to be. "Drew, your story is fantastic."

Drew eyed Den, this wasn't the response Drew was expecting, but she waited patiently and heard her out.

Den explained. "Your story is impressive. Drew, the woman that sits before me doesn't look like she's been through such a challenging journey. God truly has favored you."

Den held Drew's stare, speaking these words "The road before you hold more promises than the road behind you."

Drew sat for a moment, meditating on Den's words. Just those words alone convinced Drew that her heart's desires where on the road before her, and she wouldn't allow the hate she had for her mother to stand in the way.

Den stroked Drew's hand breaking her meditation. "Are you ok, Drew?"

"I'm good, just thinking about what you said, and it makes too much sense." Drew looked at Den and tossed her a smile. "It's time I let it go and be happy; maybe I'll hear Joy's side one day, but until then I'm going to live my best life."

Drew stood to her feet, dusted herself off, put her chin up, and her chest out. "I will not allow this hurt to succeed." Drew stated, marching around the boutique, chanting the word over and over.

"Now, this is the Drew I know." Den stood up and began to chant as well.

The ladies continued their conversation while Drew shopped; although she felt better she still treated herself. The pair were having such a good time they didn't notice a customer standing outside the door.

"Hey darling, you open," The lady cried out, knocking on the window.

Den remembered the closed sigh showing. "Yes, we are." Den hurried to flip the sign to open.

The woman entered the boutique, glanced at Drew, threw her a wink, and proceeded to the shoe section. Drew noticed it was the same lady she'd seen in the boutique before, and for some strange reason she was drawn to her.

Drew pulled Den to the side. "Who's that lady, do you know her?"

Den gave the woman a once over. "Not personally, she's been in a few times, she never says much, mostly an in-and-out shopper."

Drew eyed the woman, never turning away.

CHAPTER 22

Cold Feet

Hey beautiful," Marcus answered his phone after the fourth ring.

"Hey handsome," Drew responded. "I'm calling to make sure my sweet baby was ok." Drew always called Marcus at this time; she knew he would be done with clients and completing invoices.

"Yeah bae, I'm almost done here. How's my heartbeat?"

"Marvelous sweetheart, are you coming to Promise later?"

As much as Marcus wanted to see Drew he had to decline, the hour drive would be a little too much for him tonight. Between Drew, the shop, and the wedding, Marcus was exhausted. They had both agreed not to live in the Victorian Home until after they were married, but nights like this Marcus wished he hadn't agreed. "Not tonight baby."

Drew was slightly disappointed, but she understood. "So, I'll see you tomorrow?"

"Sure thing, future." Marcus hung up the phone and went back to work when a young boy knocked on the door. Marcus yelled out telling the young man he was closed, but he pleaded that Marcus did him this one favor and cut his hair.

Marcus peered out at the young man. 'It won't take me long,' Marcus said to self, letting the young man in. As soon as the boy entered the shop he took out a gun and asked Marcus for his money.

Marcus shook his head; he couldn't believe this was happening again. "Look man, you don't have to do this." Marcus pleaded with the young man as memories of the night his parents were shot played in his mind. Marcus was shaking like a leaf, emotions were high, fear was in control, and anger was slowly taking over.

The young man didn't say too much he just wanted the money.

Marcus eyed the young man, he could see the boy was nervous and had never used a gun, so he stayed calm, fearing being shot by this young amateur. The young man couldn't have been no older than fifteen or sixteen years old.

Marcus tried talking to him again, but the more he tried to speak, the more anxious the young man became.

"Look man, I just want some money; give me some money and I'll leave." The young man waved the gun around.

Drew walked over to the closet door where her wedding gown hung, she couldn't believe she was about to become Mrs. Marcus Tidwell. Thinking back on all the encounters they'd had in life Drew couldn't imagine she'd be marrying Marcus. It still seemed like a dream to her.

Drew chuckled remembering when she and Marcus were paired together for an eighth-grade theatre arts project. Marcus had to dramatize a story she'd wrote and told in front of the class; the project was entertaining and funny. The class really got a kick out of watching Marcus dramatize one of Drew's flamboyant stories, but Marcus didn't think so; having to jump around the stage like a frog wasn't his idea of entertainment.

Drew looked at the dress once more before turning off the light and joining Ma Tate and Den in the kitchen, where they worked hard on wedding decor. Drew got even more excited about the wedding seeing how everyone was doing their part. Even Michael had been cooperative, making sure the groomsmen stayed in line and on point.

Drew wanted her wedding to be an event where couples fell in love again, and new love blossomed, but between planning her wedding and running a company Drew was overwhelmed. She was really considering starting her own business; she and Marcus had talked about it and he backed her one hundred percent.

Drew looked around at all the wedding stuff, and by the looks of it Jay's house was overwhelmed as well; there were magazines, wedding carts, fabric, and flowers all over. Looked like a tornado had struck.

Hours had passed and the women were still hard at work; so hard at work neither of them heard Jay enter the house.

Jay looked around and couldn't believe his eyes, the living room, dining room, hallway, kitchen, and den looked like an episode of four weddings. Jay cringed at the fact he even knew what four weddings was.

Jay shook his head noticing Gabe had joined in the planning as well, sitting in the middle of the floor playing with a wedding bell and ring barriers pillow.

"GOOD EVENING, LADIES," Jay hollered out.

The trio looked up and put their heads right back down; they had only a couple days left until the wedding and couldn't afford any destruction.

Jay couldn't believe the women ignored him, he was visible and demanded attention. Looking down at Gabe, Jay placed his index finger to his mouth, telling Gabe to be quiet. Gabe looked at his father and laughed, then Jay crept over to the radio and turned it off.

"HEY, What Are You Doing, Jay Turn That Back On," The women scolded him; Jay struck a nerve interrupting the ladies listening pleasures of the Isley Brothers, but that didn't matter they could see him now.

"Jay, why would you do that," Ma Tate asked.

"Dang momma, y'all been full force on this wedding for weeks, and it hasn't given me any time with this sweet lady right here."

Jay turned the volume back up, took Den in his arms, and danced with her around the kitchen.

Den accepted the invitation, enjoying the break from diamonds and pearls, lace and satin.

"Oh yeah, Drew, why is Marcus sitting outside in the car?" Jay dipped Den.

"What do you mean sitting in the car?" Drew went over to the screen door to investigate. "What is he doing here, why is he just sitting there," Drew asked.

"I tapped on the window and told him to get out; you know yo man special." Jay laughed.

Drew looked at Jay sideways. "No sweetheart, you're the special one." Drew gave Jay a wink and walked outside.

"Marcus," Drew yelled out, but she got no response.

Drew stepped off the porch and headed towards Marcus's truck, as she got closer Drew could see something was wrong, so she called out to Marcus again, but he still didn't respond.

Marcus just sat there motionless, hands glued to the steering wheel just staring into space. The tears flowing down his face seem to be the only thing moving.

Drew tried to open the door but it was locked. "Marcus, open the door," Drew asked, but he just sit there

Drew tapped on the window pleading for Marcus to open the door until she finally gave up. Drew looked to the heavens and called on Yah; she didn't know if Marcus had gotten cold feet and wanted to call off the wedding, or if something far worse had happened.

Drew pressed her face against the glass and whispered. "Whatever it is baby, we can fix it." Tears flowed, Drew couldn't take another heartbreak. "Baby please," Drew pleaded.

Marcus's trance was broken when he heard the distress in Drew's voice, he gently opened the door, taking Drew in his arms. "I'm good Drew, it's ok, I'm ok."

Drew could feel Marcus's whole body shaking. "You're not ok, Marcus, why are you shaking like this."

Marcus tried to explain but could barely get the words to form; his voice quivered with fear. "Some kid robbed me tonight at the shop." Marcus held Drew tighter. "I was scared Drew."

Drew could feel Marcus's tears hit her tears.

"Drew, I was reliving the night my parents got shot all over again."

Drew pulled Marcus closer; he'd never really talked about his parents shooting before. Drew thought with it happening so early in his life Marcus had dealt with it and moved on, but now she could see after twenty-five years, Marcus was still traumatized from that night.

"Drew, it was so scary and surreal, bringing back every memory from that night." Marcus exhaled. "After my parents shooting I was afraid, so I made myself forget. I thought if I forgot it would keep him from coming back, so I pushed it to the back of my mind. Lost Memories." Marcus shook his head. "That's how I dealt with it as a child. But staring at that gun tonight it all came back to me. I know who shot my parents. I've seen him Drew, in the store, on the street, in the shop."

Marcus continued his story while grabbing a seat on the porch; his legs were shaking so hard he knew they would give out at any moment.

"Dad had locked up for the night and this guy came knocking on the door, just like tonight with me. The guy begged my dad to cut his hair, so my dad agreed, letting the man in the shop. I sat across from my dad watching him cut the man's hair; I watched my dad every time he cut hair." Marcus smiled at the memory. "Anyway, as my dad finished cutting the guy's hair he went into his pocket. I thought to pull out money to pay, instead, he pulled out a gun and demanded money. My dad tried talking to him, but he just wanted the money."

Drew could see the fear and hurt in Marcus's face as he relived the horrible memory.

"My mom must have felt something because she came from the back. Soon as she walked through the door the guy shot her; my dad wasted no time running to my mom, covering her from any more bullets. That's when he hit my dad. Shot him right in the back, then the guy turns the gun on me, a five-year-old little boy, scared out his mind. If he would have been one inch to the right, he would've shot me. A free haircut and eighty dollars. Drew, my mom was pregnant with Michael; how can you harm a pregnant woman?" Marcus's fear and hurt began turning into anger. "Michael could've died because of this selfish bastard. My mom could never have children again or will my dad ever walk again."

Drew couldn't speak, the story Marcus had just told her left a dent in her heart. All she could do was hold him while he cried.

Here, baby, drink this." Ma Tate handed Marcus a cup of chamomile tea and began to vent. "I can't believe someone would rob you; Marcus everyone knows you over there. You've given all the young men free haircuts once or twice. Who would be so selfish as to do this to you?"

Drew pleaded that Marcus sell the shop; she had become scared that it would happen again, but fatal the next time like his parents. Marcus tried to calm Drew and take selling the shop off her mind, because it was the last thing he wanted to do.

"Drew, it's probably a new cat out there that doesn't know the ropes or the neighborhood."

Drew wasn't trying to hear any excuses; she wanted him to get rid of the shop.

"Calm down Drew, give this man time to breathe." Jay rubbed her shoulders. "I'm pretty sure Marcus knows what he needs to do."

Jay could see Drew getting on Marcus's nerves and about to get all dramatic about the situation, so he used the wedding as an escape and suggested they get back to work before she be crying about more than the shop.

Marcus and Jay sat on the porch still trying to make sense of the whole ordeal. One of Marcus's biggest fears was having the same thing happen to him that happened to his parents.

"Jay, what if Drew had been there?" Marcus punched the palm of his hand. "Man, I can...

Jay could see the robbery was really taking a toll on Marcus. "Marcus, I know this is bothering you, and you got a million things going through your head, but you have to humble yourself and thank Yah you didn't get harmed, and Drew wasn't there."

"I feel what you're saying, but this is hitting a little differently. I know who shot my dad now, and I wanna do something about it. I couldn't do anything when I was young, but now I can keep it from happening again. This feeling I have inside will not go away. Everything in me saying let it go, but there's a small part telling me to confront this man." Marcus put his head down in shame. "I just want this fear that I've been carrying to finally be a thing of the past, and I feel the only way that can happen is confronting the man that put it there." Marcus eyed Jay. It's crazy because I feel sorry for the young man that robbed me, but I have nothing for the man that shot my parents."

As much as Jay wanted Marcus to release his fear, the idea of him confronting this guy went against his better judgment.

"You're only feeling this way because this guy hurt people you love; if he'd walked out with only the money you wouldn't be so angry. Jay clutched Marcus's shoulder. "I would say it's more hate in your heart than fear and confronting a man with that inside is not a good idea."

"Jay, I've been running that barbershop for fifteen years, even before I graduated high school, and no one has ever robbed me."

Jay pondered. "So, what are you gonna do, you know Drew's not going to let up about you selling the shop; she's scared to death, and I can't say I blame her."

Marcus thought Jay would understand but wasn't sure whose side he was on. "So, what are you saying, sell my dad's shop? Jay, that shop has been in our family for well over sixty years. I can't just sell it."

"I understand Marcus, I have a son, and it means the world to me that I'll have something to leave him when I'm gone, but not at the price of my life."

Jay took a drink from the bottle of beer he held. "Look man, you have three other shops, will it hurt you to close one? Like momma said, you practically cut hair for free in that shop anyway."

"Yeah, I know," Marcus replied. "But many of those people can't afford it, and it's like my way of giving back."

Jay understood where Marcus was coming from; they had lived in Shiloh City their entire lives, and giving back to the neighborhood was honorable, but at what cost.

"I know what you're trying to do, and I tip my hat, but Shiloh isn't the same place anymore."

Jay could remember when Shiloh City was one of the most thriving and safest cities around, but now it was overpopulated, filled with drugs, overwhelmed with crime, and ruthless. Jay knew he'd made the better choice when he moved to the rural area of Promise, Texas.

Jay's parents moved there soon after he graduated high school, so he was no stranger to the small town. It's a little over an hour's drive from Shiloh City, but that didn't matter Promise had everything he and Gabe needed. Jay went to the city for business and entertainment from time to time, but that was all. Jay knew Promise was the best and safest move he'd ever made.

Promise Texas populated about 2,500 to 3,000 people give or take. This was fine for Jay, the fewer people, the less crime.

Jay was also amused by the predominantly black community of ranchers and farmers, including himself and Marcus; the small community was always ready to give a helping hand when needed.

The Promise community was established in 1866 by formerly enslaved African Americans. It was said to have been one of the most significant Freedman's communities in Texas, wall to wall black-owned businesses, schools, newspaper and churches. Unfortunately, Promise was brought to her knees after abolishing Jim Crow laws in 1964, which caused many residents and business owners to relocate to Shiloh City; where opportunity and success came easy, thus leaving Promise with only a few people to keep it going.

Promise was your typical small country town, housing two grocery stores, a small clinic, and your usual authentic downtown; that consisted of about 25 buildings renovated and turned into small businesses. The town's schools were convenient, being that they were all on the same street, other than the high school that was only five minutes from town. Jay liked the idea of Gabe being educated by neighbors and friends; people he had backgrounds on.

The small town did have its modern upgrades like the Sonic, Family Dollar, and pizza hut, but that was about it. The people in Promise loved their small community and fought to keep it that way.

Detective Miller reviewed the results from the fingerprints taken from Marcus's barbershop and noticed the fingerprints also matched patterns from another scene. Miller read the suspects profile when noticing he was only fifteen with no priors. Miller also sees in the file that he comes from a good home, so why was he on the street robbing?

Miller was determined to find the young man before he got into more trouble. There was a small piece of him that felt obligated to help Marcus, since he was the responding officer called to the scene when his parents were shot.

Miller looked at the suspect's photo. "How does a good kid like this get caught in the streets," Miller said to himself.

Calling for his assistant to run a line on the young man Miller felt pained that another young brother was headed for the slaughter.

The woman glanced at the profile. "Wow, they're getting younger and younger."

Marcus had been sitting in his car outside the Stone Ridge apartments for over an hour; he'd been waiting on the man responsible for his parent's shooting. Marcus had spent all day researching information about the man so he could finally confront him.

"Reggie Hardaway," Marcus stated while looking down at his mug shot, displeased that he only served two years. For Marcus this wasn't enough time; this man had taken more from him, and he wanted him to pay.

Marcus also thought about Drew and if the guy came after her, so tonight he would make it his business that Reggie understood he was to never come near his family again.

Marcus's phone rang, it was Drew calling, he dared not answer; he was there to make a point, and he knew Drew would only talk him out of it.

Marcus waited a while longer, everything in him said to let it go, but the fear and hate he held for so long wouldn't allow him. Marcus thought about what Jay said, but the intervention wasn't enough to overthrow his decision to put the same fear in Reggie that he'd held all those years.

CHAPTER 23

Here and Now

Drew stood at the top of the stairs; she was gorgeous. The strapless wedding gown she wore would make the queen of England envy her. Drew's vail and train flowed like a stream of milk, diamonds hid in the dress's lace sparkled every time the light hit a gem. The *Victorian Home* had been transformed into Drew's own personal Lily garden; there were Lilies everywhere, the front yard, backyard, doors, walls, and stairs.

Drew could hear Luther Vandross's *'Here and Now'* playing, Ma Tate calling her name, Den calling her name, but she couldn't respond. Drew stood motionless staring into space as the tears flowed from her eyes. Drew tried to be strong, but the stronger she became the weaker she got.

Jay ran up the stairs, and just as he reached the top Drew fell into his arms going in and out of consciousness. Drew got flashes of everyone in a panic, Carl demanding everyone to step back, Ma Tate praying, Den crying, and Jay encouraging.

Jay stroked Drew's face with a cold towel, whispering in her ears that she was ok and had just passed out. Drew could feel the tears dropping from Jay's eyes onto her face.

After a moment Drew started to fully regain consciousness. Jay and Carl helped Drew to her feet; she could see the wedding guest at the bottom of the stairs confused about what was going on. Jay tried sitting Drew on the bench behind them, but she demanded to be taken away from the crowd.

After addressing the guest Ma Tate rushed to assist Drew, asking everyone to leave the room; she knew Drew was a private person and all the added attention would only worsen the matter, besides she needed this time alone with Drew.

Drew stood motionless, staring out the bay window overlooking the lake; she was numb, there was nothing or no one that could shake her from this hurt.

Ma Tate stood behind Drew, watching as the crushed soul tried to hold herself together; Ma Tate didn't have the words to say, so she stood there with Drew in silence, waiting to be called upon.

Drew continued to stare out at the lake, chanting in her head, *'I will not let this hurt succeed, I will not let this hurt succeed.'* Drew stated the words sternly in her head, trying to make them stick. Tears streamed down her face, the more she tried to hold them back, the harder they fought to come out. Drew didn't understand anything that was going on; everything felt surreal, and she was about to lose it at any moment.

Drew quickly searched the archives of her memory and replayed one of the funniest memories she could to calm herself. A memory from 1989; it was three days before Ma Tates birthday, and she and Jay were thinking of a way to get some money to buy her a gift, so they took all the Thrifty Nickle newspapers from the EZ-Mart and sold them to people for 50 cents. Drew chuckled to herself, recalling how furious Pop Tate was after Brother Shamir told him he'd seen us selling complimentary newspapers at the laundry mat.

Ma Tate watched Drew, and as much as she wanted to hold her she knew Drew was better with self-soothing at this point.

There was a knock at the door, Den stuck her head in and asked if it was ok if she came in. Drew didn't object; she was still chanting in her head and wasn't aware anybody had even knocked. Ma Tate gave her consent knowing Drew wouldn't mind.

Den entered the room holding a cup of tea for Drew, but she could see tea was not what Drew needed at this time, so she put the cup on the dresser and took a seat in the bay window beside Drew.

Den grabbed Drew's hand and broke her chant. Drew looked at Den with tears-stained eyes and repeated the chant, but aloud this time, so loud everyone outside the door could hear her.

"I WILL NOT LET THIS HURT SUCCEED; I WILL NOT LET THIS HURT SUCCEED," Drew's entire body shook she was so upset, and it didn't matter how many childhood memories she relived, nothing could suppress the hurt in her heart.

Den ran to the bathroom to retrieve a warm towel, hoping the cloth's warmth would calm Drew. Ma Tate hurried over to Drew, trying to calm her; it broke her heart to see Drew like this. Ma Tate rubbed Drew's chest trying to calm her, but Drew kept repeating the chant louder and louder as if it was giving her power.

Den emerged from the bathroom with the warm towel and placed it on Drew's neck as she continued to chant the words.

Ma Tate woke up the following morning; everything seemed like a dream to her until noticing they were still in their wedding clothes, snapping her back to reality. Ma Tate looked at Drew as she slept; all she wanted was for her to win in this life. The Tates had practically raised Drew, so when she hurt they hurt, and all Ma Tate wanted right now was to make the hurt go away.

Looking down at Drew Ma Tate began to pray.

"*Heavenly Father, I want to say thank you. Thank you for keeping us. Yah, I come to you asking for strength and guidance. My child needs you right now. Yah, I made a vow to her a long time ago that I would always be there for her, that I would be the stand-in mother she never had, that I would be the one praying for her because she had no one else to pray for her. Yah, I need you to please help her, give her the strength you see she needs. Yah, I've always told Drew she can trust you, so now My Father, I need you to show her that she can. Show her that she can give it all to you. The hurt Drew is experiencing right now, please help her through it. Provide us with guidance on what to do. Yah, we need you right now; please hear our cry, Todah Yah Amen.*

After Ma Tate finished her prayer she could hear a light knock at the door. Ma Tate gave permission to enter, hoping the morning guest didn't wake Drew.

Mrs. Tidwell poked her head in the door motioning for Brenda to come out. Brenda softly raised from the bed and followed Connie downstairs to the kitchen, where everyone was gathered. Soon as Brenda walked in the kitchen a flutter of questions about Drew's well-being flooded in from everyone. Brenda assured them she was fine and just needed her rest.

Joe handed Brenda a cup of coffee. After a brief scan of the room Ma Tate inquired Jay's whereabouts, and if the group had any updates on the situation.

Mr. Tidwell informed Brenda that Jay and Carl had gone to the Police station, and should've been back.

Brenda looked at Joe with worry in her eyes. "Joe, I've never seen her like this; she didn't sleep a wink last night."

"Drew's going to be just fine; our girl is strong," Joe assured Brenda that this too shall pass.

Jay and Carl stood at the reception desk at the Shiloh City Police Department trying to get information about Marcus, but the receptionist rudely ignored them. Carl could see the young lady was overwhelmed, but it wasn't a reason to be rude. Carl became impatient, tapping on the window to gain the woman's attention.

"Excuse me, Ma'am, I need to speak with Captain Shed. I need information about Marcus Tidwell."

The young lady continued ignoring Carl, and he continued to repeat Marcus's name, gaining the attention of Detective Miller after recognizing the name.

Miller walked over to Carl and Jay. "Excuse me, I'm detective Norman Miller." Miller extended his hand. "Can I help you guys out?"

"I'm Carl McCain, and I'm trying to get information about my son-in-law, Marcus Tidwell."

After Carl and Jay explained everything Miller assured them he would handle the case, and the best thing for them to do was go home and wait to hear from him.

Marcus sat in the jail cell looking at the gray painted brick; the stench from the silver bucket posed as a toilet made his stomach turn. Marcus hung his head thinking to himself, *"how could he be so stupid?"* Drew's face haunted him. Marcus imagined her beauty and the tears that followed from her eyes as the detectives drugged him away from the best day of their lives, making it the worst day.

Drew sat in the bay window overlooking the lake; she could smell the sweetness of breakfast coming from downstairs but had no desire for any of it. Drew knew someone would try to make her eat, but her belly was in knots.

Drew imagined Marcus's face and the sweet kisses he would've already given her for the morning. Drew tried making sense of everything that had happened, from the phone call she received from Marcus the night before, to the police dragging Marcus away on their wedding day.

Marcus could understand how people went crazy in jail; the gray walls, the smell of piss, the random screams, and the dampness would cause anyone to lose it.

Marcus replayed the night before over and over in his head; he kept seeing Reggie lying on the ground bloody. Marcus thought to himself, "How did he allow himself to lose control; if only he'd walked away."

Marcus knew Drew had to be devastated; if only he'd answered the phone that night and let her talk him out of confronting Reggie.

Marcus punched the wall. "How Could I Be So Damn Stupid, UGH!"

Drew's thoughts of Marcus being so selfish made her angry; how could he treat her this way? Did he even stop to think what effect this would have on her? Drew began to dismiss any love she'd had for Marcus; it was taking too much of her energy to love him, only to hate him. Besides, it would be easier to learn how to live without him, rather than *not* know how to live without him.

Drew allowed the musical therapy of the birds singing outside the window to soothe her soul, pushing everything to the back of her mind leaving it for Yah to deal with, while she meditated on his glory

Jay and Carl explained to the small group that Detective Miller would be getting back to them, and they should just sit tight and wait on his call.

Marcus's parents were still trying to process everything but didn't have enough information. Mrs. Tidwell asks Jay what Marcus's charge was, but Jay couldn't give her any information because he didn't have any to give.

Jay could see the worry in Kirk and Connie's face; it bothered him that he couldn't tell them anything, but Jay did inform Marcus's parents that a couple of nights before the incident Marcus remembered who'd shot them and was dead set on confronting the guy.

Mr. Tidwell broke down; he whaled about how he should've told Marcus that they knew who was responsible for the shooting, and the matter had been taken care of.

"You knew the man that did this to you, and you never told Marcus?" Drew demanded answers, walking into the kitchen unannounced.

Jay touched Drew's chest to calm her, but she rejected it by slapping his hand away. "How could you not tell him, Marcus has been walking around with this anger and fear for twenty-five years, and you allowed it."

Kirk tried to explain, but Drew wouldn't give him a chance; she blamed them for Marcus's breakdown as well as ruining their wedding.

"How could you be so thoughtless? Your son has been carrying this fear and hurt for so long, and all you can say is sorry. Marcus is locked up and will probably be for a long time." Drew cried hysterically; she was so upset Jay had to take her outside for air.

"I'm sorry Drew," Mrs. Tidwell cried out.

Drew had been on the deck for hours rocking back and forth in the hammock swing, only getting up to use the bath and returning to the swing. Everyone was worried because she hadn't eaten or drank anything, but Jay encouraged them to back up and give her space.

Drew peered at the stars, if she could escape this world without going through death she wouldn't hesitate, wishing for a whirlwind to take her up as it did The Profit Elijah.

Jay opened the patio doors and stood for a moment watching Drew admire the stars; he wondered how someone could take so many blows and keep going. Jay knew Marcus's reason but wasn't happy with it, so Jay's biggest disappointment in Marcus right now was he didn't think about hurting his friend.

Drew noticed Jay standing there, and although she just wanted to be alone she really needed her best friend right now. "Why are you standing all the way over there, you a spy or something," Drew yelled out.

Jay smiled, it pleased him that Drew was at least cracking jokes.

Jay yelled back. "So it safe?"

Drew motioned for him to come near.

Jay extended his hand, pulling Drew from the swing relocating her to the wicker furniture occupying the deck. Drew laid in Jay's arms and cried as he held her. Den watched the couple from the house, adoring their closeness; if only she could win Drew's heart the way everyone else had.

"Jay, I'm so sad," Drew whispered as tears streamed her face.

Jay took a handkerchief from his pocket and wiped Drew's tears. "Now, let's go look at A Different World."

Detective Miller pushed the doorbell at the Victorian Home; he felt terrible noticing the wedding decorations that beautified the home.

Everyone had gathered in the sunroom to receive information from Miller except Drew and Jay, and everyone agreed to keep it that way; they didn't want her to be devastated by any more bad news.

"Good evening folks, for those who don't know me I'm Detective Miller, I handled Mr. & Mrs. Tidwell's case years ago, and I'll be taking Marcus's as well. Marcus has been charged with aggravated assault with intent to kill. Marcus could be facing…

Mr. & Mrs. Tidwell fell apart soon as the words came from Miller's mouth. Brenda and Michael rushed in to comfort them.

Michael was devastated. "Are you serious the man that shot my parents got charged with less than that."

"I understand your concern and frustration, but evidence in Marcus's car shows this was a premeditated assault. And with his prior assault charge it doesn't look good."

"That happened when he was a juvenile. How can they use that?" Kirk contested.

"I understand Mr. Tidwell, but you know how the system works for us." Miller eyed the Tates. "If convicted, Marcus could face two to twenty years in prison, and a fine of up to ten thousand dollars."

"That's Bull!" Michael yelled out.

Miller also informed the group that a bond wouldn't be set because the judge wasn't hearing any cases due to the fourth of July weekend, and Marcus would have to sit in jail until the judge came in or until his court date.

Mrs. Tidwell buried her head in Mr. Tidwell's chest. "Why didn't we tell him, Kirk?" Connie cried out.

"How's Reggie." Mr. Tidwell asked with sympathy.

Miller shook his head. "Reggie's in serious condition, the last I heard he was in ICU at Shiloh Regional."

Marcus's parents wept.

After all the details Carl escorted Miller to the door, while in route Miller secretly informed Carl that Marcus would need a good lawyer because Judge Horn was residing the case, and he wasn't a slap on the wrist type judge. Miller also told Carl they'd better be praying the guy didn't die, because if he did Marcus could face life.

Carl shook Miller's hand. "Thanks for taking the case."

"My pleasure Mr. McCain, anything I can do to help."

Carl closed the door and shook his head; he didn't do a lot of praying, but for the first time in a long time, Carl looked up towards the heavens and asked God for help.

Drew put her wedding dress back in the protective cover and hung it in the back of the closet; her three-hour session with Jay was just what she needed. Drew wandered to Marcus, and although she was unforgivingly mad at him, Drew still cared how he was and how he was being treated.

There was a light knock at the door, Drew became annoyed; she wanted to be left alone, but she knew her request would be ignored if people were around.

Drew gave her permission for entry, and Mrs. Tidwell walked into the room. Drew sat in the bay window gazing out at the lake; she was still upset with the Tidwell's, she felt all this could have been avoided if they'd just talked to Marcus.

"Hello, Drew," Connie spoke softly.

Drew returned the greeting; she could hardly look at Marcus's mother, although Drew had been upset with them she was still embarrassed for her rudeness with them.

Connie began to apologize, but Drew stopped her, asking Connie to join her in the bay window. Connie accepted the invite sitting down next to Drew.

"I apologize for the way I acted out, it was deplorable, and I'm sorry." Drew vented to Connie about how upset and disappointed she was with Marcus, and the emotions spilled over to them. "I love both of you so much, and I'm asking for forgiveness."

"Drew, I have to admit I and Kirks' faults as well." Connie enlightened Drew that she and Kirk never told Marcus about the shooter because it was not much to tell; he served two years for shooting them, and after serving his sentence Reggie later returned and asked for their forgiveness. So, with them forgiving him they never felt it necessary to bring it up because Marcus was a child at the time, and vaguely remembered that night.

After Drew and Connie's conversation she felt better knowing the Tidwell's reason for not telling Marcus about the shooting.

Exiting the room Connie looked back at Drew and pleaded for her to stand by Marcus, but that was a promise she couldn't make.

It was quiet in the courtroom as Marcus and half the Shiloh and Promise community awaited Judge Horn's decision. Marcus scanned the room looking for Drew, he thought for sure she'd be there for the verdict, but he didn't see her sweet face anywhere.

Marcus had been locked up for three months, and Drew hadn't been to see him once.

Drew sat in her car staring at the Shiloh City courthouse, as much as she wanted to go in and see Marcus's face in the flesh she couldn't do it. Marcus was all she'd thought about for the last three months. Drew couldn't work, eat, sleep, socialize, cry, or smile without thinking about Marcus. All she needed to see were the expression on everyone's face as they exited the courthouse; this would help Drew decide what she would do, *(So she thought).*

Jay looked over at Marcus and motioned him to pull his chin up. Marcus gave him a sorrowful smile, then looked over at his parents; the hurt, worry, and fear Marcus seen on their faces was enough shame to last a lifetime, but looking at all the support from the two communities made Marcus feel good; he didn't know what the outcome would be, but their support was priceless and kept him positive.

Drew spun the engagement ring around her finger thinking back to the morning Marcus left her at the airport after burying her best friend; Drew waited for the tears to fall, seeing herself standing there with her bags, Drew waited for the tears to fall when recalling Marcus saying he wasn't going back with her, Drew waited for the tears to fall when seeing herself walking off leaving Marcus with his words and decision, Drew waited for the tears to fall remembering the sound of Marcus's voice as he called her name, Drew wait for the tears…

Drew stopped spinning the ring and touch her face, there were no tears.

Drew exhaled. "I've already been prepared for this." Drew stated, as a smile came across her face. "This is your time Yah, and you've already prepared me for it." Drew shook her head with a smile. "It's your time Yah, you are demanding it, and I hear you." Drew laughed uncontrollably. "This is your time Yah, and you want it, ok I get it." Tears streamed down Drew's face.

Judge Horn entered the courtroom; the only thing Marcus could hear was the sound of his inhales and exhales. Marcus looked over at Reggie with his family and was grateful he didn't press charges, which gave Marcus a better chance at just getting probation. The downside: Marcus knew Judge Horn was tuff and showed no mercy.

Horn read the verdict and gave his sentence. Marcus couldn't move. The lawyer shook his shoulders, but Marcus couldn't move, the judge called his name, but Marcus couldn't move. Marcus heard his mother crying, but he couldn't move. Marcus's heartbeat in slow-motion, he couldn't move. Marcus was stuck in the night he'd purposed to Drew. The smile on her face, the light in her eyes, and the touch of her soft lips were all Marcus needed right now.

CHAPTER 24

Changing & Rearranging

Drew stood back a few feet; the March winds blew through her hair, and the sun shined upon her face. Drew was boiling over with excitement, observing Carl as he put the finishing touches on the hand-crafted sign he'd made for her.

"It's beautiful," Drew yelled, while jumping around excitedly. "Serenity Meadows, Bed & Breakfast est. 2011." Drew read the sign aloud.

This was a proud moment for Drew, she'd finally followed her dream and opened her own business, a cute little B & B.

Drew ran across the street jumping up and down with excitement; she adored all the renovations Carl had done on the Victorian Home; not only was Carl a blue collared gentleman and Army Vet, but he was also a skilled carpenter. Carl had turned Drew's dream into reality.

"What do you think, baby girl?" Carl yelled across the street.

Drew was still jumping around. "It's perfect Carl, and just in time for the grand opening in a couple of months." Drew walked back across the street joining her father.

"I'm sorry it took me so long Drew, but with me selling the company and moving out here; I've been swamped."

"It's ok, Daddy, I knew you would come through." Drew kissed her father on the cheek.

Carl's heart fluttered, Drew had never called him that before; he eyed Drew for a moment while his heart melted.

"What's wrong?" Drew side-eyed Carl.

Carl blushed. "You never called me that before."

Drew embraced Carl. "Well, why not, you've proven yourself to be just that, My Daddy."

Jay sat quietly at the Shelly County Detention Center waiting for the guard to bring Marcus up. Jay observed the writing on the wall, he could see people didn't have much to say while visiting. Looking around the room Jay knew this wasn't a place for him; the smell of mildew, piss, and grief assured Jay he wouldn't survive the harsh conditions of imprisonment.

Jay notices the children in the room; for the life of him he couldn't understand why someone would bring their kid to a place like this; it was depressing. Jay had been there a million times, but each time made him more depressed. Jay hated to see Marcus locked up like this.

Marcus walked over to the window where Jay sat waiting. "How's Drew." This was the first question Marcus always asked when Jay came to visit. Marcus had been in jail almost three years, and Drew hadn't been to see him once.

"She's fine, how are you?" Jay didn't like to spend a lot of time talking about Drew; he knew it hurt Marcus that Drew hadn't reached out to him. Jay had tried a million times to convince Drew to see Marcus, but she just wouldn't budge.

"Take my love back." Marcus put a fist to the window.

"I always do," Jay replied, he didn't want to have this conversation, so he hurried to change the subject. "How they been treating you in there?"

Marcus took a deep breath. "Hey, I can't complain; I'm still here, and for that I'm grateful. I'm always going to make the best of things." Marcus gave Jay an encouraging smile. "Spending my everyday with Yah, trying to educate as many of my brothers in here as I can. How are my parents? They haven't been up in a few weeks."

Marcus's parents would usually visit him once a month, alternating days with Jay and Michael. They would also call every three days; the trip to Green Tree Texas was a three-hour drive, so mentally and physically they couldn't make the trip as often as they wanted.

"They're good bro, I talk to them a few days ago, they send their love." Jay informed Marcus that his dad has been sick.

Marcus grew weary. "He good, momma didn't say anything when I spoke with her a few days ago."

"Yeah, he good, they think it was a stomach bug." Jay pulled a folder from a leather satchel he carried. "I have the Q1 reports for you." Jay opened the folder and laid the information before Marcus; he and Michael had taken over

Marcus's businesses while he was incarcerated. Michael handled the shops and Jay handled the livestock.

Marcus was pleased to see the barbershops and livestock investment were doing well. "Thanks Jay, I really appreciate you taking care of things for me. It's the middle of March and the books already showing Q2 profits. Those investment you talked me into are paying off; the numbers look great."

Jay looked at Marcus and his heart caved. "She's doing good, bro." Jay updated Marcus on Drew, informing him that she was almost finish with the renovations on the *Victorian Home,* and getting ready for her grand opening.

Marcus was excited for Drew, he remembered the first time she'd mentioned the bed and breakfast. *Marcus looked down at Drew as he massaged her temple, she went on and on about the things she wanted in life one being a themed Bed & Breakfast.*

"You good," Jay asked, noticing Marcus had drifted off.

Marcus cleared his throat. "That's awesome, I'm happy for her."

Marcus was happy for Drew, but the changing and rearranging she explored had him a little worried.

Jay could see Marcus started to get a little choked up.

Marcus eyed Jay. "Can I ask you a something, and you be honest with me?"

"It's a thousand over here." Jay put his fist to the window.

"Has she moved on?"

The photographer snapped another picture of Drew and Mayor Stone for an article in *The Promise Say,* Promise's local newspaper. It seemed *Serenity Meadows* had become an overnight success, and looking at the turnout, not only had the B&B caught the eye of the locals, but a few Shiloh City residents also attending the Grand opening/ Ribbon cutting.

Drew's looked around at all the guests and gave Yah praise, knowing he was the reason. The Tates were also a big help; being members of the chamber of commerce and word of mouth throughout the small town, but Drew knew if it hadn't been for Yah putting her in the path of people that could open up doors none of it could've been possible.

Three years ago, sitting in front of that courthouse waiting for her happiness, Drew came to realize her happiness would never arrive if she didn't start to acknowledge Yah and put him first. So, Drew stated a courtship with Yah, and they've been going strong for three years now; Drew loved and trusted Yah more than she ever had.

"Miss McCain." Mayor Stone stated, embracing Drew. "You have an excellent turnout here, and I must say you have done a fantastic job with Serenity Meadows. I can't wait for the tour." Mayor Stone laughed out, while checking her out.

"Thank you, Mayor Stone, it's my pleasure to bring a part of myself to Promise. It's been one of my heart's desires for a long time."

Mayor Stone eyed Drew. "Well, Drew, I thank you for sharing a piece of yourself with us; this home is as almost beautiful as the woman that desired it."

Drew was a bit confused, she didn't know if the mayor was making a pass or just being nice, either way she politely gave him a soft smile and moved on. Drew believed in the words Betty Wright sang, she didn't show her teeth to every guy she met.

"Excuse me, can I get everyone's attention." Mayor Stone addressed the guest, and everyone started to applaud. "Thank you." Mayor stone raised his hand to calm the crowd.

Den gave Drew a soft nudge. "Isn't he the sexiest man you've ever seen?" Den eyed Mayor Stone.

"Shhh." Drew pinched Den.

"Ouch!" Den rubbed the sting.

Drew silently chuckled looking at the expression on Den's face. "Stop, he's the mayor."

"That hurt," Den whispered. "And who cares, he's single and gorgeous."

Mayor Robert Stone was a 40-year-old distinguished gentleman, standing about six-three; a tall glass of chocolate milk most women in Promise would say. This man was the perfect match for Drew in Den's sight; he had charisma and good looks, he was smart with a good head for business, and he had no kids, meaning no *baby momma drama.* Den couldn't understand why Drew wasn't picking up on his vibe, she could clearly see he was feeling Drew from a mile away.

"On behalf of Promise I would like to thank everyone for coming out, showing their support for Miss McCain; she's done an excellent job with this place. I remember delivering groceries to the Cooper, and I tell you this place never looked so good," Mayor Stone laughed, and so did the guest. "I would like to thank Miss McCain for sharing a piece of herself with us, so now I ask Promise to share a little of ourselves with Drew. I ask that you welcome her and his fine establishment to our community.

Drew began to get nervous; she only knew a few people from Promise, like the Tidwell's, Miss Sue, the Tates, and her father, but not enough for people to openly accept her or her bed and breakfast.

"Stop biting your lip." Den gave Drew a nudge. "It's all good girl, it's your shine day."

Mayor Stone held out his hand. "So, without further ado, the owner of this Serenity Meadows, Drewlynn McCain."

The guest applauded, Drew was amazed at how the small town accepted her; she stood behind the podium with warmth running through her veins, still amazed one of her lifelong dreams had come to life, and she had the support of the whole town.

Drew first thanked Yah and then greeted the crowd, assuring each of them she was grateful for their presence and support, and all the guests would receive a coupon for one night's stay half off.

Drew held the giant scissors readying herself to cut the ribbon when Gabe started to jumping around, demanding that he do it. The guest laughed at Gabe's determination, grabbing at the scissors trying to cut the ribbon. Drew allowed Gabe to cut the ribbon, she couldn't reject such a sweet face. Besides, Gabe had been her shadow for the last six months, picking out wallpaper curtains, wall décor, rugs, future, so why not.

"Look, daddy, I used the big scissors." Gabe looked out at Jay giving him a thumbs up.

After cutting the ribbon Drew spoke with a few more guests before starting the tour; she was amazed that everyone was so eager to help with whatever she needed, from supplies to employees.

Drew was just about to escort her guest to the front door and begin the tour when a familiar voice echoed from behind her. Drew cringed, she knew that voice from anywhere. Drew took a deep breath and exhaled; this was not the time or the place for childish behavior.

Drew turned and stood face to face with Rebecca Sims.

"Rebecca, what a surprise, it's been a long time."

The two women embraced one another; it was only right that they be cordial in front of the guest.

Rebecca gave Drew a once-over. "Wow Drew, the country life suits you just fine, I think they call that country thick." Rebecca looked Drew up and down with a smug look. "Sorry to hear about Marcus, I know these last few years have been hard."

Drew could tell in Rebecca's tone that she was trying to be derisive, but today was too important to let her ruin it.

Drew looked at Rebecca and smiled. "Which part stings the most Rebecca, knowing the man you spent your entire life trying to mutilate loved me enough to make me his wife, or the fact I'm still thriving without him." Drew gave Rebecca a wink and started her tour.

Gabe ran ahead of everyone so he could open the French doors. Drew could see he was more excited than she was, explaining each room and its theme to the guest upon entering a room. It amazed Drew, she'd watched Gabe follow her from room to room while practicing her presentation, but she didn't know he was listening to her every word. Gabe was doing a better job than she was.

Drew allowed Gabe to present the Safari Room and Music room, but she introduced the last two rooms; the last two rooms were her favorite, and she wanted to give them a glamorous introduction.

When Drew opened the door revealing the pink, gray, and white Paris room, it took the guest breath away. Drew had everything Paris in the room; the Eiffel Tower being the focus. A few guests assured Drew they would be booking the Paris room sooner than later just to lay in the antique white canopy bed (A bed fit for a queen).

The last room was a third-floor add-on. This was Drew's absolute favorite room. Drew had spent most of her time designing this room, putting all she had into it. Drew wanted a room that would bring tranquility to one's soul. A space that would make you one with nature and Yah.

Drew guided the guest up the stairs to a glass room that gave the whole experience of nature. Drew's design was unbelievable, you could see the entire sixty acres from this room, including the lake. Drew had a built-in wall fountain on the north wall; it was soothing listening to the water flow over the black rocks blending with the sounds of the rain forest coming from every direction. There was a king size bed in the middle of the floor custom made with tree branches, and a Chester drawer to match.

The guests were intrigued, never seeing a room so unique, and if Drew wanted a space that would bring tranquility to one's soul, this was definitely it. Not only were the walls glass, but the ceiling as well; you could see the clear open skies.

Drew opened the sliding doors leading to the balcony, where she had all sorts of tropical plants lining the area. The guest absolutely adored this room.

Observing the looks of excitement on the guests face Drew was pleased. Everyone seem to love this room.

Den hooked Drew's arm, smiling and squealing with excitement. "Girl, you did a fantastic job on this room." Den was just as excited as the guest, not being able to see the place until Drew was finished; nobody was.

Drew embraced Den. "Thanks gurl, this is my fav."

"Mine too, I might have to book this for Jay and me."

The two women laughed.

Den notice Rebecca's interactions with Jay. "So, who's the ten talking to Jay."

Drew looked at Den and let out a sigh. "Rebecca Sims, an old classmate."

Den could see Rebecca was a thorn in Drew's side and wanted to know the story. "So, what's up with her?"

"I really couldn't tell you; we were friends in grade school, but once we got to middle school, things changed. Then this thing about a note came up."

"What note," Den was becoming intrigued.

"I'm not sure, Rebecca came to me one day after school waving a note in my face warning me to stay away from Marcus. She went on and on about how desperate I was, and how she was going to burn that stupid note. I didn't know what she was talking about, so I asked Marcus, he told me not to worry about it and he would talk to Rebecca."

"So, what was the note about?" Den had a need-to-know craving.

"Your guest is good as mine; after that I tried to avoid her and Marcus altogether."

Den watched as Rebecca flirted with Jay by sticking her index fingers in his dimples. Den looked at Drew and smiled. "Time for a bit of intervention."

Drew glared at Den under-eyed. "Get her killer."

Mayor Stone made his way over to Drew, praising her for a well-done job, and a little flirting on the side. "Miss McCain, if I had a wife." Mayor Stone took Drew's hand. "I'd have her all up in this room."

Drew chuckled, catching the line Mayor Stone threw at her, but avoided the bait. "Well, who's to say Mrs. Stone could be in this very room; there's a lot of single women in here."

Mayor Stone kissed Drew's hand, gazing into her eyes. "A lot of single women, but there's only one single lady I have my eyes on."

Drew pulled her hand back. "Thank you, Mayor Stone, I appreciate your kind words, but I'm not shopping." Drew walked off leaving Mayor Stone with only ambitions.

Mayor Stone admired Drew as she walked off. "Not right now, but you will be."

Noticing Miss Sue, Mayor Stone hollered. "Miss Sue, let me talk to you about this year's Juneteenth celebration." Mayor Stone pulled Miss Sue to a corner.

Drew shook her head, Mayor Stone remined her of an old dirty man; he was far from old, but those were the vibes he gave Drew. Drew cringed.

Den's smiled from ear to ear as Drew walked up. "I see you over there talking to the mayor; he asks you out yet?"

"NO!" Jay stated loud enough to gain a few eyes. "Drew if you go out...

"Jay, please, no one's going out with anybody calm down." Drew smiled at the nosey eyes. "Now if you don't mind, I'll get back to my guest." Drew rolled her eyes at Jay.

Drew was really beginning to hate the big brother role Jay played. Jay had been overly protected since Marcus was locked up. Jay was scanning calls, doing pop ups, he'd even tried to give Drew a curfew, calming Gabe's sleep was being disturbed whenever she came in after his bedtime; that's when Drew knew it was time to move into the *Victorian Home.*

The home had been locked down almost a year; every time Drew passed the home she'd give it her energy, praying for the day she'd gather enough strength and courage to live in the home alone. Well, that day came when Jay demanded she be in the house by 9pm. Drew loved Jay and Gabe, but their space started to get a little crowed with, alter egos, attitudes, demands, disagreements, and control. Drew felt it was better for them all if she moved out, and although Jay put up a fuss Drew finally got him to understand Gabe was being affected by the animosity in the house.

Drew completed her tour, giving the guest full access to the B&B; she wanted everyone to feel comfortable and make themselves at home, and the only way to do that was allow the guests to kick off their shoes, and make themselves at home. Drew informed everyone there were refreshments on the deck in the backyard, and they were welcome to indulge; she also wanted the guest to bask in the essence of the outdoor comfort.

The guest dispersed over the B&B, each revisiting their favorite area of the house; some headed straight to the refreshments, others to the nature room. Drew could see everyone was comfortable and having a good time, so she did a private happy dance while watching the guest enjoy.

"Excuse me, Miss McCain," A pleasant voice summoned Drew away from her private dance."

"Yes, may I help you?" Drew quickly gathering herself.

Drew eyed the woman and instantly snapshots flashed in her memory; this was the same lady from Den's boutique she'd seen a few times before. More images came through Drew's mind; she was also the lady from Mystic Pier. The lovely lady that seemed to haunt Ma Tate, the sweet lady with the pinwheel. Drew was weirded out all this time she'd tried to remember where she saw this woman, and it didn't come back until now.

Drew was glad the Tates were out of state, now she could investigate without Ma Tate getting in her way. Drew would find out one way or another who this woman was.

The woman hesitated to speak, gazing admiringly at Drew, unsure what to say. She was taken in by Drew's beauty.

"Can I help you?" Drew asked again.

"I'm sorry I seem to have lost my thoughts." The woman blushed. "My name is Leah Reynolds, and I want to congratulate you on a job well done; you wouldn't think this was the old Cooper place, it's beautiful. I've never seen this place look better, even when they first built it." Leah chuckled.

"Thank you, Mrs. Reynolds. Did you know the Coopers?"

"Yeah, you can say they were old family friends, and please call me Leah."

The woman gave Drew a soft smile, handing her a business card. "I own Simple Design in Shiloh City, and I would like to give you an open invitation to stop by and check out some of our designs."

Drew gave the card a once-over. "Hmm."

"Drew, I really believe we can help each other. I'm amazed at what you did with this place. I could really use someone like you on my team."

Drew was elated at the opportunity, but she was done punching time clocks as for now. "Leah, I'm ecstatic that you find me talented enough to join your design team, but I just started my business and I'm going to run it myself full time."

Leah held a look of disappointment. "I understand Drew but keep my card, and maybe we could collaborate when you're ready to change things around here."

Drew looked at the card and smiled. "Thank you, Leah, I'll keep that in mind."

"NO, thank you, Drew, may you have much success."

Leah and Drew exchanged looks, Drew still couldn't understand the attraction she had with this woman. "Excuse me, I have to check on my guest."

"Of course, I must be going, but I ask that you keep Simple Design in mind." Leah gave Drew a wink and walked off.

Den sat at the antique bistro sipping a glass of wine in the sunroom, watching the quest load up on refreshments. Out of all the rooms in the house, this was Den's favorite; she'd suggested to Drew that a modern country decor would be perfect for the sunroom, but never did Den imagine Drew could bring it to life as she'd done.

Den's phone started to vibrate, when seeing the caller she became annoyed. Den took the phone and threw it in her purse as if she wanted to break it.

"So, what did that phone do to you?" Jay pulled Den from her chair and began to dance with her to the soft jazz playing from the surround sound speakers in the room.

Jay looked around the room. "Drew has this place nice, huh?"

"Yeah, it's pretty nice in here, Drew and Carl did an excellent job with this place."

Jay spun Den around. "What do you mean, her and Carl, if I can remember you had a little something to do with it too. Didn't you design this room?"

"Yeah, but Drew is the true mastermind." Den admired the leaf ceiling fans as Jay dipped her.

"Den, stop being modest, you had just as much to do with this room as Drew."

"Yeah, but Drew is who brought it to life."

Jay kissed Den's forehead, he hated when she sold herself short like that.

Den gave Jay a soft smile, poking her index finger into his dimple.

"Oh, you got comedy."

Den chuckles. "Jay, can I ask you something."

"Sure Den, you can ask me anything, and tell me anything."

Den let out a sigh. "Jay, how do you think Drew sees me?"

Jay stopped their dance. "Den, what's wrong, why are you asking me that; you've been Drew's friend for almost four years, and you don't know your place in her life."

Jay walked over to the chaise lounge and sat down, asking Den to join him. Jay could see Den wasn't herself, taking one of her braids and pulling it through her looped earring. "Why are you always so worried about how Drew views you."

Den laid her head on Jay's shoulder. "I don't know, I guess I kind of look up to Drew."

Jay didn't understand, Den was just as beautiful and successful as Drew. "Talk to me Den, what's really going on?"

Den circled her thumb knuckle with her index finger. Jay noticed she often did that when she was nervous or concerned about something.

"Well, sometimes it seems like I'm living in Shantel's shadow."

Jay grew interested. "What do you mean?"

"Drew always speaks so highly of her, making it hard to feel her shoes."

Jay stopped Den's circling finger. "Not to be disrespectful or anything, but if you're trying to fill Shantel's shoes, please stop. You can't walk this path in Shantel's shoes when you have your own. Be who you are, not who Shantel was. Den, I didn't choose you because you were anything like Shantel. I chose you because you were nothing like her. Drew speaks highly of Shantel because of Gabe; she promised Shantel that she would keep her memory alive, so Gabe would know who and what kind of person she was.

Jay lifted Den's shameful head and kissed her forehead. "I know Drew, and I know she loves you because of who you are. To be honest you'd think you're the one she looks up to." Jay took Den in his arms and whispered, "You're perfect."

Den exhaled, "Jay, I need to tell you something."

At that moment Gabe ran in, jumping up in Jay's lap. "Daddy, Auntie Drew said I could stay with her tonight."

Drew walked in after Gabe. "Yeah, after he gave me a guilt trip about helping out today, and how he should be rewarded with a sleepover; is this kid sharp or what?"

Drew walked over to Den and grabbed her hand, pulling her away from Jay. "Den, will you look at this room; this is your idea brought to life." Drew gave Den a twirl. "I love you so much I couldn't have done any of this without your help."

Den eyed Jay with a blushing smile.

CHAPTER 25

Going in Circles

Drew was preparing the Paris room when she heard the guest buzzer. "They're early." Drew looked at the Eiffel Tower clock hanging over the door, then hurried to complete the bed and put out fresh towels. *"Oh, Lord give me strength,"* Drew muttered hurrying to complete her task before the buzzer sounded again.

Drew had been running the bed & breakfast for almost two months, and business was booming; this was her twentieth booking since the opening in May.

Drew hurried downstairs thinking to herself how she needed to get some help; being that she was the check-in clerk, the cook, the bail hop, and the maid, this was exhausting. Besides, business was going well enough to take on a small staff, and with the 4th of July right around the corner Drew definitely had to do something fast.

Drew glanced in the foyer mirror and noticed she was still wearing her headscarf, so she hurried to take it off, throwing it behind the reception desk. Drew took another look in mirror, straightened her hair, dusted herself off, and slapped on a smile, while trying to catch her breath.

Drew opened the door right as the buzzer went off. "Hello, Mr. & Mrs. Filmore."

The Filmore's looked at each other, then at Drew. They could clearly tell she was out of breath.

"Did we come at an awkward time?" Mrs. Fillmore asked.

Drew laughed, assuring them they were right on time.

After checking in the Filmore's Drew led them upstairs to the Paris room. Mrs. Filmore absolutely loved it, she kept slapping Mr. Filmore on his shoulders every time she saw something in the room she liked. Drew could tell Mr. Filmore was trying to be patient because he was chewing his gum none stop.

"Stop chewing that gum like that, Larry." Mrs. Filmore slapped his shoulder again.

Mr. Filmore glared at his wife. "Now, look here Betty, you got one more time."

Before Larry could finish his sentence Betty was already lying in the bay window pretending she was in Paris. "We, We; we're in Pa-Ree."

Mr. Filmore eyed Drew and started chewing his gum even faster.

Drew put the Filmore's bags on the chaise lounge. "I'm glad you like the room Mrs. Filmore."

"Oh, Drew, I absolutely love it. It's everything your brochure said it would be. Isn't it Larry?" Mrs. Filmore slapped Mr. Filmore shoulder again. "Don't you just love it, Larry?"

Drew looked at Larry, he was going to town on his gum. Drew chuckled, she knew it was time to exit. "If you need anything don't hesitate to call me."

Drew stood at the front desk watching Larry and Betty enjoying themselves in the pool; she imagined Betty slapping Larry's wet back and cringed. Drew shook her head, she kinda felt sorry for the poor fella, not knowing when he would get a slap across the back. Drew chuckled, thinking she'd seen him dodge a few times whiles showing them the room.

The foyer door opened breaking Drew's daydream, and in jumped Gabe; Drew was thrilled to see him, he'd been in Atlanta with Loraine a week, and she was just about to start missing him.

"Hey Beetle." Drew embraced Gabe, smothering him with kisses.

"Auntie Drew, look at what I got." Gabe handed Drew a brown paper bag.

Loraine yelled out, "I wouldn't do that if I were you."

But it was too late, Drew was already running and screaming, throwing the bag at Gabe. Gabe laughed hysterically while rolling on the floor.

"I told you grandma, Auntie Drew was scared of lizards."

Loraine looked at Drew, as much as she wanted to laugh she held back. "Drew, are you ok?" Loraine batted her eyes, trying her best to hold back the laughter.

"Gabe, I'm going to kill you." Drew chased Gabe around the house while Loraine watched.

Loraine couldn't hold it anymore she laughed uncontrollably at the little game of cat and mouse.

Carl walked in, observing the chase and Loraine enjoying the entertainment. Clearing his throat, Carl hollered out, "Excuse Me Am I Interrupting?"

Loraine looked back at Carl standing in the doorway like he owned the place. Loraine continued to laugh at Drew and Gabe, trying to explain, but could hardly get the words out.

"Such a beautiful laugh." Carl extended his hand. "Hello, I'm Carl."

"Hello Carl." Loraine took Carl's hand, and he gently placed a kiss upon it.

"What a gentleman, I'm Loraine, Gabe's grandma."

Carl eyed Loraine. "Grandma, you don't look anything like a grandma."

"Well, thank you Carl, I'm flattered."

Carl Gave Loraine another kiss on her hand. "I'm not trying to flatter you, I'm trying to woo you."

Lorraine laughed, taking her hand back.

"There it is again, that unique laugh. I'm Drew's father."

"Oh, so you're Carl." Loraine nodded her head to confirm.

Carl had an awkward look on his face. "You said that like I've been talked about."

Loraine assured Carl that he'd most definitely been talked about, informing Carl that Gabe spoke highly of him, and would become a *Sarge* when he grew up.

The pair laughed at Gabe's innocence.

"You have the most beautiful laugh, it's so peculiar." Carl was intrigued by Loraine.

Gabe and Drew were still going at it when Gabe noticed Carl. "Sarge!" Gabe yelled. Gabe ran to Carl, excited to stand at attention in front of Carl, greeting him with a salute.

Carl returned the gesture. "At Ease Soldier."

Loraine was simply taken by them both; she could tell Carl had a significant impact on Gabe's life. Gabe Opened his brown bag to show Carl the lizard, then dashed off to the playroom.

Drew finally gained her composure after wrestling and running around with Gabe; she watched Carl and Loraine talk amongst themselves. Drew could clearly see Carl was taken in by Loraine, and as much as Drew loved the idea she had to let it go; the three years she'd gotten to know Carl, Drew had never seen him serious about anyone. Carl took *eligible bachelor* to a whole other level, he was quite a lady's man.

"Dad, what are you doing here?" Drew greeted him with a kiss. "And why are you dressed like that?"

Carl had on everything Stetson, from his cowboy hat to his boots and spurs.

"All black. So, are you the villain in the movie?"

Carl looked at Drew in shock, he couldn't believe she was cracking jokes about his attire. "I look good." Carl grabbed his vest, stuck out his chest, and strutted in a circle.

Carl noticed Loraine was humored by his actions, laughing at his peacock strut. "Pretty lady when I said you had a beautiful laugh, I didn't mean you could laugh at me."

Loraine gave Carl a gentle smile, trying to contain her laughter.

"Drew, I'm a rancher now, so I have to dress the part in order to get the whole experience." Carl tipped his hat to the ladies.

"Yeah, you also have to do the work," Drew stated sarcastically."

The women laughed.

"What a minute, I'm no stranger to hard work," Carl noted in his defense. "I was raised on a farm you know."

"Dad, please." Drew eyed Carl. "We both know you're not getting your hands dirty. You probably already hired someone."

Carl gawked at Drew. "I dare you, I'm a very hands-on kinda guy." Carl leered at Loraine, tugging at the oversized belt buckle.

Drew intervened Carl's stare, jumping between him and Loraine. "He has workers, believe me."

Loraine chuckled. "Well people, I have yo dash." Loraine grabbed her things from the counter.

Drew noticed Carl and Loraine eyeing each other. "Let me walk you out." Carl took Loraine's hand, guiding her to the door.

Drew wanted to stop Carl's shenanigans right then and there, but she would at least allow Carl to be a gentleman and walk Loraine to her car.

Betty was on her way upstairs when Gabe's laughter summoned her to the playroom, so she crept slowly down the hall trying not to scare the sweet child as she eavesdropped on his play session.

Standing in the doorway memories immediately surfaced; Betty could remember a time when her son played with his imaginary friends, in his fictional world just like Gabe.

Betty was so consumed in her memory she didn't feel Gabe tugging at her hand, so he kissed it, breaking her trance.

"My Auntie Drew always says when happy tears come out Yah's about to show out."

Betty dabbed the escaped tears and covered her heart, giving Gabe the biggest smile. "Your aunt is an extraordinary lady. What's your name sweetheart?"

"It's Gabriel Yahime Tate, but everyone calls me Gabe."

Betty's heart was warmed by Gabe's charm and sunken dimples. "Please to meet you Gabe, I'm Betty."

Gabe looked up at Betty with his bright almond eyes. "What's your grown person's name? My Auntie Drew says never to call a lady in her prime by her first name, unless they say otherwise."

Betty was stunned by Gabe's comment. "Gabe, may I ask how old you are?"

"Yes ma'am, I'm four, but not for long." Gabe crashed the two cars he held in his hands. "I'll be five on November fifteenth, that's in five months," Gabe held up five fingers.

"Well, Gabe, you're a very intelligent four, almost five-year-old."

"Why were you crying?" Gabe asked.

Betty fell in love with Gabe's innocence, kneeling down to explain. "Well, Gabe, I had a son about your age, but he's no longer with us."

Gabe wiped Betty's face, "But he's with you in your heart; my mommy's in my heart too, because she's not here either. Her name was Shantel; my daddy says just because she's not here for real doesn't mean she's not in my heart." Gabe ran off to continue his playing.

Betty was amazed at Gabe, her heart filled with joy as she continued gazing at him in wonder, wishing for one more hug from Jacob.

“So, that’s Gabe’s grandmother?” Carl asked, after walking back in from escorting Loraine to her car.

Drew eyed Carl, she could clearly see he was asking for his own personal investigation. “Dad No, Loraine is off-limit.” Drew walked off to her office.

“What, is it a crime for me to ask about Gabe’s grandmother?”

Drew laughed, looking at her dad as if he should already know the answer.

“So, is she married?”

“Dad, I already told you no.”

“No, she’s not married?”

“UGH,” Drew stated her case. “Dad, I’ve known you almost five years, and I’ve never seen you serious about anyone.” Drew held up her index finger. “But I’ve seen you with plenty of women to know you're not the settling down type."

To be honest Drew felt Carl was still in love with Joy, and that's why he hadn't gotten serious about anyone. Drew knew Carl would never admit it, but he needed to close that chapter of his life, so he could move on.

"I resent that." Carl looks at Drew sideways, explaining that he had no problem settling down, he just needed the right woman.

Drew was nonchalant to Carl's explanation, she’d seen him with plenty of women in the past to know that explanation was bogus; it wasn’t the women it was him.

"Loraine has something different."

Drew paused her work, glaring at Carl. "Stay away from Loraine, daddy, promise me."

Carl gazed at Drew, the love and respect he had for her wouldn't allow him to carry out his plot, so he agreed, kissing Drew on her forehead. "She still looks good."

The grandfather’s clock chimed breaking Drew from her trance; she’d been working on the books for hours, and somehow found herself sharing an intimate moment with Marcus in her head. "It's about time for me to call it a night," Drew said to herself, wrapping up the invoices for the day.

While going over the books Drew was thrilled to see she could bring on a small staff for the B&B but dreaded the interviewing and hiring process. Drew remembered *Unlimited Resource Solutions,* her dad's recently sold staffing company, so she searched her desk for the new owner's information Carl had given to her just in case she ever needed their help.

While scrambling through her desk Drew came across a picture of her and Marcus. *"How did this get here,"* Drew said to herself; Gabe being the only person she could think of. Gabe would always ask Drew about the man in the picture; he said Drew looked her happiest in it.

Drew took the picture from the desk and reminisced about the night she and Marcus took it. (Jay and Shantel's wedding). Drew smiled at the photo, she always admired the picture.

While deep in thought Drew's phone rang, startling her. Drew said to self, "Who could be calling at this hour." She didn't recognize the number. "Hello," Drew spoke softly. A animated voice announced, *'You have a collect call from the Shelby County Detention Center from Marcus, if you except press one, if you…*

Drew took the phone from her ear and looked at it, bewildered and frozen. Drew's mind was going in circles, the sound of Marcus's voice opened Drew's stomach, and her heart fell in.

Drew was so deep in thought she didn't realize the phone hung up until she heard it ringing again. Drew scrambled to answer the phone. *"Hello, Marcus."* The recording repeated the same statement, this time Drew picked #1. Drew didn't say a word, she didn't understand why she'd even answered the phone and accepted the call it in the first place.

"Hey baby, I know it's been a while, and I know I'm the last person you want to hear from. Drew, I need to see you," Marcus pleaded. "Baby, say something, I love you Drew."

A single tear fell from Drew's eye, she took a deep breath, exhaled, then hung up the phone.

The Fillmore's were about to retire for the night when they saw Drew coming from her office. "Good night, Drew," Betty whispered.

"Good night you guys, I really hope you're enjoying your stay at Serenity Meadows."

Betty took Drew's hand. "Drew, I'm having the time of my life; I was telling Larry about little Gabe, he's the cutest thing."

"I'm sorry, has Gabe been bothering you guys, I've told him not to disturb the guest."

"No, Gabe hasn't been a bother at all; actually he's been a sweetheart. I was telling Larry how much of a gentleman he was."

Drew laughed. "Yes, he does have a certain charm."

Larry laughed out, still chewing that gum. "Gabe sounds like a well-mannered kid, I'd like to meet him before we leave."

Drew gave Larry a wink. "Sure thing."

Marcus laid back on the bunk in his cell, the sound of Drew's sweet voice had given him life. Marcus took a photo of him and Drew from the wall and smiled, recalling the night at Jay and Shantel's wedding.

A thunderous voice came from the bunk across from Marcus. "Somebody got some good news."

"Yeah man, she answered." Marcus continued leering at the picture, smiling.

"Well, tell me what she said." The man seemed to be more excited than Marcus."

"Cool out, Chad, she didn't say much of anything."

Chad looked disappointed and confused. "Now call me crazy but is that something to be happy about, she didn't say anything."

Marcus tried to remain optimistic. "It doesn't matter if she said anything, the fact remains she accepted the charges."

"Marcus, look, I'm not trying to be a ballbuster, but that's really not telling you anything, besides...

Marcus cut Chad off. "She accepted the charges, Chad." Marcus didn't care what Chad said, Drew accepted the call, and that was the fuel he needed to keep his fire burning. Marcus knew Chad's heart was in the right place, but he needed this moment of positivity, and he would hold on to it.

"You know I'm just looking out for you, right?" Chad hated when Marcus got himself all worked up over Drew.

"Yeah, I know you've been looking out for me since I got here, and I appreciate it."

Chad was a beast, standing about 6'2, weighing two hundred thirty pounds, and solid. Marcus knew Chad from the old neighborhood in Shiloh City, so it came naturally for Chad to look out for him. Chad was about 15 years older than Marcus and had been in and out of jail for twenty-seven years, so you could say he'd been Marcus's mentor the three years he'd been locked up.

Chad lived with lots of regrets, leaving a wife and two kids on the outside, never getting to spend time with them for always being locked up. Chad often spoke of his kids telling Marcus they were the only thing in life he did right. Marcus would often feel sorry for Chad; the whole time he'd been locked up with him Marcus never once seen Chad's children; not even on photos. Marcus once asked Chad about his bare pitiful wall, and Chad explained, the outside world was easier to deal with if he didn't acknowledge it.

"Hey young cat, I'm not trying to piss on your parade, but a year in here is five for them on the outside."

Marcus heard what Chad said, but he trusted that Yah was setting things in place.

CHAPTER 26

Learn To Live With It

Drew called out to Gabe for the third time and he still hadn't responded, so she headed down the hall to the playroom. Midway Betty and Gabe emerged from the playroom. Betty began to apologize, informing Drew she and Gabe had been so busy playing they didn't hear her calling.

"I hope Gabe's not a bother, he's not supposed to hassle the guest." Drew poked Gabe's dimples.

"Gabe isn't a bother at all." Betty stroked Gabe's face. "He's such a sweet angel."

Gabe loved all the attention Betty was giving him.

"Gabe reminds me of my Jacob." Betty told Drew about her late son.

"Betty, I'm sorry to hear that."

"Thanks Drew, it's been eight years tomorrow, and it never seems to get easier."

Drew consoled Betty, telling her about the Tates and the loss of their son. Betty was calmed when hearing someone else's story and how they'd conquered their hurt.

Betty looked down at Gabe. "Losing a child can really put injury on a marriage."

Drew couldn't help but feel sorry for Betty and Larry, so to keep Betty's mind off Jacob's death she decided to let Gabe stay until the Filmore's were gone.

Drew looked down at Gabe. "How about you spend a few days with Auntie Drew?"

Gabe was overjoyed, jumping around with excitement; Gabe had grown fond of Betty. "Cool, let's play." Gabe grabbed Betty's hand, dragging her back to the playroom.

Drew laughed wishing Betty good luck; she knew Gabe would have Betty in the playroomall day playing cops and robbers or reacting scenes from Toy Story.

Larry and Betty sat at the breakfast table talking amongst themselves, Drew could see it was a hard morning for them as she glanced out of the swinging kitchen doors at the couple. This would make another year their son Jacob was gone, so Drew tried to make them as comfortable as possible, starting them off with a nourishing homestyle breakfast. Drew whipped up a breakfast with chicken fried steak, gravy, eggs, grits, hash browns, biscuits, and pecan pie. Drew wanted the Fillmore's to take this day to relax & reconnect.

The Fillmore's continued talking amongst themselves when noticing Gabe entering the breakfast room, wrapped in his Toy Story pajamas, guided by his Buzz Lightyear house shoes that stated, *'To Infinity and Beyond,'* every time Gabe took a step. Woody swung loosely in his hand as he rubbed the night's sleep from his eyes.

"Good morning Gabe, how's my buddy?" Betty rubbed his back.

"Good morning, My Betty." Gabe managed to get the words out, still trying to wake up.

Larry was taken in by Gabe the moment he laid eyes on him; his sweet soul reminded Larry so much of Jacob. Larry recalls Jacob coming to breakfast in the same state most mornings.

"Good morning Gabe, my wife has told me a lot about you." Larry shook Gabe's hand.

"My Betty told me a lot about you too; did you know she's lonely and cries a lot?"

"GABE!" Drew yelled out, emerging from the kitchen doors with a breakfast tray for the Fillmore's. "I'm sorry, he's a very outspoken kid." Drew scolded Gabe once more. "That's not polite, Gabe."

Betty ran to Gabe's defense. "It's ok Drew, Gabe was just going off our conversation and tears about Jacob, he meant no harm.

Drew started to tickle Gabe. "Yeah, but he needs to learn discretion."

"DISCRETION," Gabe yelled out, storing the word in his head.

Drew took Gabe by the hand. "Let's see about getting those teeth brushed, while I teach you discretion." Drew chuckled.

Larry and Betty sat on the deck enjoying the country scenery; all Betty could talk about was Gabe. Larry loved the way Betty's face lit up when she talked about the boy, he could see Betty simply adored him, and it made Larry want to give her another child even more. Larry always felt if he and Betty had another child it would feel the emptiness she had for Jacob, but Betty refused to have more children, taking her birth control faithfully every night.

Larry took Betty's hand, he could see tears gathering and knew a memory of Jacob was resting on her heart.

"Larry, I miss Jacob so much. The more I try not to think of him the more I do. Larry, when will this pain ever stop?"

Larry wiped the tears from Betty's eyes, remaining silent.

"Larry, it's been eight years today, and it seems as if the pain has gotten worse; unbearable at times."

Larry got up to look out over the deck; the young man didn't want Betty to see the tears fall from his eyes. Not only was Larry still hurt behind Jacob's death, but the guilt of not being the supportive husband he should've been was also eating at him; when Betty needed him most Larry found comfort in another woman, which almost led to their divorce.

Larry cleared his throat, swallowing the tears. "We're going to be ok Betty."

Larry always left Betty confused; she couldn't understand why Larry still hadn't released his hurt after eight years. Often, Betty would find him in Jacob's room going through his toys or smelling his clothes, but never had Betty seen him cry. Betty walked over to Larry on a mission to comfort her husband, but he quickly rejected it, claiming he needed to get a workout in, leaving Betty on the deck with her thoughts.

Joe and Brenda searched the B&B but Drew was nowhere to be found. Brenda yelled out, trying to remember if she'd told Drew they would be back from Tanzania today or tomorrow; anyway, Brenda suggested Joe and her split up and search the home in hopes they'd find a clue as to where Drew was. The Tates never liked Drew living in the home alone, running a business that housed strangers. The Tates told Drew plenty of times to at least get cameras, but Drew refused thinking cameras wouldn't allow her guest to feel relaxed and at home.

Brenda looked out the French doors sweeping the backyard when she saw Betty. Brenda quickly went to inquire of Drew's whereabouts from the young lady.

"Hello, I'm Brenda Tate, would you happen to know where I can find Drewlynn McCain?"

Betty informed Brenda that Drew, and Gabe went to the store for supplies and would be right back.

Brenda sighed and smiled. " I've said to that girl a million times, get some help."

Betty laughed. "You must be Drew's mom?"

"No," Brenda blushed. "But you could say she's like a daughter to me, a daughter that needs a chewing out for leaving her guest alone."

Brenda gave Betty a smile she could see the young lady had been crying.

"It's fine, Drew asked Larry and me, that's my husband, if we could watch things until she got back. We didn't mind Drew is such a sweet lady, and she's been more than good to us, Gabe as well."

Brenda was pleased to hear such a favorable report. "Well, I guess I'll have to wait. Do you mind if I join you until Drew returns?"

Joe searched the entire house for Drew but came up empty, so he went to find Brenda when hearing the clinging of metal coming from the exercise room. Joe went to investigate, hoping to find Drew.

Joe touched Larry's shoulder startling him. "Excuse me, young man, have you seen the owner of this place?"

Larry quickly pulled the earbuds from his ear. "Excuse me Sir?"

"I'm sorry young man, but I'm looking for Drewlynn McCain, the owner of this place."

Larry told Joe the same thing Betty told Brenda.

Joe observed the weights Larry was lifting, remembering his days in the gym. Joe began to tell Larry about his glory days when he could bench press 300lb. Larry was impressed, he could tell by Joe's statue he'd done a little lifting in his day. Larry also found Joe to be hilarious as he demonstrated how he did it.

Brenda and Betty were hitting it off like they'd known one another for years. The more the women talked the better Betty felt. It was terrific how Brenda had lifted her spirits; she had given Betty so much insight on life, death, love, and lost.

"Brenda, it's been refreshing talking with you; you're an angel sent by God."

Brenda blushed at the statement. "No, I'm just doing what Yah has purposed me to do here my short time on earth."

"You know Brenda, Gabe has really made our stay here at Serenity Meadows worth it; your grandson is one of a kind."

Brenda notices Betty looking off into space with the saddest look upon her face every so often as if she was burdened by something.

Brenda notice Betty's sad eyes. "If you don't mind me asking, why are you so sad at times."

The tears fell from Betty's eyes before she could catch them. As Betty told Brenda about Jacob, she knew Betty's pain all too well and felt obligated to share her story, hoping it would give her a little light in the dark tunnel she was stuck in.

"Joe and I lost a son sixteen years ago." A tear began to flow from Brenda's eye.

Brenda told Betty about the accident, the hurt, the distrust, the hurt, the confusion, the hurt. Brenda told Betty the hurt never stops you just lean to live with it; she also told Betty about Joe's infidelity; not that she was trying to discredit him, but these were all the trials she had to endure.

"Thank you, Brenda." Betty wiped lingering tears from her eyes. "I've never had anyone to understood what I was going through or how I felt, not even Larry. Brenda you are an angel in disguise, no one but another mother can understand a mother's love and a mother's tears.

Larry chuckled watching Joe trying to recapture his youth, pulling the cable for the nineteenth time, struggling.

"Hey man, you're good." Larry asked.

"Yeah, I'm good." Joe shook trying to pull the cable out.

"You sure?" Larry grew concerned that Joe would hurt himself.

"Twenty," Joe yelled, dropping the 200lb weight. "Yeah, I Still Got It." Joe jumped up from the bench and started to dance around. 'That's what fifty-five look like."

"Ok, I see ya Joe." Larry gave Joe some dap.

"Me and my boys use to get in that back yard every day when they were coming up."

"You got boys?" Larry lowered his head.

Joe noticed Larry falling from a hundred to zero. "Yeah, I had two boys, but Yah saw fit to take one; it's been about 16 years now."

Larry lifted his head and eyed Joe, he didn't look like he'd suffered a loss at all. "How did you get through it?" Larry told Joe about Jacob and the affair.

"Yah (God) was the only one that got me through it. I remember the day we were told; my life hasn't been the same since. I remember going to look at the car, I remember identifying the body, I remember picking out the casket, I remember burying Shawn." Joe shook his head. "After that, I don't remember anything. I was at the bars drunk more than I was at home, and work. I almost lost everything, including my family, so I started going to a support group; that's when I met The Test.

The Test lost a son two years before I did; she was the sweetest lady I'd ever meet, had all the right words and compassion."

Joe shook his head in shame, remembering his disloyalty to Brenda and Jay. "My life was already upside down, my oldest son was gone, my baby boy was in the streets more than I was, and my wife wouldn't say two words; all she did was sit in the window and cry. Brenda stopped cooking, cleaning, parenting, wifing; she just stopped living, so I sought companionship in The Test, and I failed. I failed Yah, my wife, my son, and my community. Then one day, Yah called me out on my mess." Joe eyed Larry. "All of it, the women, the booze, the lack of trust I had in him, all of it. Next thing I know I'm at home, curled up in my wife's arms crying my eyes out. Yah broke me down, only to build me back up stronger and wiser. Son, the day Yah sent me back home to my wife he'd already spoken to her, telling her not to turn me away. Joe smiled. "I thought she was the one broken, and the whole time it was me. With her praying and being still got us through the hardest time of our lives.

Joe looked over at Larry, the front of his shirt was soaked with tears. Larry cried out, asking Yah to forgive him. Joe could see the young man had finally released the pain of losing his son, and the shame of not being there for his wife.

The two men talked a while swapping stories about the life and loss of their sons. This was just the therapy Larry needed, it really lifted a lot of the burden he'd been carrying; the tears also released his load. Larry hadn't felt that light in a long time. Larry was amazed at how strong Joe was physically and mentally.

"Joe, your story is impressive. Sometimes I ask myself will I ever get over this hurt."

"Well, son, you really never get over it, you just learn to live with it."

"How do you know your wife whole heartedly forgave you?" Larry was convinced Betty still held some resentment towards him.

Joe pointed at Brenda and Betty sitting on the deck. "It took some time, but we found our way back to each other.

Larry and Betty held Gabe's hand as they walked to the check-out desk; he was educating them on his theory of how dinosaurs became extinct. The couple had been there three days, and it still amazed them how brilliant Gabe was.

Larry looked down at Gabe in disbelief. "So, Gabe, you're telling me you don't believe the dinosaurs were destroyed by a meteor."

"NOPE!" Gabe pranced around. "I think they were damaged when Yah made it rain a lot, and he told Noah to make the big boat."

Drew could see Larry was chewing his gum much slower now; somehow Gabe had managed to calm both him and Betty. Drew was pretty sure the Tates had something to do with it too, but anyone could clearly see Gabe was the reason for the reconnection.

Betty grabbed Drew's hand. "I absolutely hate to leave, these have been the best 3 days ever."

"I'm so glad you enjoyed your stay, and feel free to come back anytime. I really enjoyed having you both." Drew hugged Betty assuring her everything would be ok.

Betty kneeled and caressed Gabe's face. "Thank you, Gabriel Yaheim Tate, you are my best friend, and I will never forget you. Gabe, you have given me something back I never thought I'd have again; the desire to be a mother."

CHAPTER 27

Oil & Water

Good morning, Serenity crew," Drew greeted the workers she'd hired to assist her at the bed & breakfast. As much as Drew wanted to do it alone it was too much for one person, so she set aside her pride and hired a crew.

"I would like to thank you all for coming in today." Drew smiled at the 3-man crew. "As we all know this is the 4th of July weekend, and we'll be extra busy. Serenity Medows will not be doing anything special, but Promise will, which means business for us."

"So, what does that mean for me in the kitchen." Miss Sue flipped a cup towel over her shoulder.

"Carl will be here Friday to barbeque, nothing special just a barbeque so you can relax for the Sabbath, but I have a favor before your rest." Drew threw up one finger, giving Miss Sue a big smile.

"Oh, my, what's the damage." Miss Sue knew what the smile meant.

"Could you add three sides and two deserts."

"I thought I could rest?" Miss Sue smacked her lips.

Drew gave Miss Sue pouty lips promising to give her Sunday off, while batting her eyes innocently.

"I don't like you, little girl." Miss Sue thumped the tip of Drew's nose, agreeing to the task.

Drew laughed to herself, then turned to face an inpatient older man. "Mr. Pete, I need you right here when the guests arrive; I don't want anyone carrying their own bags."

Drew glanced at Mr. Pete, she knew he would rather keep the grounds than deal with the guest. Mr. Pete wasn't much of a people person, spending most of his time in the greenhouse teaching Gabe about different plants, amongst other things. Gabe was fond of Mr. Pete; Drew didn't know if it was from all the treats he would bring Gabe, or if Gabe felt his disconnection from the world.

Mr. Pete nodded his head and walked off, grumbling. Drew shook her head walking over to the front desk with Rainn in tow. Drew instructed Rainn to go over the guest book once more to ensure each guest had called to preregister.

"Yes Ma'am, Rainn ran to get the guest book.

Drew let out a deep breath. "Whew, my, can you please keep an eye on Mr. Pete?"

Rainn laughed softly. "Sure, Miss Drew, I'll make sure he's here to get the bags."

Drew shook her head; out of the three people she'd hired Rainn was the only one that followed the rules.

"Miss Drew, I was going over the guest registry and Mr. Styles booked the nature room for a week but didn't send a copy of his id, and he's due to check-in today at 2:00pm. He didn't preregister either."

Drew cringed. "I thought his check-in was at 4:00pm, I'll be in Shiloh City around that time." Drew rubbed her face, becoming frustrated. There's no way I'll be back in time to greet him. I'm just gonna cancel."

Rainn could see Drew becoming overwhelmed, she'd been trying to get an appointment for months with the investor, and now she had to cancel.

"No needs to worry, I'll greet Mr. Styles. Besides, he asks not to disturb his entire stay anyway, so maybe a personal greeting isn't necessary."

Drew was puzzled by Mr. Style's request. "Who comes to a B&B and isolates themselves anyway, that's especially strange, don't you think?"

Rainn chuckled. "Not really, especially if it's peace you're seeking. Isn't that what Serenity Meadows' about?"

Drew eyed Rainn before giving her the biggest hug ever. "That's it Rainn, that's it."

Rainn was obtuse, not having a clue as to what Drew was talking about. "Huh."

"The statement you made, it's my slogan." Drew threw her hands in the air repeating the words Rainn stated. "Serenity Meadows Your home away from home, your peace seeker."

Rain was amazed how Drew came up with the pitch from the few words she'd given. "Wow, I see why you're known as the queen of advertising."

Drew blushed, giving Rainn a shy smile. "I'm a little rusty."

&

Drew pulled into Jay's place when noticing the new sign on the entry gate. "Zion, wow, he finally named it," Drew said to herself. Jay had finally given his ranch a name after six years.

On the way up the drive Drew observed all Jay had accomplished, land and home, livestock, farm equipment, and now a name. Drew was so proud of Jay; he'd birthed the ranch into a very successful business.

Gabe ran out to greet Drew. "Auntie Drew," Gabe jumped into her arms.

"Hey, Beetle." Drew kissed Gabe on his cheek, handing him a bag. "Got you something."

Gabe hurried to explore the bag. "Thanks, Auntie Drew," Gabe pulled out Jessie from Toy Story. "Now she can be with her friends." Gabe jumped with excitement.

Drew knew how much Gabe loved Toy Story, so she bought him a charter from the movie every chance she got.

Gabe ran ahead of Drew to show his father the new toy. Drew was pleased with Gabe's gratitude every time she got him something.

Drew followed Gabe to the barn where he led her to Jay. "Greetings, my dear friend," Drew stated jokingly.

Jay was so busy cleaning the stalls he didn't hear her, so Drew called out again.

"Hey, Mr. Tate, how are you?"

Jay jumped when Gabe tugged at his shirt, ripping the earbuds from his ear. "What's up son, you ok?"

Gabe pointed at Drew while laughing at his father.

"Damn Drew, I didn't hear you come in."

Gabe pulled the toy from the bag and jumped around in the stall excitedly. "Look daddy, it's Jessie; Auntie Drew got her for me."

Gabe explained to his father who the charter was while Jay eyed Drew, wondering why she kept buying Gabe toys after he'd told her to stop.

Drew shrugged her shoulders. "He likes them." Drew walked over and brushed hey from Jay's head. "Dang, are you swimming in the hey?"

The pair laughed.

"Yeah, I got one hell of a backstroke. What are you doing here?" Jay asked.

"Oh wow, it's good to see you too, I'm well." Drew stated sarcastically.

"My bad, how are you today, are you feeling ok." Jay corrected his rudeness.

Drew gave him a smile. "I'm fine on my way back to the B&B, just met with an investor."

"Really, how'd it go?" Jay started back cleaning the stall.

"I think it went well; Mr. Kingston wants to come out for the whole experience the second weekend in August before deciding, but it's looking Promising."

Jay was impressed, Drew had been in business almost three months and already had investors.

"Drew, I'm so proud of you, I've watched you overcome obstacles people fail at; you have taken the talents and ability Yah's blessed you with and built your brand. I'm happy to call you friend." Jay stopped cleaning, eyeing Drew. "Now, can you do me a favor."

Drew already knew what Jay wanted, she exhaled.

Jay pleaded, "Drew can you please hear me out."

"No, Jay, there's nothing to hear, I'm not going."

"Drew, how can you be so cold?"

Jay walked over and placed his index finger on the tip of Drew's nose. "Drew, you're wrong, Marcus has been locked up for three years, and you haven't attempted once to visit him."

"How do you know, Jay." Drew yelled, starting to get frustrated. Jay had been bugging her about visiting Marcus since he'd been locked up.

"Drew, you're wrong." Jay stood in the middle of the stall going on and on about her disloyalty.

Drew looked around to see if Gabe was present, but thankfully he'd runoff.

"Ok, Jay, I understand how you feel." Drew spoke firmly. "But that's enough."

"Do you Drew, because I don't think you do," Jay said harshly. "Marcus asks about you every time I go for a visit. Drew, he made a mistake, how can you blame a man for honoring his parents?"

Drew stood before Jay in disbelief. "Are you serious," Drew yelled. "I don't blame him for that Jay, I blame him for not thinking of me first." Drew was about to walk out but paused her steps. "What did you tell me years ago?"

Jay was puzzled, he'd told her a lot of things.

Drew reminded Jay of his words the night of his wedding. “Give love a chance, allow Marcus to love you." Drew mocked Jay. "Isn't that what you advised me to do? Well, Look Where It Got Me, Jay."

Jay exhaled, speaking to Drew in a calm voice. "Drew, I understand you’re hurt, but you would think after three years.” Jay eyed Drew. "Out of everyone in Marcus's life, you should’ve been the one with understanding."

Drew screamed in her head, how could Jay side with Marcus. There was a moment of silence between the two.

“Daddy and Auntie Drew arguing again.” Gabe hopped on the stool at the kitchen counter.

Den turned and looked at Gabe. “Are you serious, again; those two have been like oil and water lately.”

“Yep, Daddy mad because Auntie didn’t go see the man that’s in jail, the man that’s on auntie’s picture in her desk.

"Drew, I know Marcus should’ve thought about his actions first, but will you allow this to come between yall."

"It already has."

Jay hated when Drew became this difficult to deal with.

"It's easier for me this way, Jay. Why can't you understand that?" Drew stormed from the barn; Jay had run her hot, and the best thing for her to do was get away from him.

Yeah, runoff like you always do.” Jay yelled out making his way to the house.

“UGH,” Jay growled. “Drew makes me so angry when she's this difficult to deal with." Jay slammed the refrigerator door after grabbing some water.

Den hesitated to give any advice, she hated getting between him and Drew. "Here baby." Den handed Gabe a sandwich she’d prepared for him.

Jay paced back and forth in a continuous rant about Drew not visiting Marcus, and how hard-headed and stubborn she was.

Den and Gabe eyed each other, both shaking their heads; they'd gotten used to these little arguments between the two.

"Daddy's always mad at Auntie Drew."

"NO, Baby, he's not mad just a little upset." Den rubbed Gabe's head.

"Doesn't look like a little to me." Gabe chuckled, taking a bite of his sandwich.

"Jay, you need to calm down, you're making something out of nothing."

Jay paused. "Making something out of nothing."

Den stood firm. "Yes, Jay, something out of nothing. You know Drew better than anyone, so you know if Marcus is out of sight, then he's out of mind for her. Jay, you know Drew and how she deals with things. If she doesn't see Marcus, talk to him, or even smell him; she doesn't have to deal with him or the pain."

Den walked over to Jay standing by the fridge and kissed his nose. "I know you want to see them together, but you have to let that be their decision. Have you ever considered how much it would hurt Drew to see Marcus locked up like that. Have you ever considered she may have tried to go for a visit and just couldn't bring herself to do it. I love you Jay, but I really think you need to be selfless at this point."

Mr. Styles looked around the B&B while Rainn checked him in, he couldn't believe the elegance of the place it was breathtaking.

"This place is fantastic. How long have y'all been operating?" Mr. Styles continued his observation.

Rainn admired Mr. Styles' poise. "I believe Miss Drew's been in business a few months now."

"Is the owner in?" The gentleman inquired.

"No, she's not, but I could let you know when she's back on the property if you like."

Mr. Styles became anxious. "That won't be necessary, under any circumstance am I to be disturbed."

Rainn looked Mr. Styles over, he was gorgeous; Rainn didn't know what was more eye-catching, his long locks, his salt & pepper beard, or the biceps bulging from under his shirt.

"Excuse me, Miss." Mr. Styles interrupted Rainn's examination.

"I'm sorry, it's Rainn, you can call me Rainn."

Mr. Styles could tell the young lady was admiring him, but he could only see a child standing before him. "Can I have the key?"

Rainn giggled, handing Mr. Styles his room key. "I hope you enjoy your stay, Pete will show you to your room."

Starting towards the stairs Mr. Styles paused, informing Rainn that he'd be taking his meals in the room, and the tray was to be left outside the door. Rainn assured Mr. Style that it wouldn't be a problem and the staff would comply.

"Mr. Styles, the B&B's having a barbecue...

Mr. Styles stopped Rain in mid-sentence. "Under any circumstance should I be disturbed."

Mr. Styles grabbed his laptop, retiring upstairs with Pete in tow.

Rainn said to herself, "Cute but weird."

HOLD ON, THERE'S MORE....

Drew and Rainn were sorting out recites when Drew noticed Miss Sue approaching the stairs with a dinner tray in hand.

"Excuse me, Miss Sue, are not all our guests attending the barbecue this evening?"

"No, Mr. Styles informed Rainn he would be having dinner in his room. I tried getting him down for the barbeque, but he declined." Miss Sue had a quizzical look on her face. "The young man is wired if you ask me, with one heck of an appetite." Miss Sue laughed out. "He ate when he got here yesterday, he ate again last night, and if you didn't eat the last of the fried chicken, I'm pretty sure he ate that too."

Rainn looked at Miss Sue sideways. "How do you know he ate the chicken, there are other guests here.

"I know because the guests eat from the guests refrigerator, this was taken from the house refrigerator."

Drew became even more curious about this mystery man and who he was. "Miss Sue, it's okay, I'll take Mr. Styles his dinner tonight."

Miss Sue gladly handed Drew the tray. "Be my guest hunny, if you can get that door open you're doing better than me; I've been up there twice already, and it's always the same response, leave it outside the door." Miss Sue smacked her lips. "The guy might be good-looking but not that good-looking."

Drew was intrigued by Miss Sue's statement. "So, you've seen him as well?"

"I didn't actually see his face because he was already headed up the stairs, but hunny." Miss Sue smacked her lips." He a manly man, you hear me."

Rainn agreed with Miss Sue. "Yeah, he's like a fine hobbit or something."

Drew laughed. "You two are a mess." Drew started up the stairs on a mission to deliver nutrients and be nosey.

Drew knocked for a second time, but still no response; she thought maybe Mr. Styles would finally get off his high horse and come join the barbecue, and she'd get a chance to find out who she was housing.

"I should've gotten those cameras, then I'd know who he was." Drew walked back down the nature room stairs grumbling.

"Sit it on the table, please." Mr. Styles asked.

"Finally, a response from the mystery man." Drew said, starting back up the stairs. "Mr. Styles, it's Drewlynn McCain, the owner, I have your dinner."

"Leave it on the table, thank you."

Drew paused. "Mr. Styles, I would like to apologize for not being here to greet you yesterday."

Mr. Styles pressed against the door, Drew's sweet voice pulled him closer; he wanted to look upon the face connected to the sweet voice.

"Put it on the table, please." The mystery man requested once again.

Drew was puzzled and suspicious about who this man was, and hearing the mystery in his voice made the situation more intense and mysterious. Drew was up for the challenge. "I will find out who you are."

Drew and Rainn were in the office going over the schedule when Jay walked in with a box of donuts. "Truce." Jay sits the donuts on Drew's desk.

Drew looked at Jay, and as much as she wanted to stay mad at him, she couldn't. "How can I refuse a truce with donuts as a bribe." Drew got one of the donuts and took a bit.

Rainn didn't say a word, standing in a trance staring at Jay. Jay had been in the B&B a hundred times, and she'd sat with Gabe one hundred and one, but every time Rainn saw Jay it was like the first time.

Jay noticed Rainn's trance. "Good morning, Rainn." Jay greeted her with a smile, his dimples roping her and pulling her in. "Would you like a donut?"

Rainn hears the question but can't process the answer, stumbling her words. "Oh, no, Mr. Tate, I'm fine, thank you."

"Rainn, I've told you over and over call me Jay."

"Ok, Mr. Tate, I mean Jay." Rainn hurried off, she could hardly contain herself.

Jay chuckled, he thought the little crush was cute. "I'm thinking about buying a truck." Jay showed Drew a photo of a 1981 chevy pickup on his phone.

"Wow, Jay, this is nice."

"Yeah, I thought you'd like it. Dude only asking fifteen for it, so I thought I may go look at it on my way to Atlanta."

"Go for it Jay, you only live once." Drew never took her eyes from the computer.

"Drew, I want to apologize for yesterday."

Drew tried to assure Jay it was fine, but Jay wouldn't have it, continuing to apologize.

"Drew, I understand why you can't see Marcus."

Drew looked at Jay with Tears In her eyes. "It hurts Jay."

Jay leaned in and kissed Drew's forehead. "I know, Drew."

Mr. Styles was about to enter Drew's office when he heard Drew and Jay talking.

"Marcus called me Jay."

"Marcus called you?" Jay looked at Drew wide-eyed. "Wow, when?"

"About a months ago."

Jay was shocked that Drew hadn't said anything to him. "Why didn't you say something?"

"Because I knew you would try and guilt me into going for a visit."

Drew began to cry. "Jay, when I heard Marcus's voice it shattered me. I didn't know if it was guilt or sympathy."

"It's ok to be confused about your feelings that come naturally with heartbreak, remember the kiss?"

Drew laughed. “How can I forget the kiss."

Mr. Styles stood outside the office door; the conversation between Drew and Jay seemed to be getting a little more personal, so he started back up the stairs when he ran into Pete.

"Um, excuse me, Mr. Pete, I was looking for Rainn."

Pete could see Mr. Styles was embarrassed he'd been caught eavesdropping. "You need me to get Miss Drew, she right there in her office."

Mr. Styles moved quickly, trying to get back up the stairs. "No Mr. Pete, that'll be quite alright, she's busy right now, and I don't want to interrupt."

"It's not a problem." Pete was eager to get Drew for Mr. Styles.

"That will be just fine." Mr. Styles disappeared up the stairs.

Pete watched the young man rush up the stairs like he was in fear for his life. "That boy is weird."

Drew was busy changing the towels in the *Music Room* having a peaceful conversation with herself when she heard footsteps leaving the lounging area; she quickly dashed from the bathroom trying to catch a glimpse of the mystery man. "Ouch," Drew cringed after hitting her pinky toe on the wooden chest that sat in front of the bed.

Mr. Styles paused when hearing thumping noises coming from the room, so he walked over to investigate. Mr. Styles put his ear to the door when he heard a woman silently fussing. Unsure what was going on Mr. Styles quickly pulled himself away from the door and headed back upstairs to the nature room, not wanting to risk getting caught by Pete again.

Still in pain Drew jumped over to the door trying to get a look. Unfortunately, by the time she made it to the door the mystery man was already headed back upstairs; the only thing she saw was the long dreads flowing down his back.

Drew sat on the chest rubbing her toe, she had a sound mind to go up to the nature room and demand he speaks with her, but Drew held back thinking it might be a critic or someone Mr. Kingston sent to check the place out.

CHAPTER 28

Mystery & History

Drew hurried to her office to get scissors so Den could get started on her braids; Den had finally talked Drew into changing her hair, although Drew found nothing wrong with her shoulder length, natural, silked wrapped, layered Bob, she was willing to try something new.

Drew searched her desk for the scissors when hearing the floor crack upstairs. Drew paused her movement to get a better listen. "What is he doing at 2am." Drew asked herself.

"What are you doing, what's taking so long." Den stood at the office door, almost sending Drew through the window from the abrupt entrance.

"Oh my gosh, Den." Drew quickly put a finger to her lips, telling Den to be quite so she could continue ear-hustling on her mystery guest.

"Drew, what is it?" Den whispered, walking into the office taking a seat on the chaise.

"It's the mystery man from the nature room."

"Drew, you still haven't met that man?" Den asked with concern.

"Shh, I think he's doing laundry."

"Drew, aren't you scared; this guy has been in your house for two weeks and hasn't had the decency to introduce himself." Den eyed Drew. "There's something weird about that."

"Pete's here, I have nothing to be worried about."

Den looked at Drew sideways. "Pete's old, girl."

"Listen, He's on the move." Drew jumped up from her desk and followed the footsteps outside her office.

Den watching suspiciously, not understanding how Drew could be so calm. "Drew," Den called her name quietly, trying to get her back in the office, but Drew ignored Den and continued her mission.

Den jumped up from the chaise to accompany Drew, because she could see Drew wasn't turning back. Noticing a bat behind the check-in counter Den grabbed it. "If he comes down here, It's on."

Drew looked back at Den holding the bat. "Give me that." Drew snatched the bat from Den's hand, knocking over the crystal candy dish that sit on the counter.

"Dang, Den." Drew silently scolded her, motioning her to calm down.

Den paused, tapping Drew and pointing to the top of the stairs. "It's him," Den stated with no vocals.

Mr. Styles stood at the top of the stairs; the shattered candy bowl had his curiosity about what was going on downstairs, so he walked to the edge of the stairs and called out. "Hello, who's there?"

Mr. Styles peered down the dark stairs when he saw a shadow. "Hello, who's there," Mr. Styles grew concerned, knowing Drew lived on the property, so he headed down.

Reaching the bottom of the stairs he noticed the shattered candy dish, so Mr. Styles continued his investigation, heading down the hall to Drew's room.

Den and Drew hid out in the exercise room; they could hear Mr. Styles' footsteps echoing off the wooden floor coming down the hallway.

"See, I told you," Den whispers. "Why is he coming to your room, Ohhh, he gone kills us, he gone kill us." Den put her hand to her mouth, trembling with fear.

"Hush Den, before he hears us." Drew nudged her.

Mr. Styles stood at Drew's bedroom door, and as much as he wanted to knock and make sure she was ok he didn't. Mr. Styles didn't wanna look like a crazed idiot.

Den whispered. "Why is he just standing there?"

"Hello, Miss McCain, are you ok?" Mr. Styles softly knocked at Drew's door; he would instead look like an idiot than something be wrong with her.

Den stuck her head out from behind the home gym she and Drew used for cover.

"What are you doing," Drew asked.

"Shh, I'm trying to see if I can see his face."

Den leaned further towards the door trying to make out the mystery man's face, but it was too dark to see anything.

Mr. Styles knocked once more but didn't get a response, so he figured Drew was asleep and didn't hear a thing, so he headed back upstairs.

"Oh My God, Drew, that was close, he almost caught us spying on him."

The ladies came from behind the exercises equipment and shared in a good laugh.

Drew paused. "Den, didn't his voice sound familiar?"

Den reflected on the sound of his voice. "Nah, not really."

The two women eyed each other and laughed again.

Drew closed the door behind her, still pumped up about their mini-mission and almost getting caught.

"What would you have done if he'd seen us, Drew?" Den plopped down on Drew's bed.

"I don't know, I asked myself that when we were hiding." Drew laughed, retrieving braid hair and Oreos from the dresser, joining Den on the bed. "Thanks for staying with me tonight."

"No problem, it feels like a slumber party." Den took an Oreo from the bag. "I notice you eat a lot of Oreos."

"There's a funny story behind my obsession with Oreos." Drew chuckled. "I'd never had Oreos until I met Shantel, and she tricked me into trying them along with some Ramen Noodles, assuring me it would be the best thing I'd ever ate; boy did she lie, I've never eaten noodles again, but I love me some Oreos."

Den envied the tale, wishing she and Drew could be as close as she and Shantel was. "Shantel seems to have been the light of everyone's life around here."

Drew was thrown by Den's comment. "Why do you say that Den?"

Den looked for a quick lie to cover up the insensitive statement she'd made, but the truth instead escaped her mouth.

"You and Jay speak so highly of her; she was perfect in y'all sight, perfect wife, perfect mother, and perfect friend."

Drew could see the little green monster sitting on Den's shoulder.

"Shantel wasn't a perfect person, Den, none of us are. Shantel was a unique person in her own way; she meant a lot to this family but she's gone now, and all we have are memories that we try to keep alive because of Gabe."

Den felt stupid; how could she be jealous of a dead woman? "I'm sorry Drew, I didn't mean to sound envious of Shantel." Den gave Drew a half grin.

Drew eyed Den. "Don't be so hard on yourself, comparing comes naturel for women."

"Drew, can I tell you something."

"Sure, Den, you can tell me anything."

Drew sat in silence awaiting Den's revelation when they heard a loud bump and Mr. Pete swearing from the hallway.

The ladies rushed to see what the ruckus was. Drew flipped on the light, finding Mr. Pete on the floor.

"Who made this mess and didn't get it up?" Mr. Pete growled.

Den and Drew exchanged looks, they were both laughing so hard on the inside if they'd opened their mouths Shiloh City would hear them.

IT'S ABOUT TO GET GOOD....

Get Outta Here Kid, You're Fired, Teach You To Sleep In My Storeroom." Mr. George yelled out.

Drew was loading her grocery when she noticed the conflict between Mr. George and a timid young man. It took everything for her not to get involved, but the look on the young man's face made her weak. Besides, Mr. George was known to be a bully, not only to his employees, but also to certain customers.

"Hey, kid, you ok," Drew yelled from the trunk of her car, but the young man kept walking; Drew could see he was embarrassed by the public humiliation. "Hey, kid, you ok," Drew yelled out again.

The young man looked back at Drew, his face filled with disgrace. "Does it look like I'm ok, I just lost my job, lady."

Drew disregarded the smug comment seeing the young man was just fired. Drew eyed the young man. "Tevin, is that you?" Drew recognized the young man from previous engagements.

Tevin squinted his eyes looking back at Drew. "Miss McCain, I mean Drew."

Leaving her groceries Drew walked over to Tevin, observing him head to toe. Drew was heartbroken to see Tevin wasn't the thriving kid she'd seen before; this young man looked like he'd been living on the streets and hadn't had a meal in months.

"Tevin, what are you doing out here?" Drew embraced him; the stench of his body almost made her vomit, and the condition of Tevin made Drew wanna cry.

Tevin didn't say a word, and he didn't have to, Drew could see from the tears of frustration the young boy was tired and weary.

"Eat up, sweetheart." Drew sat one of Miss Sue's famous meatloaf platters in front of Tevin.

"Wow, thanks Drew, it's been a long time since I had a meal like this." Tevin licked his lips, his eyes were big as headlights.

Drew could tell by his actions the young man wasn't lying about not having a meal in a while.

"Mm, I'm about to smash; meatloaf, mash potatoes, mac & cheese, greens, and good ole sweet cornbread." Tevin dove right in, not taking a breath between bites.

"Slow down Tevin, it's not going to grow legs and walk away."

Drew eyed Tevin: she had an idea why he was sleeping in Mr. George's storeroom, but she needed to hear it from him. Drew was curious; Tevin always seemed to be a well-kept kid; it never dawned on her that he was homeless.

"Tevin, why were you sleeping in Mr. George's storeroom?" Drew could see the question made him uneasy.

Tevin poked at his meatloaf. "I didn't have anywhere else to go, so I slept there."

"What do you mean, Don't you have a family?"

Tevin shied away from Drew's question. "Do you have more cornbread?"

Drew could see the question made Tevin anxious, so she offered to get him more cornbread.

Drew stood up from the table to leave the young man alone; she figured he could enjoy his meal better without the interrogation.

"Before I go, Tevin, I'm extending an invitation for you to stay here. I'm the owner of this place, and I could use some help around here. Now, I can't afford to pay a lot, but I can offer you food and board."

Tevin looked up at Drew like he'd just won the lottery. " WOW! Are you serious, Awesome! I'll do whatever you need, I promise Drew." Tevin couldn't believe Drew's kindness.

Drew gave Tevin a wink, it did her heart well to see his excitement and gratitude.

Drew, Pete, and Rainn talked amongst themselves when Tevin walked up. "Drew, I'm done eating thanks again. Now, if you don't mind I'd like to get started."

"Wow, are we ready or what," Drew was impressed with Tevin's eagerness. "Before the work starts I would like you to meet the crew. This sweet old guy right here is Mr. Pete."

Mr. Pete mumbled under his breath. "I got ya old."

Tevin chuckled to himself; Pete was funny to him.

"Mr. Pete will show you the ropes around here; he knows everything it is to know about Serenity Medows.

Drew eyed Pete: she could tell he was unhappy with the new help; he'd rather do the work alone than having someone in his way, but Drew knew the task would eventually become too much for him.

Drew eyed Tevin, she could see he was anxious for the next introduction. "Tevin, this beautiful young lady is Rainn Jacobs, she's our front desk check-in/director. Rainn makes sure I stay in the loop."

Both women laughed.

"Hey, Tevin," Rainn extended her hand.

Tevin took Rainn's hand, it was love at first sight. Tevin stood in a daze, consuming Rainn's beauty, taking mental pictures of her in his head. Rainn's smile greeted him with grace, releasing the sweetest voice he'd ever heard. The natural glow of her mocha skin could brighten the darkest room, and Tevin loved the natural way Rainn wore her hair; the Hibiscus adding more flavor. Tevin could tell Rainn was in tune with her spirit and nature, and the energy she had he wanted parts of it.

"Tevin!" Drew yelped out.

Mr. Pete shook his head. "Say something if you're gonna hold a lady's hand that long," Mr. Pete stated sarcastically.

Tevin didn't realize Drew had called his name, nor realized he was still holding Rainn's hand. "I'm sorry, please to meet you, Rainn."

Mr. Pete looked at the pair and knew there would be trouble. "Come on, young man, let me show you what to do." Mr. Pete threw his head, beckoning for Tevin to follow.

Drew and Rainn eyed each other shaking their heads, both women knew Tevin was in for a long day with Mr. Pete.

"Drew, I almost forgot to mention Mr. Kingston reserved a stay for the last weekend in August." Rainn informed Drew.

The news excited Drew. "Yes, finally, the publicity Serenity Meadows needs." Drew paused, thinking to herself. *"If Kingston was coming in August, then who was the guy in the nature room."*

Drew opened the door to the *Music Room.* "Tevin, you can stay in here until I get the pool house situated for you."

"I'll stay anywhere. Pete worked me like a Hebrew-Slave; I think he was trying to kill me."

Drew laughed. "Believe me, it wasn't an attempt on Pete's part, besides what you know about being a Hebrew-Slave?"

Tevin laughed. "I know they were our ancestors and were slaves in Egypt."

"Okay, that's kinda it," Drew took a bible from the nightstand drawer. "Read, it's more to it than that. We were enslaved in Egypt, you're right about that, but Hebrew was our language, Israelite is our nationality."

Tevin took the bible, scanning the room, amazed at the chamber; all sorts of instruments decorated the wall, dresser, and nightstand. Tevin especially loved the *wall of fame,* which held all the music greats like the Gap Band, Teddy Pendergrass, Al Green, The Isely Brothers, and many more.

"WOW! This room is impressive, Drew; did you design this room as well?"

Drew blushed. "Thank you, and yes I did them all, thanks to Yah."

"Nice, my mom is talented like this."

"Oh, so you do have a family."

Drew could tell by the look on Tevin's face, and the way he ignored her question he knew he'd said to much.

"So, where did you get the idea from." Tevin pretended to be interested.

"Look, Tevin, to build a trusting relationship we have to be honest with each other, and that's what I'm trying to develop with you. So, I think it's time for you to be honest with me. What happened to your family?"

Tevin hesitated to answer. "Ok, I have a family, but they don't want me around."

Drew grabbed Tevin's hand. "Now Tevin, why wouldn't your family like you around?"

Tevin took a deep breath. "Because I'm my father's son."

Drew was thrown by Tevin's statement but understood him completely. "Well, anything that's understood doesn't need to be explained."

Drew eyed Tevin: she could tell the young man's load was too heavy for him to carry, and she would try and help him unload as much as she could.

"Darling, I'm right downstairs if you need anything, so don't hesitate to knock on my door." Drew gave Tevin a wink and closed the door.

Later that night Drew allowed the soothing milk bath to take her to another world, releasing every thought in her mind only to refuel it with the sweet sounds of jazz. Drew was at one with herself. Drew whispered, "Thanks Yah for this moment of peace."

After a few more minutes of soaking Drew's meditation was broken by the sudden craving for Miss Sue's sea salt caramel cheesecake, so Drew quickly rose from her bath in a hurry to retrieve the last slice of pie.

Drew started down the hall on a mission to conquer the last piece of cheesecake, still humming the jazz tunes implanted in her head. Between the milk bath and the instrumentals Drew was relaxed to the point of I don't care; she was about to devour that last piece of pie and didn't care how many calories it contained.

Drew searched the fridge for the slice of pie but couldn't find it, pushing through the milk and juice, picking up and putting down treats throughout the refrigerator. Drew thought maybe Tevin had a midnight snack attack and took it; she was disappointed in a way, her taste buds were ready for that pie.

Drew tried to replace the craving with something else, but she didn't have a taste for anything but that pie. Drew picked up a yogurt but put it back, then she looked at the bread pudding sitting on the table, then the Oreos on the counter, but nothing seemed to appease her, so Drew poured herself a glass of juice and started back to her bedroom.

Just as Drew exited the kitchen she walked right into Mr. Styles, holding the last piece of cheesecake.

"Oh my, I'm sorry, excuse me." Drew took a step back to finally get a good look at the mystery man.

Drew's pupils were dilated with surprise, her heartbeat like an African drum, and a consuming fire ran through her veins, while trying to process who she'd just fixated her eyes on.

"MARCUS!" Drew yelped out, snatching the last piece of cheesecake from his hand, then running off to her bedroom.

CHAPTER 29

Thunder & Rain

Marcus pulled up to his parent's house, he couldn't believe after fifty-six years they'd finally left Shiloh City for the peaceful country life of Promise, Texas. Marcus tried plenty of times to get his parents to sell their house in Shiloh and buy one in Promise, but they would always refuse, arguing Shiloh was and always would be their home, but all that changed when their home was burglarized a year ago, leaving his parents traumatized and ready to give up their roots for safety.

Marcus observed the small Jim Walters home, it was just the right size for his parents, not too big, and not too small. Marcus smiled when seeing the small garden protected by a fence a few feet from the house. Marcus could see his mother still made sure his dad stayed busy in his garden; it was part of his therapy.

Marcus walked up the ramp to the screen door, he could smell his mother's peach cobbler dancing in the air; the smell took him back to when he and Michael were kids, and they would grow weary waiting for a piece accompanied by a scoop of vanilla ice cream.

Marcus painted on a smile he knew his parents could sense when something was wrong, and he wasn't ready to give any details about the last two weeks just yet.

Walking through the door Marcus followed the aroma of the peach cobbler, which led him to the kitchen where he found his parents dancing to one of Bob Marley's best, *Forever Loving Jah*. Marcus watched his parents sway back and forth, it amazed him that he could look into their eyes and still see the love they held for one another; this was the kind of love Marcus wanted to share with Drew, but right now he didn't know where they stood, or even if they had a friendship. After being found out Marcus got up early the following day, left the B & B, and got a room in Shiloh City, avoiding the embarrassment of facing Drew.

Marcus touched up his smile before interrupting. "Heyy, Get it, Get it then," Marcus pranced over to his parents joining them in their dance. The

Tidwell's danced even more not realizing it was Marcus dancing with them and not Michael. Marcus's mother did a whole turnabout before looking upon the face of her son and noticing who he was.

"Oh My, It's Marcus, Kirk, it's Marcus." His mother yelled out. Connie jumped around in excitement, giving him hug after hug and kiss after kiss. Marcus's father could barely get a hug because his mother wouldn't let him go.

"OH, THANK YOU YAH, MY BABY HOME SAFE." Marcus's mother jumped around, praising Yah as the tears rolled down her face. Marcus's father couldn't stop smiling and praising Yah either; their son was home in one piece.

After stuffing his face with his mother's home cooking Marcus felt whole; Miss Sue was a beast in the kitchen, but no one could get down like his mother.

"Thank you, momma, that was so good." Marcus kissed his mother.

"You're welcome sweetheart, I'm so glad you're home." Marcus's mom kissed his cheek.

Marcus eyed his parents, the happiness in their eyes held his heart, and If he could give them back three years of joy in exchange for the three years of hurt, he would.

"So, son, you ready to get back in the swing of things?" Marcus's dad inquired.

"Yeah, thanks to Yah, you, Jay, and Michael; all I have to do is walk in."

Marcus's mother could see it was time for a father and son talk, so she got up from the table and excused herself, but not before embracing her son and blessing him with a kiss to the forehead only a mother could give.

"I'm glad you're home, baby."

"I'm blessed to be home momma." Marcus gave his mother a blushing smile.

Marcus and his dad sit in silence for a moment allowing Yah to speak their hearts.

Marcus cleared his throat and spoke. "Dad, I want to apologize for disgracing you and acting foolishly, please forgive me," Marcus shook his head in shame. "I remember every morning before leaving the house you would always have us recite Proverbs Chapter 1 verses 8 & 9. *My child, listen to your fathers' teachings and don't forget your mother's advice. Their teachings will beautify your life."*

A smile came across Kirk's face, nodding his head in agreement. "All praises to Yah, son, thank you for that apology and recognizing your foolishness; we all fall, and thanks to correction and punishment we learn to be better and do better."

Marcus exhaled, as much as he wanted to talk with his dad about Drew and what took place at the B&B he couldn't bring himself to do it. The words of wisdom his father had just given embarrassed Marcus to even think about his actions concerning Drew and Mr. Styles.

Drew rolled her eyes to the back of her head, Rainn was getting on her last nerve talking about Marcus/ Mr. Styles since she'd found out he was the *Mystery Man*, she'd been on Drew's heels for days wanting details.

"Wow, Drew, I can't believe the gorgeous Mystery Man is your Marcus, I can't believe I didn't recognize him, but I mean it has been three years, and it's not like I saw him every day to even recognize who he was."

"RAINN!" Drew yelped out. "Please, focus." Drew gave Rainn the side-eye; it amazed her how she and Marcus's situation had Rainn in an uproar; Drew was beginning to think journalism was what Rainn was born for. "And by the way, he's not my Marcus, Rainn, not anymore."

Rainn chuckled. "Miss Drew, did you have to snatch the pie?"

Both women laughed.

Drew went through her checklist, things had to be perfect for Mr. Kingston; she had to show him that Serenity Meadows was worth investing in, and with publicity like Stylish Country Living Magazine, that would be the boost Drew needed.

"Rainn, what time are Mr. Kingston's reservations set for... Oh, freak, I forgot to put towels in the Safari room. Did Mr. Kingston send his menu choice, did you email him our daily activities request sheet?"

"Drew, calm Down. I've taken care of everything."

Rainn had watched Drew for weeks, it's as if she was bombarding herself with work to avoid the whole Marcus situation.

"TEVIN!" Drew yelped out, beckoning for him to come inside.

Rainn eyed Drew, grabbing her ears. "Scream much."

Drew returned the look. "Not today, and tomorrow either."

Tevin entered the office, he hadn't known Drew very long, but he could tell her character was off, so before getting on her nerves like Rainn, he stayed out the way, doing any and everything she asked.

"What's up, Drew, you need me to do something."

Before Drew could call her orders out she could see Tevin's mind was on Rainn and not mandates. Drew snapped her fingers a couple of times to break Tevin's trance. "Hello, can you focus."

"I'm sorry, you were saying, Drew."

"Can you put towels in the Safari room and make sure the room's presentable for Mr. Kingston."

"Sure thing Drew." Tevin rushed upstairs to fulfill Drew's request.

Drew's phone started to ring, after seeing who the caller was Drew let out a sigh. "Perfect, just what I need. Hello Drewlynn McCain speaking."

"DREW DON'T PLAY WITH ME, HOW COULD YOU PUT MARCUS OUT!" Jay hollered through the phone.

"Jay, I really don't have time to discuss this with you; by the way how's your trip, glad you're safe." Drew stated sarcastically.

"Drew, he has nowhere to go."

Drew looked at her phone with disbelief. "Yes he does, with you, his parents, and his brother. Look, Jay, I have an important guest coming this evening, and I don't have time to deal with this."

Jay calmly but firmly spoke to Drew. "I Could Care Less About Your Guest Drew, You Didn't Have To Throw Marcus Out."

"JAY, NO! Marcus didn't have to float around my B&B pretending to be someone else for almost three weeks."

Drew motioned for Rainn to get out, and to shut the door behind her. Rainn was shocked, she'd heard Drew and Jay argue before but never like this. Rainn kind of got concerned, hoping Drew and Jay could work things out; it would be strange not having Jay pop up every other day.

Drew paced back and forth in her office, she was hot, it seemed she and Jay had been on the outs about Marcus the last three years, and it had really started to affect their friendship.

"Look, Jay, I know Marcus is your boy and all, but this is me, Drew." Tears began to fall from her eyes as she searched the desk for tissues. "Jay, did you ever stop to think how I felt."

There was a moment of silence. Jay could hear sniffles coming from Drew's phone.

"Wow, Drew, I'm sorry, I never took the time out to ask how you were doing."

If there was one thing Jay couldn't stand that was to hear Drew cry. Jay thought back to what Den said, he would just have to step back and allow Drew to decide about Marcus.

Rainn opened the doors to the sunroom, she could hear the keys from the piano making the sweetest sounds, and she needed to know whose magical fingers were behind the mastered sounds of Alicia Keys.

"Hey, I didn't know you played." Rainn walked over to the piano where Tevin sat, impressed with his skills.

Tevin started to play off-key just the presence of Rainn made him nervous.

Rainn laughed. "Well, maybe not."

Tevin smiled, playing another melody of Alishia Keys, but this time adding a twist of jazz, assuring Rainn she was correct the first time.

Rainn began to sing along with the keys adding more fire to *the Grammy-winning* song.

"Dang, girl you can blow, you have a beautiful voice. That of a Nightingale." Tevin stated with an English accent.

Rainn chuckled, "I play around."

"Well, from what I hear you need to stop playing and do something with it."

Rainn blushed, it wasn't what Tevin said, but how he said it. The encouraging words made her feel like she could be the next Jill Scott or Lauryn Hill. It was rare Rainn got encouraged to follow her dreams.

"My parents would kill me their dream for me is in journalism"

Tevin took Rainn's hand, pulling her to the piano bench. "What is your dream for you, Rainn Jacobs?"

Rainn paused, looking up at the ceiling as if she had to think about it. "I don't know, I've always been stirred into journalism, so I never gave it any thought."

Tevin eyed Rainn and began to play the legendary sounds of Pattie Labelle.

"Oh, this is my song." Rainn jumped up from the bench singing along with Tevin as he played.

Mr. Kingston pushed the plate back and rubbed his imaginary stomach, he'd been a guest for about two hours and Drew could see he was pleased; Miss Sue's, smothered ox tails & rice seem to always do the trick when it came to wining people over. Drew hoped the private dinner was a win with Kingston as well; she'd asked Miss Sue to prepare their meal separately, so she could have Kingston's undivided attention. Drew wasn't in dire need for publicity, but it wouldn't hurt to bring new faces from all around, so an article in one of Atlanta's most thriving magazine would be just the boost Drew needed.

"Drew, I must say your hospitality is just as graceful as this place, I've never seen a B&B quite like this one, you're very talented Drew." Kingston eyed Drew. "Beautiful and talented."

Drew smiled softly. "Thank you, Mr. Kingston."

"Drew, please call me Zae."

"Sure, Zae, if that's what you want."

"Yes, that's what I want." Zae grabbed Drew's hand and attempted to kiss it.

Drew quickly withdrew her hand. "I think I'll be retiring now, I hope you've enjoyed your dinner and stay so far." Drew caught the flirtatious vibe Zae threw at her.

"Would you like to join me on the deck, I could use a nightcap after that delicious meal you prepared."

"Miss Sue prepared, I only made the pound cake."

"Desert is always the best part, join me." Zae stood and extended his hand.

Drew hesitated, it seemed Zae was trying to mix pleasure with business, and that was a no-no, but Drew didn't want to seem rude, so she went against her better judgment and agreed.

Zae eyed Drew from across the deck before walking over to have a seat beside her. "Drew, have you thought about taking Serenity Meadows to the next level?"

"The next level of what, I'm pretty confident where I am now, are you talking about changing Serenity Meadows, because if you are...

Zae stopped Drew. "No, Drew, I'm talking about expanding."

Drew was flabbergasted, that was a ten-year goal she wasn't expecting to come this soon. "Wait, are you serious about developing Serenity Meadows?" Drew was turning flips on the inside. "Zae, thank you, Drew wrapped her arms around Zae's neck, giving him a soft embrace.

Zae cuffed Drew in his arms, inhaling her scent, becoming drunken by her sweet smell.

Can I talk to you?" Marcus stood in the doorway of the sunroom it had been a few weeks since he'd last seen Drew. Marcus thought he'd give her time to cool off and process him being an idiot before coming back.

Drew continued to read her book ignoring Marcus's presence, so he slowly walked over to the chaise lounge where she rested. Marcus knew Drew could be challenging regarding her feelings, so he handled her with care. "Listen, Drew," Marcus began to explain his reason sitting down on the edge of the chaise lounge.

Marcus and Drew's eyes met, he was still taken in by her beauty, and as much as he wanted to be excited for even being in her presence he couldn't. Maybe if he'd done the human thing and knocked on her door instead of posing as a stranger he wouldn't be in total embarrassment right now.

Marcus swallowed his three-year mistake and stated his reason. "I just had to see you, Drew. I'm sorry about the despiteful way I did it but what was I supposed to do? You refused to see me for three years, so I knew you wouldn't see me if I'd just shown up."

Marcus was having a hard time talking to Drew, she was so different now but the same, which confused him.

Zae was about to join Drew in the sunroom when he heard voices. Instead of leaving Zae stood behind the giant vase at the entrance and listened, he didn't know the relationship between Drew and this man, but it would be interesting to find out.

"Your hair looks good that way." Marcus tried to make small talk, but Drew didn't say a word, she continued to look at her book playing unscramble with the words on the page.

Marcus became perplexed searching for the right words to say, he'd never been *so* nervous. "Damn Drew, I'm sorry, I know you'll never feel the same way about me. I made a stupid decision, and I'm sorry. There's no excuse for not putting you first, leaving you out here alone." Marcus dropped to his knees. "Drew, I've died a thousand times knowing I messed up the love you had for me. I got a bad deal even my lawyer said so. Baby, you have to believe me, I'm sorry.

Drew eyed Marcus, not uttering a word; the penetrating silence pierced his soul. "Drew, say something, please."

Drew emerged from the chaise and walked out of the room.

Later that night Drew laid on the floor of the nature room watching the rainfall onto the glass ceiling. Drew would enjoy the nature room on rainy nights if a guest hadn't occupied it. Laying there watching the rainfall made Drew feel at one with Yah, imagining the rain was Yah's peace and blessings showering her life, and right now Drew needed the peace more than anything.

So many thoughts ran through Drew's head, and seeing Marcus today brought back old feelings she thought were dead, which made her even more confused. Drew knew for sure what her heart wanted before Marcus got out, but now that she'd looked into his eyes buried feelings resurfaced. Drew didn't know what to do, now she regretted not seeing Marcus, at least if she'd gone her heart would be in the right place, or she would've at least known he was getting out.

Drew quietened her thoughts allowing the satisfying sounds of the rain to soothe her soul, but the images of Marcus wouldn't stop flashing in her head; his beard and dreads gave him a mature look and Drew loved it. Marcus's physique wasn't looking too bad either, Drew didn't quite remember Marcus being that buffed.

Drew imagined looking into Marcus's eyes and how he used to kiss her lips, she could almost feel his arms wrapped around her, holding her.

Drew's thoughts were interrupted by a knock at the door. "Who can that be." Drew thought to self, Den and Rainn were the only ones that knew she listened to the rain from the nature room. Drew pulled her robe closed and opened the door. Zae stood before her with a bottle of wine and two glasses. Drew didn't know what he had in mind, but she wasn't feeling it.

"Hello Drew, I saw you coming up here earlier, and thought you might want some company." Zae looked upon Drew's tear-stained eyes.

Drew couldn't believe this guy was overstepping his boundaries like this. Drew hurriedly wiped the tears from her eyes.

"Good evening Mr. Kingston, I'm sorry you must excuse me, I've had a rough day."

"No, Drew, I'm sorry, I shouldn't have bothered you. I saw you were upset earlier, and I didn't get a chance to see if you were ok, so I thought maybe you would like to share a glass of wine."

Drew admired Zae's concern: his gesture was sweet, but she just wanted to be alone. "I'm sorry, Zae, I was about to turn in for the night."

"The night is young, have a drink with me." Zae took Drew by the hand and tried to make his way in the door; this guy was really starting to rub Drew the wrong way, and she felt it was time to put him in his place.

"Mr. Kingston, I would never mix business with pleasure, and for you to come at me like this shows unprofessionalism on your part."

"Drew, you're a beautiful woman, and from what I can see you need someone to keep you."

Now Drew was irritated. "First of all, Zae, I'm already a well-kept woman, kept by Yah. And another...

Zae interrupted. "That's not what I overheard earlier between you and the ex-con."

Drew almost lost it; how could Zae dictate to her about her life, being kept and her situation with Marcus, he didn't know her or Marcus.

Drew held a tight lip eyeing Zae, taking deep breaths and exhaling in order to stay calm. "I would like for you to leave; if you think I'm going to sleep with you for an article in your magazine, you're sadly mistaken."

"Drew, you have it wrong." Zae tried to explain.

"Mr. Kingston, I would like for you to leave." Drew was done with this clown.

Tevin must have heard the rise in Drew's voice because she could see him standing at the bottom of the stairs with the baseball bat from behind the check-in counter.

"You good Drew." Tevin asked, with no hesitation to use the bat if needed.

Zae looked down at Tevin standing at the bottom of the stairs. "Drew, it's not what you think."

"Can you please leave?" Drew asked once more.

Zae was thunderstruck. "You're going to put me out in the rain?"

CHAPTER 30

Story Time

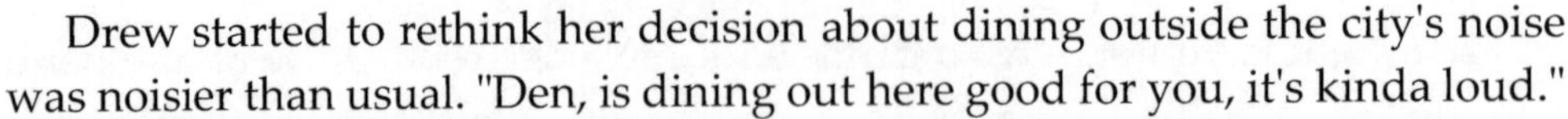

Drew started to rethink her decision about dining outside the city's noise was noisier than usual. "Den, is dining out here good for you, it's kinda loud."

Den laughed. "That's because you're out there in Promise with only the noise of frogs and crickets."

"They can get loud sometimes too, but I'd rather listen to them."

Den could tell Drew had a lot on her mind and needed to vent, so maybe they should rethink their seating options; the sounds of the city was distracting.

"We can go inside if you want, Drew." Den didn't mind, either way was good for her.

"No, it's okay, I'll deal." Drew gave Den an assuring smile.

"So, tell me what's been going on" Den was anxious to know why Drew looked so stressed.

"Whew, Chile, it's story time." Drew sighed. "Where do I begin."

It took Drew about twenty minutes to lace Den up on everything going on at the B&B the last few weeks. Den scratched her head in shock from all the drama; Marcus posing as a stranger, the new homeless help, and Drew having someone interested in her. Den was interested in the story behind Marcus, but the story behind Zae was the one she focused on. Den was shocked, Drew had been so closed off it surprised her that anyone would even be interested.

"Den," Drew called her name for the second time. "Do you think I overreacted?"

"I'm sorry Drew, processing this will take a moment." Den shook her head.

Drew let out a sigh. "So, do you think I overreacted with Zae"

Den eyed Drew. "Do you want the truth, or do you want me to lie?"

"UGH! Why do you have to be that way, Den?" Drew grew frustrated, she needed advice not options.

"Because Drew, you tend to get upset when someone tells you the truth, not all the time, just some of the time."

Drew looked at Den sideways. "WHAT?"

"I'm just saying, you tend to shy away from correction sometimes."

"Ok, forget it, just tell me." Drew started to get impatient. "Tell me the truth."

"Ok, Drew, you might have overreacted." Den could see Drew starting to struggle with her truth. "You said he was throwing hints, letting you know he was interested all day, so when he overheard you and Marcus's conversation it gave him the ambition to come at you."

"Eavesdropping," Drew said under her breath.

"See that right there, that's what I'm talking about."

"Well, he was eavesdropping, he practically said so himself."

The women shared in a laugh.

"I'm so glad you're back girl." Drew looked at Den, shaking her head.

"I'm glad to be back, Atlanta's not the place for me, I'm forever a Texas girl." Den chuckled.

"Really, Den, I felt lost without you here, and talking to Jay these days have been difficult; we haven't been on the same page since Marcus got locked up. It's like Jay stopped understanding me."

Den could finally see how much she meant to Drew, but she wouldn't make it about her and stayed the course.

"Marcus huh, Jay didn't tell me he was out, or that he was posing as a guest, wow."

"Yeah, tell me about it." Drew shook her head.

"So, how do you feel?"

"Honesty, Den, I'm not sure, it was clever and sweet, but deceitful and reckless. What if Pete had hurt him."

Den side-eyed Drew. "Girl, Pete is old."

Drew laughed out, and before she could turn away she held Marcus's stare; his come-hither look had Drew like a deer in headlights. The blood ran from her head to her heart.

Den witnessed the stare down, and as much as she wanted to intervene for Drew's sake she didn't. Den felt Marcus and Drew needed that moment; it amazed Den how their eyes talked to each other without saying a word. Den could see and feel a strong love between the two, and at this point she knew Zae didn't stand a chance.

Drew hurried to catch her tears before they fell, and Marcus disappeared in the crowd.

"It's so loud out here." Drew was unaware that Den had witnessed the interactions, so she complained about the noise again, hoping Den would suggest once more they go inside.

Den instantly caught on to Drew's persuasion tactics, so she suggested they get out of the August heat rather than talk about Drew's uneasy feelings.

After having their lunch on the inside of the Bistro Den and Drew headed back to Drew's car. Den noticed Drew searching the crowd but wasn't sure if she was avoiding running into Marcus or if she was looking for an opportunity.

Den clutched Drew's arm pulling her into a corner newsstand, hoping it would take her mind off Marcus.

"Excuse me, what are you doing."

"Come with me for a minute, I need a Red Bull that trip wiped me out."

Drew began to scold Den about drinking the energy drink, but Den completely ignored her warning, heading directly to the refrigerated area of the newsstand.

Drew looked around the newsstand, her emotions after seeing Marcus were still haunting her, so she used the newsstand for a bit of shopping therapy; by the time she and Den got to the checkout Drew had almost one of everything in her arms.

"Um, you think you got everything." Den eyed all the things Drew had on the counter, from handy wipes to lip balm. "Why so many chargers?"

"You never know when a guest will need one." Drew quickly responded.

Den was ok with that answer, but she could still read between the lines and the reason for the outrageous purchase.

"Can you grab me a few magazines?"

"Sure, which ones," Den skimmed through the magazines.

"Doesn't matter, they're for the guest bathrooms." Drew grabbed two bags of lifesavers and added them to her items.

Den didn't have time to be picky, so she grabbed a few tossing them on the counter. "There, they've been chosen."

Rainn and Tevin had been entertaining the guest for hours and needed a break, but every time they tried to steal one the small group wanted more. Rainn eyed Tevin as they both sang with intense passion; the pair leered at each other, holding an expression of love, setting the guest's mood in the room.

Drew could hear Rainn and Tevin soon as she walked into the B&B; throwing her newsstand findings on the counter Drew pulled Den by the arm. "Come with me, you have to hear this kid."

Den didn't have time to contest before Drew had her standing at the French doors of the sunroom catching the last of Rainn's and Tevin's show.

Tevin and Rainn could see the small group were finally ready for refreshments, so Rainn gave Tevin the cue to wrap it up. Tevin gave Rainn a wink and ended their song with a brief solo.

Drew eyed Den: she could tell by the look on her face that she was stunned by the young man's talent. "He's good, huh?"

"Ethan!" Den yelled.

Drew was confused about why Den called Tevin Ethan and their connection. " Den, you know...

Den ran and took Tevin in her arms not giving Drew a chance to finish her question. "Ethan, where have you been, I've been so worried about you, how are you here?"

Both Drew and Rainn were at a loss for words but had plenty of questions. Drew eyed the curious guest greeting them with a gentle smile, hoping to ensure them everything was fine.

Den gave Tevin a once-over as tears ran from her eyes. "Why did you run off, Ethan? Where have you been? Are you ok?" Den didn't give the young man time to answer one question before asking another.

"Dang, Dina, give me time to answer." Tevin pulled from Den's grasp.

Drew hurried to intervene, holding her hand in the air asking permission to speak. "Umm, before you answer," Drew pointed at Tevin, somebody please explain to me the connection between you two."

Den was so excited about seeing Ethan she forgot Drew was standing there. Den scrambled to find an explanation. Drew could tell Den was having a hard time and wondered what the hang-up was.

"Den, are you ok?" Drew asked.

"Yeah, just a little overwhelmed." Den took a seat on the piano bench.

Rainn looked around at the quizzical faces when she heard the front desk bell ringing, so she used that opportunity to escape the drama. Tevin would have to explain to her later.

"Excuse me, someone's ringing the bell." Rainn held one finger up as if to excuse herself from an overdue church service.

Drew eyed Tevin and Den confused as ever. "So, is anybody going to tell me your connection."

Tevin hurried to explain but Den took over, not allowing Tevin to state his case. "Drew, this is my brother Ethan."

Drew was shocked, but not amazed; appalled that Tevin was Den's brother but not that she had one. Den told Drew years ago she had a younger brother that had runoff.

"Wow, you have to excuse me for being so blunt, but this reunion has taken me by surprise." Drew smiled confusingly at them both.

Den knew she would have to give Drew more detail, but as of right now she needed to make sure her brother was ok.

"Ethan, where have you been?" Den asked the young man for a second time.

Tevin tried to avoid the question, but Den refused to let him.

"Answer me, Ethan." Den grabbed Tevin's arms and demanded an answer.

Drew could see Den was surprisingly upset, she'd never seen Den like this. Den was always calm in any situation, but today Drew saw a different side.

Drew took the siblings to her office so the guest wouldn't get alarmed from all the emotions running through the place. Drew didn't need those kinds of reviews.

"Are you ok?" Drew handed Den a tissue.

"I'm good, thank you." Den wiped her face.

Drew eyed Tevin. "You good, Tevin."

Tevin gave Drew a soft smile. "Yeah, I'm good."

"Ok, since we're all good, can somebody please fill me in." Drew gave them both a little bit more time to gather themselves, but that was it, after that she needed answers.

Den cleared her throat. "Drew, my brother has been missing since 2008."

"Not missing, gone." Tevin corrected Den.

Den eyed Tevin: Drew could clearly see her relief turning to anger.

"ETHAN, YOU WERE 16!" Den yelled out in frustration

Rainn flipped through the magazine, pretending she didn't hear the raised voices coming from Drew's office.

Den took a moment to calm herself. "Ethan, in the state of Texas that's missing."

Tevin eyed Den: Drew could tell he was becoming frustrated by his sister's scolding.

"Well, Den, I would've never run off if you hadn't tried to send me back to that monster."

"THAT MONSTER IS YOUR MOTHER, ETHAN!" Den yelled out.

Drew rubbed Den's shoulders to calm her.

Den exhaled. "She's been clean for years, does that count for anything?"

Drew could see the room was getting heated, so she called a time-out.

"Look, I don't know what's going on, but I do know from my experiences growing up without a family the both of you should cherish one another, even your mother." Drew eyed Tevin. "Now, I don't know what she did, but I'm pretty sure if you all talked about it the problems could be resolved; you wouldn't believe how much can be worked out if you just sit down and talk to one another and listen."

Tevin was touched by Drew's encouraging words but not enough to completely change his heart. "I hear you and all, Miss Drew, but I don't have anything to say to her clean or sober." Tevin looked at Den. "And you either,"

Tevin stormed from the office, slamming the door. Drew looked shocked, as though Tevin had slammed the door in her face. "Oh, I know he upset, but he gone have to see me about that." Drew eyed Den, giving her a wink. "Now, lady, talk to me."

Den told Drew about her mother being a recovering acholic, and she had to basically take care of Tevin when her mom was on a binge, or their father was locked up. Drew could see the explanation was tearing Den up, but she continued. Den informed Drew that she was basically the sole provider for Tevin since he'd been born, being that her mother stayed drunk 80% of the time and the other 20% trying to recover. Den revealed to Drew that her mother didn't think about becoming sober until Tevin almost drowned when he was three and spent months in the hospital, making her mom straighten up for about a year before she went on a 12-year binge.

Den let out a sigh. "Drew, my mother always left Ethan and me looking out for us so she could chase the bottle. At fourteen she made him get a job as a valet." Den shook her head. "What mother makes her 14-year-old get a job so he can help her afford her spirits. Our dad was locked up most of the time, and when he was out all he and my mom did was fight about her drinking, but I can honestly say we had more good days with my dad. If it wasn't for her he wouldn't be locked up now."

It was becoming difficult to explain, thinking back on the trauma her mother caused, but she needed Drew to know this part of her life; she had never told anyone, not even Jay.

Den grabbed more tissues from Drew's desk. "My mother has done lots of things to Ethan that's why it's so hard for him to forgive her. One night after her drinking all day my mother lay on the couch drunk, Ethan was on the floor playing with a keyboard our father had given him...

Drew could see Den's past clawing at her heart. "Den, you can stop, I don't have to know this."

Den insisted she finish. "For whatever reason, mom thought Ethan was trying to harm her, so she went to the kitchen, got a knife, and tried to cut his throat. Thank God I came in when I did because she would have hurt him if I hadn't. The neighbors called the polices after hearing all the screaming coming from our house. My mom was so drunk when the police got there she told them my father tried to kill her and Ethan. So, instead of my mother going to jail my dad took the charges and is now doing time.

Den couldn't finish at this point, so Drew suggested Den lay down for a moment, making her comfortable on the chaise. At this point not only did Den need to calm down but Drew also needed to regroup. The things Den had just revealed about her life had Drew's head spinning. Den was always humble and meek, not getting upset about anything, but now she was overwhelmed with sorrow from her past, which hurt Drew.

Drew closed the door to the office and joined Rainn at the counter. "Whew, what a day." Drew sighed. "Are the guest ok?"

"Everyone's good, doing their own thang."

Drew asked Tevin's whereabouts, but Rainn was unsure she hadn't seen him since he'd stormed out of her office.

Rainn flipped through the pages of one of the magazines Drew purchased at the newsstand. "You must have made quite an impression on Mr. Kingston's."

Drew eyed Rainn with curiosity. "Come again, what are you talking about?"

Rainn flipped through the magazine's pages to show Drew the article Mr. Kingston had written. "See Drew, it's right here in September's edition of Stylish Country Living, the article Mr. Kingston wrote."

Drew snatched the book from Rainn's hand.

Rainn looked at Drew sideways. "Umm, rude much?"

"I'm sorry, Rainn." Drew patted Rainn's hand, never taking her eyes off the article.

"Why are you so surprised, isn't this what you wanted, he got the peace seeker part and all." Rainn didn't know Drew had put the poor man out.

Drew continued reading when she noticed part of the article that shook her soul.

'Serenity Meadows felt like home, my stay was pleasant and sweet. The owner was incredibly attentive, ensuring all my needs were met, treating me like a king on my throne. The themed B&B made me feel so special my soul cried Beautiful Tears.'

"Beautiful Tears." Drew whispered; the words triggered something in Drew's mind. Airplane, Stylish Country living, Eclipse, the kiss. "OMG, Zae," Drew yelped out.

CHAPTER 31

Apologies & Apologies

Drew looked down at her phone, she knew the right thing to do was call Zae but the embarrassment she felt held her back. Drew couldn't believe she didn't recognize Zae, but it had been five years, so Drew didn't feel wrong about that; what Drew felt terrible about was kissing this man and running out on him, and then to make matters worse she put him out in the rain.

Drew put her head on the desk wishing she could disappear.

"OMG, what's wrong with me." Drew's whining was interrupted by a knock at the door. "You may enter." Drew tried to quickly pull herself together.

Ma Tate crept through the door. "Hey, my girl, are you just fine?"

The soft sweet sound of Ma Tate's voice instantly calmed Drew's soul. "MA Tate," Drew yelped out, jumping up from the desk wrapping her arms around her with an embrace of love and excitement.

"When did you get back."

"We got back last night."

"Ma Tate, it's so good to see you, I'm so glad you're back safe."

Ma Tate was shocked at Drew's perky spirit, she seemed lively and full of life. "Drew, are you ok?"

"I'm fine Ma Tate, how are you, how was your trip to Tanzania?" Drew smiled, ready for some exciting news.

Ma Tate was puzzled, Jay had told her everything that went on while she and Joe were gone, so she expected to return to a very distraught Drew but instead came home to an imposter.

"Baby, are you ok."

Drew eyed Ma Tate. "Yeah, why wouldn't I be?"

Ma Tate told Drew that Jay enlightened her on everything that was going on, and she thought for sure she'd have to come home and do damage control.

Drew gave Ma Tate a sweet smile. "Well, Ma Tate, a lot has gone on, and I must say with all your teachings and lectures we pretty much handled everything well. Some things still need to be handled." Drew thought about Zae.

Ma Tate was thrilled to know everyone had learned to deal with life and its situations independently, but the thought of them not needing her grabbed at her heart.

"Well, I see I wasn't needed here." Ma Tate displayed sad eyes.

Drew could hear the emotion in Ma Tate's voice. "Ma Tate, you know we always going to need you." Drew wrapped her arms around Ma Tates neck and began to bless her with repeated kisses.

"Oh, now, stop it, Drew," Ma Tate blushed.

"So, tell me about your trip, I heard you guys had some exciting news."

Ma Tate told Drew about all the new people in Tanzania who'd joined their organization, and they'd met an actual *Levite Priest*, who gathered males all over the world of Israelite descent once a year to honor the Passover in Jerusalem.

"Now you know Joe's already making arrangements to attend." Ma Tate laughed.

Drew was amazed that the Tates had met an actual Priest. Drew read about the Priesthood in Israel's ancient history and wondered if there were any left that kept the Covent in modern times, now her questions had been answered.

"Wow, Ma Tate, that's going to be some kind of experience for Pops."

Ma Tate chuckled. "He's planning already, although it's six months away."

Ma Tate could see Drew was just fine, but she also knew Drew was good at covering up, so she asked Drew to have a seat in the bay window, placing her in a non-judgmental comfort zone so Drew would open up to her.

Ma Tate rubbed Drew's back giving her time to receive her affection. "Talk to me sweetness, what's going on with you."

Den walked out to the tool shed searching for Tevin, she had to make sure he didn't offer Drew anymore information than she already had; she'd given the *pick-outs* of she and Ethan's story and needed to make sure he did the same. Den had given him a few days to cool down, so she hoped he'd be willing to hear her out.

"Ethan, you in here," Den called out, walking into the tool shed.

Tevin stood behind the workbench sanding down some wood to build Drew another birdhouse.

"Why are you calling me that?"

Den rubbed her hands together nervously. "How are you doing, where have you been."

"I'm fine, and I've been around." Tevin kept his cold shoulder visible.

Den walked closer. "Ethan, I was so worried about you."

"Yeah, really worried, so worried you started a whole new life out here in Promise and stop calling me Ethan."

"Why, Ethan, it's your name." Den walked over and grabbed Tevin's face. "You're never going to escape her, she's your mother. "Den eyed Tevin.

Tevin took his gloves off and sat them on the workbench. "Is that why you let her back in, because she's your mother?"

"No, Ethan, I let her back in because she needed our help. We're all she has."

Tevin took the gloves and threw them. "Dina, Wake Up, She DON'T Need Us, She Needs A Drink!"

Den tried staying humble, but it was taking a lot at this point. "Ethan, she's been clean almost four years." Den pleaded, "I just wanna be a family again." Tear streamed from her eyes.

Tevin noticed the tears coming from Den's eyes and that's all it took. "Stop crying, Bubbles."

Den hadn't heard the name Bubbles since Tevin was ten, she would always pull the bubbles out for Tevin when their mother came home wasted, taking his mind off the madness.

Den took Tevin in her arms and held him close; she could see he was still haunted by their mother. "I promise she's different this time."

Tevin pulled away from Den's embrace. "I'm not going back to Shiloh City, I'm staying right here with Drew, I'm an adult now, and this is what I choose."

Den didn't contest his reason; all that mattered was she had her baby brother back.

Rainn stood outside the tool shed listening to Den and Tevin's conversation, she knew it was wrong of her to eavesdrop, but she needed to know if Tevin was ok, and this was her reason.

Den and Tevin talked a while catching up on the last few years. Tevin was amazed that Den had finally started living for herself instead of being tied down to their mother.

"Wow, Den, you finally freed yourself from her grasp."

Den eyed Tevin, she didn't want to ruin the moment talking about their alcoholic mother and all her mistakes, so she hurried to change the subject.

"So how did you end up here with Drew.

Tevin retrieved the gloves from the floor he'd thrown before. "I don't know, I was working at this market and the owner fired me, next thing I know I'm working and living here."

Den was excited to hear that Tevin had found safety with Drew, but it also bothered her. Den didn't want demons from their past to ruin what they had in Promise.

"Ok, Ethan, I'm going to need you to be discrete about our background. These people are the closest that we've had to a family in a long time, and I don't need our pass to mess that up."

Tevin assured his sister that he would keep their past to himself, other than what Den already revealed. Tevin was just as eager to keep the peaceful lifestyle as well.

Rainn could barely hear what Den and Tevin were saying, the sound of Pete's chainsaw was making it very difficult. Rainn leaned in closer so involved with other people's business she didn't hear the roar of the chain saw stop. Rainn was getting an ear full when Pete walked up behind her.

"You shouldn't listen to people's conversations without them knowing it."

Rainn's soul left her body. Pete had scared the piss out of her, (literally). Rainn ran off to the bathroom; Pete had frightened her so badly she had to go.

Pete chuckled to himself as he watched Rainn runoff, clutching the crotch of her pants, holding her legs together trying to avoid an accident. Pete had never seen someone run so fast.

Ma Tate Laughed uncontrollably, shocked at Drew's actions with Marcus. "Drew, you took the pie?"

"I sure did, and I'm not embarrassed at all, taking that pie gave me a sense of authority. Besides, I was craving that last piece."

The women laughed at the foolishness.

Ma Tate looked into Drew's eyes and seen the life still there, pleased that Drew hadn't let Marcus's homecoming alter her mood, but this Zae character was another topic. Ma Tate knew that Drew needed to contact him regarding the article and her actions, but she was still perplexed about his feelings for Drew.

"Drew, I'm going to be honest, if you know the feelings you had for Marcus are gone, then let this man woo you. I think you should call Zae and set up a meeting."

"Why a meeting, why can't I just text him."

Ma Tate pinched Drew's cheeks. "Because you put the man out in the rain, baby."

Ma Tate and Drew started out of the office when running into Den carrying a look of surprise on her face; she didn't know Ma Tate was there, and wondered if Drew or Jay had told her about Ethan and her mother.

"Hey y'all," Den had a quiver in her tone.

Ma Tate and Drew eyed Den speciously.

"Are you ok, Den?" Ma Tate asked.

"Yeah, just had a little heart-to-heart with Ethan."

Ma Tate could see Den was rattled over she and Ethan's conversation and wanted to make sure Den was ok, but when she went in to comfort her Den pulled back, rejecting Ma Tate.

Den fidgeted with her keys nervously. "I'm good, don't worry, it's just life, you know?"

Ma Tate knew Den was used to handling things independently, but she really wanted to be there for her; Jay had informed Ma Tate on everything going on and it pained her that Den delt with this alone.

"Den, you know we can talk about this." Ma Tate offering an ear.

"I'm fine, I assure you." Den looked at Ma Tate and Drew, and as much as she wanted to open up she simply couldn't.

Ma Tate didn't want to push too hard, so she let Den's situation rest for now.

Later that night Drew lay in the bed on her fourth attempt to call Zae. Drew allowed the phone to ring three times before chickening out and hanging up. "What's wrong with you, Drew, you're just making a phone call, you got this." Drew encouraged herself.

Drew pondered a moment longer when she got the courage to finally go through with the call, but just as she went to push redial her phone started to ring. Drew was shaking like a leaf, it was Zae returning her call. Drew hesitated to answer, but it was now or never.

"Hello, Zae, how are you?"

"Hey, there, stranger."

Drew could tell by the excitement in Zae's voice he was pleased to get her call, and that was shocking. Drew knew for sure she would put her on mute.

"Hey." Drew scrambled with her words. "I just wanted to say thanks for the wonderful article, and I apologize for putting you out in the rain, I overreacted, and it was downright rude of me, and I'm sorry for our night at Eclipse."

There was silence Drew took the phone from her ear to check and see if Zae hung up; she thought for sure he'd hung up on her lame apology.

Zae finally spoke. "I'm sorry Drew, I was feeding my son, and stop apologizing everything is cool with us, I may have come on to strong, and for that I apologize."

Drew heard the apology, but did he say son. Drew asked herself. Drew didn't take Zae to be the father type.

"Wow, I didn't know you had a son.

Zae laughed. "What, you didn't figure me to be the father type."

Drew got a little choked up Zae was dead on, but she wouldn't admit it to him; she'd already made an *ass* of herself.

"Nah just...

"Let me save you the horror, you didn't."

Drew laughed. "So how old is your son?" Drew tried to back paddle from the humiliation with a question.

"Asher's two, but he has a birthday in about four weeks, September 30th."

Drew's jaw dropped. "Wow, he's named for one of the twelve tribes of Israel, and we have the same birthday. I have a birthday twin." Drew bragged. "Wow, I can't believe I'm about to be thirty-three, seems like yesterday I was only twenty-three."

Zae let out a sigh. "I know what you mean, it seems like only hours have passed since I and Asher's mother held him for the first time."

Drew didn't wanna get personal, but she wondered where the child's mother was and did she and Zae still have an intimate relationship. Drew thought twice about bringing up the child's mother, but she had already asked Zae the questions before she knew it.

"Where's Asher's mother?" Drew bit her lip.

"Asher's mother and I are no longer together; we broke up a month after Asher was born agreeing to co-parent. So, I get him every other month and holidays."

Drew was pleased with Zae's answer and even more impressed that he and his child's mother co-parented so well. Drew had a no-baby momma policy, but Zae seemed to have his BM issues under control.

Drew and Zae had spent hours on the phone talking about any and everything imaginable, from running a successful business to parenting a two-year-old successfully. The pair had connected in a way that made their first encounter a thing of the past.

Drew looked at the clock on the nightstand which read 2am, she knew they'd been on the phone a while, but this was a record. Drew hadn't been on the phone this long since she was in college, and as much as Drew wanted to keep going with their conversation she had an early morning with the guest and needed to rest up.

"Zae, I appreciate you accepting my call and continuing the article it means the world to me, and as much as I would love to continue our conversation, I have to go, I have a meditation class later this morning."

Zae wasn't at all disappointed, the time they'd already spent was much more than he'd imagined, so his heart was content.

"Thank you for sharing I and Asher's evening from dinner to bedtime, and thanks for all your wisdom on raising a two-year-old. I swear once I think I have It down something new pops up."

There was a moment of silence between the two when Zae threw the question out there.

"Have dinner with me Drew, nothing fancy, just dinner."

Drew hesitated to answer; her heart wanted to say yes but why weren't the words coming out. Drew knew the problem was Marcus; every time a man showed interest in her she would blow him off. Some how it made Drew feel like she was cheating on him. These were her same actions growing up when it came to Shawn, and now it was time to put a stop to it and allow her options to be explored. Drew knew she had to loosen herself from this hold Marcus had on her.

"I would love to accept, but I'm so busy with the B&B I don't have time." Drew shook her head, disappointed with herself.

"Make time," Zae stated softy. "How about this, I take you and Asher to Bounce Around for your birthdays, you bring Gabe, and we can call it a play date."

"Um," Drew was trying to push the words yes from her mouth, but they held on to her uvula and wouldn't let go.

Zae could see Drew having difficulty deciding, so he sugared it up. "I'll buy you a birthday cake."

Drew laughed out. "Oh no, he used a weapon, how can anyone refuse cake. Ok, I'll go."

CHAPTER 32

Admitting & Accepting

Rainn eyed Pete as he walked past the check-in counter, she could tell by the smirk on his face he still found it humorous that she'd almost peed her pants the other day, compliments to him.

"I can't stand Mr. Pete."

"What Pete do to you?" Tevin chuckled.

"He's always lurking and snooping it seems."

"What do you mean lurking and snooping, he's the groundkeeper that's part of his job, keeping an eye out for things?"

Tevin eyed Rainn as she filled the crystal candy dish. "He's not the only one lurking and snooping."

Rainn paused, thinking Pete had spilled the beans about her eavesdropping the other day, and if so how was she going to explain her deceitful behavior.

"Wow, who's the other spy?" Rainn tried to play the conversation down, fearing she'd been found out.

Tevin took one of the Lifesavers for the candy dish and popped it in his mouth, taking his time responding to Rainn's question; he wanted to see how well she'd do under pressure.

Rainn awaited Tevin's answer but instead found him more interested in a piece of candy rather than release her from the guilt and fear she suffered.

Just about when Rainn was about to confess Tevin disclosed he'd seen her peeking through the tool shed's door.

"Whew, it feels so good to get that out."

Tevin looked at Rainn sideways. "What?"

"Look, Tevin, I was about to tell you, but you beat me to it, I'm sorry I was eavesdropping." Rainn stated with no sincerity.

"Well, at least we know you're majoring in the right field." Tevin headed for the patio doors.

Rainn felt insulted, but she deserved every bit of the hell Tevin was giving her right now.

ᘐ

Drew wrapped up her morning meditation with the guest when she observed Tevin from the sunroom marching to the tool shed as if he was going to war. Drew could see that Tevin was struggling with his demons and tried to give him space to figure it out, but she saw now it was just about time to intervene. Drew peered at the guest hoping they didn't see the unprofessionalism going on; it was bad enough they'd semi-witnessed the previous altercation.

“Thanks guys, for your time, morning meditation was excellent, now if y’all are ready for some down-home cooking Miss Sue had prepared breakfast in the dining room."

The guest gathered their things, ready to indulge in Miss Sues big country breakfast.

"Also remember evening meditation starts at six o'clock if you're attending."

Drew walked over to the counter and asked Rainn if she knew what was going on with Tevin. Rainn lied and told Drew she didn't realize anything was wrong, but Drew was no fool and could clearly tell that Rainn wasn't being honest. Drew looked at Rainn unconvinced, she would allow Rainn's lie to live for now, but Rainn would have to kill it with the truth sooner rather than later.

Drew held two fingers up in a V-sign, gesturing to Rainn that she was watching her while back crabbing into her office.

Drew wasn't sitting at her desk five minutes before she caught herself gazing out the window thinking about Zae. Drew was still in the clouds over their lengthy conversation the night before. Drew thought about shooting him a text but didn't wanna seem thirsty, but she had to admit it felt good having someone to conversate with.

Just as another smile was about to grace Drew's face it was taken over by a confused frown; Drew didn’t understand why there was a *Friendly Market* van in the driveway, when she hadn't ordered any groceries.

"Rainn," Drew called out.

"Yes Ma'am, you need something?" Rainn came rushing into the office upon Drew's request.

"Yeah, there's a Friendly Market van outside. Did Miss Sue order something?"

Rainn looked out the window at the vehicle just as confused. "No, she didn't run anything by me," Taking another look Rainn's jaw almost hit the floor. "Miss Drew, look outside."

Drew looked up from the computer out the window, and saw something that she couldn't unsee. Carl standing outside the van in some khaki pants, a green polo shirt with the *friendly Market* logo on it, and an apron wrapped around his waist bearing the same logo, holding a bag of whatever in his arm.

"Oh, my goodness, what is this man up to now." Drew shook her head.

Rainn knocked at the tool shed's door, she wanted to stick around for whatever explanation Carl had for pulling up looking like employee of the month, but she needed to make things right with Tevin.

Rainn knocked for a second time but still no response, she could hear the music coming from inside, so she knew someone had to be in there. Rainn started to twirl her hair thinking how awful it would be if she'd messed things up with Tevin; she'd gotten to know him and really liked him, so it thumbed at her heart not knowing if she had ruined their friendship.

Pete shook his head as he watched Rainn give intense thought to what her next move should be. This also humored Pete, he didn't understand why young people had to think about things; back in his day if one was interested in someone they went for it and didn't worry about the what if's.

Pete was over it, all this nonsense was getting on his last nerve. "He's in there, go on in, what are you waiting for?"

Rainn's whole spirit went up to Yah, Pete had done it again, but there were no leaky faucets this time. "MR. PETE, DANG!" Rainn cried out. "Why you gotta be sneaking up on people like that, I wasn't even listening to anyone's conversation this time."

Rainn tried to hurry up and clear the air before Pete got the wrong impression.

"I really wasn't Mr. Pete."

"Well, what are you waiting on?" Mr. Pete eyed Rainn.

"I'm waiting because I...

"Ain't no needs in waiting to tell the boy how you feel, you out here telling the birds."

Mr. Pete walked off shaking his head, grumbling about how clueless and weak young people were. Rainn also grumbled to herself about how impatient and rude old people were.

Rainn slowly opened the door she could see why Tevin didn't hear her, he had the radio on and earbuds in.

Rainn crept over to the workbench where Tevin was lost in his work. Looking around the shed Rainn was amazed at all the custom-made birdhouses. There were all kinds, big ones, small ones, green ones, yellow ones; each with its own unique design.

Rainn put her attention back on Tevin; looking down at him she could tell that Tevin was broken, and all she wanted was to fix him.

"Tevin." Rainn softly called out but it didn't get his attention, so she called out even louder, but he still didn't hear her, so she did the next best thing and took his earbuds out.

Tevin almost fell out of the wooden chair when Rainn snatched the earbuds from his ears. "Dang girl, you need to knock before you enter," Tevin stated rudely.

Rainn took a deep breath and remembered she was there to salvage any bit of friendship they had, so she would allow him this one time to be an ass.

"I knocked, but you didn't hear me, Pete told me to come in."

"Well, next time, knock harder."

Rainn reached up to turn the ventage radio off that sat on the shelf. "You could probably hear me if you turned one of these radios off."

Before Rainn's hand could touch the knob Tevin had jumped up taking her hand guiding it back to her side. Tevin and Rainn stood face to face, holding each other stare, at that moment Rainn could have gotten him to do whatever she wanted, except messing with Pete's radio.

"No, don't touch that, I don't wanna hear Pete's mouth that's why I wear my buds. Don't Ever Touch That Radio!"

Rainn could tell by Tevin's tone there had been some problems behind that radio.

Rainn looked around the shed bringing up the birdhouses to open the floor for conversation.

"Did you make all these?"

“Yeah, everyone."

"Wow, you do good work, who taught you?"

"My dad, the little while he stayed out of jail."

Tevin grew frustrated taking a metal ruler slapping it on the workbench. "What do you want, Rainn?"

The sound of the ruler slapping against the metal workbench startled Rainn, her first thoughts were to run but the anger and hurt she felt from Tevin's actions had her confused in some way; anybody with good sense would've just left, but for some strange reason Rainn stayed.

"I'm trying to be your friend."

"Did I ask for your friendship?"

Rainn snatched the ruler from Tevin's hand and slapped it on the workbench, "How does that feel." Trying to catch her calm Rainn spoke in the sweetest, softest voice she could find hidden under the anger she was feeling.

"Listen to me Immature, throwing your little temper tantrum isn't going to solve your problems, so stop feeling sorry for yourself, using your misfortune as a crutch. We've all gone through something in life, some more than others, so what makes you better than anyone else that you THOUGHT you didn't have to." Rainn took a deep breath and exhaled. "I came out here to apologize and salvage what little friendship we had left, but since you out here throwing a pity party, I'll run and fetch you some balloons." Rainn handed Tevin the ruler. "My loyalty can't be measured, ETHAN." Rainn left the shed leaving Tevin with his thoughts.

Rainn took her place behind the counter trying to calm herself, at this point she didn't care if she and Tevin still had a friendship or not; the way he'd just made her feel threw up a major red flag.

Rainn checked to see if any guests had made any requests in the request basket. Drew thought this was a good idea if the staff wasn't around and the guest needed something.

Rainn heard laughter coming from Drew's office, now she regretted leaving before hearing Carl's explanation for the grocery store outfit; it would've been more entertaining than being humiliated by Tevin.

Drew was in tears laughing so hard at her father as he modeled off his check-out boy uniform. "I can't believe you bought the Friendly Market, what were you thinking, you don't know the first thing about running a grocery store."

"What are you talking about, I ran my own business for years." Carl smoothed out his apron.

"Dad, that was a staffing agency, not a grocery store; there will be a difference."

"Staffing agency, grocery store, it's all the same."

Drew shook her head, there was no need to try and talk her dad out of it he'd already signed the papers and designed new uniforms.

Drew walked over to her dad and wrapped her arms around his neck. "Congratulations, dad, may your business prosper." Drew kissed his cheek.

"Thank you, sweetheart." Carl returned the kiss. "Can we have a conversation?"

"Sure," Drew took a seat on the chaise lounge; she knew the conversation was about to get deep by the way Carl cleared his throat. "Yeah, we can talk."

"Drew, you know I've never tried to get in your business or tell you what to do, I never felt entitled to, but through the years I believed I've gained a little entitlement, at least enough to give you a little sound advice."

Drew made herself comfortable, she'd heard everyone else advice why not one more. "Sure, dad, why not, it's nothing like getting advice from your old man." Drew rubbed Carl's hand.

Carl wanted to take Drew in his arms, but he needed to stay on track. "Drew, I talked to Marcus, and what he did was reckless; now I can't argue his reason, but I'll tell you this baby girl, sometimes a person can get so desperate they'll try anything."

"Dad, I don't need him to try anything I need him to think, my gosh he was locked up for three years for not thinking."

"I can't argue with that." Carl chuckled. "But I can say Marcus is sorry and regrets what he did. I suggest a conversation to clear the air.

Drew peered out the window, she knew the advice her father gave was dead on, but the fear of knowing Marcus would no longer be part of her life scared her.

Carl eyed Drew. "The faster you do it, the easier it will be for things to fall in place."

Drew gazed out of the window, she knew the advice her father gave her was dead on, but the fear of knowing Marcus would no longer be part of her life scared her.

CHAPTER 33

Miracles & Blessings

Drew hurried from her office grabbing her raincoat and keys; after a few days of praying she'd finally made up her mind to see Marcus. Although Drew was still somewhat nervous about meeting Marcus she knew it had to be done. Drew rushed past Rainn on a mission to complete her task.

"Um, slow down, let me find out you're excited about seeing Marcus," Rainn said jokingly.

"Let me find out my guests were neglected while I was out." Drew returned the comedy giving Rainn a fake smile.

Just when Drew was about to run out the door she ran dab smack into Jay and Den.

"Slow down, slow down, where are you going in such a rush." Den inquired, giving Drew a hug.

"Ewe, you're wet, and I'm late for a meeting."

"Would this meeting be with Marcus?" Jay chuckled.

"Oh, the gossip in this town has to stop." Drew said with disgust.

"That's my boy, you know he's gonna tell me." Jay stated.

"Yeah, don't I know it," Drew stated sarcastically.

Den nudged Jay. "Isn't there something you need to say to Drew?"

"Will you give me time." Jay gave Den a sideways look.

Jay hadn't talk to Drew since their argument about her putting Marcus out, and Den couldn't stand it.

Jay took the raincoat from Drew's arms and draped it over her shoulders, trying to find the right words to say; Jay knew he'd been an *ass* to her, and now it was time to take responsibility for his actions.

"I'm sorry, Drew." Jay gave Drew sad eyes.

"I know you're sorry, now you can apologize."

Drew looked up at Jay giving him a smile that could bring light to the darkest day. "Look, I have to go, will you guys be here when I get back?"

"Sure, we can be, Lorraine is dropping Gabe off later, I'll just tell her to bring him here."

"Cool beans." Drew looked back at Rainn before she walked out the door, giving her the V-sign, letting her know that she was watching her.

Den and Jay laughed at Drew's actions, especially after seeing the look on Rainn's face.

"Trouble in paradise?" Jay asked.

"Trouble, trouble isn't the word." Rainn let out a sigh, telling Jay and Den that Drew had been on edge since Marcus got out and everyone around the B&B was walking on eggshells other than the guest, and that was only because Drew put up a front for them. Rainn also told them the only thing that seemed to put Drew in a good mood was when she was on the phone with Zae.

When Rainn mentioned Zae, Den immediately began motioning for Rainn to be quiet, but Rainn paid her no mind as she went on and on about Drew and Zae's courtship. Jay must have felt the wind coming from Den's hand gestures turning around only to catch her in the act of trying to motion Rainn to be quiet.

"What are you doing?" Jay asked Den calmy.

"It was a fly, I was trying to get the fly out my face." Den stood there with a blank look on her face.

Jay could tell Den was lying through her teeth. "OK, Pinky and the Brain, what are yall hiding?" Jay looked back at Rainn. "Who is this, Zae?"

Den and Rainn eyed each other, Rainn went to speak but Den cut her off scared she'd out the rest of Drew's business.

"That's not our business to tell Jay." Den eyed Rainn.

Jay eyed Den. "Ok, I respect that, it's not our business, but the cat's out the bag now." Jay waited for the ladies to speak, but neither said a thing. "Ok, but know this, I will get answers."

Jay smiled at the ladies to assure them one or the other would talk.

"Now come on woman, introduce me to your brother." Jay put his arm around Den's shoulder and lured her off.

Den looked back at Rainn in disappointment, shaking her head.

Drew could barely see the road from all the rain falling, it seemed the faster the windshield wipers went the more rain fell. "OMG, I should've given Marcus a rain check, literally," Drew said to herself.

Drew aligned everything she would say to Marcus in her head, from the most important to the least important. Drew tried to take three years of questions and narrow them to an hour.

Marcus sat in a booth at Brooklyn's waiting for Drew to arrive, he was more than excited that Drew wanted to meet with him. It had been almost two months since he'd talked to her, but Marcus didn't mind the intermission had given him time to get his businesses together and back under his control.

Marcus looked up at the tv mounted on the wall, and by the looks of the weather report the storm was only getting worse. Marcus thought about calling Drew for a rain check, as much as he wanted to see her Marcus didn't believe risking Drew's life was worth it.

Drew wiped the windshield trying to clear the frost from the window, although she had the defrost on full blast it was useless; the windshield had fallen victim to the stormy weather. Drew thought. *"This is senseless."* As much as she wanted to clear things up with Marcus the weather was totally against it.

Drew listened to the weather update on the radio the storm was getting worse, and headed straight towards her, so Drew felt it time to call in for that rain check.

Marcus looked at his phone puzzled as to why Drew wasn't picking up, he'd attempted to call her several times to cancel, but he got no response. Marcus was beginning to worry, but before he jumped to any conclusions he would give her a few more minutes to call back or show up.

While nervously waiting for Drew's response Marcus overheard a couple informing the waitress about an accident that had traffic at a stand still due to a care flight landing. Marcus tried to hear more of the details but the yelling from the crowd made it difficult, and as much as Marcus tried to block out any thoughts of it being Drew he couldn't, not until he was sure. Marcus pulled a fifty dollars bill from his wallet and left it on the table. He would only have peace if he knew Drew was at the B&B safe.

Den watched Jay and Tevin get to know one another, thrilled that he and Jay were hitting it off so well. Den had always wanted Tevin to have someone to look up to, and Jay seemed to fit the image Den was looking for. Jay was a landowner, business owner, and a great dad.

Den chuckled watching Jay request song after song, and Tevin honoring his every request, quenching Jay's thirst for the sweet sounds of the old school music.

Den applauded as Tevin finished up his last request. "Encore, Encore," *Den* yelled clapping her hands as if she was at Carnegie Hall.

Jay looked at Tevin still amazed he could master the piano so well.

"That's what I'm talking about," Jay gave Tevin some dap. 'That's talent you have, Tevin."

"Thanks Jay, it's just a lil something I play around with."

Den rolled her eyes at Tevin. "Something he should be taking more seriously, instead of putting all his time into those useless sculptures," Den stated scornfully.

"Wait a minute, you sculpt too, I sculpt as well." Jay was impressed.

Tevin was amazed that he and Jay had an eye for this form of art in common.

"Yeah, I have a few pieces in the shed, you wanna check them out."

"Hell yeah, let's go." Jay got excited.

Den rolled her eyes again, it frustrated her that Tevin would rather mess around with wood and metal, shaping and carving rather than master his talent for the piano.

"It's raining out we can do that some other time." Den eyed the two men.

"It's cool, a little rain ain't never hurt nobody," Jay responded.

"Yeah, I know, but why don't we just wait, Tevin can show you some other time."

Both Jay and Tevin could feel Den's negative vibe towards the useless art, and neither of them liked it. Tevin wasn't surprised at her attitude this was how she always acted when it came to his craft. On the other hand, Jay didn't understand, and needed an explanation for her nonsupport.

Jay was about to address Den's attitude when Gabe rushed into the room out of breath, wet, and excited.

"Daddy, we saw the helicopter and a car wreck, it looks bad too." Gabe announced with excitement.

"That's nothing to be excited about son, what if someone is hurt?"

Gabe looked at Jay with sad eyes. "Maybe we can ask Yah to make them ok."

"That will be just fine Gabe, let's ask Yah to make them ok." Jay embraced Gabe, whispering in his ear. "Yah, let them be ok."

Jay looked back at the door. "Where's your grandma?"

"She's talking to Rainn about the accident."

Jay became curious about the accident, so he and Den left Tevin and Gabe in the sunroom to find out more detail.

Tevin attempted to teach Gabe a few keys on the piano to occupy Gabe's time.

Jay and Den walked over to the counter where Lorraine was still giving Rainn details from the wreck. Jay could look at Rainn and tell the accident was terrible by the look of disbelief on her face.

"Hey Lorraine, you just fine?" Jay asked.

"Yes hunny, I'm just fine." Loraine embraced Jay and Den. "I was just telling Rainn about the accident on 97."

"Yeah, that's what Den and I were coming to ask you, Gabe was trying to explain. So, what happened, who had a wreck?"

Lorraine caught Jay and Den up on all the details, informing them that the accident was about 45 minutes from the B&B, and traffic had been stopped so the care flight could land. Jay's face held the same disbelief as Rainn's when Lorraine told them the victim had to be lifted.

"Wow, did you see what the car looked like?"

"No, I didn't, the car was flipped over and surrounded by first responders."

Jay thought about Drew and hoped that she was sitting in front of Marcus dry and warm, but it didn't matter how much Jay tried to be optimistic about Drew's whereabouts his soul wouldn't settle until he knew for sure Drew was sitting in front of Marcus.

Just as Jay went to call Drew a call from Marcus came through. Jay's heart dropped into the pit of his stomach.

HOURS LATER....

Jay pushed the button on the vending machine, his heart trembled with fear; the last time he'd been in Shiloh Regional this scared Yah had taken Shantel.

"UGH, REALLY!" Jay yelled at the machine that held on to the bag of chips he'd just purchased.

Den noticed the altercation between man and machine and hurried to assist. "Hey, babe, you good?"

Jay continued to kick the machine. Den could tell Jay was taking his frustrations and fears out on the device, and she needed him to get a grip before they were all kicked out.

"Jay, you need to calm down, here take this." Den tried to hand Jay a dollar.

Jay looked at the dollar Den held in her hand. "I'm good." Jay walked off leaving Den standing there holding the dollar.

Den was mortified, thinking how could Jay just walk off on her like that. Den took the dollar and put it back in her purse, as much as she wanted to scream Den held it in.

Marcus watched Jay's actions with Den and noticed the look on her face; the image looked familiar to Marcus as he thought back to the day Shantel died, and Drew rejected him the same way.

Marcus tapped Jay on the shoulder handing him a bag of chips. "I thought you might want these."

Jay turned and looked at Marcus taking the chips. "Thanks bro, the dang machine took my money."

"So, you took it out on Den. I saw what you did, and it wasn't cool. Den's just trying to be there for you. Remember how I tried to be there for Drew when Shantel passed, and she rejected me?"

Jay threw a chip in his mouth thinking back on that day and felt terrible. Jay shook his head with disappointment looking over at Den standing by the vending machine. Jay gave Marcus some dap, walked over to Den and apologized.

Marcus looked over at Sarge and could see the fear and hurt in his eyes. Out of all the people in the room Marcus thought for sure Sarge would be the strongest, but he was just as shaken by the fact Drew was fighting for her life just beyond the double doors as everyone else. Loraine tried her best to comfort Sarge, but the tears wouldn't stop falling from his eyes.

Marcus looked over at Jay's parents, his parents. Pete and Miss Sue, they seem to all be in their own personal conversation with Yah, so Marcus felt maybe that was something he should do as well. Marcus left the group in search of a quiet place to pray.

After a brief search Marcus found himself sitting on a bench in front of the fountain outside the hospital, it seemed to be the only place he could be alone. Marcus inhaled the fresh air and exhaled his fears as he began to pray.

"What's up Yah, I want to first say thank you. Man, I know if it had not been for you I wouldn't be sitting here now. Yah, I need you right now man, we all do but especially Drew. Yah, I need you to work on her behalf. I know we not deserving, but I'm asking for you to have favor over us. Man, Yah I don't know what to say or ask for, usually I'm on top of my stuff, but right now I'm lost. I can tell you all the things I'll do if you let her stay, and I can tell you all the things I want do to ever hurt her again, but I'm not. I'm going to ask you to give me strength to accept your will, and to give me guidance if your will honors my prayer. Guidance to follow you and allow me to be who you need me to be. Yah, I love that woman in there fighting for her life, and I haven't always put her first, and I know I don't deserve to have her as my own, and if that's your will I understand, but Yah please don't take her from me, from us. My trust is in you, I ask you give the doctors and nurses the knowledge to help her. I ask that you…

Marcus could no longer hold it together, before he knew it he was head down crying his eyes out. Marcus didn't care who seen him he needed this cry; the three years locked up, losing Drew, and now Drew fighting for her life, Marcus was long overdue for a good cry.

After returning from his prayer Marcus could see not much had changed, everyone seemed to be in their own world and space. Marcus guessed the news came as a shock to everyone, and they were still trying to process it.

Marcus noticed Sarge standing by the vending machines so he walked over to ensure he was in a good mindset.

"What's up, Sarge, you good?" Marcus clutched Sarge's shoulder for a bit of touch therapy.

"Nah, man, I ain't no good right now this is tearing me up. I haven't had enough time, I...

Marcus stopped Sarge. "You still have time."

"I don't know, it's not looking too good, Marcus."

"Look, Sarge, I know you don't get the whole Israelite way of life and that's understandable, but you serve the same God I serve, he watches over those who put their trust in him, and know for sure Drew puts all her trust in Yah; she has since she was a kid. Palms 91 has always been her favorite, and when I think about the passage I know Yah's going to take care of her because Drew wholeheartedly believes what it says."

Sarge eyed Marcus and the words he spoke ruffled his heart because he remembered a time he believed just like that, and for the first time in a long time his heart was beginning to humble before God once again. Sarge thought about all the obstacles Drew had faced since he'd been in her life and the ones before he entered her life, and it was nothing short of a miracle that she was still standing, so the words Marcus had just spoken confirmed it was Yah carrying her the whole time.

Sarge cleared his throat. "Thanks, young buck" I needed those words. If Drew can have that much trust in Yah with all she's been through, why can't I."

The double doors opened, and a doctor emerged asking for the family of Drewlynn McCain. Everyone stood at attention, waiting to hear good news. The doctor informed the group that Drew had to be put in a comma state because of the bleeding on her brain, and she would have to remain that way until it stopped. He also told them that she had spinal trauma that could cause penalization if the swelling didn't go down and that she suffered a broken leg as well.

The doctor looked at the hopeful group and shook his head in disbelief. "Miss McCain is beyond blessed to still be here. I've seen accidents like this before, and they're usually fatal. The impact alone should have killed her."

After the update the group flooded the doctor with questions. Marcus advised everyone to calm down and allow the good doctor to answer one at a time. By the time everyone asked their question, it was basically everything he'd already informed them about.

Walking into the hospital room looking at Drew hooked up to all the wires hurt Jay to the core of his heart it seemed like millions of wires to him, but Drew was only hooked up to three. Still, it killed Jay to see Drew this way; he'd been to see her every day since her accident, but it hadn't gotten any easier.

Jay sat down in the chair beside Drew's bed watching the monitors, looking at all the flowers, cards, and pictures Gabe had drawn. "Todah Yah for saving my friend." Jay whispered looking down at Drew. A single tear came from his eye as he began to praise Yah; he was so involved in his praise he didn't feel Drew sat up in the bed.

Drew leaned over towards Jay, then took her finger and placed it in the middle of his forehead.

"Imagine that a dime, and I'm asking for the thoughts on your mind."

The sound of Drew's voice sent a jolt of electricity through Jay's heart. "DREW! Jay yelped out. "What are you doing, lay down." Jay gently laid Drew back on the pillow, then took the controller and raised the head of Drew's hospital bed.

"Thanks Jay, you're my hero." Drew chuckled.

"Drew, I'm sorry, the thought of being mad at you for protecting your peace when it came to Marcus is spanking my heart; how could I be so deliberately obtuse when it came to your feelings." Jay shook his head in disappointment.

"Wow, just jump right in there."

"I'm for real Drew, I was a complete hole, and I ask Yah if he let you stay with us that would be the first thing I did."

"Yeah, you were a complete A-Hole, and I didn't like you." Drew gave Jay a wink. "But you've already apologized and it's ok."

Jay shook his head in disbelief. "What happened, Drew?"

"I'm still not sure, I went to call Marcus to cancel our meeting, and next thing I know I'm waking up here. The Doctor and nurses came in about an hour ago, checked my vitals, told me I was in an accident, rechecked my vitals and left. They told me they would be back to run a test, but that was over an hour; I guess they're taking their time." Drew chuckled.

The tears began to fall from Jay's eyes uncontrollably as he held Drew in an intense embrace. Jay hugged Drew so tight she could hardly breathe. "Todah Yah, he allowed you stay with us."

Drew indulged in the embrace, but she was slightly confused about why Jay was so emotional and why he held her so tight.

"Jay, I'm fine calm down, you act as if I died and came back."

Jay released Drew from their embrace. "Drew, you really don't remember?"

"No, Jay, I don't remember. Can you tell me what happened?"

"You almost died, Drew."

"What do you mean almost died?" Drew was confused at the words coming from Jay's mouth.

Jay looked at Drew in amazement. "Drew, you hit a light pole, flipped three times, broke three bones in your leg, and flatlined three times before they got you here; you had to be put in a comma state because of the bleeding on your brain, and you could've even been paralyzed."

Drew looked at Jay shocked she'd been through all that. "How long have I been in here?"

"Three weeks today."

"Are you serious, other than this cast and a little fatigue, I feel just fine?"

Jay shook his head, he was looking at a living miracle. "Wow Drew, this is unbelievable, the entire family has been here around the clock: me, momma, daddy, Sarge, Den, and Marcus. Gabe drew you all these pictures, momma and Den loaded you with the flowers, and everyone's else kinda hung around and made sure you were comfortable."

Drew looked up towards heaven and the biggest smile rolled across her face. "Miracles and blessings, Todah Yah. Those who go to Yah for safety will be protected by Yah all-powerful. I will say to Yah, you are my place of safety and protection. You are my God, and I trust you. Palms 91." Drew looked at Jay and smiled.

CHAPTER 34

Prayer & Patience

Miss Sue was busy preparing lunch for the guests when Rainn walked into the kitchen. Miss Sue looked over her glasses at Rainn, she could tell the young lady had a lot on her mind, and this was a plea for help.

"What's the reason Rainn?" Miss Sue asked.

"I hate Miss Drew's down this place doesn't feel the same."

Miss Sue continued to eye Rainn, she knew her excuse for being in a funk was a cover-up and knew precisely the problem.

"You know Rainn, it would be easier if you just talk to Tevin."

Rainn looked at Miss Sue sideways. "Huh, what are you talking about, this has nothing to do with Tevin."

Rainn tried to deny the charges, but Miss Sue wouldn't allow her to back out on her feelings.

"Don't you huh me, I know exactly what's wrong with you. It's that Tevin fella he has your whole mood in his hand, he's a lot difficult than what you intended him to be huh?" Miss Sue laughed.

Rainn shook her head, she didn't know how but Miss Sue knew exactly what was going on, and she was right, her whole mood for the past few weeks had been because of Tevin.

"I just wanted to be there for him Miss Sue, but he acted like I did something bad."

Rainn went on and on about Tevin, and Miss Sue listened. After about ten minutes of Rainn's venting Miss Sue spoke.

"I don't understand why young people make the courtship so hard." Miss Sue shook her head. "Back in my day conversation ruled the nation, now young people text three words and act like you've said something."

Rainn took a deep breath and exhaled. "But Miss Sue, I've tried talking with Tevin, but he shut me out."

"Did you talk to him or at him. Rainn you must speak to a man calm and sweet, almost like you're talking to a baby, then when you get him to the point where he's expressing himself allow him to do that with no interruptions. Now, this may take some time but be patient, and ask Yah what you can do to help the situation."

Miss Sue looked at Rainn and raised a brow. "Prayer and Patients sweetheart, learn this now for the future because life will require lots of Prayers and Patients; this will lead you to Peace."

Rainn gave Miss Sue a soft smile. "Thanks, Miss Sue."

"You're welcome, now put this snack tray on the breakfast table." Miss Sue handed Rainn a snack tray filled with all sorts of treats.

"Wow, now this is what I call a snack tray, the guests are going to love this." Rainn swiped an olive from the tray, tossing it into her mouth.

"That's not for the guests it's for Drew, she asked for that tray, a small cake, and a pint of ice cream."

Rainn looked at Miss Sue and chuckled. "Dang, when Drew said she was going to enjoy her birthday alone this year she didn't lie."

Rainn took the tray and headed to the dining room. Miss Sue chuckled, looking at the young lady prancing away with a smile did her heart well, knowing Rainn felt better and saw things a little clearer.

After a couple of hours of transferring files from Drew's prehistoric desktop to her new laptop Rainn was in much need of a mental break; she didn't know so many files could be stored. Drew kept a file on everything from Q tips to stovetops.

Rainn shook her head as she pushed back from Drew's desk. "Oh lord, I'm tired boss," Rainn said to herself before grabbing her phone from the desk then proceeding to the front counter.

Rainn was enjoying a private photoshoot with herself when she suddenly felt a presence staring at her, and just like she figured it was Tevin standing in the middle of the floor chuckling to himself.

"I don't think your phone can hold all that beauty."

Rainn sat her phone on the counter and readied herself for battle; Tevin was on her turf now and she wasn't having none of that ruler slapping on her counter. Rainn paused thinking back on Miss Sue's words as she eyed Tevin standing in the middle of the room; It had been a few weeks since their last decent conversation, so this was her chance to put Miss Sue's theory to the test.

Rainn eyed Tevin, and in the softest voice she could speak thanked him for the compliment, adding a smile, a smile that weakened Tevin like kryptonite weakened Superman.

Tevin took the smile as an invitation to move closer, and as he did he started to apologize for taking his frustrations out on her and being an *ass*. Tevin vowed to Rainn if she forgave him, he'd show her his loyalty in return.

Rainn eyed Tevin: the sincerity in his apology had her heart doing flips. Miss Sue was right, the kindness alone had Tevin acting like a totally different person. Rainn grabbed her phone from the counter and asked Tevin to pose for a picture.

Tevin laughed. "Oh, so now we gotta capture the moment."

"Yeah, of course, this is the beginning of our journey."

Tevin gazed at Rainn, and before he could stop himself he'd planted a kiss on her cheek.

"What's that for?" Rainn blushed.

"Just being you."

Rainn smiled, continuing their photoshoot.

Marcus chuckled looking at Rainn and Tevin pose for the camera, he'd been standing there for about five minutes and the pair hadn't noticed him yet. Marcus cleared his throat to gain their attention. Rainn immediately put her phone away when she heard the thunderous hint given by Marcus.

"I'm sorry, Mr. Styles, I mean Mr. Marcus, I mean...

Marcus could see Rainn was nervous about getting caught taking selfies on company time, so scared she was still using his fake name.

"It's ok Rainn, Marcus will be fine." Marcus then looked back at Tevin. "What's up man, you good?"

Tevin nodded his head, ensuring he was good.

Marcus peered at Tevin for a moment. "Hey, do I know you from somewhere?"

"I can't say I've seen you before, Mr." Tevin gave Marcus a half-smile.

Marcus continued to look at Tevin, but this time squinting his eyes. Marcus wasn't sure who the young man was, but he knew their paths had crossed somewhere before.

"You gotta excuse me youngin, but your face sho looks familiar."

Tevin was literally shaking in his boots remembering Marcus from the night he'd robbed him at the barbershop. Tevin wanted to go ahead and repent his sin to Marcus because he knew Drew cared for him, and she always told him to be honest with her, and right now he wasn't holding up his end of the bargain.

Marcus shrugged his shoulders. "Maybe you just have one of those familiar faces. What's up man, I'm Marcus."

"Good to meet you Marcus, I'm Tevin."

The men gave each other dap.

Marcus then looked back at Rainn and asked was Drew in. Rainn wasn't sure if Drew wanted to see Marcus, so she was hesitant to send him to her location.

"Um, let me call her first." Rainn ran off to Drew's office to confirm with her that it would be okay for Marcus to come back.

Marcus looked at Tevin and shook his head. Tevin could see that Marcus was nervous about the answer he'd receive by the way he taped the box of flowers waiting for Rainn's return.

"Relax, she'll say yes Drew's kind like that."

Marcus gave Tevin a smile. "Yes, she is, sometimes too kind."

Marcus took another look at Tevin; he wasn't sure who this young man was, but he could tell he cared for Drew. "So, how you know Drew."

Tevin's mind went blank, not expecting a question to come after his comment. "It's a long story, let's just say she's my earth angel."

Marcus was impressed with Tevin's answer, not satisfied but impressed. "Wow, you can't add anything to that."

Tevin looked at Marcus and smiled, delighted he'd gained some *brownie points;* then maybe later if he was found out it would go smooth.

The men talked amongst themselves until Rainn came back with a response. Both Tevin and Marcus stood at attention when she entered the room. Rainn eyed the two men she could feel both their anxiousness.

"Goodness, relax, the both of you look as if you're about to receive results from a paternity test."

The two men looked at each other and laughed, neither of them could deny the allegations, the ten-minute wait felt like an eternity.

"What did she say?" Tevin asked, he was excited and curious to know the answer. Tevin had been at the B&B for over a month, and from the stories he'd heard about Marcus, and his encounter with Zae, Tevin had already put money on Marcus being Drew's pick.

Rainn smiled at Marcus, just as much as Tevin was team Marcus so was she. Rainn had only known Drew to love one man and that was Marcus, so Rainn wanted to keep it that way.

"Miss Drew said she will see you."

Happiness bounced in all three of their hearts.

"Drew's in the sunroom." Rainn looked at Marcus and smiled.

"Thank you, Rainn." Marcus gave her a gentle smile and Tevin some dap before proceeding to the sunroom.

Rainn and Tevin watched Marcus as he went to reclaim his love for Drew, both pleased that this could be the step Marcus needed to take in order to reclaim his woman.

Drew sat in the bay window enjoying a book from one of her favorite authors, *Elisheba Yisrael* eating a bowel of grapes; she'd been home a few days and could get used to the fuss everyone was making over her. Drew had barely lifted a finger to turn the pages of her own book.

Marcus stood back indulging in Drew's beauty, stunned by the strength and dignity Drew held, she had been knocked down more than a few times, but here she stood just as firm as before; it was nothing short of amazing to Marcus, and this is one of the reasons he loved her.

Marcus knocked on the door frame to gain Drew's attention. "Hey, how are you."

"I'm just fine Marcus, come in and have a seat."

Marcus sat down beside Drew and handed her the box of flowers.

"Wow, Lilly's how sweet of you, they're beautiful."

Marcus smiled at Drew bashfully. "Of course, beautiful flowers for a beautiful woman."

There was a moment of awkward silence between the two, neither of them knowing what to say. Drew admired the lily's trying to avoid the elephant in the room. This would be the first time she'd seen Marcus since before her accident. Jay told her he was there at the hospital around the clock putting everything on pause, but Drew didn't remember any of it. Marcus even paid Drew's hospital bill, asking the hospital and Jay to keep it anonymous.

"I don't think I've ever received Lilly's from anyone before. Thank you, Marcus."

Marcus fluffed the pillows under Drew's leg. "So, how's the leg, how are they treating you here?"

"They're treating me like a princess and a handicap." Drew laughed. "And the leg is coming along; I was told once it started to itch that meant the healing process was beginning."

Marcus picked up the customed made clothes hanger lying across the table. "And I see we have the suitable device for the job."

Drew laughed. "Tevin made that for me, he's such a sweetheart and can you believe he's Den's little brother?"

"Wow, are you serious, maybe that's why he looks so familiar. Anyway, I met him a few minutes ago, it's good you have a young man around here. I can tell he's very fond of you."

"Yeah, him and Rainn or my protectors, so they think."

Marcus nodded his head in agreement. "No doubt, I almost had to go through a whole background check before I could see you."

Marcus peered out at the guests on the deck enjoying the warmth from the chimenea, and Drew observed him. All she wanted to do was release the hurt she held for Marcus. Drew knew if this was done she could move on from him, but Drew's heart was staggered.

Drew couldn't believe how much Marcus had changed, being incarcerated had really matured him in ways Drew couldn't even imagine. She could tell in his walk, talk, and in his touch that he wasn't the same man, and for this reason a small part of Drew didn't wanna let him go. That part of Drew wanted to know who this new person was and if he could finally love her the way her heart desired.

Drew stroked Marcus's arm breaking his trance. "Thank you for being there, Jay told me you were always there." Drew swallowed her tears. "I'm glad you're home safe Marcus."

Marcus wrapped his arms around Drew consuming every bit of her. Drew melted like butter in his arms there was almost none of her left before she remembered this was the very thing she didn't want controlling her anymore.

Drew pulled from Marcus's embrace. "Marcus, wait, there's something I need to say."

Drew paused, and just as she was about to speak Zae walked through the door holding a giant teddy bear and a package of Oreos.

"Happy Birthday Drewlynn McCain," Zae yelped out.

Drew was mortified, and by the look on Marcus's face he was as well.

Zae paused his words and steps, eyeing the pair, shocked to see Marcus there and sitting so close.

Drew wondered where the *hell* was Rainn and Tevin and which one authorized this, knowing Marcus was there. Drew knew they were behind this monstrosity, and they would pay.

Marcus took a deep breath and exhaled, gazing into Drew's eyes, their heartbeat the same rhythm. Marcus didn't care that Zae was there, he'd asked for this time, so he took it.

Marcus went into his pocket and pulled out a box. "Happy birthday Drew." Marcus kissed Drew on the cheek, stood up, and proceeded to the door, but not before stopping to greet Zae. Marcus knew this man *existed,* because Jay knew this man *existed*, and this was cool, there was no need for panic. Marcus knew what he'd ask Yah for, and now he would have to be patient and wait.

"Enjoy your evening Drew Boo." Marcus gave Drew a gentle smile.

Drew quickly put the gift in her jacket pocket and turned her attention to Zae. "What are you doing here?"

Zae shook the little green monster off his shoulders and continued as if Marcus was never there.

"Aww, look at you, I'm sorry it took me so long to get here, I had meetings for days." Zae tried to make Drew more comfortable, explaining his reason for not being there sooner.

Drew noticed Zae trying to make himself a bigger deal than Marcus with the extra care and explanation that wasn't needed.

"Zae, stop, you don't have to do that, Marcus was just here checking on me."

Zae couldn't believe it was evident that he was annoyed by Marcus being there. "I'm sorry, Drew, seeing you with Marcus kinda made me feel some type of way, dang I don't wanna lose you before I have you."

Drew was impressed that Zae wasn't hesitant about staking claim to her. "Zae, what are you doing here?"

"Well, I had to bring you this." Zae handed Drew the gifts.

"Aw, Zae, you didn't have to do that." Drew gave Zae a hug.

The affection from Drew's hug sent Zae into orbit. "I couldn't miss your birthday, and with you being stuck in the house alone didn't sit right with me."

"Aww, you're special, Zae."

"No, you are," Zae went into his jacket and pulled out a DVD, then handed it to Drew.

"OMG, Zae, A Different World, where did you find this?" Drew loved the gift, it meant a lot that Zae took heed to a conversation they'd had about their favorite show as kid, and Drew telling him her was ADW. Drew also told him she'd had the show on VHS, but between her move from Atlanta, to Jay's, and then to the B&B it was lost.

Zae knew he'd struck gold when he heard the excitement in Drew's voice and the smile on her face. "I got my connect."

"Wow, I've looked everywhere for this." Drew examined the DVD. "I will be in my room for the next three weeks, nobody bothers me." Drew said jokingly. "And it's all six seasons."

"I'm glad you love it, now can I join you for the next three weeks?" Zae stroked Drew's face and gave her the sweetest kiss.

Drew pulled away from Zae, not expecting the kiss. "Zae, I think we needed a friendship line."

Zae looked at Drew puzzled. "What's a friendship line?"

"A line that can't be crossed when it comes to us. A line that will protect our friendship."

"So, is this line invisible, or can you see this line?" Zae leaned in closer, kissing Drew once more.

Drew sat in the middle of her bed with her injured leg propped on a pillow, enjoying all the treats she'd asked Miss Sue to get for her private birthday celebration. Not only did Miss Sue get the goodies Drew asked for, but she'd also decorated Drew's bedroom. Miss Sue had emerald and silver balloons everywhere and a cute little table set up in the middle of the room draped with emerald and silver beads and streamers. The table held party favors and a tiny cake; you would have thought Drew had friends over.

Drew's eyes were glued to the television; although she'd seen this episode a million times for some reason this watch had her thinking about herself, Zae, and Marcus. Was she wanting Marcus and Zae like Whitley wanted Dewayne and Julian? Drew tried to shake the thoughts from her head, but they were coming in one after another, so many that she'd stop watching the tv show and started episodes of her own.

Drew evaluated herself, her actions, and her life, and as strong as she tried to be at that moment she broke. Drew's thoughts went four months back, even farther than that, but the events she seem to be resting on were Serenity Meadow's birth, Marcus getting out, Tevin and Den's dysfunctions, Zae and his article, the accident, and Turning 33.

"I have too much to be thankful for, but why do I feel so empty." Drew said to herself with tears in her eyes.

Drew turned the tv off and stretched out her arms, pleading for Yah to give her strength and guide her in the direction he wanted her to go. Drew had been standing strong for so long; she forgot how it felt to break.

Drew was determined that this time with Yah be filled with true intimacy, so she hoped from the bed to the floor and lay prostrate before Yah, confessing all her sins and shortcomings. Drew cried out for Yah to help guide her on the new journey, she cried out that Yah would help Den and Tevin with their mother, she cried out that Yah shows her what to do about Zae and Marcus. Drew cried out in Praise for Serenity Meadows, she cried out in Praise for Yah sparing her life in the accident, she cried out in Praise for her family and friends, she cried out in Praise for Yah's mercy and grace; Drew's mission was to lose herself in Praise, and that's what she did.

Drew had been lost in Praise for a moment when she finally found her way back, exhausted and needed hydration, so she lifted herself from the floor and back to the bed. Drew was drained but never felt better; she hadn't felt that light in a long time, and she loved it. Drew couldn't believe she'd lost focus that fast. Looking towards heaven Drew sincerely apologized to Yah for the fall and vowed she would be careful to pay closer attention to his will and not get so distracted by things that kept her away from him.

CHAPTER 35

Decisions & Decisions

Drew stood on the porch awaiting her guest's arrival, finally her leg had healed, and she was back to the basics; although Drew missed being waited on hand and foot she was somewhat glad to be back to the usual.

Drew watched the black Lexus pull into the driveway, at the same time looking at her watch. "Prompted, I like that" Drew stated, she was excited to have one of the most significant design teams hired for her new project. Drew had decided to turn the pool house into an entertainment area/ apartment for Tevin and needed quality. Drew knew just the person for the job, Leah Reynolds, owner of *Simple Design*, the number two design team in Shiloh City. Drew knew going with Leah was her best option. Due to the accident Drew had to stop the expansion of *Serenity Meadows* and focus on adding more attractions to the Promise B&B. At first it ruffled Drew's feathers, but she knew it was all a part of Yah's plan, so she excepted it and kept moving.

Drew watched Leah as she exited the car, she didn't realize how beautiful she was; she'd spent so much time trying to figure out who the lady was and never noticed.

Rainn called Tevin's cell phone she knew if he wasn't there to get Ms. Reynolds bags Drew would flip.

“You rang?” By the second ring Tevin was emerging from the lounge area.

"Yes I did, Miss Drew's guest is here, The Fabulous Mrs. Reynolds."

Tevin looked at Rainn sideways. "And what's so fabulous about her?"

Rainn could tell Tevin wasn't impressed by her introduction. "Are you serious, Mrs. Reynolds is like number two in the design world."

Tevin looked at Rainn and shook his head. "I have no clue."

"Wow, I can't believe you don't know who Mrs. Reynolds is; she started her business only four years ago, and already designed over 3,000 homes and businesses. And we're not gonna talk about the number of celebrity homes she's designed; a lot of them could be seen on Celebrity Cribs.” Rainn eyed Tevin, hoping he’d got the brief bio.

“Anyway, I was calling so you'd be here to get Ms. Reynold's bags; you know how Drew is about the bags."

Tevin walked over to the window and peered out, he wanted to see what was so fabulous about Mrs. Reynolds. As Tevin looked out at the lady and Drew exchanged pleasantries Tevin's blood warmed, he started to sweat, and his lunch was making its way out aggressively.

Tevin looked back at Rainn holding his stomach. "I gotta go." Tevin hurriedly ran off to the bathroom in a panic.

Rainn shook her head as she watched Tevin disappear down the hall. "I guess when you gotta go, you gotta go."

Drew and Mrs. Reynolds walked through the door, and Rainn just knew Drew was about to throw a dramatic fit when she noticed Tevin was *MIA*, but Drew was so busy cozying up to Mrs. Reynolds she didn't see, nor did she comment on Tevin's whereabouts.

"This is Rainn, my front desk clerk/Director."

"How Are You Mrs. Reynolds!" Rainn was boiling with excitement. “I just wanna let you know Mrs. Reynolds I love your work; what you did in Lexy's house was fantastic, and...

"Ok, Rainn, Mrs. Reynolds is only staying a few days." Drew gave Rainn the eye.

"It's ok Drew," Mrs. Reynolds smiled at Rainn. “Thanks for following me Rainn, it's always my pleasure to meet a fan of my work."

"Mrs. Reynolds, since it's no problem can I ask you something?"

"Sure, Rainn, ask away."

"Is Lexy really a whiner?" Rainn waited anxiously for the response.

Drew was shocked but not surprised by Rainn's question, she'd spent so much time in the *star's* business she barely could tend to her own.

"Rainn, not today, I'm sorry Leah, sometimes Rainn can be a little outspoken."

Drew grabbed Leah's bags and proceeded up the stairs looking over at Rainn shaking her head.

As Rainn watched Drew and Mrs. Reynolds walk up the stairs she also shook her head. Rainn tried her best to keep Drew's mind off Tevin not being there but wasn't sure it worked. Drew still didn't say anything or ask any questions about him, which scared Rainn because she knew Drew's silence was deadly.

After showing Leah to her room and the layout of the pool house Drew was in Rainn's face inquiring what happened to Tevin and why he wasn't there to get the bags. Drew was hot; the lack of responsibility Tevin had shown had her blood pressure through the roof.

"And another thing." Drew yelped out, Rainn was getting the lashes meant for Tevin and boy was she loaded, but Rainn didn't say a word while Drew fussed and ranted about Tevin's lack of responsibility; she let it roll off her back but Tevin had to come see her.

Sparks were really flying as Ma Tate and Den stood at the check-out counter listening to Drew give someone the business.

Gabe shook his head. "Somebody got Auntie Drew mad, I bet it was daddy."

"Shh, Gabe, that's not our business." Ma. Tate nudged his shoulder.

"Well, why are we listening then?"

Ma. Tate and Den eyed one another.

Drew emerged from the office, the trio eyed her, scared to say a word. Drew looked as if she could bite the head off a snake. Gabe was the only one brave enough to speak up.

"Hey, Auntie Drew, why are you fussing?" Gabe jumped into her arms. "Did my daddy make you mad again?"

Drew kissed Gabe's cheek. "I'm sorry baby, Auntie Drew wasn't fussing, and your dad's on aunties good side for once."

"That's not what it sounded like to me." Gabe fondled Drew's earrings.

Ma Tate embraced Drew. "Did we come at a bad time?"

Drew put Gabe down and rubbed her head. "Nah, I'm just trying to get back into the swing of things; there's a lot I need to strengthen out around here starting with the help."

Drew eyed Rainn as she emerged from the office in humiliation. Drew started to feel bad about how she'd handled Rainn, it wasn't her fault Tevin was slacking.

"Rainn, I'm sorry, that lashing was meant for Tevin, and I took It out on you."

Rainn assured Drew it was okay and she understood, but now Den was a little frazzled with Tevin.

Den looked around the B&B. "Where is Tevin, I'll talk to him for you."

"Nah Den, It's okay, he's my employee and my problem."

"Are you sure, Drew, because I can ruff him up for ya?"

The women laughed.

"Nah, I'm going to let Rainn have him," Drew looked over at Rainn giving her a wink.

Gabe opened the door to the shed, he didn't waste any time telling Tevin that Drew was upset with him. Tevin gave Gabe some dap and asked him about everything that was said.

After Gabe told Tevin all that he'd seen and heard Tevin knew for sure Drew would be all over him. Tevin started to sand down a birdhouse thinking about the lashing and Gabe watched closely, taking a piece of extra sandpaper from the workbench attempting to sand down a scrap piece of wood.

Tevin noticed Gabe trying to mimic him, so he took Gabe's hand and guided it up and down the wood. "Do it like this." Gabe giggled, he was excited to be learning something from Tevin; Gabe really looked up to him so Tevin always tried to show and tell Gabe the right things. That's why Tevin knew he had to make it right with Drew.

Tevin looked down at Gabe. "So, your Auntie pretty mad huh?"

"Yep, she was hollering at Rainn and everything."

Tevin shook his head. "Dang, now Rainn gonna be mad."

"Sure is." Gabe shook his head.

Tevin laughed out. "What you know about it."

Gabe chuckled. "I know a lot about that because when Den mad at my daddy he has that same look you got on your face right now." Gabe laughed out.

The women were gathered in the sunroom trying to figure out what to do for Gabe's fifth birthday. Gabe had pleaded for a *Spider-Man* party; now the issue was where to have it. Den suggested the Pier, but Drew informed her Gabe had already made it clear that he didn't want a party at *Mystic Pier* this year but instead wanted a big boy party, somewhere *Spider-Man* could hang from the ceiling.

The woman laughed at Gabe's innocence, but Drew blamed the growth on Raleigh, Gabe's new best friend. Drew told the ladies since Gabe started school this little girl had clutched on to him, changing his mind about everything; he'd traded *Woody and Buz* for *Spider-Man*, the *Pier* for *Urban Air*, and his *French fries* for *apples*. Drew didn't really know where the last one came from, but she blamed that on Raleigh too.

Ma Tate laughed, "Wow, Drew, doesn't that sound familiar." Ma Tate told the ladies when Drew moved in next door Jay just about forgot about his brother Shawn for Drew; the games they played, the movies they watched, and the foods they enjoyed.

Ma Tate chuckled. "I remember one day Shawn storming in the house, he was in a rage, venting that Drew was trying to steal his brother from him, and all Jay wanted to do was what Drew wanted to do."

The women laughed at the story but Drew thought back on that day, she remembered Shawn getting mad because she wanted Jay to go on a mission to find ET and Shawn wanted him to play kickball. Drew never knew Shawn felt she was stealing Jay from him. Now it all made sense to her; it wasn't that Shawn didn't like her, he was jealous of her and Jay's relationship.

"Wow," Drew said to self. *"If only Shawn had told me."*

"Drew!" Ma Tate called her name for the second time finally breaking her trance. "What do you think about Gabe's party being here?"

"That's fine, Ma Tate." Drew was still joyed by the insight she'd just received from Ma Tate's story.

The women talked amongst themselves when Tevin and Gabe walked into the room. The women were so busy discussing the party they didn't hear the young men enter.

"Excuse me," Tevin yelped out. "Drew, can I speak with you?"

Drew looked up from the discussion and eyed Tevin, she could tell by the look on his face he was scared and unsure about approaching her.

"You have a lot of explaining to do Tevin, where were you earlier?"

Tevin fumbled his words while Gabe held on to his hand. Gabe could tell that Tevin was scared because of the sweat coming from his hand. Gabe pulled his hand from Tevin's and proceeded to show Drew his wet hands, revealing to her how scared Tevin was and she should just forgive him before he melted.

Gabe had the women in tears from laughing so hard at his statement. Drew looked at Tevin, then back at Gabe, how could she refuse such a sweet face.

"Ok, I'll give you a pass because your stomach was messed up, but Riann took your lashing and that my dear you're gonna have to take up with her."

Drew looked over at Rainn, giving her a wink accompanied by a devious smile.

"Yeah, answers, I need answers, baby." Rainn yelped out.

Tevin thanked Drew for her pardon, but the fear of facing Rainn was still there, and when he looked at her and didn't receive a smile it frightened him even more.

"I'm sorry," Tevin stated the words to Rainn only using his lips.

"You owe me," Rainn responded only using her lips.

No one else noticed the conversation between the two but Gabe did, watching them bot closely.

Den looked over at Tevin, she could tell something more than his stomach was bothering him by the nervous look on his face, and the awkward way he stood there as if he wanted to say something and didn't know how.

"Ethan, are you just fine?" Den asked.

Tevin took a deep breath. "Can I speak with you privately?"

"Sure, Ethan." Den removed herself from the discussion and followed Tevin.

Den and Tevin walked out to the pool house to be alone; she didn't understand why Tevin wanted to come all the way out there when it was plenty of rooms in the B&B.

Den had a quizzical look on her face. "What's good Ethan, you, ok?"

Tevin stared at Den with a brooding look on his face. "She's here."

"Who's here?"

"Your Mother." Tevin paced back and forth.

Den's heart fell into the pit of her stomach, startled by Tevin's words. "What do you mean she's here?"

"She's here Den at the B&B, she's designing this pool house for Drew."

Den began to pace back in forth in sequence with Tevin, nervously. "Did she see you?"

"No, I faked a stomachache before she came in."

Den paused a minute, messaging her temple. "OH MY God, why is she here?"

"I'm here because Drew wants me here." Leah walked from behind the plastic dividing the room. Den and Tevin were frozen in shock from their mother's voice.

The pair turned around to see Leah standing there holding wallpaper samples. Leah stretched out her arms, giving her children an open invitation to an embrace. Den hurried to hug her mother, but Tevin held back; he hadn't seen his mother in almost four years, and matter how much Den said she'd changed, he wasn't falling for it.

Leah looked over at Tevin disappointed that he still didn't trust her.

"Oh, come on baby, momma has missed you."

"Naw, I'm good." Tevin didn't move; he knew he loved his mother but he didn't trust her.

Tevin stood in place watching Den and his mother indulge in each other presence. "Why you always gotta mess things up?" Tears fell from Tevin's eyes as he stormed from the pool house.

Leah looked into Den's eyes while gently caressing her face, she knew how Tevin felt about her, but Den was her support, her go-to. "I've missed you, Dina."

As much as Den wanted to be excited about the reunion with her mother she wore the same feelings as Tevin.

"Ma, what are you doing here, I haven't seen or heard from you in months."

Leah walked over to the wall matching the wallpaper samples. "I was doing my own thang, giving you kids a break, then Drew called and needed my assistance with this pool house."

"Ma, how did she even know to contact you?"

"I was here at Serenity's grand opening; if you had answered your phone that day you'd known that."

Den couldn't deny the charges she'd ignored all of Leah's phone calls that day, avoiding any drama she was trying to bring her way.

"You're right, I didn't answer that day because I didn't want to get caught up in any of your mess. Why are you here Ma, to mess up our lives again?" Den shook her head in disappointment. "Drew knows what type of mother you are, Tevin told her after I found him living and working here for her. Drew asked questions after discovering that we were siblings, so Tevin and I gave her a rough draft of our life with you. Ma, Tevin and I are good here; Drew's good to Tevin, Jay's good to me, so please do your job and leave us alone."

Leah was in tears from the request Den made. "Wow, I've worked my ass off for years getting clean and sober, building my business for my family, and this is the thanks and congratulations I get?"

The words Leah spoke made Den furious. "Congratulations, I'll give you that much, but Thanks, woman are you crazy? I have taken care of you, daddy, and Ethan most of my life; if anyone deserves any thanks it's me."

Den got in her mother's face. "Do your job and leave us alone."

Den stormed from the pool house leaving Leah in tears. Leah tried to calm herself, but the realization of how Den and Tevin felt about her was too painful to bear.

Leah hurried to retrieve her phone from the counter in a desperate plea for Den to forgive her.

GET SOME POPCORN AND SIT TIGHT....

Drew watched Gabe and his little friends enjoy the *Spider-Man* bounce house, she was grateful the party had gone as planned; about twenty kids were in attendance enjoying the festivities, and there wasn't a wet eye in sight.

"Everyone seems to be enjoying themselves." Drew took another look at the cake, then assisted Ma Tate with the plates.

Ma Tate put a hot dog and caramel apple wedges on each plate. "Yeah, we've been lucky so far."

"Tevin is going to be a hit; I know Gabe will be amazed." Drew stated.

"Speaking of Tevin, I think you better check on him."

Drew left Ma Tate with the children to see how Tevin was coming along with the Spiderman costume. Drew loved how Tevin was always willing to go the extra mile for her; it didn't matter if it was putting on a crazy outfit or cleaning the toilets, Tevin never complained about anything Drew asked him to do, and he always made sure he did his best.

Drew walked through the B&B humming, in search of Tevin when she noticed Den and Leah in the lounge area talking. Drew wondered what their conversation was about but didn't worry about it she needed Tevin.

On Drew's way upstairs to find Tevin Marcus walked through the door with his arms full of gifts.

"Aww now, don't run off, beautiful." Marcus gave Drew a charming smile.

Drew looked at Marcus and returned the smile. "Good afternoon, Mr. Tidwell, the parties in the back."

"Can I get a hug or something?" Marcus didn't care when it was, or where it was he took every opportunity given to wrap his arm around Drew.

Marcus sat the gifts on the counter, and Drew took her place in his arms. Marcus held her just right and Drew received the embrace openly. The pair basked in the essence of each other's aura, recharging off each other's energy, sparking a current that was just about to start an *electrical confusion*.

Marcus and Drew were in the middle of their embrace when Zae walked through the door. Drew was shocked to see him there he hadn't given her a definite answer about attending the party, but here he stood; him and Asher.

Drew hurried to pull from Marcus's embrace, she couldn't believe Zae had caught them interacting once again. Drew knew Zae was insecure about Marcus, so she tried her best to be discreet whenever they were in the same place, which wasn't often but Drew respected her situationship with Zae.

"Wow, you made it." Drew kissed Zae on the cheek, then squatted down to greet Asher. "Hey there sir, you must be Asher." Drew gently took the child's hand.

Asher quickly took his hand back, then hid behind his fathers leg scared to greet Drew.

Marcus didn't want to be a blocker, so he greeted Zae and excused himself, but before Marcus left Drew asked if he would check on Tevin upstairs. Marcus was honored to run in circles for Drew, especially in front of Zae.

"Yeah Drew, I got you." Marcus ran upstairs to complete his mission.

Drew took the gifts Marcus brought for Gabe and escorted Zae and Asher to the backyard. Drew called Gabe over to meet Asher, and he came running with Raleigh in tow. Drew hoped that Gabe would be considerate and take Asher under his wing, but to Drew's surprise Raleigh was the one to do that. Taking Asher by the hand leading him to the treat table.

Drew laughed. "I guess she's gonna take care of them both."

Ma Tate, Loraine, Den, and Rainn had their eyes fixed on Drew *and* Zae. Neither of the women could believe their eyes if they'd taken them out and exchanged them for new ones; Drew was actually entertaining another man besides Marcus.

Drew took Zae by the hand and introduced him to the nosey women first and then the men. Drew knew everyone there was team Marcus, so she hoped everyone would be friendly and accepting.

As the party went on Drew was somewhat shocked by the crew's acceptance, she thought for sure they would make Zae feel out of place, but they were all getting along just fine, even Marcus was a good sport. Everyone enjoyed themselves, from the kids to the adults. The men were in one corner and the women in another.

Drew glanced over at the men when she noticed Marcus *and* Zae eyeing her. It was unreal, how could she ever have a relationship with anyone else long as Marcus was around.

Den nudged Drew and whispered, "Decision, Decision."

Drew gave Den a half-smile and shook her head.

Ma Tate and Drew cleaned up the deck; the party was a success and now it was time for clean-up.

Leah emerged from the pool house and took a nice long stretch and deep breath, allowing the brisk country air to refresh her; she'd been working around the clock trying to get the pool house finished for Drew.

Ma Tate looked over and noticed Leah standing there, becoming shocked and bothered she asked. "What is that woman doing here?"

"What woman?" Drew looked up and noticed Leah standing on the porch of the pool house. "She's designing the pool house for me."

Ma Tate eyed Drew. "You ought to be careful who you let in your house."

Drew cringed from Ma Tate's statement and tone, she felt it came from a place of anger. Drew didn't know the history between the two women, but this was her day to find out.

"Ma Tate, what's the deal with you and Leah, do yall know one another? She seems like a lovely lady to me."

"Everything that glitter ain't gold, Drew." Ma Tate responded sarcastically.

Ma Tate caressed Drew's face realizing how negative she must have sounded. "I'm sorry baby, just know me and that woman go a long way back, and she's done some unforgivable things."

Drew wanted more of the story, but she didn't push because she noticed how upset it made Ma Tate. All kinds of scenarios went through Drew's head, but the only one lingering was Leah had to be the woman Pops cheated on Ma Tate with.

Ma Tate grabbed Drew's hand startling her. "Listen to me Drew, you watch yourself around this woman, ok."

Drew sat a half-eaten cake on the kitchen counter, eyeing it, making plans for it later that night.

Zae stood in the doorway laughing. "Something tells me you've made future plans for that cake."

Drew chuckled. "Wow, how did you know."

Zae walked over to Drew and planted a kiss upon her lips with no hesitation. "I've been waiting to do that all day."

Drew blushed from Zae's actions. "Hey, that's crossing the friendship line. Do you remember the friendship line?"

"Who cares about the friendship line?" Zae took Drew in his arms and kissed her again, but this time with more passion.

Drew's heart raced, and the adrenaline pumped; it wasn't soon enough when Rainn came rushing through the door, sending Zae to one side of the kitchen and Drew to the other.

Rainn paused glaring at the pair, first at Drew, then at Zae. Rainn didn't witness an actual kiss, but she could tell their lips had been locked. *'It was a good one too.'* Rainn thought.

Rainn smiled bashfully at Drew. "Miss Drew, there's a lady here to see you, and you too." Rainn eyed Zae.

The pair eye each other wondering who would want to see them both, then Zae remembered he'd made arrangements for Asher's mom to pick him up there.

"I'm sorry Drew, but I asked Asher's mother to meet us here, I hope it's not a problem."

"It's fine, I'll get Asher."

Drew walked into the B&B after retrieving Asher, and to her surprise his dear sweet mother was no other than Rebecca Sims. *"You got to be kidding me,"* Drew said to herself.

Asher ran to his mother when noticing her standing at the check-in counter.

Drew was still in shock, she never knew Rebecca had a kid, and from the way Zae talked about his child's mother she didn't need one.

Rebecca looked up at Drew after completing a full body check on her son. "Wow, you just can't get a man of your own, can you."

Drew took a deep breath and exhaled. "Rebecca, I had no idea."

"Sure, you didn't, you never do."

Drew looked dagger at Zae waiting for him to step in, but he stood there like Rebecca had a spell on him.

Rebecca looked over at Zae. "How long has this been going on, Zae?"

Zae stood between the two women speechless and motionless, Asher pulling at his shirt, Rebecca in his ear, and sweat running down his face.

Drew and Rainn eyed one another, both wondering the same thing, Why wasn't he saying anything.

"Well, Zae, how long?" Rebecca poked at his chest.

"We can talk about this later." Zae eyed Drew as to say help.

Drew hurried to intervene. "Yes, talk about it later, you two can talk about it later."

Drew took a gift bag from the basket on the counter and handed it to Asher. "Thank you so much for coming Asher, I hope to see you again."

Rebecca let out a sigh. "I don't think so."

"Thanks for bringing him." Drew gave Zae a hug and sent him out the door with Rebecca.

Drew eyed Rainn. "You see, that's why."

Rainn nodded her head in agreement, now she knew precisely why Drew didn't date guys with kids and baby mommas.

Drew sat on the deck cozied up to the firepit relaxing when her phone went off. Drew looked down at the vibrating phone and shook her head; it was Zae again, this was his eighth call & eighth message, and Drew still wasn't answering. It was unappealing to Drew how Rebecca had Zae wrapped around her finger. Drew could understand being a good dad and supporting male in Rebecca's life, but this was ridiculous; Zae was like a scared child in the presence of Rebecca, and Drew couldn't deal.

Drew looked down at her phone as it started another round of vibration, she couldn't believe she'd gotten caught up with yet another one of Rebecca's men. Drew shook her head thinking back to Zae just standing there too scared of his *baby momma* to defend her honor.

Drew leaned forward to tease the fire when she felt something poke her; putting her hand in the jacket's pocket Drew pulled out the gift Marcus had given her on her birthday. Drew had forgotten all about the present, distracted by the DVD Zae had given her. Drew opened the box and pulled out a piece of paper that looked like it had been in the box for years. Drew's eyes got big and her mouth fell open when she started reading the words on the paper.

Date: 3/24/91

Time: 8:45pm

Song: I Love Your Smile

Where: Bedroom

Why: Thinking about you

What's up, Drew, I know you probably gonna throw this letter in the trash, but I don't care. Drew, I know I go with Rebecca, but I don't like her like that anymore. Since you and I have been working together on our Theater Arts project, I have wanted you. You are a lot different than what I thought. Your smile is pretty, and you are kind. You have been very patient with me, and I'm glad Ms. Draper paired us up. I know I gotta break up with Rebecca to go out with you. So, if you like me, please tell me so I can break up with Rebecca and go with you.

P.S. Do you like me? YES or No

P.S.S I really like your smile. Marcus

Drew couldn't believe her eyes it was the note Rebecca was so upset about. Drew examined a burn on the lower left corner of the note. Drew went back to that day after school when Rebecca confronted her about the note, and after telling Marcus about the altercation. Rebecca never said anything else to her about the note. Drew was smitten by the note; she couldn't believe Marcus held on to it after all those years, and why?

Drew was teary-eyed sitting on the deck holding the note, Marcus had always found a way to keep her loving him. Drew folded the letter to put it back in the box when she felt something else. Drew removed the green tissue paper which revealed the engagement ring Marcus had given her the night he proposed. Drew had left the ring at Jay's house forgetting all about it.

Drew shook her head, she could see Marcus was out to prove his love one way or another, while Zae couldn't make up his mind if he wanted to be loved by her or controlled by Rebecca. Drew looked down at the ring, slipping it on and off her finger.

"Looks like someone has some decisions to make," Leah stated while watching Drew fondle the ring.

Drew let out a sigh. "Decisions, Decisions, but not tonight."

Leah smiled at Drew, asking if she could join her. Drew welcomed Leah with open arms making room for her on the swing.

"Wow, you're working late."

"Yeah, trying to get it done; I know a week will be long enough for me to be in your hair."

Drew smiled at Leah. "Take your time it's no bother to me, honestly it's been nice having you here. Now, Tevin on the other hand will probably be glad you're gone."

Leah started to become nervous fearing Drew knew who she was. "I'm sorry, have I given Tevin something to dislike me about?"

Drew chuckled. "Oh no, you've done nothing, Tevin sleeps in the pool house and I know bunking with Pete hasn't been the easiest thing for him, so I'm sure he'll be happy when you're finished."

Leah laughed out, relieved that Drew was still clueless about who she was. "Oh, gurl, then let me be quick because Mr. Pete scares me."

The women laughed at the statement.

Drew eyed Leah thinking about the statement Ma Tate made earlier, and as much as Drew wanted to get down and personal with Leah she left it alone.

"What a nice night." Leah tried to find a better conversation other than Pete and Tevin.

Drew looked up at the sky. "Yeah, pretty nice for November."

"You know, Drew, the decision doesn't have to be as hard as you're making it," Leah stated while watching Drew continue to fondle the ring. "Just write down all the things you like about one and all the things you like about the other, then make your decision from that."

Drew eyed Leah with a quizzical look on her face. "How do you know about my situation?"

Leah laughed out. "Gurl, I watched you run in circles all day behind those two men."

Drew was embarrassed, if it was that obvious to Leah then she knew Marcus and Zae noticed it as well. Drew let out a sigh. "UGH, I'm so confused."

Leah eyed Drew; she had nothing but compassion for her, thinking back to a similar decision she'd made.

"Look Drew, we don't always make the right decisions in life; lord knows I've made plenty of the wrong ones." Leah shook her head in disappointment. "When I was in my twenties I was in love with this guy but our situations wouldn't allow us to be together, and I had to let him go. That was a decision I made and haven't come back from yet, not because I left him, but the trickle-down effect that came later in life. I tried to go back and make it right, but by then it was too late, he was gone. So, be careful, because most decisions are permanent."

Drew was touched by Leah's advice and started to look at the whole Marcus and Zae situation differently, because far as Drew was concerned it would be a permanent decision.

"Thanks for sharing with me Leah, it's really given me new light on my situation."

Drew sat on the Deck with Leah for hours talking and having a good time. Drew didn't understand how someone could have a problem with Leah; she was sweet, fun, and sincere. Drew didn't know the history between Leah and Ma Tate, but she could tell whatever it was Leah had put it and a lot of other things behind her and chose to live her life carefree of all the mistakes she'd made.

CHAPTER 36

Love & Happiness

Carl kissed Drew's cheek before letting the lace vale down over her face. Drew was honored to have her father give her away, it was the way she always imagined it.

As Carl led Drew down the boardwalk at *Mystic Pier* she looked upon the faces of her friend and family; the Tate's, Miss Sue, Pete, Jay, Den, and Leah was even there. This was the day Drew had always dreamed of. This was the day she'd become someone's wife, and although Marcus came in the middle of the night trying to change her mind, confessing his love, Drew knew this was the right thing to do, and looking at the tears coming from Zae's eyes confirmed it.

Drew gave Zae a soft smile; the way she felt at this moment was priceless and she wasn't going to allow the actions of Marcus to ruin it. Although the kiss he'd given her was still fresh on her lips, today she would become Mrs. Kingston.

Mayor Stone started the ceremony by asking who gave this woman, and although Carl was team Marcus he didn't contest and gave Drew over to Zae.

Zae and Drew stood in front of everyone confessing their love when the Ferris Wheel began to turn, exposing Marcus and Rebecca in one of the passenger cars shouting. Marcus begged Drew not to marry Zae, and Rebecca gave Zae all types of orders, from washing the floors to taking his ring back.

Drew and Zae looked at each other lost and confused, neither could believe Marcus and Rebecca's actions. Drew started to panic when Ma Tate stood up holding a little girl, telling everyone to be quiet and listen because the little girl had something to say, so Ma Tate put the little girl down in front of the Ferris Wheel and took her place back in the crowd.

Drew crouched down looking into the eyes of the little girl when seeing a reflection of herself as a little girl, crying in the arms of a lady with no face, then the little girl states, *"Be careful of the decision you make because some of them are permanent."*

Drew backed away from the little girl startled she held that memory of her as a little girl. Drew was hunted by the memory she saw in the little girl's eyes, because it was the day her mother left her at the pier.

Drew looked around trying to find Zae in search of comfort, but to her surprise he was literally wrapped around Rebecca's finger. Then Drew looked back at the little girl and she was pointing at the crowd, so Drew looked in the direction the little girl pointed when she saw Ma Tate on her knees, bawling her eyes out asking Drew for forgiveness.

Drew walked over to Ma Tate and placed her hand upon her shoulders ensuring her that it was ok, and she forgave her; that's when Ma Tate pointed at Marcus kneeling on one knee with a ring in his hand, proposing.

Drew looked over at Zae to see if he would stand for Marcus's foolishness, and that's when he got on the Ferris Wheel with Rebecca. Drew ran towards the Ferris Wheel to stop Zae when Marcus grabbed her by the hand and slid the ring on her finger.

Marcus pulled Drew closer to him, caressed her face, looked into her eyes, and screamed. "WAKE UP, DREW!" Marcus scream the words over and over.

Drew fought to come from her sleep, sitting straight up in the bed, sweat covered her body, her heart thumped like a drum, and she could hardly catch her breath, shaken by the dream and the words coming from Marcus's mouth, that were really coming from her phone. *'Wake up, wake up,'* the alarm was still chiming.

Drew grabbed her phone to shut off the screaming alarm. Drew let out a sigh, she didn't know if the crazy dream came from the last episode of A Different World or the late-night snack she'd eaten just after midnight. Either way the deranged fantasy had her heart racing and mind wandering.

Jay was in the bathroom taking care of his morning grooming when he heard Gabe singing along to the Sponge Bob theme song; Jay shook his head when catching himself singing along. "Oh no, not today, Gabe." Jay ran to the living room and suggested they spend the day fishing instead of watching *SpongeBob* all day. There was no way he'd spend another day with Patrick, Squidward, Sandy, and Mr. Krab.

"So, you good with us doing a little winter fishing?" Jay took a bowl from the cabinet and grabbed a cereal box from the pantry, hoping Gabe wouldn't suddenly change his mind about going fishing and he would be stuck in the house again looking at that ridiculous cartoon.

"I'm better than good," Gabe danced around with excitement. "Can Tevin, Mr. Pete, and Uncle Marcus come too?"

Jay chuckled. "Ok son, we can ask, but I thought maybe it could just be you and me."

Gabe put his index finger to his temple and thought about it. "Um, maybe next time, daddy."

"Oh wow, you think you could've let me down a little easier, son." Jay handed Gabe a bowl of cereal.

"Thanks daddy, but Den puts berries in them."

"I don't think we have any berries." Jay searched the kitchen for the berries but couldn't find them.

Gabe shook his head as he watched his dad open every cabinet in the kitchen, searching for the berries. "They're up there, daddy." Gabe pointed to the hanging basket in the corner.

"Now you tell me; why would she put them there?" Jay muttered.

"Because it makes them sweeter, that's what Den says."

Jay eyed Gabe suspiciously, and for the first time he realized Gabe really cared for Den and the things she did for him.

"So, son, you really like Den?"

"NO, daddy, I love her." Gabe put a spoon of cereal in his mouth.

Jay was shocked at Gabe's answer. "Why do you love her, Gabe?"

Gabe looked at his dad sideways. "Are you kidding me, she's cool and she always makes sure we put new flowers on mommy's grave."

Jay was speechless, he never knew that's where the flowers were coming from; he assumed they were coming from Drew seeing he'd fallen behind on getting flowers every week.

"So, you like Den being around?"

"Yes, daddy, I don't see why she can't be here all the time; why can't she be here all the time daddy?"

Jay rubbed the top of Gabe's head. "I don't know son, maybe I should ask her if she would like to be here all the time."

Drew picked and poked at the food on her plate still puzzled by the dream she'd had; the little girl, Zae, Marcus, and the lady with no face made no sense. The more she thought about the stupid dream, the crazier it seemed.

"Drew, are you just fine?" Ma Tate asked after noticing Drew's absence.

"I'm just fine, Ma Tate." Drew continued to poke at her plate.

Ma Tate noticed Drew didn't look up once when answering her question, so she motioned for Den's attention, speaking to her with silent lips "what's wrong with Drew?"

Den shrugged her shoulders, speaking back with silent lips. "I don't know."

"There's nothing wrong with me," Drew stated, catching the women in their silent conversation.

Ma Tate eyed Drew. "Welcome back, how was your trip?"

"Wow, you're funny Ma Tate."

"Yeah, I could've been a comedian, now tell me what's ailing you, and don't say nothing, because clearly we can see your bodies here with us, but your mind is on the other side of town."

"I had the most bizarre dream last night,"

Drew explained the dream hoping they could give her some insight into what it meant. Den seemed to think the confusion between Drew, Marcus, and Zae was because both were trying to prove their love to her, and the crying girl was the fear of her being left alone again. Drew kinda understood where Den was coming from, but the explanation Ma Tate gave made more sense. Ma Tate told Drew the clash between her, Marcus, and Zae were because she knew it was time to decide, and the pros and cons she'd listed in her head were coming in the form of a dream, and the crying girl was something she was about to face from the past.

Drew thanked both ladies for their input, but she was still unsure about the dream. Drew thought it could be from the extra stress put on by Marcus and Zae, and if it was she needed to deal with this situation quickly.

The ladies were enjoying their lunch when Drew noticed Rebecca walking in. "Oh lord, the queen of drama," Drew said under her breath.

Den heard Drew's comment and looked directly at Rebecca, and while Den observed Rebecca she noticed Zae come in behind her. Den hurried to block Drew's vision but it was too late, Rebecca had already seen them and made it her business to come over and entertain.

Rebecca clutched Zae's arm; Drew could see this was all a part of Rebecca's role in being the victor, winning the man, but that didn't bother Drew. The thing that bothered Drew, Zae did nothing to stop the gloating Rebecca did; he'd been calling her non-stop for the past few weeks, and now here he stood like he'd never seen her a day in his life.

"Wow, this town is too small." Rebecca said sarcastically.

"Way too small, Rebecca," Drew replied while counting in her head, trying to block the mess Rebecca was throwing her way.

"I was just telling Zae how lucky he was that he didn't have to see his past on every corner or in every restaurant like here in Shiloh." Rebecca sneered her nose at the ladies.

Drew would usually be boiling at this point, but she was taking the encounter and smug remarks very well for some reason. It was probably because at that moment she knew where her stress came from. Drew took this as a lesson learned, especially looking at Zae and noticing he was still unwilling to stand up for her, nor did he intend on letting Rebecca know where they stood in their situationship.

Drew looked over at Zae. "I'm glad to see you and Rebecca have worked things out, it's been my pleasure helping you find your way back to her." Drew took a drink of her Mimosa. "I mean with you not being sure if ever being with her was worth it. You're welcome, I wish you both nothing but love and Happiness."

Zae was motionless, the only thing moving was his blinking eyes, you would've thought a dust storm was in the place by the way he batted his eyes.

Rebecca glared at Zae, upset he would say those things to Drew. "Are you kidding me, Zae?"

"Can we please find a table, Rebecca?" Zae tried to be as polite as he could, but Rebecca wasn't trying to hear it; she bowed him in the chest and walked off in a rant. Zae tried to stay behind and explain to Drew, but neither her, Den, nor Ma Tate tried to hear his excuses.

Jay laughed so hard he couldn't reel in his catch; not only did Mr. Pete's statement crack him up, but the look on Marcus's face was priceless.

Marcus looked at Pete sideways; the condensation coming from his nostrils looked like that of a raging bull.

"I can't believe you just said my game was weak, Mr. Pete."

"I call it like I see it," Pete stated sarcastically, throwing his line back in the water.

"So, you're saying the way I've been coming at Drew is weak?"

"That's what I said, weak and tired. Let me tell you something about Drew, she's a woman of action, you gotta show her things not just tell her." Pete looked over at Marcus. "You'd know that if you paid attention to her. Now, when you first come to the B&B you showed Drew just how much you wanted her; the way you done it was bogus but it was an action she couldn't refuse, not even on your worst day."

Marcus thought about what Pete said.

"Pete may have a point," Jay stated, still struggling to bring his catch in. "Just make sure next time you leave Mr. Styles at home."

The men shared in a laugh.

Tevin looked over at Marcus and shook his head. "Look Marcus, I've only known Drew eight months, and man you gone have to step it up. I watched her put oh boy out in the rain, and he still wrote a bomb article about her in his magazine. I'm just saying bro, you got a little competition on your hands."

Jay was still laughing about the situation, taking the fish off the hook. "Hey, their right, Drew's changed; she's not that same girl you left four years ago. Drew's found herself, and you know once a woman does that she ain't taking nothing short of almost perfect."

Marcus thought about what the men were saying, everything made sense. Marcus looked down at Gabe who sat beside him on the dock fishing with his *Spider Man* reel.

"What do you think about your Auntie Drew and me, you think my game is weak?"

Gabe tilted his head to the side thinking about Marcus's question. "Um, I think you should just be her friend."

The men looked at Gabe shocked at his answer.

"Why you say that Gabe?" Marcus was interested in Gabe's explanation, because he believed what it said in Isaiah, *'That a child will lead them,'* and right now if Gabe's advice could lead him to Drew, he was willing to follow.

"Well, I ask Auntie Drew who you was and she said Uncle Marcus and you used to be her friend, so maybe you could just be her friend again and she'll like you again."

Gabe's words blew Marcus's mind, he realized at that moment he wasn't trying to be Drew's friend, he was trying to be her man and that wasn't working. Marcus knew what he had to do now, and that was go back to the beginning, not pick up where he'd left off.

Drew hurried to put her things away, yelling at Den to grab a bottle of wine from the downstairs cellar. Den threw her stuff on the lounge area's sofa and quickly went to retrieve the wine.

Drew threw her bags on the bed and quickly changed into something more comfortable. After a day out in Shiloh shopping, eating, and rude encounters, both women craved the peace and serenity that awaited them on the deck with a bottle of wine.

Den grabbed a bottle of wine from the wine rack when she heard voices coming from outside on the deck. Den was sure this was Drew's guest free weekend, and if so why were there voices coming from the deck, and who did they belong to. Den headed back upstairs to investigate.

Drew threw on a black sweater, a pair of gray yoga pants, and her fleece slippers. Looking at her image in the mirror Drew said to self. "Ok, girl, tonight you chill, no calls, no thoughts, just chill, free yo mind and let the rest follow."

While giving herself the little pep talk Drew heard laughter coming from the backyard; she knew there weren't any guests there, so who was in the backyard. Drew grabbed the bat from beside her bed and went to investigate.

Den shut the door to the cellar, trying to be as quiet as she could.

Drew walked down the hall headed to the back door, trying to be as quiet as she could, and just about the time Drew walked into the house's opening so did Den, both women were about to take off until they noticed who the other was.

Drew put her index finger to her lips motioning Den to be quiet and follow her so they could continue their investigation; the two women crept to the back door, Drew's hands wrapped tightly around the bat, and Den ready to assist her with the bottle of wine if needed.

As the women got closer to the doors they noticed flames coming from the deck. Drew dropped the bat and hurried to open the door, yelling at Den to turn the water on. Den ran to turn the water on, and Drew grabbed the water hose, both women in a panic to put the fire out.

Drew ran to the deck with the hose wide open, aiming right at the fire; she screamed when the flames got bigger; instead of the water putting the fire out it made matters worse.

Drew was so focused on putting the fire out she didn't notice or hear the men calling her name, it took Den turning off the water to gain her attention.

Drew covered her mouth with one hand and held the hose in the other. The men glared at her soaked and shocked. Drew examined each of them, Jay, Marcus, Tevin, and Mr. Pete.

Jay calmly walked down the deck's steps, took the water hose from Drew's hand, and beckoned for Den to turn the water back on. At first Den refused but Jay demanded her, so Den complied and turned the water back on.

Drew pleaded for Jay not to spray her, and the men chanted for him to do it. Drew ran and took cover behind Den in hopes Jay wouldn't spray, but that didn't work he sprinkled them both. The women yelled for Jay to stop, but he didn't until they were just as soaked as the men.

The men watched and laughed as Jay sprayed the women with a gentle mist. "Yeah, get them, Jay." The men yelled out. It did them good to see justice being served.

Drew and Den pleaded for Jay to stop, and after a few seconds more he finally gave in. Jay turned the water off, then handed the group towels he retrieved from the poolside storage cabinet.

"What the heck were you thinking, Drew? "Jay shook the water from his head.

"I saw fire and panicked." Drew took the towel and dried herself.

"And I was just following Drew's lead," Den confessed.

Jay looked up at the cold-fussing men on the deck and shook his head. The men were all in an uproar about Drew and Den's actions; not only did they give them a shower, but they also put out the fire for the fish fry.

Jay took the towel from Den and dried her face. "Oh, baby, you're all wet."

"I know, you wet me." Den gave Jay pouty lips.

Drew looked at Den sideways. "Are you kidding me?"

"What?" Den asked, with a slight grin. Den respected Drew for being her girl and all, but Jay had fire in his arms.

"You're going to get in bed with the enemy?"

"No, I'm just going to kiss him, and let him warm me up." Den gave Jay a soft kiss and took shelter in his warm arms..

Drew shook her head. "Where is the loyalty."

Drew stepped up on the deck and apologized to the men as they tried to get the fire started back. The men eyed Drew, hesitant about accepting her apology until she gave them her pitiful look; A look where she bats her eyes, then tilts her head to the side and eyes you, displaying an innocent smile. That's all it took and the men where putty in her hands.

The group had been sitting around the fire pit for hours enjoying each other's company, sharing stories and wisdom, eating, and drinking. The women didn't mention what happened with Zae and Rebecca, and the men kept silent about their conversation (the part about Drew).

Marcus excused himself from his, Tevin, and Mr. Pete's conversation to get a beer when he looked over at Drew in conversation with Rainn, who'd just walked up with Gabe. Marcus consumed Drew's beauty in slow motion, from the way she motioned her hands when she was involved in a conversation, to her sweet smile assuring you that she was paying attention. Marcus thought about the conversation he'd had with the men earlier, and knew now he'd have to think outside the box when it came to Drew; she was a different woman now and it would take a different approach, so Marcus took his phone from his pocket, googled *Musiq Soulchild's Love,* and shared it with Drew. After sending the text Marcus stood back to watch her actions when it came through.

Drew took her phone from the table and checked the alert, a smile came across her face when seeing the song Marcus sent her. Drew searched the deck for Marcus finding him smiling at her by the spread table. Drew was in the mood for a bit of adult entertainment, so she searched her Google and returned the text, sending Marcus *Musiq Soulchild's "Teach Me How to Love."*

Marcus checked his phone; when seeing the song Drew sent a smile painted his face remembering the first time he'd heard it; that night at Brooklyn's when Jay and Ami tried setting him and Drew up on a reconnect date. Marcus remembers holding Drew in his arms that night, hoping and praying for the chance to hold her forever.

Rainn noticed the text exchange and couldn't help but write the happy conclusion to their love story ending in marriage and kids. Rainn could clearly see that Drew was no longer engaging in their conversation about her working part-time at the *Friendly Market,* so she excused herself and went to sit with Tevin.

Everyone was engaged in their own conversation when Den startled the crowd with a scream full of excitement. Everyone's attention was on her as she jumped around uttering the word yes repeatedly. Drew caught on to Den's actions quick, and when she looked over at Jay and the smile he held confirmed it, he had just proposed. Drew was overwhelmed with excitement jumping to her feet joining in Den's happy dance; once Rainn caught on she also joined in, leaving the men clueless for a moment.

Marcus looked at Jay then at the women, and when putting two and two together he knew what had just taken place. Marcus walked over to congratulate the couple never losing sight of Drew; Marcus was excited for Jay, but he had Drew's attention and didn't want to lose it.

Drew eyed Marcus remembering how excited she was when he proposed to her in that same backyard, and although years had passed Drew still got butterflies when thinking about that night.

Tevin and Gabe eyed Mr. Pete seeking an explanation; both were still confused about what was going on. Mr. Pete shook his head looking at the young man not knowing any other way to explain. " Yep, well, look like you about to have a new momma, and you Tevin a new brother. Meet your Uncle Tevin, Gabe."

Mr. Pete laughed and walked off, leaving Gabe and Tevin sitting there with their thoughts.

CHAPTER 37

Fears & Tears

Drew went over her checklist waiting for Gabe to unlatch his seatbelt. Gabe had been withdrawn all day which bothered Drew; she tried to give him space and wait for him to come around, but today he held back and kept his distance.

Drew took a dime from the cupholder and handed to Gabe. "A dime for what's on your mind," Drew stated softly, lifting Gabe chin so she could see his face; it hurt Drew to see his little mind dealing with so much.

Gabe took the dime and threw it. "I don't wanna talk."

"Gabe, what is wrong with you, why would you do that?" Drew scolded Gabe, hurt by his actions.

Gabe looked at Drew. "I'm mad, and that dime not going to help my mad."

Drew grabbed patience and understanding placing them on her heart, she'd never seen Gabe act out like this.

"Gabriel Yahime Tate, you better have a good reason," Drew stated sternly.

"Because she's trying to take mommy away from daddy and me."

"Who's trying to take mommy, what are you talking about, Gabe." Drew was confused.

"Den, she's going to be my new mommy, right." Gabe was panting he was so upset.

Drew took her hand and placed it on Gabe's chest. "Calm down Gabe, take a deep breath, and gather your thoughts."

Gabe took a deep breath, looking up at Drew with tears in his eyes. "When daddy gave Den that ring it made her my new mommy and Tevin my new uncle. I'm happy about Tevin being my new uncle, but what happens to mommy if Den is going to be my new mommy? Because Mr. Pete said so."

Drew could see the whole engagement had Gabe confused and scared. "Aww, Gabe, Dens not going to take your mommy's place; Shantel will always be your mommy no matter what. Yall have the same eyes," Drew wiped the tears from Gabe's eyes. "Yall have the same ears," Drew pulled Gabe's ears.

"The same nose," Drew poked the tip of Gabe's nose, and the same heart," Drew rubbed Gabe's heart. So, you and your mother will always be connected, and no one can ever take that. Sweetheart, Den is just gonna help your mom out because she can't be here."

Drew took a handy wipe and wiped the tears from Gabe's eyes. "Don't you like the way Den helps mommy?"

"Yeah, but why didn't Yah just leave mommy here to do it?"

Drew searched for the right words to say so Gabe could understand.

"Well, umm, you see, Yah needed your mommy to bring you into the world, and when she did he took her, because he had something else for her to do. That's why Yah sent Den in her place. Isn't it wonderful he left us with all the great memories of your mom, and now you can make new ones with Den."

Drew hoped Gabe understood, and she hadn't confused or traumatized him with her explanation; she didn't want to scare the poor child for life.

"So, how did mommy bring me into the world?" Gabe looked up at Drew, starting a whole new conversation, expecting answers. Drew wasn't ready for any of these questions; she knew the day would come but not this soon.

"Ok Gabe, let's go talk to Sarge, and we can talk about this later with Jay." Drew hurried to use Sarge as an out to set Gabe's mind on something else.

"Yay, let's see Sarge." Gabe yelped, jumping from the car charging towards the *Friendly Market.*

Drew yelled for Gabe to slow down, but by the time the words came from her mouth Gabe had already run smack dab into Marcus, knocking him back a few steps.

Marcus crouched down before Gabe taking a Goalkeepers stand. "Whoa, you push back hard G, you're gonna have to play soccer for me when you turn six. You wanna be a Jaguar?"

"For real Uncle Marcus, I can be a Jaguar?" Gabe wore a big smile.

Gabe turned to look at Drew screaming that Marcus said he could be a Jaguar. Drew could hear Gabe ranting about something, but she was more focused on finding her phone; every time she drove Jay's truck she seem to lose it. Drew was grateful to Jay for letting her use his chevy truck; his pride that he restored, but between Jay checking for scratches and the truck stealing her phone, Drew was ready for her own transportation.

Gabe whispered to Marcus asking him to speak with Drew about the offer. Marcus agreed, giving Gabe some dap before he continued his mission to the doors of the *Friendly Market.*

Drew walked towards Marcus; the thoughts of *Musiq Soulchild* came to mind as Drew thought back on the night Jay proposed to Den. After everyone had gone home that night she and Marcus spent the rest of it and part of the morning texting various songs to one another, having a conversation through the artist's lyrics.

Drew hollered at Gabe to wait before entering the store, so Gabe occupied his time by greeting customers as they walked in and out of the market.

"Good afternoon Mr. Tidwell, how are you?" Drew gave Marcus a smile that could light an entire house.

"I'm awesome now that I've had a chance to look upon your beautiful face, Miss McCain," Marcus bowed to a blushing Drew.

Drew returned the gesture by giving him a curtsy speaking to him in an English accent. "Mr. Tidwell, how delightful are your words, you're such a gentleman, and what is this Gabe ranting on about?"

The pair laughed at the imitation as they gazed into each other's eyes.

"Yeah, I was just telling Gabe he can come play soccer for me when he turns six."

"Well, you're gonna have to take that up with Jay."

As much as the pair tried to fight their attraction for each other they simply couldn't; the energy that pinged off them could charge a car.

Marcus chuckled when he noticed a leaf hiding in Drew's braids. "Um, you been rolling in leaves?"

"Wow, thought I got them all. Gabe and I did a little rolling around today." Drew laughed taking the leaf from Marcus's hand.

Marcus held on to Drew's hand, never taking his eyes from hers.

"So, what's the plan for the New Year?"

"Nothing, you know I don't do the pagan holidays."

"Cool, just checking, making sure your head was still in the game."

Drew blushed. "You know when it comes to following the Torah, I keep my head in the game."

Marcus rubbed his beard, Drew loved when he did that, it gave her the idea that he was really putting thought into what he was about to say, and it was downright appealing to her.

Marcus rubbed his beard once more. "Brother Mykel's hosting a talk that same night in Shiloh City at the Renaissance about the difference between Holydays and Holidays. It's supposed to be a catered event too."

"Are you asking me on a date, Mr. Tidwell?" Drew picked up on Marcus's hint.

"Yes, Miss McCain, I am."

As much as Drew wanted to accept she had to stick to her vow of not always being available, besides she'd already promised Gabe a movie night. "I'll have to rain check."

Marcus was shocked by Drew's answer, he just knew she would accept, Drew always accepted. Marcus stood there with a quizzical look on his face he didn't know how to respond. Marcus was relieved when he heard Gabe calling out for Drew, it gave him time to think of something while she answered him.

"Ok baby, hold on, I'm coming," Drew brought her attention right back to Marcus. "I'm sorry Marcus, but I promised Gabe a movie night.

"Shot down for a five-year-old."

Marcus gave Drew a smile that made her consider changing her plans, but she couldn't do that to Gabe, he'd been begging for a movie night for months.

Drew looked over at Gabe still greeting the customers and decided to use him as an excuse to leave the conversation, seeing how she was a millisecond from changing her mind. "I gotta go before Gabe gets harassment charges."

Marcus lifted his hand and pulled another leaf from Drew's hair. "The next time you and Gabe decide to have a roll in the leaves, give me a call."

"Sure thing Mr. Tidwell." Drew gave Marcus a wink and walked off to fetch Gabe.

Gabe skipped down the isles heading straight to Carl's office, shaking every worker's hand he saw, complimenting them on a job well done. Drew shook her head, she knew Gabe's actions were coming from watching her father; Carl always made sure his employees felt appreciated. Carl had been the grocery store's new owner for only four months and had already made many significant changes. The food stock was better and fresher, the staff was friendly, and the building's maintenance was much better; Carl had made many changes inside and outside the aged structure.

Drew walked into her father's office where he and Gabe were already exchanging salutes, and Gabe telling him about being on Marcus's soccer team.

"Good afternoon, sweet princess." Carl greeted Drew with a kiss. "Marcus just left, did you see him?"

"Yeah, I just talk to him before coming in."

"So, what do you think about the shop he's opening, good idea, huh."

Drew was clueless about what her father was talking about. "He didn't tell me anything about opening a new shop."

"Yeah, right here in Promise, he's renovating one of the storefronts in the square." Carl pointed in the direction of the town's square. "I think it used to be the old bakery shop."

"Wow, good thinking Marcus," Drew said with excitement.

"That's what I told him, besides closing down his grandfather's old shop is going to save him a lot of money and hassle."

Drew was surprised to hear Marcus opening a new shop but even more surprised that he was finally selling his grandfather's shop. "Wow, he didn't tell me that either."

Drew started to feel '*some type of way*' about not being included in Marcus's life; she knew certain things they didn't share anymore, but why not tell her about the shops. This was a big shock to Drew, so she knew Marcus had to be struggling with selling his grandfather's shop.

Drew was so deep in thought she didn't realize she'd left the conversation with her dad and started her own.

Carl snapped his fingers. "Hey, think long, think wrong."

"You're absolutely right." Drew gave her father a soft smile and gathered her thoughts, remembering why she was there.

Drew made herself comfortable on the black futon next to Gabe playing a game on his tablet.

"So, Rainn tells me she's going to work here part-time."

"Yeah, she came in last week and asked me. Now, I did tell her to make sure it was fine with you first." Carl specified.

"She did, and I told her it was fine if she could handle the workload."

Carl took a bite of his sandwich. "She said it's extra money for college, so I'll help her any way I can."

Drew helped Gabe with an alphabet game on his tablet giving her father time to finish his lunch; she needed his full attention for the question she was about to ask.

"So, what brings you in other than questions about Rainn working here." Carl put what was left of his lunch on a corner table.

Drew took a deep breath and exhaled, she hated bringing up the past to Carl, but she needed some answers about that day at the pier 29 years ago. Maybe it would shed some light on the dream she'd had a few days ago. "I needed to ask you something about the day Shelia called about me."

Carl thought back to that day trying to remember, it had been so long ago that his memory was a bit foggy. "I think it was mid-afternoon when I got Shelia's message. I thought it had to do with our mother because she was down sick with cancer, and my dad had run off and left her."

Drew's heart fluttered, she'd never heard Carl mention either of his parents before, so this was a first for her. Drew knew his mother had died but didn't know when or how.

"I hurried to call Shelia nervous and scared our mother had died, but when I got Shelia on the phone she told me about you." Carl shook his head. "I went from nervous and scared to terrified and shocked. Not only was I young and dumb, but your mother had been the only woman I'd ever been with."

Drew was shocked as many women as she'd seen her father with she knew for sure her mother hadn't been his first. "Wow, Joy was your first?"

"She was going to be the only hadn't she ran off on me. My mother always taught my sisters and I to honor our marriages no matter what, and that's why I've never gotten married. Marriage is a sacred honor to God, and it's something I'll never play with."

Now Drew understood why Shelia stayed in her toxic marriage with Curtis; her mother taught her to do so. "Wow, that explains a lot." Drew said under her breath.

"Anyway, Shelia told me that some lady found you near the Ferris Wheel at Mystic Pier, wondering about crying for your mother. The lady and her husband contacted security, and they searched the entire pier, but Joy was nowhere to be found. The police were called, and they took you to the CPS office, putting you in temporary foster care where you stayed a month before they contacted Shelia."

Carl could see the information caressed Drew's heart and now hated he'd ever allowed her to open this book again. "If it does your heart some good, Shelia said the lady that found you never left your side; she even asked if she could stay in touch, but the social worker wouldn't allow it."

Drew told Carl about her dream and the reason for all the questions, so he offered to call Shelia for more information, but Drew declined, she hadn't reached that point of forgiveness for Shelia and didn't want to involve her.

Gabe looked up from the tablet at Drew. "Auntie Drew, your mommy left you too?"

"Yeah baby, my mom left me too."

"Well, who did Yah send to help your mommy?"

Drew looked at Gabe and a warmth came over her heart when she thought about who Yah had placed in her life, taking her mother's place.

Joe watched Brenda as she paced back and forth from the living room to the kitchen in a rant about Leah and Zae; her solution for Zae was simple, he needed to be with Rebecca and leave Drew alone, but her matter with Leah wasn't that simple, Brenda had personal issues with Leah that needed to be resolved.

Before Brenda started another tour to the kitchen she stopped and eyed Joe. "And another thing, Joe, how can you be so calm, this woman is back in our lives, and you act like it's nothing."

"That's because it is nothing, you're getting yourself worked up for nothing." Joe took his pipe from the table and lit it.

"Joe, this woman is up to no good, I can feel it; she wreaked havoc before, and she'll do it again."

Joe eyed Brenda. "The only person around here wreaking havoc is you, ranting and raving about Leah to Drew. Have you ever stopped to think that Drew and others might not see her the way you do. You're the only one that has a problem with her; don't make it everyone else's.

Brenda took a deep breath and exhaled, but before she could comment Jay and Den walked through the door.

"Hey, parents." Jay could feel the hostility in the air, and by looking at his mother's face there was a lot of it. "Did we come at a bad time, it looks like world war three is about to pop off."

Brenda put her ranting to the side long enough to give Jay and Den a hug. "I'm sorry Jay, I'm just a little upset about a small matter."

Jay knew his mother was lying about the small matter; if he knew his mother, Jay knew nothing was small when she was upset about it. Jay looked over at his dad waiting for him to spill the bean, but his father avoided eye contact, never looking in his direction. Jay could tell his father was not in the mood for entertaining his mother's dramatics. More than likely his father was probably hoping the conversation would cease that way he could enjoy his pipe and football game in peace.

Jay and Den took a seat on the sofa, both eyeing *The Parents,* waiting for the right time to intervene. Brenda stood in the middle of the room watching Joe, and Joe continued to watch the football game, ignoring Brenda.

Jay and Den watched the silent augment between *The Parents.* It made Den a little uncomfortable she'd never seen this side of the Tates. Den whispered to Jay that it might not be a good time to tell them about the engagement. Jay could understand Den being reserved about the announcement, but he felt *The Parents* could use some good news.

Jay stood to his feet extending his hand for Den to join him; Den blushed as she stood to her feet. "Ma, Dad, I have something to tell you."

The Parents gave their complete attention to Jay; his father took the pipe from his mouth and muted the tv, and his mother calmed herself.

"Is everything ok, son?" His father asked.

"Yeah dad, everything is fine, we just wanna let you guys know we're getting married."

Brenda stood in the kitchen doorway with her bottom jaw to the floor, and Jay's father was smiling from ear to ear. The issues *The Parents* had before were a distant memory.

Jay's father rose from his recliner and congratulated the two while his mother stood in place, still in shock over the news.

After a moment of processing the news Brenda finally spoke. "Babies, we're going to have more babies."

Jay and Den laughed out.

"Is that all you can say, momma?" Jay kissed his mother's cheek.

"No, I mean yes, oh Jay I'm happy for yall." Brenda embraced them both. "But this does mean more grandchildren."

The pair laughed, knowing Ma Tate had been hinting around at them both for grandkids.

"So, Den, have you figured out a date, do you want a summer or a fall wedding, I've always loved fall weddings." Ma Tate paused. "I'm sorry Den, here I go taking over, I'm just so excited for you guys." Ma Tate excitedly led Den to the kitchen giving her all sorts of ideas.

Ma Tate asked Den to have a set while she prepared some tea.

"I'm happy you're happy about it." Den rubbed her sweaty palms.

"And why wouldn't I be, you're everything a mother could want in a daughter."

Ma Tate's words summonsed tears from Den's eyes. "Wow, thank you."

Ma Tate raised Den's chin and dabbed the tears with a cloth. "Why do I feel those are tears of relief."

Den hesitated to explain her reason, unsure how Ma Tate would take her honesty. "Well, I thought you maybe wanted someone different for Jay and Gabe. You know a motherly type of woman. A woman that knows and studies the Torah."

"Den, nothing upsets me more than a woman that takes away from herself."

Den eyed Ma Tate with a quizzical look on her face. "I don't understand."

Ma Tate took a mirror from the cabinet drawer. "Look at yourself and tell me what you see."

Den eyed her image for a moment. "I see me, Dina."

"Den, When I look at you I see more than just Dina, I see a special young lady that has come into my son and grandson's life and made a difference. Not only did you accept Jay and Gabe, but you accepted everyone that came along with them. You are kind, sweet, intelligent, beautiful inside and out, and if you can't see that you've been looking at the wrong image of yourself. And far as the Torah, that will come with time. Yah has a time for everything remember that."

Den embraced Ma Tate. "Thank you, those words meant a lot to me."

Pop Tate eyed Jay from the corner of his eye while puffing on his pipe; it was the third time Jay's father had looked in his direction with the same smirk on his face. Jay straightens himself resting his arm on the back of the couch, knowing his dad had something to say or ask, so he readies himself.

Pop Tate muted the tv but continued to observe the game. "Son, let me ask you something."

"Here we go," Jay said under his breath.

"Jay, I know some of us tend to go along with these western traditions when it comes to marriage, and that's understood every woman wants a beautiful proposals and wedding. I guess what I'm trying to ask is have you enjoyed the honeymoon already."

Jay blushed, he felt this was the question his dad was going to ask. Pop Tate was big on not sleeping with a woman unless you knew for sure she'd be your wife. Pop Tate didn't care about the western traditions when it came to marriage; he felt it was all a scam for tax purposes, but he did believe if you uncovered a woman's nakedness then she should be good enough to become your wife.

"Well, son, have you?" Pop Tate waited on an answer.

Jay laughed with a slight blush. "We're getting married Pops."

Pop Tate eyed Jay and unmuted the tv.

The women spent the next couple of hours putting together ideas for the wedding. Den was honored Ma Tate had taken an interest in helping her plan when thinking about the mother she had to deal with.

Ma Tate pulled out some old magazines and scrapbooks from the cabinet that belonged to Drew and sat them in front of Den. "Good thing we didn't do away with these things."

Den looked through the books thinking back on Drew's wedding day. "Drew's wedding was like a fairy tale in a floral garden. I'd never seen so many Lillies in my life, and red ones at that."

"Leave it to Drew," MA Tate stated.

Both women laughed.

Ma Tate Didn't want to take the attention from Den, but she needed to do a little prying into Drew's life, and who better to ask than Den. "Den, how well do you know this Leah woman Drew's taken a liking to?"

Den eyed Ma Tate puzzled about the question; did she know Leah was her mother, had Drew told her something, had Leah said something to Drew.

Ma Tate waved her hand in Den's face to gain her attention. "Earth to Den, come in Den."

"I'm sorry, I had to process the name, I don't know much about her just that she designs homes and offices; she came in the boutique a couple of times, and she's done work for Drew. Other than that, I don't know her."

"Well, I know Leah, and her hanging around with Drew doesn't sit well with me."

"If you don't mind me asking, what did she do?" Den was determined to find out what her mother had done to these people.

"Let's just say our paths crossed a long time ago, and I should've dealt with her then."

Den hurried to leave the conversation by pointing out a teal green flower arrangement in one of the magazines, but she could see Ma Tate's mind was no longer thinking about wedding plans but trying to find Leah's reason for hanging around.

CHAPTER 38

Mother & Daughter

Den pulled into the friendly Market when she noticed Leah going into the storefront Marcus rented for his new shop, and as much as Den wanted to avoid her mother she needed to know why Leah was still hanging around, and what she'd done to the Tates. Den looked for Marcus's car and didn't see it, this gave her the perfect opportunity to confront her mother.

"Good morning, Leah." Den stood in the doorway.

Leah turned to see Den standing in the middle of the room. "Hey, darling, what do I owe this pleasure."

"Cut the crap, Mother, I want to know why you're hanging around and what did you do to Brenda Tate?"

"Wow, couldn't you be more pleasant. I'm here because Marcus asked me to be here, and I don't have a clue as to who Brenda Tate is."

Den eyed her mother, and as much as she wanted to catch her in a lie she could tell Leah was telling the truth.

"Well, Ma, why does Jay's mother dislike you so much, are you trying to ruin my life intentionally?"

Leah shook her head. "To be honest, baby, I don't know Jay's mother or the reason, and I'm not trying to mess anything up for you. If needed, I'll talk to Jay's mother, and we can get to the bottom of it.

"NO!" Drew yelped out. "Stay away from Brenda I'll get to the bottom of it I don't need you staring things up."

Leah walked over to Den holding her stare. "I'm not going to do anything to mess up what you and Ethan have here, but baby I'm your mother, and I would like to be part of yalls lives."

The tears that fell from Leah's eyes weakened Den. "You are Ma, it's just so much has happened."

"So much that you couldn't tell me you were getting married." Leah caressed Den's face. "I'm your mother, you're my daughter, does that count for anything?"

Den looked at her mother puzzled, how did she know about the engagement. "How did..."

"Drew told me." Leah rolled her eyes.

"Why are you still in contact with Drew." Den let out a frustrating sigh.

"She contacted me about this job for Marcus, and I accepted."

"For who's convenience, yours or Marcus's." Den got in her mother's face, never taking her eyes from hers. "Stay Away From Us Ma, I Mean It."

Marcus stood in the doorway eyeing the ladies, confused as to why Den was there, and why she was in Leah's face like that.

"Good afternoon ladies, everything good?" Marcus inquired.

Den was startled by Marcus's presence, "Oh, Marcus, how are you?"

"I'm good, but you don't look good, what's going on here?" Marcus waited for an explanation.

Den looked for a quick lie to cover up her actions. "I'm good, I was just talking to Miss Reynolds about some designs she'd done on the boutique."

Marcus eyed the two ladies, and as far as he could see Den was upset about the work Leah had done.

Den gave Marcus a smile then turned her attention back to Leah, assuring her they would continue their business later before she walked out the shop.

Marcus eyed Leah, he could see she was haunted by whatever Den was comforting her about; he didn't wanna make it his business, but the awkward silence and the look of disappointment on Leah's face bothered his peace.

"You good, Miss. Reynolds?"

"Yeah, I'm just fine, some people are never happy with the work you do." Leah grabbed her things and headed to the back of the shop before her tears revealed themselves, leaving Marcus wondering what had just happened.

Drew tossed the National Enquirer magazine on the futon and yelled back at it, "WHAT ABOUT HER DAUGHTER!" Drew had enough about the death of Whitney Houston. It had been a little over a month, and the only thing the tabloids were worried about was how she died and her alleged drug addiction.

Drew slid on her slippers and headed to the kitchen. Looking over the B&B Drew was pleased to see the guest taking advantage of the peaceful sounds of the rain forest. Drew was big on peace and meditation, so for an hour starting at six o'clock Drew would pick from various calming sounds and play them throughout the house. This was called *Serenity Time.*

Drew pushed through the swinging door of the kitchen finding Miss Sue and Mr. Pete sitting at the table eating strawberries. Drew eyed the pair as she headed to the refrigerator for a light raid; she chuckled when thinking about the love affair the couple thought they were keeping secret, unaware that Rainn had already informed her that she'd seen them holding one another in the tool shed a few months ago. Drew didn't mind the courtship, they were both close to retirement age, so why not start something new and retire together later.

Drew scanned the refrigerator disappointed with her choices. "Ugh, there's never anything good in here," Drew looked over at the guest refrigerator and thought about scavenging it, but what kind of host would eat their guest's food.

Miss Sue and Pete watched Drew go through the cabinets, the pantry, and the refrigerator *twice* in search of a snack. Miss Sue shook her head, knowing when Drew went on an eating binge she was usually upset about something.

"What's bothering you, Hot Potato?" Miss Sue asked.

Drew eyed Miss Sue and smiled, remembering where the nickname came from. '*Darwin Smith,*' the eldest son of Charles and Tina Smith had given Drew the name almost three years ago when she and Miss Sue catered to the family after becoming homeless due to a fire. Darwin would always love to hear Drew talk about the Torah and Israel's history; he told her she was a real *Hot Potato* when it came to Yah, and she should never let anyone or anything change that. If it hadn't been for Darwin's encouragement Drew would probably still be sitting behind a desk at Cambridge. Darwin told Drew she was a natural when it came to caring for people; a year later Drew started renovations on the Victorian Home, determined to put all she had into *Serenity Meadows.* So, whenever Miss Sue called her *Hot Potato,* Drew would get warm inside thinking about Darwin and his family.

"I shouldn't have read that stupid tabloid, especially during Serenity Time."

"Well, what's the problem, we still have twenty minutes of Serenity Time left, don't you wanna enjoy it?" Miss Sue asked.

Drew sat down at the table joining Miss Sue and Pete. "You know what sickens me?" Miss Sue and Pete waited to hear Drew's response. "The fact that the whole world is worried about how Whitney Houston died but has anyone's considered how Bobby Kristina must be feeling."

Miss Sue could see Drew was upset about the matter, and she could also see it went deeper than Bobby Kristina. "Drew, what's really bothering you."

Mr. Pete eyed the women, he could see they were about to have a heart-to-heart, giving him a cue to leave, so he raised from the table giving Miss Sue an eye only she was supposed to catch, but Drew got a glimpse of it as well, leaving her wondering how long this love affair had been going on. Still, she respected their privacy and would wonder until one or the other came clean.

"Good night ladies." Mr. Pete grabbed his hat from the chair's back and exited through the back door.

Miss Sue watched the old man until he had completely vanished, then turned her attention back to Drew. "Now, Hot Potato, tell me what's going on."

"Here lately I've been remembering even dreaming about the day my mother left me at the pier, and I guess thinking about how alone and scared I felt is causing me to sympathize with Bobby Kristina." Drew took a granola bar from the basket on the table. "I know she has to be scared and feeling so alone right now, just like I did when Joy left me; the only difference is her mother's never coming back. At least I have a chance to maybe one day see mine again."

Miss Sue knew Drew's story, but this was the first time she'd heard her speak on it or her mother, so she made sure to choose her words wisely, for she knew this could be a sensitive conversation.

"I'm pretty sure Bobby Khristina has a lot of family surrounding her at this moment, and I'm positive you'll see your mother again one day." Miss Sue tried to find the sincerest words to comfort Drew.

"But, what if she's dead, what if she died years ago and I just don't know it."

"Well, have you ever tried to find her?"

"Yes Miss Sue, I've tried any and every method I could, but can't find anything, it's like she never existed."

Miss Sue eyed Drew for a moment. "Let me ask you something Drew, are you ready to see your mother when the time does come?"

Drew thought about the question and examined her heart. "Yes, I can honestly say that I'm ready; I've come to realize there's a story behind every mistake we make, part of forgiveness is being willing to listen and understand."

Miss Sue was impressed with Drew's wisdom. "I'm glad you feel that way sweetness, it shows maturity on your part."

Drew let out a sigh. "Yeah, maybe so, but I don't think I'll ever find Joy to put it through the test."

"You will baby, give it a little time. Yah's not ready yet, it'll happen when he prepares you. Understand something Drew, we can be sure we're ready for certain situations all day, but only Yah knows if our hearts are truly prepared for what we're asking him for." Miss Sue patted Drew's hand for a means of comfort.

"Thanks for the ear Miss Sue, I really pray Bobby Kristina is ok."

"You welcome baby, and she is, you will be too."

Miss Sue grabbed the bowel of strawberries and headed for the back door.

"Wait, where are you going with the berries?"

"Oh, baby, don't worry about these berries, you got enough to deal with."

Miss Sue continued her exit with the berries. Drew was in dismay thinking about where Miss Sue was going with those strawberries.

IF YOU THINK THAT'S SOMETHING, WAIT.....

Brenda sat in her car outside *Simple Design*, she needed to get a few things straight with Leah, and this was the perfect time. Joe was out of the country in Jerusalem for the Passover, and Jay was with him, so there was no one to stop her from addressing Leah.

Brenda got out of the car and walked to the door, praying for courage thinking of different ways to present herself to a woman she'd had a problem with for years. Turning the doorknob Brenda noticed someone had left the keys in the door. "What good does it do to lock the door and leave the keys." Brenda said to herself while unlocking the door, hoping to find someone to retune the keys to.

Upon entering Brenda noticed all the lights were on so it had to be someone there. Brenda walked through the office admiring all the different room designs, the stage props really showed Leah's talent. "Hello, is there anyone here," Brenda yelped out searching the office, but no one responded. The only thing she could conclude was someone either left in a hurry, or they were very careless.

Brenda headed back to the entrance ending her search when she heard music coming from one of the back offices. Brenda had scanned the open office space for souls but not the private offices, she felt that was going too far, but now that Brenda heard signs of life she walked back to check it out.

Brenda knocked at the office door but no one answered. Brenda could hear music playing and someone singing along, but she never got permission to enter, so she stood at the door a few moments and listened to the slurred singing voice before knocking again.

"Hello, it's Brenda Tate, someone left these keys in the door, and I was trying to return them." Brenda talked through the door hoping to gain access, when she hears a thump like someone had fallen.

"Is everything ok, do you need help." Brenda knocked at the door.

"Put them on the counter and leave, please."

Brenda could tell in the woman's voice she was toasted, and this was probably the reason for the keys left in the door. "Are you ok, it sounds like you may need some help."

There was salience from the room other than the radio playing which scared Brenda, she didn't know who occupied the office and what was going on behind the closed door, but a thump and silence were never good.

Brenda remembered the keys in her hand, so she tried each one until she found the right one. Brenda slowly entered the office. "Hello, are you ok, I'm trying to return some keys." Brenda scanned the office; the elegance of the decor was breathtaking, everything from the office furniture to the mouse pad was chocolate brown trimmed in red.

Brenda looked around the office mumbling to herself. "I know I'm not crazy, I know I heard a voice coming from outta here."

"You sure did, and it's coming from under the desk." The voice let out a drunken laugh.

Brenda hurried to the other side of the desk where she found Leah on the floor between the chair and wall.

"Oh My God, Are You Ok!" Brend pushed the chair back and tried helping Leah up.

"No I fall down, and I can't get up," Leah said in a whiny voice while giving Brenda pouty lips.

Brenda could see Leah had been hitting the Patron she held in her hand pretty hard, so she took the bottle from Leah and set it on the desk, then pulled Leah from the floor and guided her to the leather sofa. Leah tried to get up and retrieve the Patron from the desk a few times, but Brenda wouldn't allow it; instead she got her a bottled water from the mini fridge in the corner of the office.

"Here, drink this, it's going to be way better for you." Brenda tried to hand-feed Leah the water ensuring she got some down, but Leah rejected the water knocking Brenda's hand back. Brenda grew frustrated with Leah's actions and rejection, so she pinched her nose and poured the water down her throat adding some to her face. "I'm sorry hunny, but you'll thank me later."

Leah started to choke from the water fighting it from her face. "What a minute, you trying to kill me?"

"No, I'm trying to sober you up, here drink some more water."

"Look here lady, I don't need your help." Leah pushed Brenda's hand back trying to stand but fell right back down. "Well, maybe a little bit."

"Would you prefer coffee over water?" Benda asked. "Because I can make you some if you like."

"I need for you to get outta here and leave me alone, Lady." Leah snatched the bottled water from Brenda's hand and took a swig.

Brenda grabbed patience and understanding sitting them on her heart, because she knew the spirits were in control of Leah's actions right now.

"Who are you and what are you doing in my place?" Leah demanded answers.

"I'm Brenda Tate"

"I don't know Brenda Tate, and I don't know you."

"I'm Brenda Tate, I'm aware you don't know me, but I need to speak with you."

Leah paused thinking about Den and the name she'd mentioned before. "Oh, you're Brenda."

Brenda eyed Leah: the comment she'd made had Brenda feeling like she'd been discussed, and if so with who. But that would have to wait because Brenda needed Leah sober, so she got Leah up from the sofa and led her to the kitchen to prepare some coffee.

"Would you like cream and sugar, or would you like it black." Brenda set the cup down in front of Leah.

Leah took the coffee and sipped it, not saying anything to Brenda for about ten minutes. Brenda felt Leah needed time to relax and allow the coffee to work, so she sat at the small round table and didn't say a word.

Leah eyed Brenda suspiciously pulling a pack of cigarettes from her breast, then taking one out and lighting it. "You that jazzy lady from Drew's spot, yeah I seen y'all having a little disagreement on the deck when I was there."

"I don't know about jazzy, and it wasn't a disagreement, but yes that's where you saw me amongst other places."

"Yeah, what other places I don't know you lady."

Brenda took a deep breath and exhaled. "No, you don't know me, but I know you."

Leah laughed uncontrollably while puffing on her cigarette. "Lady, you don't know me, hell, I don't know me. I'm sitting here drunk after four years of sobriety. I didn't even know me well enough to know I would be sitting here wasted at my own pity party, talking to my only guest, The Stranger."

Brenda eyed Leah: she knew listening and understanding were critical in this situation, remembering when her sister suffered from alcoholism. Brenda also knew relapsing after four years of sobriety meant something had to be weighing heavy on Leah's heart, and maybe if she handled the situation correctly Leah would shake back from this relapse.

"Who's your sponsor, you need me to call them?"

"Ha, sponsors are for the weak, I got these four years on my own."

"Yeah, with a lot of help from Yah," Brenda said under her breath.

"Look lady, I don't need no sermon or no sponsor. What I need is for you to find your way to the door."

"I will once I state my case."

"Please go ahead, state your case, make your point, and leave." Leah lit another cigarette.

At this point Brenda had grown tired of Leah's stank attitude and would no longer consider her feelings. "Leah, I need you to understand who I am and what I'm doing here. Twenty-nine years ago, my life changed forever when I found a little girl scared to death at Mystic Pier crying for her mother; a mother that had gone off and left her unprotected. A mother watching in the distance to see if anyone would find the little girl. A mother that thought more of herself than that of her little girl."

Leah didn't move, she didn't blink, Leah didn't even breathe, thinking back on that dreadful day.

Brenda walked around Leah hoping that every word she spoke pierced her heart. "Yeah, I saw you that day watching in the distance, making sure your daughter was found before driving off in a white Cadillac. I could've pointed you out, but for what, if you were that selfish and heartless to leave your baby girl alone like that, then maybe she was better off without you in her life."

Tears poured from Brenda's eyes when remembering the fear and hurt she saw in Drew's eyes that day. "I spent seven hours trying to comfort that beautiful soul, and CPS just ripped her from my arms. Although she kicked and screamed begging the lady to let her stay, they took her anyway, not allowing me any access to her. For years that haunted me, not knowing if she was ok, or if her mother ever came back for her. Until one day four years later my prayers were answered, and she moved next door to me. I promised that day when seeing her sweet face jumping from the U-Haul that I would fight hell and high water to make sure she was protected, and I'm here to make good on my promise."

Leah eyed Brenda before getting up staggering back to her office. Brenda knew precisely where Leah was going, so she whisked pasted her and retrieved the Patron bottle from the desk. Leah begged Brenda for the bottle, giving all kinds of excuses for why she should comply, but Brenda refused. After a moment of begging Leah finally gave up and staggered over to the sofa crying out, "My baby, how could I leave her like that?"

Brenda observed Leah and felt sorry for her; although she'd gone there to be stern and warn her about hurting Drew, now all Brenda could do was have pity on her.

Brenda sat down beside Leah holding her why she cried. Brenda was Drew's protector and went there with her in mind, but right now Leah was a wounded soul that needed a lot of TLC.

"You're my angel." Leah looked up at Brenda. "I saw you that day as well, finding my little girl taking care of her. I prayed that day like I never had before. I prayed that God would keep you in her life to take care of her, love her, and be the mother I couldn't be. Although I put contact information in that purse for my parents and her dad, I always wanted and wished she was with you." Leah shook her head in disgrace; the guilt was unbearable. "My baby, how could I leave my baby. I was so lost and confused at that time in my life. My parents disowned me and wanted nothing to do with me. Drew's dad was a sweetheart and I know he loved me, but he couldn't take care of a baby and me, so I took off without telling him I was pregnant. A few months after that I met my ex-husband. He wined and dined me at first and made me feel like a queen, but all that changed a year into our marriage, he started abusing me and drugs.

Leah fell to the floor overwhelmed with sorrow as the tears poured from her eyes. "I didn't want him to hurt her, so I took her to the pier like we did every Sunday, and I left her not for the love I had for him, but for the love I had for her. I know it was heartless, and I'm sorry but it was to keep her safe. I knew what I wanted for Drew, and it was everything I saw in you. I'd watched you every Sunday for over a year; the way you loved your family was surreal, so I took Drew to the pier that day only planning to leave her if I saw you, and after an hour of riding the Ferris wheel over and over, there you stood waiting to board the ride; that was my sign that she would be ok. If you hadn't shown up that day I was gonna take my baby and leave."

Brenda couldn't say a word, the revelation alone had her speechless. Brenda got up from the sofa and began to pace back and forth, it seemed like every time she went to speak the words wouldn't come out. Brenda sat in the office chair, but not long before she was back on her feet pacing the floor once aging.

"You watched me for a year?"

Leah nodded her head. "Yes, I knew from the first day I saw your family that's what I wanted for Drew. I couldn't give it to her, and my ex didn't feel obligated to give her that kind of family structure, so I chose you."

Brenda helped Leah up from the floor. "I'm honored you chose me Leah, but from your poor choice, you almost destroyed Drew's life."

"It's not anymore destroyed than mine, two weeks after abandoning Drew I found out I was pregnant." Leah shook her head. "Now I was stuck with this man, and as much as I wanted my baby back I knew she was better off."

Brenda sat in silence processing all Leah told her, now she saw Leah in a different light; she wasn't this heartless soul leaving her baby for a good time, but a soul that had been broken and rejected in need of healing.

CHAPTER 39

Donuts & Handcuffs

Drew sang along with Gabe and Raleigh to the inspiring school song coming from the radio. The radio station played the track every morning at 7:30, motivating school kids on their way to school and Drew loved it. The fifteen minutes it took her to get from the B&B into Promise was just enough time for the song and her morning prayer with the children.

Drew finished her prayer just before driving into the drop-off lane. "Ok, you two have the best day ever, and remember to be kind and obedient."

"Yes, Ma'am," both children yelled out ensuring Drew they were listening and would comply.

Gabe opened his door and jumped out, but before closing the door he turned and tipped his hat to Drew, blowing her a kiss. Then Gabe walked to the back door of the mid-sized SUV and opened the door for Raleigh. Raleigh jumped from the vehicle and gave Gabe a bow, thanking him for the chivalry. Drew smiled at the two youngin's actions, it did her heart well to see the *Village Teachings* revealing themselves.

After dropping the kids off at school Drew decided to stop by *Good Mornings* to treat herself to coffee and donuts. While in route she saw Marcus going into his shop, Drew immediately started to tease her hair and wipe the night's sleep from her eyes as if he could see her.

After getting her order Drew pulled up to Marcus's shop. Drew figured she'd use checking on the shop's progress as a chance to spend some quality time with Marcus before she got her day started. Drew let the visor's mirror down to conduct a quick face and breath check before exiting the vehicle. If Drew was gonna put herself out there like that, and this early, she needed to make sure she was on point.

After pushing the bell Drew waited for an answer but didn't get one, so she pressed the buzzer again looking out at Marcus's car. "I know I'm not crazy, I did see Marcus go in here." Drew said to herself, that's when Marcus's opened the door. Drew held up the coffee and donuts. "Breakfast, anyone."

"Hell Yeah." Marcus unlocked the door and welcomed Drew in.

Drew walked into the shop sitting the donuts and coffee on one of the stations, then looked around to see if they were alone.

"Whoa, this place looks good, Leah is really doing her thang."

"She was doing her thang," Marcus stated with a slight attitude.

Drew gave Marcus a quizzical look. "What do you mean?"

"I haven't seen or heard from Leah in two weeks, I've tried calling her, texting her, I left messages and everything, but she doesn't answer or reply."

Drew handed Marcus a bear claw and a cup of coffee. "Wow, that's strange, did you go by the office?"

"Man, I have done everything." Marcus took a bite of the bear claw chasing it with coffee. "Omg," Marcus's indulged in the sweet taste of the bare claw mixed with the hazelnut coffee. "Just my thang in the morning. Thanks, Drew."

"You're welcome, I had some time to spare," Drew sipped on her coffee inspecting the half-done job on the shop, she couldn't believe Leah was being so unprofessional.

"When Leah gets done with this place, it's going to be nice."

"Yeah, if she ever gets done."

Drew could see Marcus was frustrated with Leah. "I'll give her a call today, I'm sorry she's not doing a good job."

"You don't have to apologize for her, I just see why now Den had a problem with her."

Drew eyed Marcus. "What are you talking about."

"Oh, yeah, I forgot to tell you Den was over here a few weeks ago and when I say she was giving Leah the business, she was giving her the Bizznezz."

Drew's eyes were glued to Marcus's lips, "What happened, why did she do that?"

"Dang, you still nosey as *HELL,"* Marcus chuckled.

"Ha-Ha, you're funny, now tell me the rest."

"There is no rest. Den confronted Leah about some work she'd done at the boutique, and then she left."

Drew wondered what Leah could have done so wrong at the boutique that Den had to find her at Marcus's shop and confront her. Drew stored the thoughts and questions in her mind for later, but as for right now it would have to wait because she was more interested in Marcus.

Drew rubbed the marble countertops of the workstation eyeing Marcus. "So, are you going to make your 34th birthday special this year?"

"Only if a friend will make it special with me." Drew blushed at Marcus's answer. "Well, can my friend make it special with me?"

Drew stood before Marcus. "You have lots of friends which one are you referring to; Jay, Mikel, Michael." Drew taunted Marcus.

"It's only one friend I have in mind." Marcus invaded Drew's personal space standing so close she could smell the sweet smell of hazelnut coming from his mouth.

"Only if you promise me one thing." Drew held up her index finger, placing it between her and Marcus's lips. "We have to do something extra fun."

"Sure thing, I can promise you that."

Marcus and Drew held each other's stare, the energy between the two was off the grid, and before either of them crossed the line and found themselves in a passionate kiss they hurried to pull away.

"Well, I better be going, I have so much to do." Drew walked towards the door trying not to fall victim to her flesh.

Marcus followed close behind her, reminding himself to stay in the friend zone.

Drew turned and held Marcus's stare once more. "I came, three times." Drew held up three fingers clearing the way for the tears that had run from her eyes to the back of her throat. "The first time was at the courthouse. The second time was six months after you went in, and the third time was when I decided to quit my job and open Serenity Meadows. I tried so hard Marcus; I sat outside that jail for hours trying to muster up enough heart to get out and come in, but it hurt too bad. All I could do was think about you and matters how hard I tried not to... Drew shook her head as the tears flowed from her eyes. "I'm so sorry Marcus for not coming, for not sticking with you. I was so mad at you, so hurt."

"I understand Drew." Marcus kissed Drew's forehead pulling her in for an embrace.

Drew put her head back and inhaled, the smell of the rain coming was refreshing and the touch of the wind caressing Drew's body gave her goosebumps. Drew indulged in the spring weather sitting outside *The Gates* a nice little Jamaican restaurant on the pier, listening to Rainn and Den go on and on about Mr. Pete and Miss Sue's love affair. Drew thought about her morning with Marcus and got goosebumps on top of the ones she already had; the courtship alone had her head in the clouds. Drew wasn't sure where things were going with Marcus, but she was enjoying the trip.

During her morning recap of Marcus Drew also thought about Leah and wondered why she'd disappeared, which led her back to the questions she had for Den. "Hey Den." Drew interrupted her and Rainn's conversation.

"Yeah Drew, what up?"

"How do you know Leah Reynolds?"

Den's mobile ability was destroyed, the question struck her body like lightning; she didn't understand why Drew was asking her this, had she found out about their secret. "I don't know her."

Drew was confused, Marcus's story didn't line up with Den's answer.

Den eyed Drew and could tell she questioned the answer she gave, that's when Den remembered her visit with Leah at Marcus's shop. "Oh, you're talking about Leah Reynolds over at Simple Designs."

"Yeah, that Leah Reynolds, who did you think I was talking about?"

"Gurl, I don't know, I guess the name wasn't registering." Den chuckled, trying to laugh off the humiliation. "Yeah, she did some work for me a few months ago, the sitting area."

"Wow, I didn't know she did that, it looked perfect. What problems did you have with that?"

Den hurried to make up something hoping this would be the last question Drew asked. "Just little things like the bench and some of the paintings."

Rainn eyed the women taking her phone from her purse excusing herself from the conversation.

"Anyway, I stopped by Marcus's shop this morning and he told me you had come by the shop to talk with her, so I thought maybe you knew her personally, and had another number for her other than the one I have."

"I have the number on the door, sorry."

Drew let out a sigh. "Well, I guess Marcus will have to find someone else."

Den grew concerned with Drew's statement. "Why, did she mess something up?"

"No, she hasn't shown up. Marcus said he hasn't heard from her in a couple of weeks."

Den's concern grew knowing Leah hadn't been heard from. When her mother usually went MIA it meant one of two things: she was on a binge, or her dad was out.

Drew snapped her fingers. "Den, are you ok?"

"Um, yeah, I was just...

"Good afternoon ladies." The trio looked up to find Mayor Stone standing before them. Den hadn't been happier to see the mayor then at that moment; he'd given her an escape from Drew's interrogation.

"Good afternoon, Mayor Stone." The woman said simultaneously.

"What a beautiful sight, I swear you ladies bring out the beauty in the pier."

The women blushed at Mayor Stone's statement.

Mayor Stoned eyed Drew for a moment licking his lips and rubbing his beard. "Drew, you know I was waiting on an anniversary party for Serenity Meadows."

"I'm sorry Robert, but I'm going for the fifth year, any business can do good in the first year, but to still be thriving after the fifth year is an accomplishment to me, so if Yah says the same Serenity Meadows's fifth year will be our year to celebrate,"

Mayor Stone nodded his head in agreement giving Drew the eye. "Sure thing Drew, you just let me know the time and place, and I'll be there." Mayor Stone tipped his hat to the ladies before walking off. "Lady's."

Den and Rainn eyed Drew, "Robert," they both said.

"What, y'all act like it's a problem with me knowing his first name."

"Well, not everybody can be on first name bases with the mayor." Rainn chuckled.

"Rainn please, it's not that type of party."

"Well, tell us what type of party it is." Den asked while giving Rainn some dap.

"Oh wow, you to Den?"

"Yeah me too, everyone can see the crush he has on you."

"Ok, pump your breaks, I don't have time for a man right now."

Rainn and Den laughed hysterically, gaining the attention of the restaurant's customers.

Drew motioned for the ladies to calm down. "Shh, people are starting to stare, and what's so funny?"

"You're funny Drew," Rainn stated taking a sip of her Mojito. "You've been out with Marcus every night for the last month, and you don't have time for a man. Well, it's pretty hard to tell."

"And let's not forget the game night partnership," Den added.

"Ok, first of all it hasn't been every nigh Rainn, and you guys always couple up on game nights, leaving Marcus and me our only choice, Den."

Den and Rainn continued to taunt Drew about her time with Marcus, and Drew continued to defend herself. This went on for about five minutes before they were interrupted by a crowd gathered by the Ferris Wheel.

"I wonder what's going on over there." Rainn inquired.

Den took a closer look at the crowd. "I don't know, but there go the Pier Police."

The ladies watched from their seats as the police broke up the crowd. They had never seen that much action on the pier before; it was like a celebrity had made a special appearance by the way the public hollered.

The ladies continued to watch the action as the police pulled a lady from the crowd kicking and screaming, trying to get her to calm down, but it was useless, the woman was drunk and unruly, so the police slapped handcuffs on her and attempted to load her into the car. That's when the ladies got a glimpse of her face.

"Omg, it's Leah." Drew yelped out.

Jay eyed Marcus grumbling to himself after hanging up the phone with Drew; Jay knew the two had been seeing one another on the regular for a few weeks and thought things were going just fine, but by the way Marcus hung up the phone and grumbled Jay worried there was trouble in the land.

"What's up man, you good?" Jay asked.

"Yeah, I'm good," Marcus said with disappointment.

"You sure, cause by the look on your face...

"Nah, man it's nothing like that we good. Drew just told me Leah, the lady I hired to design the shop was just taken to jail."

"For real bro, what happened?"

"Drew said she was stoned drunk at Mystic Pier making a scene, and the law's hauled her off for public intoxication." Marcus picked up a bale of hay and tossed it to Jay who stood on the hay trailer.

"Damn, if it ain't one thang it's another." Marcus vented.

"It's not that bad just find someone else." Jay suggested.

"Nah bro, it's not that bad, it's worse. Detective Miller came by the shop for a cut, he told me after four years they finally found the guy that robbed me."

Jay was puzzled. "Isn't that good news, now you know who did it."

"Man, I wish I didn't know." Marcus shook his head in disappointment. "It was Tevin."

"Dang man ain't this some ish." Jay shook his head.

"Yeah, I know, now how do I confront Tevin and tell Drew."

"Tevin is a good kid, and I know you have to address the matter but go easy on him, because from what I understand he and Den had it pretty bad growing up with an acholic mother and a felon for a father."

"Dang," Marcus uttered, rubbing his head perturbed about the decision he had to make.

CHAPTER 40

Breaking The Rules

Hold on Ma Tate." Drew asked as she jumped from the step ladder to retrieve her phone. "Hello." Drew smiled when hearing Marcus's voice.

Ma Tate held her position on the ladder until she saw Drew getting involved in her conversation, so she took the opportunity to fold some cloth napkins. She and Drew were readying the pool house for Jay and Den's engagement party later that night, and she had no time to spare if everything was to be done by eight.

"I'll see you in a little bit." Drew ended her call with Marcus then jumped back on the ladder. "I asked you to hold on, Ma Tate."

"Girl, I don't have time to hold on while you and Marcus cupcake on the phone."

Drew laughed out. "What do you know about cup caking?"

"I know more than you think I know. Now come over here and help me fold these napkins."

Drew dropped the sign. "I wonder what Marcus needs to talk about, he sounded kind of anxious."

Ma Tate eyed Drew and smiled. "Maybe he wants to get more serious; I mean you guys have been spending a lot of time together. By the way how did the birthday outing go?" Ma Tate gave Drew a wink.

"Oh my gosh, Ma Tate, it was awesome." Drew looked up at the ceiling with a blush and dreamy look on her face. "First we went to the pier and rented bikes, then rode them to Kings park where we enjoyed an outdoor jazz concert. After the concert we went back to the pier and returned our bikes, then to the lake where we camped out until the next morning; it was super nice."

"I must say you guys had an exciting night." Ma Tate eyed Drew. "I'm so happy for you Drew, it's good to see you smile."

"Thanks Ma Tate, I thank Yah for this moment of peace, and I thank you for warning me about Leah.

Ma Tate's heart skipped a beat. "Why, did she do something or say something?" Ma Tate hoped Leah didn't try and contact Drew about being her mother.

"Yes, she did a lot. First, she didn't finish the work on Marcus's shop and he had to hire another designer, second she was at the pier a couple of weeks ago and the police had to restrain her. Leah was yelling like she'd lost her mind, I felt sorry for her, it's like she was really sorry for something, but why public humiliate yourself."

"Did she see you?"

Drew was puzzled by the question. "No, we were at The Gates, why do you ask?"

"I just thought with you two being so close and she seen you, it might have calmed her down. I never want to see anyone down like that."

Drew seized the opportunity. "Ma Tate, if you don't mind me asking, what's the bad blood between you two?"

Den, I know you're upset but will you please listen to me, I wasn't drunk, I had a breakdown. Leah pleaded her case. "Everything was so overwhelming to me, and I didn't know how to handle it."

Den stormed from her bedroom in a rage yelling at Leah about her behavior at the pier. "Didn't look that way to me Leah, the laws had to drag you outta there."

Den, I'm sorry but...

"Sorry isn't going to work this time Ma." Den pulled Leah up from the green love seat by her arm. "It's time you go, I don't know why you're here anyway."

"Wait Den, listen to me." Leah pleaded once more.

"State your reason Leah, you got one minute."

"Ok, I'm not going to lie, I relapsed, but."

Den cut Leah off. "See, I knew it, you will never change."

"Den please hear me out. I did relapse, but it was only one time, and it was way before that day at the pier. Den that day at the pier my demons had finally caught up with me, and I thought going back to the place my life went dark would help me in some way, and it did. It made me realize how horrible I was as a parent and how I needed to make things right with my children. "I sat at the Ferris Wheel and my whole life replayed in my mind; all the mistakes, failures, pain and lost. I just want to make things right. Den it's time I make things right."

"Look, Ma you can't make it right, I don't care how hard you try, you just can't make it right. You have ruined our lives and yours, so why don't you just leave us alone before you do any more damage. As for Drew, she doesn't know you're her mother, and I suggest you keep it that way. Besides, she wouldn't want anything to do with a good for nothing, washed-up, unfit, alcoholic mother anyway. Look, I have an engagement party to prepare for, so if you're done can you leave." Den walked over to the door and opened it, not giving Leah a choice.

Leah tried to speak, but the words from Den's mouth cut deep. Leah kissed Den's forehead then walked out the door, not saying a word.

In tears Den slammed the door and ran back to her bedroom, pulling a floral box from under her bed; the box was filled with pictures of Drew from a baby to the present day. "Why can't I be more like you?" Den looked at a picture of Drew when she graduated high school. "Why didn't she give me away too, maybe I would have gotten a better life like you. She always loved you more. UGH!" Den screamed. "She always loved you more."

Marcus stood in the doorway shaking his head, it seemed like every time he came to the B&B, Rainn was involved in her own personal photo shoot.

"Good afternoon, Raindrop."

Rainn gave Marcus a soft smile. "Good afternoon, Mr. Tidwell."

"Rainn, why every time I come in here you got a photoshoot going on?"

"Because she's addicted to social media, and it's gonna get her a full-time position at the Friendly Market," Drew responded sarcastically, standing behind Rainn in the doorway of her office.

Rainn hurried to put the phone in her purse, she knew Drew was bluffing but better safe than sorry, she'd already threatened to fire her three times that week.

"Sorry, Drew, I love you."

"Yeah, I'm sure." Drew looked at Marcus and gave him a wink. "Come on back Marcus, let's leave Rainn to her work. I know she's more than excited to get back to updating Serenity Meadow's website."

Marcus looked at Rainn and chuckled; her and Drew's relationship was always humorous to him, like a big sister little sister thing.

Marcus took his phone from the leather holster and pretended to take pictures of Rainn before going into Drew's office.

"Ha-ha," Rainn gave Marcus a fake laugh. "You got comedy."

"What's up baby. " Marcus made sure the door was shut before he grabbed Drew and lavished her with kisses. "Mm, you smell so good."

"Will you stop," Drew pulled back from Marcus's grasp.

"Why do I have to stop, I thought you said I could kiss you."

"That was only for your birthday."

"Well, can we pretend like it's May10th again?" Marcus pulled Drew back in for more kisses.

"No, we can't Mr. Tidwell, because it's June 15th, and I have an engagement party that I'm hosting tonight, so I don't have time to fight you, besides I'm pretty sure Rainn has her ear to the door."

"Well don't fight me, just let it happen." Marcus kissed Drew once more.

The pair laughed but Marcus didn't hold his smile long when remembering why he was there. As much as he wanted to keep the robbery matter between him and Tevin he needed to tell Drew; that way she could give him an idea on how to approach Tevin.

Drew noticed Marcus's absence. "What's up, you good, you checked out on me."

"Yeah, I'm good." Marcus took Drew by the hand leading her to the chaise. "Let me talk to you for a minute."

Pete had been standing at the check-in for about three minutes and didn't say a word, he wanted to see how long it would take for Rainn to notice him standing there.

"Ahem, excuse me, when you get done exposing yourself for the public's eye can you tell Drew I got the lights up."

Rainn eyed Mr. Pete. "I'll tell her when she comes out."

"Tell her you been back on that phone taking pictures too, didn't you get fired three times already?" Pete chuckled as he walked off shaking his head.

Rainn snared her nose at Pete as he walked away. Disregarding his warning Rainn returned to her photoshoot, not noticing the gentleman standing in the doorway.

"Excuse me, Shawty." The thunderous voice startled Rainn as she hurried to put her phone away. "I'm sorry Shawty, I didn't mean to scare you."

"It's ok, I'm ok." Rainn tried to calm herself without revealing that she was embarrassed for being caught. "How can I help you, name on the reservation."

The gentleman laughed. "I'm sorry sweetheart, I don't have a reservation, I'm looking for Ethan Cole."

Rainn paused wondering if she should tell this strange man Tevin's whereabouts; besides it had been almost a year since Tevin came to the B&B, and no one had ever been in asking for him, and this guy looked speciously dangerous with the never-ending tattoos, the gold teeth, and the basketballs under his skin. "Um," Rainn hesitated to answer.

"Maybe you know him by Tevin." The man assumed the hesitation had something to do with the name he'd gave.

"Um, let me get my boss you're gonna have to talk with her." Rainn grabbed her phone to call Drew, but it wasn't needed she and Marcus were already coming from the office.

"Rainn, can you get Tevin up here, I need to speak with him?"

"Sure Miss Drew, but this man is also looking for him."

Drew eyed the man. "Can I help you?"

"Chad!" Marcus called out.

The man looked at Marcus. "Marc, well I'll be damn, it's a small world."

The two men embrace one another while Drew and Rainn question the connection between the two.

Marcus was surprised to see Chad standing before him. "What are you doing here, I thought you had five more years."

"I guess the Warden felt sorry for me and let me out."

The men laughed.

"Wow, I can't believe you're here." Marcus looked at Drew and noticed she desired an explanation and introduction. "I'm sorry for my rudeness, let me introduce Drewlynn McCain."

Chad eyed Drew. "My lady, I've heard so much about you."

Drew gave Chad a soft smile. "Have you now?"

Marcus could see Drew needed a more entailed introduction. "I'm sorry baby, this is Chad, he watched out for me on the inside when I was locked up."

"It's nice to meet you Chad, this is Rainn."

Rainn gave Chad a quick wave, she was still questing his interest in Tevin.

"So, what are you doing out here in Promise, bro?" Marcus inquired.

"I came to see my son Ethan, well y'all might know him as Tevin."

BRACE YOURSELF....

Send Jay and Den to my office soon as they get here." Drew hurried to her office where Chad waited for her. "I'm so sorry Chad for pulling you away from your reunion with Tevin, but we need to talk."

Are you sure you're up to this?" Jay caressed Den's face: he could see Den was overwhelmed by the news that her father was out and at Serenity Meadows. "We can cancel the whole thing if you want."

Den held Jay's stare giving him a gentle smile. "No, I want to celebrate our love. Am I shocked that he's here, yes, but I'm not mad. How can I let anything get to me right now, I'm about to marry the man of my dreams." Den gave Jay a soft kiss on his lips.

You're correct Drew, me showing up like this was unexpected. I didn't come to ruin anything or hurt my children. I came to make amends; I just chose the wrong day. Damn it, I just need to make things right with them." Chad lowered his head in shame and disappointment.

"That's why I'm not asking you to leave, and I ask Den if she could come before the party started so you two could talk; she's outside."

Chad looked up at Drew, his heart was touched by Drew's acts of kindness. "Wow, you're amazing, I'm glad Den and Tevin found you, and I thank you for being nice to me after all I've done."

Drew gave Chad a soft smile. "Hey, we all got something to be sorry about."

There was a knock on the door, Den and Jay entered. Den couldn't believe her eyes, it was her dad standing before her after ten years. "Wow, you're really here, how did you find us?"

Chad embraced Den excited to see her, but Den refused the embrace allowing her dad to enjoy the moment alone. Chad released Den from the embrace answering her question. "I found yall on that thang called Facebook."

Drew could see this was a private moment, so she used the party to escape. "I need to go check on the guest, I'll leave you guys to talk." Drew looked over at Jay. "Jay, you wanna come with me to check on the guest?" Drew eyed Jay hoping he would catch on and follow her out the office, but Jay didn't budge until Den assured him that it was okay, and she would be fine.

Drew and Jay stood at the pool house doors greeting the guest as they arrived. "What do you think is taking so long, they've been in there almost thirty minutes." Jay eyed Drew with a look of worry.

"It's going to take longer than thirty minutes for their issues, but I do hope they wrap it up soon before the guest gets anxious. "Thank you for coming," Drew greeted one of the guests.

"Yeah, me too." Jay shook his head. "Maybe this a sign or something."

"Aw, now don't start, I ain't even got time for that. This is not a sign it's a glitch, and glitches can be fixed, so please don't start."

Jay eyed Drew and laughed. "I love you girl."

Drew and Jay greeted a few more guests when *The Parents* walked up. "Heyy, Are We Ready To Paar-Tay?" Ma Tate yelled out as she and Pop Tate approached the pool house.

Drew and Jay laughed at his mother as she danced her way into the building, Pop Tate following behind smiling, bouncing his head doing a jig of his own.

Drew eyed Jay as he looked towards the house waiting for Den to emerge from the French doors. "She'll be on, let's get the party started."

Jay addressed the crowd thanking them for sharing the moment with him and his bride-to-be. The group looked around in search of Den, Jay assured them that she would be with them shortly.

Ma Tate nudged Drew inquiring about Den's whereabouts. Drew told Ma Tate about Den's father, and her heart went out to her as she volunteered to go check on the matter, but Drew assured her it was under control.

Drew scanned the room for Tevin but didn't see him anywhere, so she went to his backroom apartment in the pool house where she found him speaking with Marcus. Drew didn't know what the men were conversating about, but whether it be about the robbery or Chad, she hoped Marcus would be understanding and helpful.

When Drew made it back to the party Den had arrived. Drew was sure Den would be sad and not in the partying mood, but Den had a totally different face; she was smiling, interacting with the guest, and introducing her father; it was like nothing had happened, and Drew was thrilled. The last thing she wanted was for Den to allow her evening to be ruined.

Drew walked over to Den, blessing her with a kiss to the cheek. "Hey, you ok?"

"I'm just fine, how can I let anything, or anyone ruin my night? This is beautiful Drew, you and Ma. Tate did yalls thing." Den admired the purple, lavender, and silver decor.

Drew walked over to the counter and grabbed two glasses of wine, handing one to Den. Drew stroked Den's face holding her stare. We're not going to let anyone ruin this night.

"Good evening, Darlings," Leah stood before the crowed drunk out her mind holding up a bottle of opened champagne. "I Would Like to Make A Toast."

The crowd paused, everyone stared in shock as Leah walked over to Den and Drew who were stupefied "Ahh, it's your night baby girl, and I toast to you." Leah took a swig of the champagne.

"What are you doing here?" Den was furious, the blood flowing through her veins was hot as lava from a volcano.

"I told you I have to make it right." Leah set the champagne bottle on the table and stroked Den's face.

Drew eyed Den and Leah, confused by the connection.

Tevin was freaked. "Ma, what are you doing here?" Tevin asked from the back of the room.

"Ma," Drew asked herself before looking back at Marcus.

"I'm here to make it right. A very wise lady told me that I had to make it right in order to move on." Leah looked at Ma Tate and gave her a wink.

Ma Tate shook her head, silently asking Leah not to continue.

Leah scanned the room when she noticed Chad. "Ahh, Dina, I see you made it a family affair and welcomed your dad." Leah walked over to Chad placing a drunk wet kiss upon his lips. "Baby, why didn't you tell me you were getting out? Doesn't our little girl look beautiful, and wait, this is Jay." Leah ran and cuffed Jay's arm pulling him to Chad. "Did you get a chance to meet Jay because I didn't, Den didn't think I was good enough."

"Come on Leah stop this, let's get some air." Chad tried to take Leah outside but she refused.

"NO, I'm staying right here. I let you take me away from my baby once, but not this time." Leah eyed Drew giving her a wink.

"What is this, Den?" Jay asked.

Den held Jay's stare with tears in her eyes not able to utter a word.

Leah looked over the crowd. "Is this a party or what?" Leah danced around snapping her fingers to music that didn't exist. The crowd watched in silence.

"Come on baby, dance with me," Leah ran and grabbed Tevin by the hand pulling him to the middle of the floor dancing a drunk jig around him.

Tevin looked at his mother with tears in his eyes. "Why you always gotta mess things up." Tevin ran back to his apartment with Rainn in tow.

"He never liked dancing with his mom." Leah said while continuing her solo performance.

Drew and Den ran to Leah trying to calm her. Leah looked at the two women placing a hand on each of their cheeks. "All I ever wanted was for you to know one another, and look here you are, best of friends, My Girls."

GIRL GET UP

How did I get here? Is that even a question? Look at all the time that has passed.

You sit back and you waited, it's not that you failed but you where continuously on repeat, always coming back from a defeat.

This life is what you make it, so receive it, but not without action and not without a fight.

Girl get up, didn't you know you'd have to fight, battling demons day and night.

Prayer in the morning, prayer will get you by. Pray in the evening, prayer without a cry.

Girl get up. Chin up, chest out; now you step. Step with the pain, step with the hurt, step with the fear, never forgetting Yah is near.

Nothing here is easy, and if you sit back long enough, you'll miss your season.

It's doesn't matter the age time is always ticking. If you want change go get it, you've been hurt those are life lessons, so take it all as one big blessing.

Remember the past will always be the same, you can do this, you can maintain.

Why are you afraid, what's out here will be, forget what they said, forget what they made you believe. You will be what you're destined to be, get up girl.

Tennisa Davis,

Made in the USA
Middletown, DE
26 November 2024